An Unbreakable Bond

Mary Wood

Published in 2009 by New Generation Publishing

A CIP catalogue record for this title is available from the British Library.

Mary Wood was born in Maidstone, Kent, in 1945. She is the thirteenth child of fifteen children. Repatriation after the war saw her family being re-settled in Leicestershire. Most of her childhood was spent in the villages of Ullesthorpe, where her family lived in ex-Army huts, and in, Claybrooke, where they lived in a three bed roomed Council house. Mary slept in a double bed with three of her sisters, but gradually made it to a bed of her own as each sister left to get married. She was educated at St Peter's RC School in Hinckley, where one particular teacher, when setting composition titles, used to say to her: 'Mary Olley (her nee name) I want one page and one page only, not a novel!' And yet, another teacher, of whom Mary has fond memories, Mr Tom Payne, encouraged her to write all she could and even remarked that he thought she would one day be an Author! It took a long time, but at last Mary has achieved this. After leaving school Mary attended the Hinckley Technical College of Further Education where she studied Office Skills. Mary and her husband of forty six years, Roy, originally settled in Leicestershire living in both Sharnford, Nr Hinckley and in Lutterworth. After their fourth child reached school age they ventured into the licencing trade and eventually ran a Public House in Enderby, 'The Plough'. This was a venture that spread over almost fifteen years in various venues in the Midlands and also in Lancashire, after they moved to Blackpool in 1981. Mary has spent the last ten years working for The National Probation Service in Lancashire as a Probation Service Officer. Mary now has a large family of her own. Three of her four children have married and given her and her husband eight grandchildren and four step-grandchildren, four of these grandchildren have children of their own and Mary & Roy now have seven great grandchildren, one of whom, Jacob, lives in heaven and is a shining light and inspiration to all the family and very much missed. Mary is very happy to be retired at last, and to concentrate full time on her writing. This is her first published novel. A prequel is planned.

To find out more visit Mary on www.marywood.com

Acknowledgements

My first and foremost thank you is to my husband, Roy, who has supported me in this project through tears and tantrums and the burning of the midnight oil and still loves me despite it all. My children, Christine, Julie, Rachel and James, how you read so many versions I will never know. Your support and encouragement has been unstinting and much valued. Christine, thank you for helping me to edit the book and for all the research you did for me, this book would not exist without it. Thank you to my brother- in-law, Bob, who, many years ago when I first started writing, lent me his precious computer and has believed in me ever since. To my sister, Magdalene, who has always been a tower of strength and support to me and to my sister, Felicity, who has badgered me to keep writing ever since she read my first novel, the manuscript of which has long since been abandoned to the attic. I thank my niece, Lynda, who also helped me to edit the book and my nephew, John Skillen, author of, *EXTRA CHILI SAUCE*, for his encouragement to remain positive throughout. Thank you to every member of my family and family-in-law though not mentioned by name, you have always shown an interest in my writing and encouraged me. And to friends and colleagues, you are too many to mention, but all of you are important to me and I value your faith in me. Thank you to: 'YouWriteOn.com', a fantastic website for aspiring Authors, and to their members who have critiqued my work and been of great help to me. My last and biggest thank you is to New Generation Publishing, your innovation has given a chance to many more writers to accomplish their dreams than would ever have been possible. I hope I have done you all proud.

PART ONE

INNOCENCE LOST

1913

CHAPTER ONE

The draughty, stone-walled corridor echoed their journey to the Reverend Mother's office.

Megan and Hattie paused by the internal window just feet from the huge oak door. The window served as a mirror for last minute checks of their appearance.

Satisfied both hers and Hattie's grey serge frocks were crease free and their starched white collars were buttoned up under their chins, Megan tried to tuck the stray unruly locks of her auburn hair under her mobcap. Hattie giggled at her attempts. Megan made a face at her. Hattie's smooth, dark hair always looked neat for next to no effort.

'Enter!'

Reverend Mother's tone cracked Megan's already frayed nerves. Hattie squeezed her hand.

The small comfort the gesture gave died instantly with the silent tread of the deep carpet and the smell of wax polish. A stark contrast to the flagstone floors and the carbolic soap and boiled cabbage stench that clung to the corridors and rooms they, and the rest of the orphaned, abandoned or born-of-sin children, occupied.

They waited to be acknowledged. Megan's eyes fixed on the butterfly wings of stiff white linen cascading from each side of the Reverend Mother's bent head. The sudden lift of the head made her jump. She tugged Hattie's frock to bring her attention back from looking around the room.

'Well, Megan Tattler and Hattie Frampton, you are now thirteen years of age and you are to leave us. And, I don't have to ask to know how pleased you both are, do I?'

Neither of them answered. Though, Megan knew if either of them did it wouldn't be to say they were pleased. Not altogether pleased. There was a lot of sadness in them at the thought of being separated.

'You, Hattie, go later today I understand? And, Megan, you are to leave tomorrow.' The Reverend Mother's eyes, shrouded by a brow squashed into a bulge by her veil, darted between them. Her smile pinched her face.

'Now, Hattie…' Hattie's body stiffened.

'I see you have a very fitting placement in the household of Lord Marley's country residence. You are going to be a scullery maid. Very good! Are you prepared?'

'Yes, Reverend Mother, but…'

'No buts, Hattie. Lord Marley is one of our biggest benefactors and has given many of our girls a good start in life by providing them with jobs. It's up to you to make something of yourself.'

'Yes, Reverend Mother.'

'Good! Now, Megan Tattler… It seems to me you think you can take up a placement far above your station. It is unheard of that someone of such low status be taken on as an apprenticed seamstress!'

The insult and the look that went with it froze Megan's hopes. Hattie found her hand and squeezed it.

'I would not have thought of letting you go.' Reverend Mother continued, 'had it not been for Sister Bernadette's persistence on your behalf and the fact that after being told of the sin you were born from Madame Marie is still inclined to give you a chance. She states in her letter she is taking you on merit because of the talent you show in the drawings and the sample of stitches shown to her by Sister Bernadette. However, she makes it clear you will be expected to know your place and to keep it at all times. You are not to try to engage with any of the young ladies who are training there. You will have a room in the attic away from the others. Do you understand?'

'Yes, Reverend Mother.'

'I hope you do as it is on these terms and these terms only, I have decided you shall be allowed to take up this placement.'

Megan struggled with the joy surging through her, but knew Reverend Mother, aggrieved at having allowed her to take up the apprenticeship, would take it away from her if she gave her an excuse to do so. She kept her, thank you Reverend Mother, as stiff and correct as it should be.

Reverend Mother inclined her head.

'You may go. But remember, whatever you make of yourselves is up to you. If you work hard and stay true to the teaching you have received here you will prosper. If you don't…' The pinched smile reached her eyes, 'the gutter is where you will find yourselves as many have before you.'

There were no goodbyes. Megan hadn't wanted any and knew the same feeling would be in Hattie. The uppermost thought in Megan's mind was to be free of the tense atmosphere of the office and to be able to give a release to her feelings. But they hadn't gone far along the corridor when Hattie's words dulled her joy.

'Will we ever see each other again, Meg?'

'Aye, we will. We'll make sure of it. We'll write regular. As soon as we get our first wage we can get paper and stamps...'

'I'm not for working in service, Meg. I'll be off from there just as soon as I can.'

'What...Why...'

'Because, I'm scared of ending up like Daisy.'

'Daisy? Why, what's happened to Daisy?'

'She's left her placement. I saw her on the day as I had to go into Leeds to have me tooth pulled. Sister Bernadette made me wait outside a shop. I wandered up the street and there was Daisy.'

'You didn't say...'

'I know. I should have, but I were a bit shocked, I'm sorry, Megan. Anyways, Daisy's working the streets. She were hungry so I gave her cab fare Sister'd given me in case we got separated. I told Sister as I'd lost it.'

'Oh, Hattie, is that the gutter as the Reverend Mother spoke of, this working the streets?'

'Aye, I reckon it is by the looks of Daisy. But she said as things'll get better for her. She's being accepted on the patch and has a couple of customers of her own.'

'But, what is it she has to do, is it cleaning or something?'

'Oh, Meg! You daft ha'p'orth!'

Hattie doubled over in a fit of giggles. Megan couldn't help but giggle with her though she felt there was something Hattie was party to which she didn't know of.

'They sell themselves. You know... to men. They let men do things to them.'

'What things?'

Hattie giggled again. 'Things as men do to make you have babbies. Only they don't keep having babbies, because they have ways to stop that happening.'

'How do you know of such things, Hattie, and why is Daisy doing it? Why didn't she stay at her placement?'

'Daisy told me everything as a sort of warning because she knew I'd most likely end up in service and she wanted me to watch out for meself. She told me her master forced her to do it with him so she had to run away. She made her way to Leeds and was helped by this girl who was working the streets. She had no choice but to do the same.'

'Poor Daisy. You know something, Hattie? I don't even know how...Well...how babbies happen. I've been on with thinking about it since we started our bleeding and Sister Bernadette sent us to the laundry room and Mrs Hartley showed us how to use the rags.'

'I know. I was curious after that. It was her saying we were to watch ourselves and not let boys have their way with us else we'd end up pregnant. I wondered what a boy's way is, but I know now. I could tell you if you like.'

Megan said nothing, wanting to know, but not wanting to say so.

'Well, Daisy said, the man...'

A tickly feeling in her private part, as Sister Bernadette called that part of them they were never allowed to expose, shocked and embarrassed Megan as she listened to Hattie. And all she could think to say was, 'Does it hurt?'

'Daisy said it did the first time, but it isn't bad after that.'

'I suppose it can't be because women keep having babbies, don't they? Anyroad, happen as poor Daisy were unlucky in her placement.'

'But I'm scared, Meg. Daisy told me that the girl who helped her said it happens a lot. She said, some top-drawer folk like to take a young maid's flower and the master Daisy'd worked for were known for it.'

Megan didn't ask what a flower was. She didn't want to know. Instead she asked, 'Where was Daisy's placement?'

'I don't know. I was so shocked I forgot to find that out... Still, I shouldn't be going on. Your placement doesn't sound too good either, not with that Madame woman thinking of you as she does.'

'I know, but it doesn't bother me. It'll be worth it. Just think. I'll be learning to make frocks and gowns. And, maybe something'll come of me drawings. Wouldn't that be wonderful, ay? To see me drawings being made up out of satins and such like...'

'Aahh, Megan and Hattie, here you are.'

They both stiffened. Being caught in idle chit-chat was one of the deadliest sins. They hadn't heard the chinking of keys or the dull knocking sound of huge wooden rosary beads. Sounds that warned one of the sisters was approaching.

Megan peered into the dullness of the corridor. The voice hadn't given her which nun had caught them out. The outline of a plump figure, hazed by a flowing, cream habit came towards them. Her relief as the nun came into view was voiced by Hattie.

'Eeh, Sister Bernadette, it's you. You gave us a fright.'

'I expect I did, Hattie.' There was a twinkle in Sister Bernadette's eyes that belied the strict retort. 'I have been looking for you both this good while. Tell me, my wee ones, is it your placements Reverend Mother has been confirming with you? And are you happy now you know for sure where it is you are going?'

They both nodded. The feeling that had taken Megan on hearing of Daisy's plight, deepened. The only person she and Hattie could share their worries with was Sister Bernadette. But not worries like this. You couldn't talk to a nun about such things.

'And you, Megan. Are pleased you know at last you can go to Madame Marie's?'

'Oh, yes, Sister. I can't believe it! Ta ever so much.'

'It is the Good Lord you have to be thanking for giving you such a talent, Megan. Not that He missed out giving you something when he was at the making of you, Hattie dear. You have many virtues: Your kind ways and a willingness to help others. You will do well, too. I'm sure of it.'

Tears rolled down Hattie's cheeks as she nodded her head and Megan knew her own eyes to fill up at the sight.

Sister Bernadette patted Hattie on the shoulder. 'It is a beautiful house you are going to, Hattie. Lord Marley's Country residence is on the outskirts of Leeds on the road to Sheffield. And, Megan, Madame Marie's is in the centre of Leeds itself and her salons are wonderful...'

***

Seeing Hattie off was the worst thing Megan had ever done. Even the journey to and from the station on the motor-bus, a new experience for her, didn't lift her. The suffocating nearness of the strangers travelling with them, the rumbling and vibrating of the engine and the discomfort of the jolting over cobbled roads were an intrusion on her feelings. Sister Bernadette held her hand throughout the return journey, but didn't speak.

They were walking across the pebbled courtyard of the convent when Sister Bernadette finally spoke.

'Megan dear, I have something to tell you of and something to give you which belonged to your dear mammy.'

The words jolted an instant shock through Megan's body. Her mam had never been spoken of. Questions had always been suppressed. All she knew was she'd been born in St Michael's, a convent for sinful, unmarried, pregnant girls.

Once they were inside the convent doors Sister Bernadette took her hand and led her to her room.

11

'Now, Megan, you sit yourself down whilst I get you something that will be very special to you.'

Sister Bernadette crossed the room. There was no thick carpet to hush her steps or to dull the sound of her keys bouncing on her hip. The room was bare but for an old wooden desk in one corner, a brass bed in the other and a cane chair.

Megan sat down on the chair grateful to get off her shaky legs. Sister Bernadette sorted through her keys and inserted one into one of the drawers before putting her hand inside. A panel to the side of the desk shot open.

'Megan, my wee one, what I have in the palm of my hand is a locket. Inside is a picture of your granny and granddaddy.' She paused and made the sign of the cross. 'It is sorry I am to have to tell you, my wee one, but...' She crossed herself again and looked heavenward. 'Your mammy died just after giving you your life. I helped at the birth of you.'

The pain Megan had held in her chest since saying goodbye to Hattie came up to her throat threatening to strangle the life from her. 'She...she can't be. I have to find her. She...'

She had been about to say her mam was the daughter of a rich family who'd been turned out of the family home and only allowed back if she gave her babby away... But that had been the make-believe she'd lived along with Hattie who'd always imagined her own mam had been a princess shipped away in disgrace leaving her 'sin' behind.

'Now, now, my wee one...'

The urge to shout, 'I'm not your wee one. I'm nobody's wee one', fought with the part of her that would never hurt Sister Bernadette. But though she didn't utter the words she knew them to be a truth. She wasn't a child any longer. How could she be with what today had given her?

She took the locket. Her fingers clamped it closed.

'Look at it later if that is what you have a mind to do, dear.'

It was later, much later, when Megan opened the locket. She'd lain awake for hours her body a turmoil of emotions and confusion. But all at once, she knew it was time. She would look at the pictures in the locket. She sat up. No one questioned her. She waited. If any of the girls she shared the dormitory with were awake they would whisper something. Nothing happened.

Easing the locket from under her pillow she made her way towards the door leading to the corridor. The light coming through the window in the door was enough. She opened her cramped fingers. The light glinted on the locket.

This was it. This was to be her family. Did she look like them? Had her mam looked like them? Sister Bernadette had said her grandparents had died before she had been thought of. She was glad of that. It meant they hadn't abandoned her mam when she'd most needed them.

Turning the locket over she read, 'To Catch a Dream', inscribed into the slightly tarnished, dented silver. Had her granddad had that done for her gran? So many questions...

She opened the locket the couple looking out at her didn't look like grandparents. The picture had been taken when they were young. Her granny was pretty with huge smiley eyes. Granddad, too, had a nice look. A warm feeling took the fear and coldness out of her as she saw she had some likeness to them both.

Her granny had unruly wavy hair just like her own and the freckles on her nose were identical. Studying her granddad closely Megan could see he had some similarities to her. Her high-cut cheekbones and slightly slanted eyes were just like his.

The image was in shades of brown. But it was still possible to see her granddad's complexion was darker than her granny's. People always remarked that she had an olive skin so in this, too, she was like granddad.

Sister Bernadette had said she couldn't remember their names and was sorry she hadn't written them down. She'd hesitated over her mam's name as if she'd forgotten that, too. "Br...Brenda, that was it, Brenda Tattler." She'd said. Then she'd told her, her mam hadn't been wicked. That the conceiving of her had been the result of an attack by someone she'd trusted. She'd gone on to say, "Everything isn't straightforward in life, Megan. It is better not to be dwelling on things how you would like them to be, but to get on with what is what. Just be thankful, your mammy left you something to hold on to."

Getting back to her bed and lying back on her pillow, Megan mulled the words over in her mind. Sister was right. It was no use dwelling on the sadness inside her at being parted from Hattie and finding out her mam was dead or to think on her fear of being alone in an attic and not being good enough to talk to the others at her placement. Instead she would think of her family and talk to them. You could do that with dead people. They watched over you and helped you.

CHAPTER TWO

Laura Harvey stood at the window of her study. The stagnant view of the symmetrical lawn bordered by a tall, tailored hedge echoed what her life had become.

Beyond lay the view she wanted to see: fields coloured with crops, chimneys releasing the gasses from the bowels of the earth where the men and boys sweated long hours to bring up the coal, the mainstay of hers and Jeremy's income. And yes, the stables. Once the centre of her life, but now a painful sight since her dream had been ended.

How often she'd wanted to have the hedge chopped down. But Jeremy had laughed at her. Thinking he knew better about what privacy she would need in her own little sitting-room, as he called it. He never called it, her study.

Yes, she'd had the two Queen Anne carved sofa's brought in, smothered them with soft cushions and placed them each side of the ornate fireplace making a comfortable sitting area. But the mahogany desk on the opposite side of the room, huge in its proportions and flanked on each side with floor to ceiling shelves stacked with all manner of books and files, told of the real purpose of the room.

Her father in law's death whilst Jeremy was still a serving officer had necessitated her running the estate and had been the original reason for commissioning this room.

The hedge hadn't bothered her then. This had been a busy room for her. After all, the whole of Breckton breathes life from the Harvey Estate.

Her mind went over how she'd had to learn the ins and outs of the running of the colliery, the farm and the stables besides continuing to manage Hensal Grange, this grand twenty-bedroomed house she and Jeremy now rattled around in. On top of all of that the maintenance of the tied cottages had been her responsibility, as had the shops, the leased farms and the buildings that house businesses, such as the blacksmiths. The work involved in administering it all had been an immense task. Especially for her, a woman who had never worked in her life up to that point.

Every day had presented her with decisions and she'd risen to the challenge. Revelled in it, in fact. But now her life was humdrum. Household accounts she could do with her eyes shut and listening to the whining of the senior household staff were hardly riveting tasks. Even her marriage held nothing for her. Not since... No. She'd not dwell on that. Her loneliness would crowd her. Suffocate her!

Oh, how one hoped Emily Pankhurst would win through! Not that one altogether agreed with the woman's methods, but to be liberated enough to have the vote would help towards being seen in a different light.

Looking away from the window Laura brought her mind back to the task of today and decided it would be better conducted if she were sitting behind her desk. Observing a certain formality would be less of an intrusion on the woman's feelings.

She sighed as she sat down. Meeting with Tom Grantham's widow wasn't something she was looking forward to.

The realisation of how much Tom's death had shocked and hurt her pulled her up. She'd always thought of staff as dispensable commodities. But then, Tom had been different. He had been an expert horseman and the best damn groom in these parts. His death had made her realise that he'd become a sort of companion, even a father figure of sorts.

'God! What has one become when one has to seek companionship from one's groom? And now I'm talking to myself...'

She would have to do something. Write to Daphne. Yes, that would be the thing.

It wasn't often she envied her sister. Daphne's life as the wife of a Lord, the adorable Charles Crompton, was a round of socialising and charitable work. The charitable work wouldn't suit at all, but she could do with socialising more. Jeremy just wasn't interested since... Anyway, she'd ask Daphne to come to stay for a few days. Daphne would probably insist she visited her in York instead. She wouldn't say so, but Laura knew Daphne found the cold, polite atmosphere of Hensal Grange embarrassing, to say the least. Still, it didn't matter which. Just to be with Daphne and to talk silly talk, gossip about the latest goings on and maybe a dinner party, where she would be flirted with and told she is beautiful, noticed even...

A knock at the door interrupted her thoughts. Hamilton announced Isabella Grantham. One glance told this was a homely woman used to eating copious amounts of her own cooking. She had the appearance of one who had scrubbed her face until it gleamed, but this didn't hide the sadness and apprehension in her eyes.

Laura knew the words of condolence she uttered sounded empty. She knew from experience they made no difference. They helped the speaker rather than the bereaved. She supposed she should offer the poor woman a chair but thought she'd probably refuse.

'Mr Grantham was a very valued member of my staff, Mrs Grantham. Consequently I want to do all I can to help you. The accident was most unfortunate. There was no warning the horse would kick out in that manner. I am very sorry. It is sad, too, to think this has come at a time when your daughter is to leave to take up the placement I found her at Tom's... Mr Grantham's, request. Are you still of the mind to let her go?'

'Yes, Ma'am, I can't see her waste a chance like this. It was good of you to get it sorted for her. She leaves this afternoon.'

'A good decision. Such placements are not easy to come by. I hope your daughter doesn't let me down. Madame Marie took her solely on my recommendation. The type of employee she usually takes on are educated and from middle class families. Vicar's daughters and the like...'

'My Cissy is as good as the next one, I'll have you know. Oh... I... I beg yer pardon, Ma'am...'

Laura was taken aback. Even though the woman had apologised for her outburst it was still apparent she'd alienated her. She had no idea why. Better to ignore it.

'Now, about your own future. I understand you work at the local shop?'

'Aye, I do, Ma'am, I do three days and some cleaning for Manny's wife.'

'Well, Mr Harvey and I have decided you may stay on in the cottage. There will be a rent of one shilling three farthings per week and you will be expected to help out in the house from time to time to cover for staff sickness or any social events. We are not looking to employ a new groom in the foreseeable future so your tenancy is safe for some time to come. The new enterprise Mr Grantham and I were working on, the building of a stud farm, is not to go ahead at present.'

The act of telling someone gave Laura the reality of it. Jeremy had been adamant. Was it just another way to punish her? Or did he really believe there was going to be a war? She took a deep breath. If the woman noticed her pain she didn't show it. She only showed a relief for her own position.

'Ta, oh ta ever so much, Ma'am.'

'If we decide in the future to hire another groom we will inform you in good time and will re-house you. In the meantime, Old Henry

17

Fairweather and Gary Ardbuckle are going to manage the stable. Henry hasn't lost his skills. He taught your husband as you know.'

'Aye, Ma'am, he did. I can't grasp yet how someone like my Tom could be killed by a horse. Not with him being best in County with horses. And him being so strong.'

'Yes. It is unbelievable...'

'Me and my Tom thought as we had a lifetime together. We didn't count on that being until I was forty-five and him just on fifty. We...'

'Yes of course, I am very sorry. Do let me know if there is anything more we can do for you.'

This was getting uncomfortable. Laura didn't want or need to hear about how this woman's hopes and aspirations had gone. She had enough of her own dashed hopes to contend with. She reached behind her and tugged the bell cord. Hamilton appeared immediately.

'Do wish your daughter good luck in her position and remind her not to let me... us down. Goodbye, Mrs Grantham. Hamilton, take Mrs Grantham through to the kitchen. Give her some supplies...'

'I don't need none, ta very much, Ma'am! I have plenty in me pantry and me pots still full. Full enough for me own care anyroad, and I've no-one else to care for now, have I?'

'Come along, Mrs Grantham.' Hamilton ushered her out.

Laura was left looking towards the door in bewilderment. She shook her head. Whatever had she said to alienate the woman in that manner? Surely she wasn't blaming her for the accident?

She opened the silver cigarette case which always stood on her desk. Her hand shook as she placed a cigarette in her holder and lit it. The smoke stung the back of her throat. Coughing brought tears to her eyes. Good God! She was going to cry! Damn and blast the woman! Damn and blast everything!

CHAPTER THREE

'Which one of you is Megan Tattler?' Madame Marie looked from Megan to the girl standing by her side.

'I am, Madame.' Megan stood straight her shoulders pulled back just as Sister Bernadette had told her to, though she didn't keep her eyes to the floor. She didn't want to be seen as insolent, but then, neither did she want to be seen as something from the gutter.

Madame wasn't at all like she had imagined. Her name and what she had said in her letter had conjured up an image of a witch-like, beady eyed person with teeth that stuck out. Madame in the flesh was far from that image. She wasn't pretty. The word Megan would use to describe her would be, handsome. Funny word for a woman, but that is what she conveyed. Her features were precise, almost sharp. Her hair was dark and though held in a comb at the back it was rolled at the front. This added to her handsomeness and softened her face. Her grey eyes didn't show any emotion. They, like her voice and manner were businesslike.

'So, you must be, Cecelia Grantham?'

'Cissy...'

'Cecelia!'

'Yes, Madame.'

The girl standing by Megan's side sniffed as she answered. Megan had met her just a few moments ago at the door of the office they now stood in. They hadn't spoken; just smiled at each other. Megan had been too busy taking in the sight of the rows of benches where young girls sat bent over their sewing. One of them had sniggered and nudged the girl next to her, but she hadn't let this worry her. She'd lost herself in the smell and the colours of the fabric and the rows of shelves housing boxes she supposed held things like cotton reels and fastenings.

She had registered though, that Cissy was the prettiest and yet saddest girl she'd ever seen. Her eyes were big and round and the palest blue, which even the puffiness from her crying hadn't spoiled. Her hair was the colour of straw when the sun is on it and had the look of a mound of bubbles as it tumbled round her face in a mass of curls.

Madame Marie let out the breath she'd held and her glare left Cissy and shot between them both.

'Not that it matters what your Christian names are as from now on you will be known as Miss Tattler and Miss Grantham. And may I remind you, you are extremely lucky to be here. Especially you, Miss Tattler. Though, it is a concession on my part to have taken either of you. At least, Miss Grantham, you come with a modicum of respectability and a reference from one of my best customers. Whilst the only persuasion I have for taking you, Miss Tattler, is the talent you seem to display in design and the exquisite stitching of the samplers I was shown.'

Megan felt her body lift from her belly upwards and her head stretch on her neck whilst her eyes looked straight ahead. But though this outward sign of her pride helped her, her inner shame burned her face red.

'I will be watching your every move. Manners and attitude are just as important to me as hard work and ability. In all these you both have to prove yourselves worthy of being here.' Madame paused and stared directly at Megan. Megan dropped her head. What did it matter? She knew inside she was as good as the next one.

'I'm glad that is clear to you, Miss Tattler. I hope the way you are to conduct yourself around the ladies working here is just as clear.'

Megan nodded.

'I was tempted to put you two together, but I don't want to risk offending Mrs Harvey. So you, Miss Grantham, will be allowed to sleep in the main dormitory. But remember, the other ladies there are above your station in life and you must treat them as such at all times.'

'But...I don't...I'd like...'

'Never answer back, Miss Grantham. Never! You may only speak to me when I have spoken to you first. And then only if I require an answer. Do you understand?'

Cissy's body trembled and Megan wanted to put her hand out and take hers and give her some comfort. She felt certain Cissy was going to say she wanted to be with her. This gave her a nice feeling inside and made up for what she'd had to stand for.

'Very well! Now, you will be working in the finishing room. That is the room just outside this office where you will have observed the ladies at their work. To begin with you will practise on scrap material and won't be allowed to touch the garments until I feel you are ready to do so. You will have every Sunday afternoon off. The morning, after you return from church at 9am, will be spent cleaning the salon and window displays. Every month you will have the first Monday and Tuesday as your leave days. You will both be responsible for cleaning the workrooms after the ladies have left to have their evening meal. You will take your own meal when this work is finished and the ladies have left the dining-hall. You will be at your work benches by eight every morning and take your breakfast and lunch after the ladies have had theirs. Your salary, less deductions for your keep will be paid to you on the Monday morning of your leave. You will keep yourselves and your rooms spotless at all times.' She rang the bell on her desk.

This was so unexpected they both jumped. Cissy made a sound like a giggle being snatched back. It was nearly the undoing of Megan as the sound before it was checked was infectious, but the years of practise at keeping a straight face stood her in good stead.

A girl who looked just a little older than she and Cissy answered the bell's summons. She was introduced to them as Miss Stallton. Megan took an instant dislike to her when, at Madame's instructions to show them around, she gave them a look as if they were the dirt from the bottom of her shoe.

As soon as they were outside the office Cissy gave way to her giggling and didn't stop even when subjected to another of Miss Stallton's disdainful looks. It was all Megan could do not to join in but as Miss Stallton turned away Megan did take Cissy's hand in her own and squeeze it. This turned the giggles to tears so she slipped her arm around Cissy and held her close as they followed Miss Stallton through a door on the left of the finishing room and up the stairs.

'It'll be all right, I promise.' Megan whispered.

Cissy managed a smile at this and dried her tears.

'I believe you have been told, Miss Tattler, you are not to speak to anyone here unless you have been spoken to? Well, I am sure that even includes Miss Grantham.'

Shock stung Megan and caught her breath in her lungs. She said nothing, but Cissy did, which further shocked her as she'd had Cissy down as someone who would need looking out for. Not someone who'd be looking out for her!

'It don't include me. She can talk to me when she wants to.'

'Miss Grantham...'

'Me name's Cissy...'

'Miss Grantham! If you know what is good for you and you want to retain this position you would be wise to think carefully about your standing. Which I understand from Madame, is only just above that of

Miss Tattler's. And take your hands off Miss Grantham at once, Miss Tattler! I shall report this to Madame.'

Both Megan and Cissy gasped at this but neither of them said anything.

The smell of the corridor at the top of the stairs reminded Megan of the Reverend Mother's office. Her footsteps squeaked on the polished floor. She couldn't fit on to the narrow carpet runner that silenced Cissy's tread.

Miss Stallton stopped at the first door and opened it. 'Your bed is the fourth one along, Miss Grantham, and the washroom is through the door at the end on the right.'

Megan looked through the open door. There were four beds on the side she could see. Each had a folded screen next to it and a set of drawers displaying knick-knacks on top stood between the beds on the opposite side to the screens. The room was light and the curtains and bedspreads were of a matching pink colour. It was a welcoming, pretty room.

'Now, Miss Tattler, you see those stairs at the end of this passage? Well, they lead to your room in the attic. On the bottom step is a jug containing water. When you have washed and changed into your uniform bring your bowl down and I will show you where you can empty it in the back yard. You will get fresh water from a pump out there and... Well, there is a lavatory out there for your use. You are to empty your...Your chamber pot in the lavatory every morning.' Her body shuddered with disgust as she paused. Then seeming to pull herself together she continued, 'I will expect you at the bottom of the stairs in half an hour.'

It was no good her trying not to cry, she had been undone. She was nothing. That girl, that spiteful girl with her, Miss this and Miss that, had made her feel like she was the lowest of the low. And Madame Marie had, too.

Her tears blurred her vision of the room she was to spend her time in. She wiped them away with her sleeve and looked around.

The floorboards were bare except for a well-worn rug between the two narrow beds pushed up against the sloping wall on one side of the room. Her bag was on one of the beds and her uniform was spread out next to it. The wall facing the beds had a curtained alcove each side of the huge chimney-breast. Putting the jug down on the washstand in the centre, Megan pulled one of the curtains aside. There was a rail with hooks on it and some shelves at the bottom. She should put her things away and get herself ready but she had no inclination to do so. The relief to find it wasn't the dungeon she had imagined had done little to lift her.

The shame she'd felt at being told in front of Cissy about such private things as to where she was to go to the lavatory and the mention of the pot under her bed gnawed at her. And loneliness like she'd never known before crushed her.

She sat down on the uncluttered bed and buried her head in the pillow. What had she now? No Mam to find, no Hattie, no Sister Bernadette... 'Oh, Hattie, Hattie...'

A tapping on her door broke into her sobs. She hesitated a moment before grabbing her hankie. She wiped her tears and blew her nose, 'Who's that?'

'It's me, 'Cissy.''

The loud whisper warmed her and her body moved towards the door before she'd time to tell it to, such was her pleasure in the realisation that Cissy wasn't put off by all that had happened.

'Aren't you ready, yet? By, you'll catch it, come on.'

It was as if they'd known each other forever the way Cissy spoke as she came through the door.

'Come on, Megan, get your frock and pinny on. I couldn't wait to get mine on.'

Cissy twirled round and in an exaggerated posh voice said, 'Don't you think it is the height of fashion, Miss Tattler? The navy is the latest colour and the ankle length gives one...modesty.'

The twirl ended with her falling on to the bed giggling in such a way it would take a saint not to join in with.

The giggling felt good but it didn't last long. Cissy stopped as suddenly as she'd started and sat up. 'I'm sorry about all me blubbing earlier. Only I haven't ever been away from me mam afore and, well...me dad...me dad passed on just a few weeks ago.'

Megan didn't know what to say. She took Cissy's hand and they sat a moment not speaking.

'Anyroad, as me mam'd say, there's nothing to be gained in feeling sorry for yourself, there's always those worse off. And, we'll have each other, Meg.'

Only Hattie had ever called her, Meg, before. It was strange to hear but somehow right that Cissy should call her that, too.

'Come on. Slap that flannel round your face and get dressed. Miss What's-Her-Knickers'll be at the bottom of the stairs any minute.'

'Miss What's-Her-Knickers?'

'Aye, that's what me Mam'd call her. Besides other things that would make your lugs go red! I'll tell you of them some other time though as I'd better be off. Me and you have to be secret friends, Meg.'

As the door closed behind Cissy, Megan could have shouted out. Such was the good feeling that replaced the loneliness inside her.

CHAPTER FOUR

'By, you're up with the lark this morning, dear. You haven't wet the bed, have you?'

Hattie giggled. Cook had some funny sayings. 'No, Cook, I just thought as I'd give Betty a hand. She's lagging behind a bit and I've plenty of time to do me own chores.'

'You're a good lass. You've settled well and you only being here a few days. I've given a good report to housekeeper and she's right pleased with you.'

Cook was standing in front of the gleaming black cooking range stirring a large pan of porridge. The job of blacking the range was one of Hattie's chores she'd to do at least once a week, but she didn't mind.

To her surprise she had found she liked the kitchen work. Everything about the large warm kitchen was comforting to her. It was a busy place and not just because of all the baking that went on. It was also a social place for the staff as they gathered for meals at the large scrubbed table in the centre and popped in and out as they went about their business.

'Mind,' Cook continued, 'It don't do to be too kind you know. You could be put on. Though I'll admit as Betty needs a lift, her only having a few weeks to go till she drops her babby.'

Hattie didn't reply. She carried on gathering the bucket, brush and shovel she needed from the utility cupboard at the other end of the kitchen. She had to clean out the grates in the front room and the hall. She'd already done the breakfast room and the withdrawing room and had set fires going in both before she had helped Betty to get the sheets soaped.

'Are you happy then, lass?' Cook stopped her stirring and looked over towards her.

'Aye, I'm all right. It isn't what I want to do with me life but it's working out better than I thought it would.'

'Good. It's a while since we had someone as knew how to go on without being shown every five minutes. Daisy was the last and she'd come from the same place as you did. They teach you well, I must say.'

'Daisy! Daisy, was here?'

'Aye, she was a good lass. It was a pity and unexpected, I might say, when she ran off. Just like that without a by your leave! I hope you don't do the same, Hattie.'

Hattie couldn't speak. All in all she'd been happy. She was well fed and had a space of her own in a little room at the top of the house. She got on well with everyone. The work was hard and the hours long but she'd been willing to stick it out. But now her fear was taking her happiness away and she knew that fear to deepen at Cook's next words.

'Has Mrs Barker told you about the party next week, then?'

'No, is...is the family coming that soon?'

'Oh, aye. Lord and Lady Marley will be here come Saturday and the rest of the family, ten of them altogether with Lady Marley's sister and her brood, will be here come Wednesday. The party on the following Saturday kicks off the Christmas season. We'll have our work cut out that day, I can tell you. They'll likely be around fifty guests with at least twenty staying over. But don't be worrying you'll have your duties all mapped out and as long as you carry them through and keep out of sight as much as you can you'll be all right.'

Out of sight! Hattie had a mind to not be found at all! She stood a moment unsure what to do. Should she say she knew why Daisy had left?

The sudden appearance of the housekeeper stopped her from saying anything further.

'What's this? Not slacking, are we? There's not enough time to stand gaping into space, Hattie. Not now and certainly not when the family arrive so don't be making a habit of it, girl.'

'No, Mrs Barker, I'm sorry, I...'

'It was my fault,' Cook said, 'I was telling her of the family coming. Mind, lass has been up a couple of hours and has been giving Betty a hand so I thought it wouldn't hurt for her to slow down a bit.'

'Very well, Cook, we'll let it go this time. Now, Hattie, after breakfast come to my room. I need to talk to you about the extra duties you are to carry out whilst the family are here.'

Breakfast was a feast of creamy porridge followed by scrambled egg on thick slices of toasted bread, all of which looked delicious, but Hattie could hardly pick at. Thankfully no one seemed to notice so she wasn't asked to account for her lack of appetite.

Usually Hattie enjoyed the banter that went on amongst the staff at mealtimes but today she felt a relief when Cook called the proceedings to a halt by sending everyone back to their chores. Hattie was sent to retrieve the housekeeper's tray.

'Well, Hattie, you seem to be settling in I am pleased to see.' Mrs Barker had invited her to sit down as soon as she'd entered her office.

'Now, you know about the family coming home next week so I will run through what is expected of you during the time all their guests are here with us.'

The list of her extra chores seemed endless to Hattie. She'd to step out of her usual role whilst the house was so busy and assist the chambermaids, women from the neighbourhood, who all knew the routine well and would be in early the next day and everyday throughout the family's stay. She would be responsible for the fires, the turning down of the beds at the end of the evening and the bed warming of five of the bedrooms, including that of Lady Marley. And, she must be ready to run for trays whenever needed besides generally help everyone out.

This meant she'd be on her feet for most of the day from six in the morning till gone midnight on the day of the party and till at least eleven at night on other days with only a two hour break in the afternoon.

The work didn't bother her, but with what happened to Daisy fresh in her mind, being around the bedrooms late at night did. Lying awake in the early hours she thought about her situation and tried to quell the fear building up inside her.

Leaving wasn't an option. She had no money and her wages weren't due until her first leave days after Christmas and that was weeks away. And telling what she knew of why Daisy had left and of her own fears had become impossible. Everyone had spoken so highly of the family and the master. She'd never be believed.

There was only Betty who hadn't said anything whilst the others were going on. But then, she didn't say much at anytime. She mainly kept her head bent as if she was looking for something. Hattie worried about Betty she seemed to be very unhappy. She looked fearful and jumped if she was spoken to. No, she couldn't add to whatever troubled Betty by talking to her about her fears.

Her thoughts went to Megan. Tears stung her eyes as she lay wondering what Megan was doing. There was no one of her own age here. No one she could make a friend of. She liked them all, but it wasn't like she and Meg had been.

She brushed away her tears. She would cope. She'd watch her back at all times. Make sure the corridors were clear of folk before she came out of the rooms. At least the ones she was responsible for were all to be occupied by ladies. Even the master had a separate room to his wife and though their rooms did have a connecting door she felt sure if she came across him he wouldn't try anything in his wife's bedroom. No, she'd be safe until she left the rooms. Then she would have to watch her step.

***

Making her way to her room for her afternoon break on the day of the party, Hattie thought she'd been daft to have been afraid. She was sure poor Daisy must have been in the wrong place at the wrong time, because despite her being around the place from morning till night she'd hardly clapped eyes on the master. And on the two occasions she had seen him he hadn't even glanced at her.

'There you are, Hattie. I wanted to catch you before you went for your break.'

Hattie nearly jumped out of her skin as she rounded the corner and saw the housekeeper standing at the bottom of the stairs leading to her room.

'I'm going to be very busy here there and everywhere tonight. I wanted to make sure you know to finish warming Lady Marley's bed and have her fire well banked up at precisely midnight, having finished all the other rooms you are responsible for first. Now this is very important as Lady Marley has informed me the carriages are leaving at eleven forty-five and she and all the ladies in residence intend to leave the gentlemen just after and retire. Do you understand, Hattie?'

'Yes, Mrs Barker, I'll have it all done on time.'

'That's a good girl. Now, after you have finished I want you to make your way to the west-wing kitchen using the back stairs. You are to see if you can be of any help. If not, you may retire to your bed.'

Hattie nodded.

'Good. Make sure you have a good rest now. It's going to be a long day. A very long day.'

For one moment she thought Mrs Barker was going to take hold of her. The smile she had on her face was a funny sort of smile and she had her head bent to one side, just like Sister Bernadette used to when she was pleased with her. It was odd. But then, everything seemed odd today. Different to normal.

It wasn't just the arrival of some of the guests that was causing it. Mrs Barker hovering around the bottom of the stairs waiting to give her instructions was something she hadn't known to happen before. And, only a few minutes ago she'd seen Florrie Bateman, the chambermaid she helped, coming out of one of the guest bedrooms looking as if she had been in a fight. Her hair had been sticking out of her mobcap and she had been fastening her pinny. And yet, they'd finished cleaning and preparing that room hours ago. And where had Florrie found the coins she saw her put into her apron pocket?

With all this playing on her mind and the excitement and noise of more of the guests arriving, Hattie didn't rest well during her break. Tiredness gnawed at the bones of her as she closed Lady Marley's bedroom door having finished the last of her chores.

Turning towards the west wing she made the back stairs in time to be out of sight of the ladies she'd heard coming up the stairs. This relaxed her a little, but she hoped she wouldn't be needed to help out when she reached the kitchen.

Going down the first steep flight of stairs tired her even more. Her pace slowed as she walked along the corridor towards the last flight that would take her down to the kitchen. This corridor had the bedrooms on one side which were used to house the visiting staff.

Hattie thought about these strange beings and how they displayed airs and graces and thought of themselves as above the regular household staff. She imagined most, though probably not the ladies maids, were tucked up and snoring by now.

She had reached the last bedroom when suddenly the door opened and a large man stepped out into her path.

'Aahh, so the little lady has arrived! Jolly good, this way, my dear.'

She shrank back. 'I...I'm sorry, Sir, I...'

'Come along now, don't be shy your master is waiting...'

'But...but, I'm on me way to the kitchens, I've to help out...I...'

'That's enough! You know very well why you are here. Mrs Barker would have told you. Now come along and don't keep your master waiting. Or, you may find your pay is halved!'

The man grabbed her arm. Hattie tried to pull away, 'You're mistaken, Sir, Mrs Barker told me to go to the west kitchen...'

He pulled her into the room.

'She's here, David, and my, she's a young piece and just ripe I'd say. Pity it's your turn to go first, old chap.'

'Ha! Felix, you needn't try that one. I intend to take my rightful turn so you'll not sway me.'

Hattie looked from one to the other. Her fear banged her heart against her ribs. Lord Marley rose from where he had been sitting in a chair in the corner of the room and came towards her. His smile a smirk that didn't reach his ugly cloying eyes.

'Umm...Very young, and petite with it.'

The high voice Hattie knew him to have sounded deep, raspy and slurred.

'Come on over here, little one, and take off your clothes. I've a mind to see you first and by the looks of you, tiny firm breasts just emerging and I'd wager, a fluff beginning to sprout between your legs, I'm in for a treat…'

A scream started in her bowel, racked her throat and assailed her ears as her body cringed away from him.

'Now, now. I like a fight, but there's no need to go as far as to scream. We don't want to wake the other servants, do we?'

His body was close to hers. She could smell him. Cigars, wine and a musty perfume smell that turned her stomach. Beads of sweat trickled down his fat jowls and his hands felt wet and clammy as he grabbed her arms.

Instinctively Hattie kicked out. Her foot caught his shin. He doubled over. Then straightened and slapped her face. The sting brought tears to her eyes.

'Little bitch! Hold her Felix.'

Her shoulders burned with the pain of being pulled back from behind. She couldn't move. Lord Marley's face was still near to hers. His anger snapped from him. 'I'll stop your antics, you little vixen. You bloody well know why you're here so don't play the innocent. If you want the money you do as you are bid. Am I making myself clear?'

'I don't know, Sir…I was told I was to go to the…'

'That's enough.' Lord Marley looked above her head. 'What do you think, Felix?'

'Well, she's here now and she's definitely the one pointed out to me. I think she's got cold feet, but that's not our problem, is it?'

'No, you're right and I'm not thinking to give up now. As long as you're of the same mind?'

'I think the plaster and the cords will help our cause…'

'Good idea. Let's get on with it, then.'

Hattie fought until every bone of her ached with exhaustion. Her tears clogged her nose. The plaster over her mouth suffocated her, and yet, it seemed the more she struggled the more they enjoyed themselves. They tore at her clothes taking no heed that her uniform was being ruined. Shame took her as they gazed on her naked body before dragging her towards the bed.

She could do nothing. Her arms and legs were stretched as far as they would go and tied to each corner bed-post. There was no way she could help her cause. Moving only dug the cords deeper into her hands and feet. Struggling to breathe took all her energy.

Lord Marley stood over her and undid the buttons on his fly.

Hattie found she couldn't look away from the sight of what he fetched out from his trousers and rubbed up and down in his cupped hand. Was he really going to put that in her, like Daisy said men did? Her fear became a terror.

The bed sank as it took his weight. He knelt over her, his hand next to her head steadying him. His other hand still grasped himself.

She couldn't swallow. Her heart bled the agony of her terror. Useless prayers mocked her brain.

Lord Marley crushed her as he bore down on her. His hand touched her private. Then a stretching, ripping sensation seared a pain through her. Her mind couldn't take in the horror. Her thoughts swam away in the cold tears that ran down her cheeks and into her ears. She was nothing, nothing, nothing...

The sound of splashing water woke her. Her head hurt. Her throat burned. Her mind wouldn't give her why she was lying on this bed in this strange room. She looked over to where the sound was coming from and saw the man the master had called, Felix, filling the bowl from the jug on the wash stand.

Memory slapped her bringing back the pain and humiliation and the moment He had done to her what the master had done. The horrible smell of the cloth he had put over her face after he'd finished still stung her nostrils. Then she realised the plaster had gone from her mouth and her arms and legs were no longer tied.

She looked round the room. The master had gone.

Felix brought her attention back to him. 'When I leave you are to wash yourself. There's a new uniform in the cupboard.' He moved over to the door as he spoke. 'Tell no one or you'll be out on your arse with nothing.' Then, just before he closed the door he threw some coins onto the bed.

Hattie didn't move but her body did. It shook. Every limb and every part of her trembled. Her teeth knocked together as did her knees. It was the warm wetness dribbling down her legs and dampening the sheet beneath her that determined her to take action. Action that was born out of memory of standing for hours with wet sheets tied around her whenever she'd wet the bed like this back at the convent.

She eased herself off the bed and made as if to strip it, but the sight of the bloodied sheet and the smell of her urine renewed the terror in her. She crumpled to the ground and wept.

CHAPTER FIVE

A forced cough alerted Megan. She looked over at Cissy. Cissy nodded in the direction of Madame's office.

The words, "Miss Scot-Price, how nice of you to say you like my designs much better than Madame Marie's," flashed into Megan's head and sweated her body with fear as she saw Miss Stallton walking towards the office with a sketchbook in her hand.

Just last week Miss Scot-Price had been in the salon to choose her gowns for her debutante year. Megan had fetched swatches of material for the girl and her mother to choose from.

The colours and the feel of the different fabrics had inspired Megan. She had sketched late into the night.

Cissy had been enthralled with the designs. She'd taken the crayon and drawn a figure with a bubble coming out of its mouth with those words written in and underneath she had written, 'Madam Megan.'

The joke had grown and they'd drawn another figure with huge tears coming from its eyes and written underneath, 'Madame Marie'.

Miss Stallton's face had a look of sheer delight as she wafted the sketchbook in Megan's direction before entering Madame's office.

Megan held her breath, there was no doubt in her mind now. The sketchbook was hers. *'How did Miss Stallton come to have it?'*

'Miss Tattler!' Madame's voice boomed out from her office.

Megan jumped. The fear in her deepened. *'I'll be thrown out...'*

A movement of the bench took her attention. Cissy stood up and headed towards the office.

'No, Cissy... No...'

'It was my doing, Megan, and I'm not letting you take the blame.'

Megan jumped up and ran around the benches but wasn't in time to stop Cissy, who had reached the office, knocked on the open door and walked in.

'Miss Grantham? Get out at once! I called for Miss Tattler.'

'But it wasn't her doing, not the fun making. It was me. All Megan did was to draw the designs and...'

'Are you daring to speak to me without being spoken to and to call one of my la...Miss Tattler, by her first name?'

'Aye, I am. Megan is me friend and I'm not for letting her take the blame for something as I did.'

The fear in Megan made it hard to swallow the spittle in her mouth. She looked from one to the other. Cissy, red faced and defiant and Madame, just as red, but with a rage on her that was making her eyes bulge from their sockets.

Madame broke the stare and turned in her direction, 'Miss Tattler is this true, have you gone against my instructions and formed an alliance with Miss Grantham?'

Megan nodded.

'You are two of a kind! I should have known. I should not have given you privileges you did not appreciate, Miss Grantham.' She was silent for a moment, her eyes scanning the drawings.

'However, Miss Tattler, you have settled in well and apart from this...this...' She waved the sketch pad, its pages snapping her anger, 'I have to admit I have been pleased with your work and your manner. The pleats you stitched into the bodice of Lady Gladwyn's frock were beautifully done. She commented on them'

Megan kept her head bowed, not sure whether to say she was sorry for the drawings and the little figures in the corner or to say thank you for the praise she'd been given. The noise of pages being torn from her pad lifted her gaze.

'You have a talent, Miss Tattler, but if you think design is all about producing good drawings and having a good imagination and flair; you are very much mistaken. The drawings are only the basis of design. They need to be broken down into pieces that form a pattern. Each piece must be precisely measured to fit, not only with the other pieces to build the garment, but to the figure of the client. All the details need to be enhanced in smaller drawings for the finishers. Only then can it go to the first cutters who will make a pattern for the second cutters to use as their guide to cut the material.'

She paused and gazed at one of the drawings she had been sifting through.

'Umm, yes, well, imagination and flare you certainly do have, this is very good. However, without the technical know-how you cannot call yourself a designer. It takes years...years.'

Without her seeming to make a movement one of the drawers of her desk sprung open. She tucked the drawings into it.

'Now, Miss Grantham, what are we going to do about you? It appears from these early days that you are good at sewing on buttons, hooks and eyes and press studs and not much else. Obviously there is a need in the finishing room for someone who is good at these tasks and willing to do them. But, you are headstrong and at times very, very rude. This must change. Otherwise, I will write to Laura…Mrs Harvey and tell her that you are not suitable. I know this won't please her and, as she is a valued customer, I am reluctant to do this. Therefore, I want you to make an extreme effort.'

'Yes, Madame, I'm sorry, Madame.'

'Miss Tattler, I think you have earned the right to have a companion. You may move your things to the attic, Miss Grantham, and occupy the other bed in that room.

'Yes, Madame, thank you, Madame.'

'I do not want a repetition of what happened today. And, Miss Tattler, If you do any drawings in the future I want you to show them to me. If you continue to show such promise I may consider training you in the techniques of design.'

'Oh ta, Madame, ta very much.'

'You mean, "THANK YOU". Oh, just get back to your work and ask Miss Stallton to come to my office.'

In their hurry to get out they bumped into one another. Cissy giggled. The joy inside Megan spilled her own giggles, but the smug look Miss Stallton gave her when she came out of Madame's office deadened the feeling and uneasiness stirred in the pit of her stomach.

***

Engrossed in her work, embroidering a rose on the collar of a silk blouse two weeks later, Megan's thoughts were of Hattie. She listed the things she needed to tell her. She'd start the letter tonight then it would be ready to post by the time her leave days came and she had the money for a stamp. She could use some pages out of her sketch pad.

She'd tell Hattie about Cissy's mam's letter inviting her to go home with Cissy for their leave days. And, best of all, to spend Christmas there, too! Excitement at the thought of going to a real family home tickled her insides, but the tickle dulled into an ache as she remembered it will be her first Christmas without Hattie. She hoped Hattie was as happy as she was.

A door banged at the other end of the room bringing her out of her thoughts. The ladies were back from breakfast.

'Come on, Megan, I'm…'

Madame's voice commanding their attention stopped Cissy finishing what she was going to say. 'Gather round, ladies. This is the first of the garments for Miss Scot-Price. There is a good deal of smocking to be done.'

Megan's breath caught deep in her lungs. She glanced over at Cissy, willed her not to say anything. Cissy's mouth opened and then closed. Megan nodded at her, letting her know that she was right not to speak out.

The emerald green satin caught the light and enhanced the flounces of the skirt just like she knew it would. And the smocking would tighten the bodice in a soft way so suitable for a young lady. The frock was everything she'd dreamed it would be.

'It is superb, Madame,' Miss Stallton said, giving a sideways glance in Megan's direction. 'Your designs are always beautiful, Madame. What did Miss Scot-Price think of this one?'

'Thank you, Miss Stallton. Miss Scot-Price was enthralled with my design and when she came for the first fitting, she had tears in her eyes. Now, Miss Tattler...' Madame's eyes narrowed. Megan read the warning; knew she was being dared not to protest. 'I want you to do the smocking. And, Miss Stallton, you are to attach the lace edging around the bodice and sleeves.'

Miss Stallton let out a small laugh. 'Delighted to, Madame.'

Megan felt Miss Stallton's eyes on her and didn't have to look to know the smirk that would be on her face. Madame must've sworn her to secrecy over what she'd seen in the sketch pad.

Anger born of the knowledge there was nothing she could do welled up stinging, unshed-able tears to the back of Megan's eyes. She did not look at Madame as she took the garment.

There was no further explanation offered. There was no need of one. Madame knew she didn't have to explain where the smocking should start and end.

As she and Cissy left their benches and went towards the dining room, Megan acknowledged for the umpteenth time how glad she was of the rule that they weren't allowed to take meals or breaks with the others.

'Eeh, Megan...'

'It's all right, Cissy, don't fret yourself. I'll get me own back one day. I'll show her.'

'How?'

'I'll tell you when we're sat down, I'm starving.'

'I'll make you some toast, the fires glowing so it won't smoke the bread. There's not much left to go with it by the looks of things.' The lids of the breakfast trays clanged one after the other as Cissy made her fruitless search, 'Just a dried up fried egg and some crispy rinds of the ladies bacon and that's your lot.'

'Toast'll be all right. I'll pour us a mug of tea.'

Once Cissy had her tea in her hand she asked Megan again how she thought she could get her own back on Madame.

'Oh, it won't be for a while, but I've a dream in me and I mean to catch it.'

'Catch it? That's a saying as I haven't heard afore, Megan.'

'It isn't a saying as such...' Something stopped her from telling Cissy about the locket, it was if she would lose something if she spoke of it. 'It just means, well, yer know, like a falling star carrying your dream and you have to be ready to catch it.' She'd thought this out when she'd been thinking about the engraving and she hoped that is what it did mean, it sounded nice.

'That's grand. What is your dream, Megan?'

'To own me own establishment just like this one, where me frocks and gowns I design are known as mine and...' The tears she'd not thought she'd shed spilled over. She brushed them away. 'But, I've a lot to learn afore that can happen and saying anything about Madame taking me drawings and using them as her own won't help me.'

She knew she was telling herself as much as Cissy. It helped. Her need to cry passed. 'I have to keep doing good work and giving Madame me ideas and then hope as she'll keep her promise and one day teach me how to turn me drawings into garments.'

'But, it isn't right...It's not fair as she...'

'Aye, I know it isn't right as she's took me design as her own and I've a mind she'll carry on doing so, but it's like Sister Bernadette always said to me and Hattie, "All that's fair isn't always right and all that's right isn't always fair." Anyroad, it's not all bad, Ciss. Me drawings led to us sharing and being open with our friendship...Hey, watch that toast its scorching, there's smoke coming from it.'

Cissy rescued the toast and set things back to normal by acting the fool as she juggled the hot bread.

But though Megan laughed at her antics part of her didn't laugh. Sister Bernadette's words were true; she knew that, but unfairness, right or wrong, still hurt.

37

CHAPTER SIX

Laura Harvey looked across the table at her husband. Had she heard, right? 'You intend to rejoin your regiment! Jeremy, you can't mean that, surely?'

'I do, Laura. I have thought long and hard and it is the only way I would be able to live with myself. I can't think of my men going to war without me.'

'But, what about the colliery, and...And the farm, and the estate?' She wanted to say: *and what about me? But then, there is no 'me' anymore,* she thought.

'Laura, Laura, you know very well you can manage without me. You are the only woman I know who has a business head on her shoulders as good as a man's, besides, you have done it before.'

The scratching of his knife on his toast grated on her. It went on longer than necessary as he spread the butter to every corner giving him a reason not to look at her.

He hardly ever looked at her. And of all the bare-faced cheek, to say, just because he needed her to take over the running of the business again, that she had a good business head!

Taking a bite of his toast before laying it down and wiping his hands on his napkin, he picked up his paper and unfolded it. *Oh, why did his every movement affect her, she was like a dog waiting for a titbit at his master's knee!*

'I've spoken to Charles and he said he will oversee the financial side...'

His voice droned on. Laura's pain stabbed deeper.

Did Daphne know of his plans? Surely Charles would have told her? But no, her sister wouldn't keep this from her. Daphne had been a tower of strength to her this past year, and Charles had offered to speak to Jeremy about his treatment of her, but she had refused to let him. Of course Jeremy would have to speak to Charles, their financial matters were dealt with by his bank and Charles himself oversaw their accounts...

Jeremy's voice changed bringing her attention back to him.

'...So, what do you think?'

'This is my punishment, isn't it, Jeremy? My God! Don't you think I've been punished enough?'

'Your... punishment?'

'Yes. You've never said anything, but I've known. You blame me for the loss of our son. It's why you called a halt on my stud farm and now this...'

'Good God! Is that what you think?'

'What else am I to think? You won't talk to me about what happened. You're distant. You don't even come to my bed any more. And now you want to go away and leave me...' Tears rained uncontrollably down her cheeks. Pictures flashed in her mind. Pictures she'd denied access to for over a year: The agonising birth, the tiny, still body, the blond tufts of hair and the little fingers unable to reach out to her. Then the blackness, the sinking clawing blackness and emerging weeks later to face the truth, her child, her baby, was dead and she would never be able to conceive again!

'Laura, darling, I...I thought you wouldn't want me... I thought...Oh, my darling.'

Jeremy rose and came round the table towards her. Taking her hands he pulled her up from her chair and held her to him. 'I tried to comfort you, I tried...'

Her tears became draining sobs, 'It was too soon. I wasn't ready, but then...' She couldn't say it. She couldn't pile the pain of his distancing himself from her on to the agony of the loss she'd allowed into her heart. It was over, she was in his arms. He was whispering his own agony and his love into her hair.

After a moment he guided her to a chair, knelt down in front of her and buried his head in her lap. Her crying slowed. His pain eased hers.

'He was so beautiful, our little son... He...Leonard, was so beautiful...'

His words shocked her. She hadn't known he'd been affected in this way. Hadn't thought he could feel what she had. She'd been so selfish in her grief... My God! She had been just as guilty in shutting him out...

'Oh, Jeremy...Jeremy.' She stroked his hair. His crying stopped. He lifted his head and all she loved about him was there before her, looking up into her eyes, loving her with his very being.

'Laura, I've missed you so much, darling.'

'Oh Jeremy...'

They stood without bidding each other to do so. Joined in pain. Joined in love. They clung together.

When his lips found hers the torn seams of her world were brought together. Feelings she'd denied herself crept over her and were answered in the deepening of his kiss.

'Shall we go upstairs, darling?'

She giggled at his question. A silly, girlie giggle. 'The chamber maid...'

'Well the guest-wing, then?'

'No, Jeremy, they will know...They'll have to re-do it...'

'Stop putting hurdles in my way, Wench, I mean to have you and will do so right here if you don't find a solution as to where.'

Her giggle became a belly-laugh like she hadn't experienced for such a long time. She'd forgotten what a clown Jeremy could be. His laughter joined hers, but not for long. She was in his arms again. So close she could feel his need. Her own desire became a hunger.

Neither of them said anything. Their love didn't need a voice or any clowning around. It was reignited. Their kisses told of their feelings.

It was Jeremy who broke away, took her hand and led her across the hall to her office locking the door behind them.

'We won't be disturbed, darling. The servants know what's afoot. Didn't you hear the door open and then close again?'

She knew a moment's embarrassment but it faded into oblivion when he took her in his arms and rained kisses over her face, her neck and her breasts as he manoeuvred her towards the couch.

Undressing wasn't a slow dignified process. Garments were discarded in a frenzy of activity as their eyes told of hunger and need. No time was given to fondling. None was needed, only a joining of their bodies would satisfy their craving. A joining that came the moment the soft cushions accepted her naked flesh.

The deep intrusion was all she wanted it to be. The words of love Jeremy spoke were all she wanted to hear.

Her body took and gave back the desperate thrusting with an urgency that begged to be released. A release that came with an ecstatic pulsating that caused her to stretch out her body beneath him.

'Oh Jeremy...Jeremy. Stop, stop, darling, Pleee...ease...'

He held still as she bid. Her muscles clenched on him throbbing spasms through her that were beyond endurance.

His mouth covered hers and drank in her moans. His hands searched and caressed her breasts, her buttocks and the deep crevice of her back till finally she relaxed and took once more his deep thrusting till his body released his love into her.

They lay still locked together for sometime after, cementing their love in the stillness. Their closeness and what they had just shared said all they needed to say.

After a few moments Jeremy eased himself from her and looked down into her face. 'My darling, I love you.'

'I love you, too, My Sweetheart.'

A shadow of concern passed over his face. 'If only I'd known…'

'What is it, darling, what's wrong?'

He didn't answer her but climbed off her, sat on the edge of the sofa and pulled his trousers on.

A sinking feeling banished all traces of the ecstasy from her. 'Jeremy?'

He gathered up her clothes. 'Here, darling. Put these on and we'll talk.'

Once they were dressed he took her in his arms for a moment and then eased her down on to the sofa.

'If only I'd known before… I wouldn't have rejoined my regiment. I would have found it hard not to, the men, you know… But with everything how it was, it was unbearable. I wanted to get away. I used the talk of war as an excuse. I persuaded them to take me as soon as possible. I told them I needed to brush up on my training… To get to know the men I hadn't led before … Oh God, it's too late… Too late…'

'Oh, no! No! I don't want you to go! How could you have taken such a step without talking to me about it?'

'I felt so certain that you couldn't bear me to be around, I'm sorry, my darling, I'm sorry. Forgive me.'

'Won't they release you, darling? Can't you make some excuse? After all, no one is certain we will go to war.'

'I've signed! Oh, Laura…' He wiped the tear from her cheek. Don't cry, darling.'

He pulled her into his arms. Tears she'd always thought of as a weakness gave no head to her battle against them. It seemed her whole body wanted to weep. Weep for the feeling of loss she'd denied. Weep for the love that had been frozen. Weep for the loss she faced with not having Jeremy with her and weep for her fears for him.

Jeremy held her throughout. His love helped her till she came to an acceptance.

CHAPTER SEVEN

'You're looking under the weather these days, Hattie, is anything wrong, lass?'

'No, Cook, I'm all right.'

'Is it your bleeding, have you started with that, yet?'

'Aye, I have, and happen it's that as is coming on.' Hattie hurried out of the kitchen afraid to stand under the scrutiny of Cook for long, and embarrassed at her blunt way of talking. It was her bleeding she was worried about, but not its coming, just the opposite in fact. She'd been due over a week ago and nothing had happened.

There was no one amongst the staff that Hattie felt able to confide in. She wanted to, but it was a question of whether she'd be believed and what would happen if she wasn't. She had a plan, though. As soon as she got her first leave days and her wages, she would leave. She would go to Daisy and ask her for her help

She had thought of borrowing a stamp and some paper and writing to Megan and telling her, but the shame still burned in her and stopped her from doing so. Megan was part of her life that was clean and trouble-free. She didn't want to taint that with the dirt that had happened to her.

Every time she thought of what had happened she became more convinced in herself that Mrs Barker had had a hand in it. *Why would the master and that other one think she knew the reason for being there? In fact, they had said, "Mrs Barker would have told you... "*

Hattie had just sat down to have her breakfast with the rest of the staff when Cook questioned her again.

'Eat up, lass, you've hardly eaten anything for days now, are you sure you feel all right?'

'Aye, I'm tired, that's all, Cook. I'll be right when we get Christmas over and I get me leave days. I'm going to stay with a friend in Leeds. I'll be a different person when I get back.'

'You are coming back, then?'

This shocked her, as did the way Cook looked at her.

'We've all been there, yer know, it's not easy to come back when you have your first time away from here and with your wages in your pocket, an all. But it's hard out there. You'll not find the same protection as you have in here, especially with you not having a family.'

As usually happened, everyone was surprised when Betty spoke, but what she said now caused everyone to take a sharp intake of breath. 'Has something happened, Hattie? We know the way of it and can be of help, yer know.'

'Bet...'

Cook didn't get a chance to even finish bringing Betty's name out before the kitchen door flung open and Mrs Barker stood glaring at them. 'What is going on? I have my hatch open and...Well, it is obvious you all have more than enough to say.' She directed her gaze at Betty.

'Aye, well, you can't be at marrying this one off. She's only just on thirteen!' There was a death-like silence, the cracking of which by Betty's chair scraping along the stone floor before crashing to the ground, made them all jump.

A sobbing Betty climbed over her chair and ran from the kitchen.

Cook stood up, 'Its not still happening, is it? Be God, no! I thought after Aggie...but...Betty... and...and young-un here?'

Sweat beads trickled a shiny path down Mrs Barker's colourless face.

'God! You've something to answer for, Jean Barker,' Cook said, 'Well, this time you can answer to Madam, because I'm going to do as I've told you I'd do if it happened again. I'm going to tell Madam what's happening and what part you play in it, and, how you profit from it, too!'

There was a moment when Hattie thought Mrs Barker would crumble, her body shook and swayed from side to side, but she pulled herself together and walked out of the kitchen.

Cook took charge. 'Right, off with you, go on all of you. Get to your work. And you, too, Jimmy. And close your mouth before flies can take root in there.' The stable boy did as she bid without his usual back-chat. 'Florrie!' Cooks commanding tone stopped Florrie just as she was going out of the door. 'Find Betty and send her back in. Tell her I want her to help me with Hattie. I'm going to get to the bottom of this.'

The silence after the commotion clawed at Hattie. Cook came round the table to her.

'Eeh, Hattie lass, tell me what happened.'

Hattie couldn't speak. Her stomach lurched. Her head swam. The heat of the kitchen dragged at her. She was sinking...sinking...

'Come on, Hattie lass. Everything'll be all right, we'll help you.'

The soothing voice that met her as she came out of the blackness spilled her tears.

'There, there. Let it all out. Hold her a mo, Betty. There's, a good lass. Come on now, tell us what happened.'

Hattie knew a feeling of safety surround her. She could tell them. There would be understanding. She leant heavily on Betty and told them what she could, though the shame of it only allowed some of it to be spoken of.

'Same thing happened to me', Betty said. 'It were the start of the summer season. Mrs Barker made me pass this off as Cory's.' She jabbed at her stomach. 'She knew we were talking of being wed, but Cory hadn't done anything to me. He isn't the same with me. He married me because he was told he'd lose his job if he didn't. He wanted to be first, as it should be, but now, well, I don't know which one fathered me babby...'

'Oh, Be God, she'll not get away with this! I caught her out before. Years ago. It was a young lass by the name of, Aggie. In fact, she came from the convent you've come from, Hattie. Anyroad, you know how tale goes. Well, young Aggie came screaming to me in the night. I had Mrs Barker about it and she played the innocent, though I always suspected she had a part in it as Aggie had said. And she was flush for a while after. Going off and buying new clothes. She said it wouldn't be happening again as she'd make sure it didn't. I didn't want to, but I left it at that and haven't had reason to suspect anything since. By, but she's been clever with it.'

'It happened to Daisy, an all,' Hattie told them. 'I didn't know it was here she'd worked until you told me, Cook, but Daisy told me the master of the house where she worked had forced her to do it. That's why she ran off.'

'Right, that's it! Betty, get on with clearing this lot. You help her if you feel up to it, Hattie. I'm going to see Lady Marley.'

When Cook had left the room, Betty asked, 'Are you worried over anything else, Hattie? Have you started having your bleeding? And...and did they hurt you badly?'

'Aye, me bleeding hasn't come and...and it was bad... '

'Oh, dear. You could be caught. Aye, I know as you're only young, but once you have your bleeding, then you can get caught for a babby. Look, don't worry. Cook'll sort something out.'

'I'm not coming back. Don't tell Cook about me bleeding not coming, Betty. She'll not be able to help me and if they know, I'll be shipped off to some convent and I couldn't bare that. I have a plan. As soon as I have me wage I'm off. I'm going to Daisy.'

'Aye, happen as that's best. I s'pose as I were lucky having Cory, even though everything's been spoilt by it all. But, Hattie, you can come to me and Cory if you get stuck anytime. We understand and'll help you all we can.'

'Ta, Betty.' The words could hardly be heard. Hattie's unshed tears took their own course. Betty cried with her. They held each other, each finding some comfort in the understanding of the other.

Two hours hadn't passed before Mrs Barker left taking all her goods and chattels with her. Her parting shot to Cook was to flash her handsome pay off money as if she had triumphed. But, Jimmy saved the day. He brought the trap round to the back of the house for her, but he didn't help load her boxes and everyone laughed every time she dropped one of them.

Lord Marley followed shortly after as did all the other guests, leaving only Lady Marley and her sister, Lady Carter, in residence.

In the hushed household, the sound of Lady Marley's distress filled the corridors until later that evening when the doctor arrived and she became quiet. Not long after, Lady Carter sent word for Cook to bring Hattie to her. She would see them in the housekeeper's office.

As they were about to knock on the door Cook patted her on the shoulder and said, 'Speak up, Hattie, don't be afraid. If there's anything you want I'm for thinking you will get it in exchange for your silence. I'm going to see as Betty's looked after, an all.'

***

Desolation filled Hattie as she boarded the train early the next morning. The ten pound silence money tucked into her blouse pocket and what was left of her wages, after deductions, in her purse, did nothing to console her. She had been given the opportunity to stay or to leave, but then, neither Lady Carter nor Cook had guessed what was in her belly and if she had stayed and they'd found out, she knew, it would've been St Michael's for her.

Cook had done her best to persuade her to stay, but had been comforted by Hattie telling her she had a friend to go to. She hadn't said that friend was Daisy or what Daisy did for a living.

She sat back on the hard wooden bench. The passing countryside and the sudden darkness of going through a tunnel had no impact on her. Nor did she register when the scenery changed and the big houses on the outskirts of Leeds could be seen on the horizon. But when the rows and rows of smoke blackened, poorer dwellings and the tall, City buildings and factories came into view she knew Leeds Central was the next stop and this caused her to clasp her hands against the anguish and fear beating her heart and to whisper a silent prayer: *'Please God, help me to find Daisy and let her know what to do to help me.'*

One thing she knew for sure; she wasn't going to St Michael's Convent and though she wanted to with all her heart, she knew, too, she couldn't go to Megan. Not yet she couldn't, not till everything was sorted. Oh, Megan...Megan...

CHAPTER EIGHT

A week later, Megan turned into the road that would lead to Daisy's place with a feeling of dread in her that was shaking her body. What would she find? The thought that hadn't been far from her mind visited her again. 'Was Hattie having a babby?' It must be that. In her letter Hattie had said that her master had done that horrid thing to her, just like he did to Daisy, so she must be having a babby!

Thoughts, of what she'd heard of St Michael's, deepened her dread. No, she wouldn't let Hattie go in there, she'd find a way. She could get a job in one of the factories and find a room they could share. But then, what of the babby? She couldn't think about it. It was all too much.

The run-down building in front of her and the street it was in shocked her. She checked Hattie's note again, but no, she hadn't made a mistake.

'Hello, you must be Hattie's mate. I've been told you were coming.' The door had opened without her knocking and standing smiling down at her was a girl of the like she'd never seen before. She had long blonde hair tied with ribbons the way a child's hair would be tied and her face painted with rouge, glowed red from her cheek to her eyes. Her plump figure bulged out of the top of her blouse.

'Me name's Phyllis, I'm a mate of Daisy's. And I don't bite.'

'Oh, I'm sorry, I'm, Megan.'

'I know, come in, I'll take you to Daisy's room. Hattie's there, but she's not well. That woman Daisy took her to was no better than a butcher. Mind she's picking up a bit. Well, at least she hasn't haemorrhaged and that's a good sign.'

Megan didn't understand, but didn't ask questions. She followed Phyllis through narrow passages and up a steep flight of uncarpeted stairs. The dirty, gloss painted, un-plastered walls, closed in on them the higher they went. The dank smell hanging in the air sickened her stomach. Her worry for Hattie increased with every step and every word Phyllis spoke.

Daisy met them outside a room on the left of the top landing. 'Hello, Megan, Hattie's in here.'

An embarrassment took Megan as she looked at Daisy, but she managed to give her a cheery greeting and a smile as she followed her into the room.

'Megan, Oh, Megan...'

'Hattie, what's happened to you?' The bed creaked as she sat down on it and leant over to hold Hattie. Hattie looked tiny. Her face was pinched with pain. Megan pulled back the grubby sheet, but Hattie pulled it back as if to hide as much of herself as she could.

'I...I told you, in me note. It was awful, Megan.' A tear dropped on to her cheek.

'It'll be all right, I promise. I'll find us a place and I'll get a job in the factory, in fact, why don't we all find a room together, Daisy and...'

'No, you've got to stay where you're at. It's what you want to do. Just as soon as I'm better I'll get meself right, don't be worrying.'

Megan wanted to ask if Hattie'd had an operation or if there was a babby on the way but she felt awkward so all she said was, 'I brought some money with me for you. I've a mate at the salon and she lent it to you. She said not to worry over when you can pay it back.'

'Ta, Megan, it's needed, I can tell you. I wouldn't have sent a message to you, only we haven't eaten since yesterday morning. This mate of yours sounds right nice. Tell her as I'll pay her back as soon as I can.'

'Here, I've brought some butties, too. Me and me mate; Cissy she's called, made them up whilst we were having our break, we're the only ones to work on a Sunday, so nobody knew.'

'I'll go and put kettle on,' Phyllis said. Come on Daisy, you can help me. A pot of tea'll go nice with them butties. '

This relieved Megan. She hadn't been able to talk properly to Hattie whilst the others were in the room.

'Are you really all right, Hattie? I mean...did...well, yer know...that thing as they did to you, did it make it that you'll have a babby?'

'Aye, Megan. It did...It...' A sob like a hic up jolted Hattie's body. She rolled over and turned away. Megan snuggled up behind her and held her to her.

'Hattie, don't cry. We'll manage. You'll not go to St Michael's and babby won't go in no orphanage, we'll care for it. I've thought on it and it can be done...'

'It can't, Megan. Who's going to let a room to two young-uns like us and besides, there is no babby now. Daisy took me to a woman and she got it away from me...'

Sobs trembled through Hattie's body. Megan held her even tighter. Tears wanting to be shed were denied by the cold feeling the shock had given her. She hadn't ever heard of a babby being taken from someone's inside before. Was the babby still alive when it'd been taken out? Her stomach turned over. 'Oh, Hattie...'

'I'll be right. I'm going to stay with Daisy and do as she does.'

'No! Please don't, Hattie...'

'I've no choice, Megan, I've nowhere to live. If bloke as owns this place finds me here Daisy and Phyllis will be for it unless they say I approached them to introduce me so they brought me in. It's this or the workhouse, Megan. I've no reference. I had chance of staying in me placement, but I knew then as I was in for a babby, so I left. They gave me money for me silence, but that's gone to that woman and to a doctor as come to see me, well he wasn't a proper doctor, Daisy said he was a quack, but he looks after the girls for a price and I think as he saved me life.'

'Oh Hattie...' She couldn't talk of what Hattie'd have to do. 'What will happen if you are hungry again...?'

'Daisy said they only get hungry at this time of the year. It'll be all right when Christmas has passed. They both have regulars, gents as work in the city, but with Christmas just around the corner, they can't get away so easily from their wives as they have a lot of social events. Anyway, Daisy's regular is coming tonight, he sent word to her and she's going to ask him to give her a bit to tide her over. He thinks a lot of her and doesn't know as she isn't fed right. She said she'll take a chance and not hand over all as she should.'

Despair settled in Megan when she left Hattie. All her pleading had done no good. The Hattie of her childhood had gone. Life as she'd thought of it had gone. Nothing was simple anymore. But, no matter what, she'd not ever, ever give up on Hattie. She'd always be her friend. She would visit her every Sunday and make sure she had enough food and money. Oh, if only they were older...But then, she did feel old. Old inside.

The next day it felt to Megan as if she'd visited Hell and now was about to step into Heaven.

The sign on the station with pots of greenery around it stated they had reached Breckton, a small town on the way to York where Cissy lived. She could hardly contain herself. But, knew she had to. Her mind questioned for the thousandth time, what it would be like. She'd never in her life been in a real home. She had seen sketches in books, but to actually go inside!

'Come on in, love, by, I thought as the day'd never come.' Cissy's mam held Cissy in her arms for an age and tears fell down her cheeks. At last she released her and looked at Megan.

'You'll be thinking I'm a rude old biddy, come in, you're very welcome. I've cooked a pie and beat all me rugs in your honour.'

A giggle escaped Megan. It seemed a funny thing to say, but it warmed her and made her feel at home.

'Mam, you're daft, yer know. Come on, Megan. I'll take you up to me room.'

'Don't be long, love, I'm not on with joking about pie, it's in oven and I've table all laid.'

Megan looked around her. It was like she was in one of the books she'd read. Everything about the room made her feel happy. In fact it made her feel like she'd never felt in her life. She looked at the grate with the fire roaring up the chimney and the oven to its side, from which came a delicious smell. On top of the oven, pots bubbled on the gleaming black hob. Each side of the fire stood a chair with a rag-rug between them made of bright colours edged with black and lain on a red-tiled floor so scrubbed it shone. In the centre of the room there was a table, draped with a dazzling white cloth and laid for three. There was a pot sink in the corner with a chequered curtain prettily pleated round it, and a dresser on the opposite wall polished until you could see your face in it. It was…It was…A home.

Her throat tightened. If only…

An arm came round her and she felt herself being pulled into a soft fleshy body. 'Think of yourself as being at home, love. Oh, aye, I know as you've never had a home afore, but you have one now, lass. You have one now.'

She thought of Hattie. And, how, just a few short weeks ago they'd been so young. Poor, Hattie. Would she ever know anything like this?

Cissy's mam wiped her tears with the corner of her pinny. It smelt of starch and cooking and…and love.

PART TWO

THE LETTING GO

1918

CHAPTER NINE

Hattie stood with her back to the wall, trying to shield herself from the wind. The cold seeped through her thin coat and tiredness ached her limbs. She had been on her patch since two and it was now on four. She'd only had one customer, a regular, who hadn't had much time, but feeling his need and knowing there'd be nothing doing at home, had asked for her to fetch him off with her hand. She was good at that, knew how to make it last if that's what was needed or could make them come in seconds.

Hattie had gone into the ginnal with him and done a quick job as he'd asked her to, but then, he'd halved what he knew were her charges. Saying as that's all it was worth. *A measly two bob!* She hadn't argued; she knew better than that. He was one that could cut up rough after it was done. There were a few blokes like that. It was guilt or something that got to them. Them as came too quick or couldn't get it up were the worst. They blamed the lass they'd hired for their own shortcomings and used them as a punch bag to vent their frustration. Hattie had been lucky lately, but Phyllis, poor lass, had copped for a good beating a couple of weeks back.

A shiver trembled Hattie's body. Oh God! She hated her life and everything about it. No, that wasn't true; she had Arthur. He was something that was good in her life. He loved her and she thanked God it was her he'd happened upon. She doubted if any of the others would've taken him on. Not looking like he did. And with what he'd suffered, further rejection, particularly by the likes of her and the lasses, would've been more than he could have stood.

No matter how much she told him he'd no need to be he was always so grateful to her. He was a lover, not a customer, though he made her take her due and a good bit over. She was getting a good stash together because of him and she was still able to tip up plenty to Bobby Blackstaff to keep him happy.

She thought of Megan. Five years had passed since they'd been together. *'Oh Megan, Megan, if only...'*

Their being apart wasn't down to Megan. She had never given up trying to find her, Hattie knew that. At first, after the bed and breakfast place had burnt down and she and the other lasses had been moved, Megan had come every month and traipsed the streets. And even now, after all this time had passed, she still came into the area every few months or so, looking for her. But she wasn't for being found. She didn't want Megan mixed up in the life she led.

Hattie had seen Megan on a couple of occasions, but had managed to dodge out of sight and had asked one of the lasses to make her go away by threatening her. How Megan felt about this played on Hattie's mind. But it wasn't safe for lasses like Megan to be in these quarters. Bobby Blackstaff looked out for 'fresh meat', as he called it, all the time.

'You bastard! You're one of them! You thieving, murdering whore!'

The screaming voice shocked Hattie out of her thoughts. She turned to see a woman staring out at her from eyes sunk deep into dark sockets. Desperation sagged the woman's body. She slumped against the hedge and wept.

Hattie took hold of her and guided her into the ginnal. 'You're right, Misses, I am a whore, but I'm no thief and I'm definitely not a murderer. What's this all about, ay?'

She held the woman's body close to her. The woman didn't resist. Her tired sob's tore at Hattie's heart. 'Come on, love, tell me what it's all about.'

'It was him as you work for, everyone knows it was him, he's done it afore, and more than once…A few times. Young-uns, not…not passed their Da's knee. Snatched! And…and, you lasses help him, you know you do. You make friends with the young-uns, and then, he moves in. And…And young-uns are never seen again. Oh God! I can't bear it. I want my Janey! I WANT HER!!'

Hattie took the blows. The woman pummelled her with her fists till her chest burned, but the shock of what she'd heard held her still. After a moment she caught the woman's hands. 'Don't…don't, I know nothing of what you're saying. I promise you, I know nothing.'

The woman stopped fighting. Her body once more slumped against Hattie. Quiet, hollow sobs racked her body.

'Look, love, let's go to Ma Parkin's for a cup of tea. She brews a good pot for a penny and I've enough on me for that. She's got a back room where she let's us go if we want privacy with a customer. Well, I mean, not for, well, yer know. But, some of them want to talk some afore they…Well, anyrod, come on, it's warm in there and like I say, it's private.'

The woman didn't say, yes, but she didn't resist as Hattie led her away.

'Me name's Hattie, what's yours, love?' They were in Ma Parkin's back room and had a pot of tea in front of them. The woman had gained some control and sat staring at Hattie.

Hattie poured the tea. The ache and cold seeped out of her as her worry for this woman filled her.

'Susan, Susan Clough. I live over Chapel End. Me and me young-uns. Me man was took in the war. He didn't have to go. Him working down pit exempted him, but he wanted to do his bit.'

'Aye, him and a million others. I'm sorry to hear of that, if I could get me hands on that Kaiser bloke! Anyroad, tell me of Janey and them others.'

Susan took a deep breath before she answered. 'It started a few years back. After war'd been on about a year. There's mostly only women looking after young-uns and a lot of them are trying to do a job as well. I work at the cotton mill on the early shift. Anyroad, a young lass of only seven years went missing and not long after a ten year old and there's been more heard of from over other end of the city. Nothing's ever been seen of them. It's said by other young-uns that they were took by a woman. These young-uns knew the woman to be a prostitute, though no one can find her, at least that's what the police say. Mind, some say as police are in it, as they don't give it much attention. Then, three weeks back...My Janey...My Janey...'

She dropped her head. After a moment she continued her voice not much more than a whisper.

'She's only just on nine and...and...they say they take them for the gentry. They say good money is paid for...for...Oh God! Janey! Oh God!'

Hattie shuddered. Memories turned her insides over. The bile rose in her throat threatening to choke her. She heard herself spit the word, 'No!' But, as she said it she knew it was possible, that what was said was true. And it was something she could put down to Bobby Blackstaff. There's an evil in that man. An evil that seeps through his pores and lives in his blackened soul.

'You say it's been on three weeks since she's been gone?'

Susan nodded.

Hattie tried not to show it, but her thoughts told her this was a hopeless quest. Three weeks was a long time to keep a child hidden and if she'd served her purpose she'd most likely be got rid of. It would be first pickings that would be of value. But, she'd have to give hope to Susan, even if that hope was in vain. 'Look, I've a friend in the police, he's a Sergeant...' She didn't say he was more of a customer than a friend, but her thought was that she could use her knowledge of him to get him to do something about what was going on. 'He'll help if I ask him, he probably knows of something.'

'Oh God! Do you think you can find my Janey?' Susan leant over and took hold of Hattie's hands.

Hattie felt an overwhelming urge to take her in her arms and say she wouldn't rest until she had found Janey. But deep inside she feared it was too late, so she just patted her hands.

'I trust you, lass, I trust you. I'm sorry I called you them names. I know you're one of them, but somehow I know as you're not, not really, not where it matters, in your heart. You're not one of them in your heart.'

'No, I'm not, Susan, and a lot of the other lasses aren't either. For most of us it was just circumstances that led us this way, but then, once someone like Bobby Blackstaff gets hold of you, you're trapped. Come on, let's get you home. I'll walk with you so I'll know where to find you if I get to know anything.'

Susan didn't object. Hattie held her arm as she rose. There was no flesh on her bones. 'Come on, lass, lean on me. I'll get you home.'

On the way Susan told her she had another child, Sally, who was just six years old. A neighbour was looking out for her. 'I'm afraid for her, Hattie. What if they come back?'

'Don't think on it, love. Something'll be done to stop them, I promise.'

But, what if they know I have another lass and are watching me comings and goings? They'd know as I leave her every morning to go to me shift!'

'You mean she's left on her own?'

'Aye, I have a fear in me and I wished it was different, but if I don't work we'll starve...'

'Look, you said you're on early shift, that's six whilst ten, isn't it? I could come over and watch out for her. I don't go on me patch until two-ish, unless Bobby Blackstaff has someone lined up for me earlier, but it's never afore twelve.'

Susan was quiet for a long time.

Hattie sighed. 'It's all right. I know how you're thinking. After all, I really could be the one befriending young-uns. You've no way of knowing for sure, you've only just met me. Don't take on about it. I'll get on with asking around and I'll talk to Sergeant Jackson. I'll come back as soon....'

'No, no, it isn't that. I do trust you and I don't think...well, to be honest I don't know what to think.

'I know, love.'

They had reached a row of cottages and had stopped at the steps of one of them when Susan said, 'I've a picture of Janey. It's just the one. Tally man took it on her Communion day. Have you time to come and look at it? Only, if you know what she looks like you can look out for her.'

The picture caught at Hattie's heart. The golden-haired little girl smiling out at her looked like an angel in her white veil and with her hands clasped as if in prayer. A hate welled up in her for Bobby Blackstaff and his cronies and she vowed she would do all she could to try to stop their evil game.

The sound of Susan's sobs brought her attention back to her and she put an arm around her and held her. She had no words that would help her.

The click of the back gate opening brought Susan up sharply. She took herself from Hattie's arms and grabbed a piece of towelling from over the rail above the fire and rubbed her eyes. No sooner had she done this than the door opened.

'I see you're back then, Sue. Any luck, lass?'

'No, Vera, well, not luck as such, though I've met up with Hattie here and she's going to help me. Hattie, this is me mate, Vera. She's been looking out for Sally.'

Vera looked from one to the other.

'Aye, I know what I am, there's no need to look at me like that. Like I said to Susan here, a whore I am, and not of me choosing, but a child snatcher and murderer, I'm not. I knew nothing of young-uns going missing. But now I do I'll not rest till those responsible are caught. And, I have more chance of doing something about it than all of you have.'

'Well, I beg your pardon, but I was just shocked to see you in here, seeing as how it's one of your kind as has a hand in all this.'

'I can understand that. I don't blame you or Susan for not trusting me, but I'll be at trying to prove to you as best I can as to me motives being the same as your own. I'll go now, Susan, but like I said. I'll be in touch as soon as I know anything. And think on about me watching out for your little Sally.'

'I've thought on and I'd be grateful, Hattie. Ta. I'm on shift every Monday to Friday morning, so if you could come tomorrow?'

She'd no time to answer before the door, which had been left ajar, was pushed open and a head of fair curls popped round it. The child's face mirrored the one in the picture. But, this face wasn't angelic; it was very cross. 'Mam, you didn't come for me! I saw you come down the road and waited and waited, and then, Aunty Vera left me behind...Who's this?'

'Me name's Hattie. What's yours?

'Sally. Have you come about me sister?'

'No, well, not altogether. My business is with you. I'm being interviewed by your mam. She's thinking of taking me on to look out for you in the mornings.'

'I don't need no looking out for. I'm six and a half, yer know! I can look out for meself!'

'Sally! Don't be so rude!'

'It's all right.' Hattie laughed out loud. 'She's got the same spirit as I had at her age. I can see as me and you are going to be mates, Sally. I like someone as can look out for themselves. It means they can look out for me, an all.'

'Do you need looking out for, then?'

'Aye, I do. And, I can't think of anyone better to look out for me than you. How about I come for breakfast every morning when your mam goes to the mill?'

'I'd like that. We could toast butties on the fire. Me mam says as I'm not allowed to do it when she's not here, but she'd let me if you're here, won't you, Mam? We have a long fork and...'

'Aye, all right, Sally. That's enough. Hattie knows how to make toast. Now, get out back and get swilled down under the tap ready for your tea, there's a good lass.'

Sally went to do as she was bid, but as she got to the door, she turned and said, 'Will you be here when I wake up in the morning? Only mornings are getting darker and me mam won't let me light me candle. She says as I have to keep me eyes shut until it gets light, but it never seems to get light and I don't like the dark. Not when I'm on me own, I don't.'

Hattie laughed again. The spirit the little one held in her was not enough to stop her fear of the dark. 'That's something else then, as me and you are alike in, because I wasn't for being on me own in the dark when I was a young-un. I'll be here. I promise. And, I'm not afraid of anything now I'm a grown up.'

As Hattie walked back to her patch she thought over what had happened. The sick shock she'd felt was still in the pit of her stomach. If she knew anything the one who'd befriended the young-uns was most likely to be Doreen.

Doreen was known as Bobby Blackstaff's woman, though he didn't have real feelings for her, or any woman for that matter. Doreen was more for show, a cover up for the real type he was, or at least that was the rumour. He wasn't above putting Doreen to work when it suited him. Her being a beauty she caught the eye of the fellas and if the one who was asking could be of some service to Bobby, then she had to do his bidding.

You could feel sorry for the lass in some ways as it was clear she adored Bobby, but she was a sly one. She kept her eye out for anything she could report back to him and she was the cause of many a lass being beaten or even disappearing.

Hattie's thoughts turned to the stash she had. She had a fear in her where that was concerned. Doreen had been watching her lately. Turning up on her patch and hanging around her room. She'd have to be careful that she didn't get to find out about her looking out for Sally. Mind, Doreen was never about much before two-ish on account of her 'duties' as she called the fact as she had to serve drinks and was at the beck and call of Bobby Blackstaff and whoever he was playing cards with till the early hours.

It was rumoured as sometimes she was taken down by every bloke there and in full view of the others! By, she'd been brought low at times from what was said.

Hattie sighed. Happen Doreen was more to be pitied than blamed, even though she lived far better than the rest of them. But, if she was mixed up in this rotten business, she'd not get any pity! God! It didn't bear thinking on.

CHAPTER TEN

The envelopes came on the same day. The regiment's buff one, with the crest indented on the bottom corner came first, causing Laura's heart to skip a beat.

There was so much talk of 'the last push' and if it was successful the bloody war would be over. She felt certain Jeremy was writing to say he was coming home! She didn't take the letter to her room as she was used to doing, but eagerly ripped it open as soon as she picked it out from the other post laid on the silver tray by her breakfast setting.

Her eyes scanned over the words. There was no mention of the war's progress or of when he would see her. But then, why had she expected there to be? She knew putting such things in letters was forbidden in case they fell into enemy hands.

The pages spoke of his love and how he missed her. He told her how much her letters meant to him and how they kept him going in the darkest moments as did thoughts of her and of them together.

'I hope it won't be long now, my darling, I count the seconds with the beat of my heart, which is easy when I am thinking of you because then, it thuds so loudly.'

As she read this she pressed the letter to her own heart. 'Oh, Jeremy, Jeremy.' His name was a whisper on her lips, but an agonising pain of longing, in her heart.

Jeremy had been gone for three and a half years now and every day had held fear for her as well as loneliness and longing. Please God, let it end soon and please send him home to me safe and sound.

The prayer had hardly died on her lips when Hamilton came up to her. The silver salver in his hand shaking.

'Wha...What is it, Hamilton?'

'A...A tel...Telegram, Ma-am.'

He lowered his hand the brown envelope on the salver screamed the news she'd dreaded every day. The moment froze. She didn't move, neither did Hamilton. The clock on the mantel shelf took over the space, its ticking taking her towards her doom. Killed in action...Killed in action...Killed...Killed...The scream started in her bowels and went with her into her blackness.

***

'Lord and Lady Crompton are here, Ma-am. Shall I...'

'Thank you, Hamilton, there is no need to stand on ceremony today.'

Hamilton turned and looked surprised that the guests had followed him through to the sitting-room. He bowed his head to acknowledge Lady Crompton's words, then turned sharply and with an air of disapproval, left the room.

'Laura, Oh, my dear, I'm so sorry, I...'

'Yes, old thing, a bad business. Sorry we couldn't get here sooner. Poor Jeremy and poor you. What happened? Have they told you?'

Laura looked helplessly from one to the other, her sister, distraught and lost, not knowing what to say or do and Charles her dear brother in law, uncomfortable, but trying to take some control. But, how could he? How could anyone take control of this bloody awful situation? 'I haven't heard anything, just...just...'

'Leave it with me, old thing. I'll telephone George, he works in the war dept, he'll find out all the facts and if, well, if they are bringing Jeremy home.'

Daphne's arms came around her. She sank into them. The tight knot that was holding her together didn't release. Would she ever be able to let it? A bitterness she'd battled with since the news had come in two days ago resurfaced. 'Why him? Why? We had so much to look forward to. Why couldn't it have been young Garry Ardbuckle? What use is he to anyone? But, no, he'll come back fit as a fiddle and...'

'Laura! Don't talk like that, don't even think it. Of course, Gary...whoever, has a right to live and I'm sure he is loved by someone, his mother...'

'I know, but, every young man that went from this village is safe, and for what? What do they have to give? Nothing! They only take, but Jeremy...'

'Come on, old girl, you're not thinking straight. It's to be expected. Has your doctor been in to see you?'

'I am thinking straight, Charles, and I don't need a doctor.' She lifted her head. Jeremy smiled down at her from his picture hung on the wall between the long windows. She drew strength from him. 'I've been making plans. I want to start up the stud farm again, just as soon as this lot is officially over.'

'But, Laura!'

'No, Daphy. I know you mean well and God knows I'd like nothing more than to curl up in your arms and just cry and cry and be comforted by you, but that won't help. I know from experience that it won't. I need something to focus on. The stud is just the thing, it was when I lost my son and it will be again.'

Charles coughed. 'Yes, my dear, you are right, it is a good idea for you to have something to occupy you, but I would have thought you have enough on your plate at the moment and you will have to concentrate on selling off Hensal Grange Colliery and...'

'No! Don't even think about it, Charles. No, no! Jeremy would want me more than anything to hang on to the Mine and the Estate. But, it isn't enough. I have an excellent Manager, as you know. The day-to-day running of the Mine goes ahead without me, not like the old days when I was needed everywhere. Jeremy, with your help of course, had everything running so well, My involvement is only to oversee and to make final decisions. But, as for the Estate, I find that work tedious and will be grateful for any suggestions you can make regarding the running of it.'

'All right, darling, but promise me you will give yourself some time. Come and stay a while with us until...'

'Yes, Laura, you need time, and...' Charles pulled at his moustache, 'Look, I'd no intention of speaking to you about this yet, but as you are making plans I think I should. I've been thinking about your Estate as a whole just lately and I must admit the possibility of, what would be the best for you if you were in the situation in which you find yourself.' Again he paused. Laura had seen the disapproving look Daphy had given him.

'No, don't stop him, Daphy. This is just what I need to talk about. It is all worrying me. I know, I've coped pretty well, but it was meant to come to an end. It won't now. I need to have a plan to enable me to face the future, at least then, I will be able to let go of the business worries and give myself the time you are right in saying I need. After all, the plans I have for the stud farm cannot take place just yet. Go on, Charles.'

'Well, my dear. I can appoint an Estate Manager to take care of the day-to-day running of the Estate, the letting of properties and hiring and firing. That sort of thing and I can oversee all the business and make sure you are not cajoled into making any decisions you don't really need to take. You know I have your best interest at heart.'

'I think that's an excellent idea.'

'That's settled, then. Leave it all to me. I have a young man in mind. He will make a first-class Estate Manager working as a mediator for the bank and the estate. He had great prospects before the war, but he was badly injured. He needs a position that will be flexible and an office of his own, situated in his own home. I was thinking, maybe the gatehouse? I know it hasn't been occupied for some time, but it wouldn't take much fixing up. He has a young family, so that would be perfect. It means he will be near enough to you if he needs to discuss anything with you.'

'Good gracious! You have been thinking about this, haven't you? Well, it all sounds fine to me and I can't tell you how relieved I feel.'

'Good. I tell you what, I'll put into place what I can and I'll try not to bother you too much with the details. But, these other plans you have. Well, I'd suggest you give a lot of thought to them, make your plans, and then, Daphne and I will stay over after, well, after…You know, old girl, the funeral or memorial service, which ever it is to be.'

'Charles!'

Daphy's face was a picture! Laura couldn't help smiling at her. 'Don't worry darling, Charles matter-of-fact way of dealing with things is just what I need. You know you don't have to pussy-foot round me.'

She took a cigarette from the silver box on the occasional table in front of her and put it in her cigarette holder before offering the box to Daphne and Charles. They each took one and Charles did the honours and lit them. Laura relaxed back and inhaled deeply. It felt good to talk about the future and to make plans. None of them had done that for so long.

'Right! That's settled. Now, how about some refreshment? I don't know about you two ladies, but I could do with a stiff drink. I'll go and telephone George while you organise it, Laura, and whilst I'm at it, I'll see if he has any indication of how we are doing over there and if the promised end is in sight.'

Hamilton had left the room having brought in the drinks tray. Daphne had poured the drinks and they were settled back on the sofa. 'Laura, whilst Charles isn't here I want to talk to you. I've been thinking too, about what would happen if this was the outcome. Darling, you have been under so much stress this last few years ever since you lost little Leonard. You need a break. You're living on your nerves. Look, in a few weeks when everything is settled why don't we go away together? Caroline is always asking us to go and stay with her on her South Sea Island, whatever it's called. I think this would be a good time to take her up on that offer. We could stay for three months or so, what do you think?'

Laura didn't answer for a while. She put her drink down and snuggled back into Daphne's arms. Could she take time out? Would she cope with lounging around doing nothing? Long days with nothing to do but think? But then, perhaps that's what she needed to do.

Perhaps there was something in this, giving yourself time... 'Yes. Yes, Daphy, I will, I will come away with you...'

'Really! Oh, Laura, I'm so glad, Oh darling, I can't believe it. I'll help you. I'll look after you...'

'Now, Daphy, I don't want you planning to mother me and fuss me, you know I don't like that, but I need to talk. Talk about everything, get this knot of pain undone and sometimes I will need to be allowed to be weak and to cry and cry...Oh. Daphy...'

CHAPTER ELEVEN

Hattie closed the gate and removed her gloves.

The house looked like any other in the street where all the buildings were tall, three storied dwellings with small enclosed gardens to the front. Half net curtains shielded its every window and a sign on the gate pronounced it as being a hostel for young ladies. The other residence knew the real business of the place, but none of them gave them any trouble. Bobby Blackstaff owned most of them in one way or another, him being a loan shark, amongst many other dark and darker dealings.

The girls living there each had their own rooms. Some rooms were more pokey than others as the larger ones had been divided into two. Furnishings were few but each girl made what they could of their own space. Hattie was proud of hers, she had some good pieces, some she'd bought herself and some were from Arthur, oddments he didn't need. This had been commented on, but as the money coming from him was more than any other client, Bobby let it go.

Hattie opened the door with confidence, some of the stealth she'd used when she'd first started to look after Sally two weeks ago had left her. No one had seemed to notice her comings and goings. Though, her mind was troubled by the fact that nothing was happening to find Janey, despite the information she'd given and Arthur getting his solicitor involved.

Daisy's door opened as she went up the stairs.

'Hattie, quick! In here. Come on.'

'What is it, Daisy? What're you doing up at this time? You're not usually around until noon or after.'

'I'm not the only one up, shush, come in quick, lass'

As soon as they were inside the room Daisy closed the door and motioned to her to come over to the window. Hattie's throat tightened at what she saw. Doreen leant around the corner at the bottom of the road, looked towards the house and then hurried forward.

Daisy pulled her away from the window. 'She might look up! We don't want her to see us!'

'Oh, Daisy, do you reckon as she followed me?'

'Aye, I'm sure on it, she left just after you. I've been up most of the night with running out back to the closet. Then, come five-ish I heard someone on the stairs and the front door closing so looked out me window and saw the back of you go round the corner. You'd only just got out of sight when Doreen appeared and hurried out the gate after you. What took you out so early? Have you been to see Arthur?'

'No, I look after me mate's little lass...Oh, Daisy, what am I to do?'

'Well, if that's all it is as you've been up to, I don't see you have anything to worry over. I thought you were at deceiving Bobby. Making a bit on the side he didn't know of. Anyroad, who is this mate? I didn't know you had one outside of this house! Well, not since you dropped off seeing Megan.'

Hattie hesitated. But no, she couldn't tell Daisy, it'd be too dangerous. 'I've to go, Daisy, I'll tell of it some other time. I can't let Doreen think you know where I've been...'

'But why? I can't see as Bobby could object to you helping a mate.'

'Just leave it, Daisy love, I've to go. Doreen mustn't be at thinking you're involved.'

'But...'

Hattie gave her no time to say anything further. She was through the door and skipping along to her own room just as she heard the door at the bottom of the stairs closing.

Once in her room she found her body wouldn't settle itself. Her stomach churned with fear. She paced up and down. *What could she do? What could she do? If she said all she was doing was looking out for a mate's young-un, they'd not believe her. Not if they know her mate is Janey's mam! Oh God! What if they found out she'd been making enquiries of Sergeant Jackson? Or that he'd had meetings with Arthur and Arthur's solicitor?*

One thing gave her hope; the cowardice of Sergeant Jackson. He was likely to be mindful of his own skin and that's what would keep her scheming from being found out by any of Bobby's lot. Thinking about it, it was probably Sergeant Jackson's cowardice that was holding things up. He'd be afraid to move until he was sure of trapping the whole gang as he knew if even one of them was left free he'd be dead.

Bastard, that he was, he deserved to be, too'.

He was little better than they were. Hattie's skin crawled at the thought of lying with him. Of how he sweated as he pounded her and of the things he wanted her to do to him. And, for no payment. At least, not for her. It was his pay-back for favours owed to him by Bobby. But, that aside, what sickened her the most was how he got a night with her. He'd pick her and a few of the lasses up. Lasses who were getting past it and Bobby wanted rid of. They would be thrown into the cells. But, she would be taken to his office to pleasure him. In the morning the lasses would be up before the magistrates and end up being sent to a workhouse, or worse, rotting in some prison! She'd be let free with no charge! There was nothing she could do about it, it just happened to be her he wanted. The lasses knew how it was for her and knew how much it hurt her to be the bait that helped Bobby to get rid of the others. They didn't hold her to blame.

In fact, if she knew anything, it was more than a good bet that it was the Sergeant who'd alerted Bobby to her goings on. He'd not say he knew what she was up to. He'd not dare. With Arthur's solicitor knowing everything, he'd be caught out. No, he'd just say he'd seen her out and about in the early hours and was wondering.

The more she thought about it the more it seemed likely. Getting her stopped from prying was one way he'd be released from doing anything about Janey and the other young-un's disappearance.

'One day she'd get even with that bloody sod! In the meantime she'd have to think of something; she'd have to!'

The knock on her door stiffened her body. Opening it and seeing Doreen leaning against the wall, her arms folded across her middle and a look of triumph on her face sank any small hope she might have harboured that the worse wouldn't happen.

'Bobby wants to see you.'

Just that, "Bobby wants to see you," but it was enough. Enough to strike such fear into her that her body broke out in a sweat. But she wasn't for showing Doreen that. 'All right, I'll be up in a minute, I'm just taking off me outdoor things.'

'I wouldn't be long if I was you. He isn't in a good mood.' A sickly smile shone a gleam from her eyes.

Anger replaced some of the fear in Hattie. An anger that urged her to hit out at this vile woman, but if she did she'd not stop beating her until one of them was broken. And that wouldn't solve anything. But she'd not spare her the lashing of her tongue.

'Why's that? Haven't you been at licking his arse all night, then? Because you might as well as it's known as you'd do his bidding no matter what that bidding be. By, Doreen, you've been brought low. So low you're not fit to clean the shit off the closet the rest of us use, and that's at saying something!'

Doreen faltered, her shock at the attack registered on her face. But she didn't take long to recover. 'We'll see about that, shall we, when you're begging for mercy and I'm watching. We'll see who's been brought low then, ay?'

'So, it's a beating as I'm in for, is it? Well, well, and it'd have nothing to do with you snooping in what doesn't concern you, would it? You're a bastard, Doreen, a vile bloody bastard!' As she said this last she slammed the door in Doreen's face. The action helped some, but as soon as it was shut she slumped against it.

She knew she hadn't long. Knew it'd be worse for her if she kept Bobby waiting. Her mind attacked every avenue she could think of that might convince him she didn't know anything. But in her frantic state she had no answers and she knew in her heart it was hopeless.

'Aahh, Hattie!'

Bobby's greeting surprised her. He didn't seem in a bad mood. He was slumped in an armchair, the like of which she was more used to seeing in Arthur's house, but which didn't look out of place with the rest of the stuff that furnished this light and airy room. He was cleaning his nails with a long thin paper knife. Smoke curled up from an ashtray on a polished table next to him. He picked the cigarette up and drew heavily on it. The smoke came out of his mouth and down his nostrils as he spoke, causing his eyes to squint.

'I hear you are taking a little walk every week-day, Hattie.'

'I look after me mates young-un, whilst she's at her shift, she lost her man in the war.' In an instant she decided she couldn't not mention the missing child, In fact, it'd be better if she did. It would make him think she didn't know he was involved. 'And her other young-un's gone missing so she's in a state.'

'Gone missing? Well, well.'

He swung his legs to the floor and stood up. He moved towards her. She couldn't think what he was up to. This sickened her fear even more.

'And, where do you think she's gone; this other one?'

He was close now, very close. He grabbed her hair and yanked her head backwards. The suddenness of his action shocked rather than hurt her as it hadn't been in keeping with how he'd been with her.

'I think you know only too well where she has gone, Hattie, don't you, ay?' He still had hold of her hair as he walked slowly round her turning her as he went. She winced with the pain of it as he pulled harder and harder.

'No…'

'Oh, I think, yes. And, I can't have the likes of you lying to me now, can I?'

His other hand grabbed her left arm and twisted it up her back. His face was near to hers. So near she could smell him. Smell the feminine perfume of him that spoke a truth to the rumour that he liked company of his own sex more than he did of women. It shocked her to think of this at this moment and to have the fleeting thought that she was right in the times she'd pitied Doreen.

Just as quickly as he'd grabbed her, he let her go. He walked away from her and picked up his cigarette again. He was like a cat, graceful in his movements, and yet, menacingly ready to pounce.

'Well, let me tell you something, Hattie. The first chicken I took from your mate's nest served me well. She made me some good money, and now, you're going to help me pluck the next one.'

'No!'

'Oh, yes. I think you will bring the pretty little thing to me. In fact, I have already put out the word of her coming and have a customer waiting. I can't believe how easy it is all going to be.'

'No! I'll not! I'll not do it!'

'You have no choice. Bring her here and you live. Don't and you die. It's as simple as that! Oh! Actually.' He blew his inhaled smoke in her direction. 'It isn't that simple, because your death wouldn't be pleasant, or quick!'

He'd moved closer to her again, his expression mocking her. As if on impulse, his hand whipped out and caught hold of hers. Her skin seared with pain as he ground the stub of his cigarette out on her arm.

Using all her strength she pulled away from him, 'I don't care what you do to me. You Bastard! You'll not get me to bring Sally here, not ever!'

'Sally, is it? Pretty name. And, I'm a bastard, am I? Well now, whilst we're on to names, let's see. What was the other one called?'

Again his body reminded her of a cat as he stretched forward and rang a bell that stood next to his ashtray. 'Hum, Janey...yes. "Janey's me name, Sir." Ha, Ha! A treasure! A little treasure! What pleasure she gave. So much that I think I could charge double for the younger version.'

He was talking as if Janey was dead! She swallowed hard. His words had taken her fear and cleared her head. If she could settle her stomach she could think clearly as to what to do. She had to do something. Something that would make Bobby Blackstaff pay and would save Sally!

The door across the room opened and Doreen came through. Her satisfied smirk unmasking her inner evil

'Fetch Wally and Doug, please, Doreen.'

'Yes, Bobby.' As she looked at Hattie, her eyebrows rose in a gesture that said, 'I told you so.'

The gesture gave Hattie no feelings. Her mind was far above what Doreen felt or did. She knew what she must do. She'd to take as much of the beating coming to her as she could bear and appear to be broken and ready to do Bobby's will. Bobby knew her, knew she had spirit. He'd not believe her if she gave in at the threat of being hurt. He'd suspect she had a scheme of sorts. Once she was trusted she'd set something up that would trap them all. Arthur would help her. He'd find a way to keep Sally safe and get the just deserts to this lot.

When the door opened again and Wally and Doug came through, her newly found courage all but deserted her. They were brutish and had no feeling for the pain of others. She'd heard the screams coming up from the basement when they were at their work. And, she'd helped in the nursing of the bloodied and beaten lasses who'd displeased Bobby in some way. Even worse, there'd been times when the screams had died down, then of a sudden, stopped, and the lass being beaten hadn't come back up the stairs or was ever seen again! Oh God! Would she be able to hold out long enough to convince them?

Bobby gestured towards her with his head. 'Just until she agrees, I don't want her dead, not yet. Make it last a few days if you have to. Only call me if she's near to death and hasn't agreed. I make the decision on her living or not. Is that understood?'

'Yes, Boss.'

Bobby's tone changed and he looked over at her, 'Now then, Hattie, you are about to find out for yourself just what a bastard I am!'

The men had moved across the room. The fear she'd let go of gripped her in a tight knot.

Without warning, Wally, the small fat one, punched her in the stomach causing her to bend over double and gasp for breath.

'Make her holler loud enough for me to hear, boys, I like the sound of pain. And, I like my whores to hear as well, gives them a lesson.' Again, Bobby was near to her.

'You look at the boss when he speaks.' Doug grabbed her, twisted her arm up her back and yanked her head so she was looking into Bobby's evil eyes. She could do nothing, her stomach cramped with pain. Her arm burned. 'Don't, please, don't...' No one answered her or even acknowledged she'd spoken.

'Try not to mark her face. It hasn't got a beauty to it, but some of my more useful customers seem to like it. And, leave her intact where it matters. She's good to have a go at, so I'm told. You could sample it and let me have your opinion. Yes, that would be fun. I've heard too, as she'd do anything rather than let her arse take it. Give her some of that; get her ready. You do it, Wally. The size of you will definitely loosen it up. Sergeant Jackson often complains that he can't get her to let him up there. I think he'd be pleased enough to tell me more of what she knows if he thinks it's been made ready for him.'

The spittle gathered in her mouth. Her hatred of him spat from her. 'Fuck you!'

'You, fucking whore!' His hand whipped out and stung her cheek, but the pain was worth it to see her spittle running down his face.

'You'll pay for that, you filthy bitch!' he wiped the spittle with his handkerchief. 'Use the chair after you've raped her. Take it to its limit.'

As they dragged her along the corridors and down flights of stairs none of the doors of the bedrooms opened. When they approached Daisy's room Hattie clamped her lips together and stopped resisting. She didn't want Daisy getting involved.

A cold shaft of air brushed her face. The door of the cellar clunked open. They shoved her into the dimness. Her foot missed the step. She couldn't save herself from crashing onto the stone floor. Wally lit the gas mantel. The light took time to reach each part of the cellar. Her fear dried her mouth. The implements of torture snarled at her. Straps, whips, knives chains and unidentifiable objects lay on a huge wooded table. In the far corner a chair. The chair that wasn't a chair mocked her senses. Made of wood and iron it spoke of pain and death. Leather clamps positioned on the arms, feet and at chest height hung ready to hold a victim like a vice. But what etched the terror into her heart was the cage-like contraption fixed to the top of the chair. Please God they weren't going to put her head in that!

Fighting didn't help. Just one of these men would have been too much for her. With every article of her clothing torn from her body they dragged her to the table. With one swipe of his hand Wally sent the implements clanging across the room. Doug forced her over the edge of the table.

She wouldn't beg. She wouldn't kick out or utter a sound. To do so would heighten their pleasure. She closed her mind. Doug took his turn first. It was nothing. Wally goaded him on. It was over in no time.

'Well done, Doug.'

Doug laughed.

'Now move over and let the big boy in.'

Doug laughed again, a high stupid laugh. He took her hands from Wally. Hattie clenched her fists. *She mustn't think. She had to keep relaxed.*

The pain tore through her. She screwed up her eyes. Her breath hissed through her gritted teeth. Spittle ran down her chin. Every thrust

75

ripped her, but as it went on it felt as if each sore was being rubbed with sandpaper.

It was done. Doug threw her on to the floor. He and Wally hugged and shook hands, their talk that of schoolboys congratulating each other on scoring a goal.

Hattie screwed up into a ball. Her body trembled. A tear trickled down her cheek. If she had a mam she would have called out to her instead she thought of Susan and little Sally. And knew a reason why.

'Right, now you're going to pay, whore, for spitting at the boss, get her in the chair, Doug.'

'No...no. Don't, I'll do it. Tell Bobby, I'll do it...Tell him I'm sorry...'

'Aahh, but it's not about that now, bitch. No one gets away with what you did.'

Her screams bounced off the wall and slapped back at her. The nut crackers clicked in her face glinting in the flicker of the mantel before crushing the bones of her fingers.

'This little piggy went to market....'

The pain caused her very soul to scream for mercy. But, there was no mercy.

Her mind sank into the vilest of places, where she knew the despair of despising God and her very own being.

But then, the pain eased and a blackness took her. She was in a deep, dark, closed part of her mind. There, the laughing, mocking faces of the hated, Reverend Mother, the vile, filthy, Lord Marley and Felix and the rotten to the core, Mrs Barker, yo- yoed at her. And she knew she had started a descent into her own madness.

The shock of the icy cold water dragged her back. The acrid taste of smoke clogged her throat. Heat burned her nostrils. Her confused mind gave her the terror of a room of fire, but as her head cleared she saw Doug holding a lighted torch. He wafted it backward and forwards before her eyes. He smiled down at her before brushing the torch along her arm.

She opened her mouth to scream, but only a hoarse moan came from her.

CHAPTER TWELVE

Megan clutched the crumpled note in her pocket.

'Megan, I need to see you. Forgive me for losing touch. Please come. I'll meet you at six, down at the end of Fell Lane, next Sunday. You know where it is, it's the one as you turned off to go to the guest house. Please, please come. All my love. Your friend, Hattie x.

Going over the words Hattie had written gave Megan the courage she needed to turn the corner and go along the dark ginnal that would take her into the streets where Hattie, and the lasses who plied the same trade, did their business. To think Hattie had made contact at last! Just when she was thinking of giving up trying to find her and resigning herself to having lost her for good.

As she turned into Fell Lane, Megan saw a shadowy figure of a woman pacing up and down. At last! Her steps quickened as the woman turned towards her.

'Hattie? Hattie, is that you?'

'Aye, it is, Megan. Eeh, Megan…Megan…'

'Oh, Hattie, Hattie!

They clung to one another in desperation, laughing and crying.

Hattie winced with pain and then stood back and said, 'Quick, step into the ginnal, don't let anyone see you….'

'Who? Are you all right? Are you hurt, Hattie? Is someone…' She went to take Hattie's hand and was shocked to feel the bulky bandages. Hattie pulled her hand back

'Don't worry, I'm all right. Come on, love, let's get off the street. Oh, Megan, it's good to see you.'

'I tried to find you, Hattie, I looked…'

'I know you did, love, but I wasn't for being found. I'll tell you of it all. I promise. First we have to get ourselves to a safe place.'

They walked in silence and kept as close to each other as they could through the narrow pathways, but no matter how narrow the ginnal became, they stayed with their arms linked and walked sideways rather than let go of one another.

Hattie'd asked her to link with her left arm as that wasn't as badly hurt as the other. Even so, she could feel the bandages through her coat and wondered again, with a deepening worry, what had happened to Hattie. And, it wasn't just her injuries that were causing her to worry.

Their progress was slow as Hattie would suddenly gesture to her to get into a doorway and motion to her to keep quiet. Their journey took them through ginnals and along back lanes where the stench of poverty clawed at her and as ever she felt the pity of what had become of Hattie and thanked God and Sister Bernadette for her own fortunes.

As they crossed over a muddy road the air became fresher and was tinged only with the smell of the horse dollop they'd had to weave around. On the other side of the track were the gates to a park, dimly lit by gas lamps. Hattie visibly relaxed. 'Nearly there, love, just got to cross the park. We'll be fine now. I have a friend, well... He's a sort of friend. He started as one of me customers and got fond of me. He's a gentleman. He was hurt bad in France. Lost a leg and part of his face and his wife won't have anything to do with him. Anyroad, he came looking to satisfy his needs and that's how we met. He's took this house just round the corner from other side of the park and he's helping me to get away from fella as controls patch I work on.'

Megan didn't know what to say. Everything Hattie had said was so far from what she knew of.

She wanted to say she was pleased for Hattie, but on the other hand she didn't want Hattie to be used by any man, whether he was a gentleman or not. It was easier just to squeeze her arm gently and smile at her.

'Me man's name is, Arthur. He isn't easy to look on with his injuries, but I know you'll be like me and take that in your stride. He's after me moving in with him. But, I've other plans. I want to look out for all the lasses on the patch. And, I have an idea for a business that would help them and could see me right, an all.'

They'd crossed over the park and now stood in a street so well lit it seemed it was daylight. The houses lining it were of the type that folk lived in who were far above hers and Hattie's station. Hattie looked at her and smiled. She smiled back but couldn't find anything to say.

Words were even harder for her to find when they stopped in front of huge ornate gates and Hattie said, 'This is it,' then, opened the gates and there before her stood a large house. Hattie led her to the front door!

The door opened and a tall upright young man smiled a welcome. 'Hello, Hattie. Is this your friend, then?' His voice didn't go with his accent. It was like as if it had a posh tinge to it.

'Aye, this is Megan, Harry.'

'Pleased to meet you, Megan, I'll take your coat. Captain Naraday is still at his rest, Hattie, but I've a fire lit in the front room. If you and Megan go through I'll fetch some tea in to you.'

Megan handed him her coat and smiled at him, then watched as he helped Hattie off with hers. 'Are you feeling any better, lass?' he asked Hattie.

'Aye, I'll be right. It'll all be worth it in the end,' Hattie answered him.

There was an obvious friendship between them and for the first time Megan felt her insides warming. Hattie had folk who cared for her and that was good to know, no matter what the circumstances.

The welcome had taken away her awe at where she found herself. The hall they'd stepped into had been beautiful in a manly kind of way. The dark mahogany of the doors and banister stood out against the background of the cream walls. Framed photographs of men in uniform hung in military straight lines, and the stairs, which wound up from the centre, were carpeted in a rich brown plain carpet.

The room they entered was different. Its grandness made her catch her breath. The deep red carpet, and gold and red drapes formed a backdrop to pink and gold cushioned chairs and sofas with elaborately carved, arms and legs. The tables scattered about were of a deep mahogany and they too, had carved and beautifully curved legs.

'It's grand, isn't it, Megan? And, it could all be mine if I wanted.'

Hattie's smile didn't reach her eyes and there was a touch of bitterness in her words. Her friend's thinness, her sunken eyes and the bruise she saw for the first time on Hattie's cheek, brought Megan back to reality. 'Oh, Hattie, your face! And your hands! What happened?'

'Don't worry, love, I had it coming to me. Fella as I told you of as owns patch I work, wanted me to do something and I wasn't for it. But, I thought on how I could do it and get him caught for what I'd found out. Taking me beating and not giving in until he'd near killed me, made him think I'd agreed because of that and hopefully kept me scheme from him.'

Megan clutched her stomach. Hattie was in a world she didn't understand. It was peopled with folk who would beat her and others that would use her and, then again, kind people like Harry. But what of Harry's master, this Captain bloke, what would he do to her?

'Tell me what's been happening with you, Megan. You look well. You've not changed. Only, I didn't think as you'd make such a beauty.' Hattie laughed as she said this and it lightened the moment.

'Go on with you! I'm no beauty. You should see Ciss; by, she's something. I've never seen anyone prettier. Mind, you've not turned out so bad yourself. Though, you're a mite thinner than you should be. Oh, Hattie, I've missed you. Why haven't you been in touch till now?'

'I wanted to, I did, but me life wasn't what I wanted you mixed up in. Lasses as threatened you when you came looking were doing so at my bidding. It's a dangerous place where I live, Megan. Lasses like you, innocent lasses, are snatched regular and raped and such, then, put on the game. And, not only lasses of an age...Megan, I know things. Things I shouldn't know of and I'm...'

Harry came in at that moment with a tray laden with tea, sandwiches and cakes. 'Thanks Harry, is Arthur up, yet?'

'His bell rang just as I was crossing the hall. I went up and he's asked for a tray. He said as he has a headache and sends his apologies. He won't be joining you. Though, he hopes you can go up after your business with your friend is done. Now, if I pour for you both, will you give Hattie a hand, Megan? She's not a good patient so be careful you don't lose a finger or two!'

They both laughed at this and as he left the room Hattie said, 'That means Arthur isn't up to meeting you after all. Poor Arthur, it's hard for him looking like he does. He's afraid of meeting folk for the first time. Mind, he's lucky to have Harry, he's a good man. He's been with Arthur for all of his army career. He was his batman and he'll not leave him now. Especially how he is.'

Again there was a note of something that Hattie wasn't telling of.

'Well, tell me how things have worked out at that Madam Marie's place and then, I've a lot to tell you of.'

'It's worked out better than I thought it would, Hattie. In fact the war has made me life better, which isn't a good thing to say seeing as how so many are suffering. But, business took a bad turn with the war. It wasn't as if folk hadn't got the money, more that it'd not be right to have parties and things. Even weddings are quiet affairs.' She giggled then as Hattie looked puzzled. 'I'm not at making much sense am I? I can see as you're wondering how all this doom and gloom has been of benefit to me.'

'Aye, I was at wondering.'

Megan helped Hattie take a sip of her tea and lodged a sandwich between the only two fingers that were showing through the bandages then, taking a sip of her own tea, she began to relax. It was easier to talk about her own life than to listen to Hattie's tales about hers.

'Well, it's like this. Me and Ciss'd thought at first as we'd be down the road when Madame started cutting back, but it was the others, the posh lot, she let go. She had us in her office and said as she'd keep us on if we took a dock in our wages and learnt other skills so as we could help out where needed. I was that glad to think I was going to get a chance to learn things like cutting of patterns and making up and I was ready to agree straight off, but Ciss! Eeh, Hattie, you'd like Ciss, you wouldn't think it to look at her, but she's got some clout. She only ups and says as me and her'll only be agreeing to staying if the rules were relaxed some. Madame'd looked right put out, but it was like Ciss'd said later, she'd not have been able to ask the posh lot to take a dock and do all the other work, an all. So we were her only hope. Anyroad, Madame took on what Ciss'd said and now once our work hours are done we can come and go as we like and we get to go home every three to four weeks or so...'

'Home?'

'Aye, I've a proper home, Hattie. Like me and you always dreamed of. Issy, that's Cissy's mam, she treats me like a daughter and Ciss has become...well...I mean...'

'It's all right, love, I'm happy for you. I know as you've never forgot me. Don't go feeling guilty. It was my fault we've not kept in touch and I know you're still like a sister to me, an all. You thinking on Ciss in that way won't affect me. I'm just glad your life's going so well. And, I've never forgot Cissy's kindness in lending me that half a crown that time. Tell her I have it for her and with some interest on it, an all.'

Hattie had reached out and taken Megan's hand as best she could as she said all this. Megan let it lay in hers, wanting to ask, and yet, not wanting to know, how she'd been so hurt and how badly hurt her hands really were.

'Now, I've something to tell you.' Hattie said. 'I'm for giving up this game, well that is, in part. I mean as I'm not going to sell meself to all and sundry, but I will still be Arthur's...mistress, sort of.'

'Oh, Hattie, that's good news, I can't stand to think of you doing what you've been doing. But, are you sure you want...well, yer know...'

'Aye, Arthur's a good man, but I'll not come to him on his terms and he knows that. Anyroad, he's helping me. Not just with money, though I need that as me own stash isn't enough for what I'm planning. No, he's helping me with all the legal stuff and with the police...'

'The police! Are you in trouble, Hattie?'

'No, well not as such, not with the police that is. But, what I am involved in could go either way. I mean it's very dangerous and I could be killed...'

'Hattie! No! Oh, Hattie, Oh God!'

'I'm sorry, love, I wasn't for wanting to shock or hurt you, but I had to see you before I do what it is I have to do.'

'Oh, Hattie, whatever it is, don't do it, please don't do it. Look, I've got some money saved and it sounds like you have, too. Let's find a place, a little house, you me, Ciss and Daisy...'

'It wouldn't work, love. Me and lasses would be hounded down till we were found, then punished or even murdered as an example to others not to try to get out. I have to do this thing, I have to. It's me only way. Now listen, I need to tell you what I want you to do if anything happens. Me stash is with me solicitor. Eeh, that sounds grand! Me solicitor!' She giggled and it sounded good, but the fear and pain inside of Megan wouldn't let her giggle with her.

Hattie didn't hesitate for long. 'He's Arthur's solicitor really, but he's acting for me in the business I mean to set up. I've been at saving for a long time. Holding back what I could, whenever I could and stashing it away. And then, when I met Arthur, well, he always paid me over the odds. He's always wanted to get me off the game. He thinks a lot of me, Megan, and he's willing to put in a lot more money, an all.'

'What business are you talking of, Hattie?'

'I mean to buy a house, a good sized one and in an area where it's pretty decent, but won't have neighbours as such so there'll be no young-uns about or folk to upset. I've seen just the place. It's at the end of a cul-de-sac. Houses line one side of the road leading down to it and the canal on the other. Houses used to be homes, but are now used as offices for solicitors and such like. It's ideal for me purpose because it's still in the city, but it's not a thoroughfare or place as police go on their beat.'

Still mystified, Megan just waited for her to continue; she had so many questions and fears, but they were all tangled in her brain. She didn't know if she wanted to know of the business, her part in it all, or the thing Hattie had to do that could get her killed!

'I can see as I've put you in a stew with me going from one thing to another, Megan. Look, me business is going to be a home for the lasses, a safe place, a clean place, a place where gentlemen come to them and they don't have to walk the streets. They'll have regular meals and medical treatment. That quack as I told you of as helped me, do you remember? Back when I first come back from being in service. Well, it turned out he was a doctor who'd been struck off. Something to do with a married woman as was his patient. Well, he's good, so I'll be taking him on to look after the lasses. Lasses will pay me a percentage to have all this provided for them plus a bit on top as'll be me profit. Mind, I won't have any visitors meself, only Arthur, and sometimes I'll be staying here with him. And it isn't like I'm going to be a pimp or anything like that. I won't be selling the girls or enticing others to be prostitutes. I'll just be providing proper conditions for them as are already doing it. Them as have no other choices.'

'It sounds good, Hattie. Well, that is if it's what you want. I'd be more glad if you said you were opening a tea shop, though. But, is…is there something stopping you taking up Arthur's offer? Wouldn't that be better for you?'

'No. Why do you ask that, Megan? I'd have thought you'd have known.'

Megan felt surprised at this answer and afraid she'd said something to upset Hattie.

'I didn't mean…'

'I know. But well, I never planned it like it's happened. I'm no different to you, Megan.'

Megan saw the bitterness again.

'I've just not had the chances. I don't want life as I lead, but, well, it still wouldn't sit right with me. I always thought that when I went to a man it'd be as his wife. And, that's still what I want. You know, someone like Harry, someone of me own class. I'd come here gladly and live in servant's quarters as Harry's wife.'

'You mean; you love Harry?'

'No, that's just it, I love Arthur. I do, despite everything. He's good, he's kind. The man inside the broken body is everything I've ever wanted. But, when I found him, he's everything I can't have. Not proper like. Not as could take me to be his wife and let me live a decent life, like we were brought up to do.'

'I don't know what to say, Hattie. I've always carried a guilt at how things have turned out. You'd never take me up on ways I thought we could have got by…'

'Don't, Megan. You're the best thing in me life, and'll always be. I know you'd have given everything up for me. But, I couldn't have bettered meself at your expense. I would have dragged you down. I'm sorry. Me moaning about how me life's turned out isn't fair on you. I could have had chances. You tried to give me some. I could've set up in a cottage or something with you…'

The silence between them wasn't comfortable.

Megan tried to think of something to break it. It was as if they were at odds with each other, something that had never happened before.

'This house as you're getting will change things for you, love. I know it isn't life as you'd really want it, but it sounds like next best thing and I'll be able to visit you regular.'

'Aye, you will. I'll have me own private rooms! You should see it, Megan. It's grand. I'll have a good life there, I know I will, and don't worry over other things as I've said, I'll be happy. I've long since learned to be happy with me lot. I don't know what prompted me to bring all that stuff out. It must be being with you. We were always able to say what was in our hearts. I've missed that, Megan.' She smiled her lovely kind smile and Megan gently took her in her arms and held her. It felt good.

'We'll never be separated again, Hattie. Never! I'll come regular, I promise.'

'I can't wait, Megan.' Megan felt a shudder go through Hattie's body and drew back.

'Are you all right now, love?'

'Aye, it's this other business I've to get that out of the way first. Every time I think on it me body shudders.'

Megan had been dreading this moment, but she didn't say anything just waited to hear what Hattie had to say.

'I need to tell you what I want you to do. If anything happens to me. I want you to go to me solicitor. Me money as I've left with him is to be yours. You're to use it how you want, though I'd like you to see as Daisy and Phyllis are all right. Arthur would help you sort it all out.'

'No, Hattie! I couldn't...I don't want your money. I want you to be right.'

'I know, love. And, I hope to be. But, if the worse happens I'd be happy knowing as you and Daisy and Phyllis are at being all right.'

'Oh, Hattie, I can't bear it. I can't think on you being in so much danger. Do you have to do this thing as you're talking of? Isn't there no other way?'

'No, there's no other way and when I tell you of it you'll understand, like Arthur does. He knows and you will, as I couldn't live with meself if I did nothing.'

CHAPTER THIRTEEN

The fear and agony in Susan's face clicked an uncertainty into Hattie. Was Susan going to stop the plan going ahead?

'It'll be all right, love, I promise, I'll not let anything happen to her. This is the only way. And, it's like I said, Sergeant Jackson'll have a dozen police in plain clothes around and about. None of them are local, so'll not be known by Bobby Blackstaff or his cronies.'

'But, what if they get away with her? I'd not bear it. And, what if they don't find Janey?'

Susan's thin drawn face had a tinge of yellow to it, as did her eyes. It was the colour of failing health, of desolation and..., Hattie shuddered. She couldn't give her thoughts to it. But, that didn't stop her worrying.

Susan was always being sick and complained constantly of pain in her stomach. The little flesh she had on her bones sagged as if the life had already left it. The simplest of chores took it out of her. She'd stopped going to the factory weeks ago and lived on the parish relief and whatever she would take from Hattie. Thank God that had been more lately as Hattie had convinced her it was for Sally. No matter what, Sally couldn't be allowed to go without.

'I'm getting me doctor friend to come and have a look at you when this is done, Sue. Now don't protest. I know as you're a proud woman, but you need help and who else can you take help from if not from your mates, ay?'

Susan managed a smile. 'Aye, and you've been a good mate to me, Hattie. I'd have not got through without you. I can't believe what you had to go through, with what they did to you. And, all to help get that lot caught and to get me Janey back. I'm just worried over Sally. I'm worried what it'll do to her, she's bound to get a big fright when they come to take her. It don't seem right to put her through it no matter what it might mean.'

'They won't frighten her, not if I know anything they won't. It won't serve their purpose to. After all it'll be a sight more difficult to take a screaming young-un. No, I think as they'll get her to go willingly. Doreen can put on a kind and gentle side when she wants to and she has a knack of making people like her. I've seen her with new girls Bobby's brought into the game. Everyone's taken in by her till they get to know what she's really like. She'll probably tell Sally she's going to get some tuffies and'll promise her she'll bring her back afore I return. The police will follow her and if all goes to plan, catch the lot of them.'

'And, Janey? They'll make them tell where Janey is, won't they?'

'Aye, of course they will. It's hoped as they'll be able to uncover the whole bloody show Bobby Blackstaff and his lot run: selling young-uns to gentry, taking money for protection, prostitution and God knows what else. And, while we're on mentioning His name, pray to Him that they all get their just deserts and are hanged!'

Though, she hoped her words about Janey brought comfort to Susan, she didn't feel inside that she would be found. Not alive anyway. But, she hoped with all her heart that she would and she couldn't think of what might happen if Bobby Blackstaff didn't get caught, or if he didn't get the death penalty because he'd know she was the one who had planned it all.

As the plan was to go, she and Sally had been in the park for about ten minutes when she saw Doreen walking towards her. 'Look, Sally love, I'm going to leave you for a mo, I've to pick something up from me mates'. She just lives around the corner. She's got some medicine as might help me with me hands.'

'But, me mam say's as you're never to leave me alone, Aunty Hattie. She'll not have it, yer know. Why can't I come with you?'

'It's not a place for young-uns, me mate's man don't like anyone round.' This wasn't working out. Sally usually did as she was bid. She'd no choice but to involve Doreen. That was the last thing she'd wanted to do, it would look to Sally as if she was giving her to the woman who'd take her off, instead of leaving her unattended and the woman persuading her to go! She took a deep breath. 'Eeh, look there's another of me mates, her name's Doreen, I'll ask her to watch you for me.'

'I don't want her to watch me! I want to go with you!'

'My, what's this? A cross little girl? Are you cold, love?'

'Hello, Doreen. This is Sally. The little girl as I told you of. I look after her when her ma needs a rest. She's a good un really, but she don't want me to leave her. I'll not be a mo, can you watch out for her?'

'Aye, I tell you what, how about me and you go over to Ma Parkin's, Sally? She'll have done her trays of tuffies by now and they'll be cooling on the wires in the window. We can buy a farthing's worth and be back here munching it afore Hattie here gets back.'

'Can I, Aunty Hattie?'

Though, it feared her to do so she nodded. 'Aye go on with you, I'll see you in about ten minutes.'

Sally tucked her hand in Doreen's and looked trustingly up at her. 'We'll have to hurry some, Dorween, if we're to be back. Ta rah, Aunty Hattie.'

It's Dor..reen!' Doreen laughed out loud as she shook the little hand in hers causing Sally's body to shake and making her giggle. 'You're a cute little thing, aren't you?'

Sally smiled up at her.

Doreen smiled back. A smile that would make the devil love her. Then looked up at Hattie, 'Bobby's going to be really pleased. You've done well, Hattie.'

Hattie thought she was going to retch. It was all she could do not to snatch Sally and run, but there was so much at stake. So many pretty young-uns who might be in danger in the future, and then, there was always the hope of finding Janie.

She turned and walked away as fast as she could, not daring to look either way to see if anyone was following Sally and Doreen but praying to God they were.

***

Hattie couldn't stop her body shaking as she looked in disbelief at Sergeant Jackson, 'But, you said as Sally'd be away in no more that a few hours! Oh God! I can't believe as she's not home yet. Why? Why?' She heard her own voice screeching in her ears and felt a sick fear in her belly. She clutched the back of the nearest chair.

'Try to keep calm, my dear, everything will be all right, I am sure. Let the Sergeant explain.' Arthur leant on his crutch and put his arm around her waist. A flicker of what looked like disgust passed over the Sergeant's face and Hattie's desolation turned to anger. She glared at him. He shuffled from foot to foot, coughed and twiddled his helmet in his hands. She felt a disgust of her own enter her. Disgust over how he'd used her. His vileness grated on her. He should protect people. Stop the filth that happened. Not contribute to it. And he dared to stand in judgement of her!

The sweat of anxiety stood out on his forehead as he spoke, he'd known her thoughts. His discomfort gladdened her.

'Bobby Blackstaff didn't show up, so we couldn't make a move. He was followed to London a couple of days ago and seen outside a gentlemen's club talking to Lord Marley, him as has a country residence not far from here...'

Hattie drew in a sharp breath.

'What is it, dear?'

'That's him! You remember? I told you of him. He and his friend...'

'Lord Marley! You didn't say it was him! You only told me...'

'Does that gentleman have some significance in all of this?' Sergeant Jackson asked.

'Yes, he does. I know of him. I know from me past experience that he likes young lasses. He used to take young-uns into his service from the convent I was brought up in. Then, he'd rape them. He was stopped at his games when the cook found out and told Lady Marley of his antics. Oh God! Do you think as this could mean he's getting young-uns through Bobby Blackstaff?' Her head reeled. Memories turned her stomach over so forcibly she felt she'd be sick.

'Sit down, my dear. This is all too much for you...'

'No! I must go to...to Sally...Susan. Oh God! I don't know which one to go to. Poor Susan she'll be out of her mind. And Sally! Sally'll be scared and...'

'You can't go anywhere. It isn't safe. They'll know as you didn't return to the house. They'll smell a rat. Our worry is they don't go through with it and get rid of young-un...'

'No!'

'We've got to see that as possible, though unlikely, before Bobby Blackstaff returns. He'll be one as says what goes. But, it's a risk as we had to take, getting half the gang wasn't going to do no good. It's got to be all of them...'

'You bastard!'

'Hattie!'

'I'm sorry, Arthur, but he is. He stands there saying he'd sacrifice a young-un to get them all. And, I know and he knows the reason for that. No! No! I'll not stand for it. Tell me where she is and I'll go there. I'll...'

'You'll be doing no such thing. They'd kill you as soon as look at you.'

'My dear, the Sergeant is right. You will be in too much danger and you going there won't save Sally, it will only serve to have you both killed!

'I can't bear it. What have I done? Oh God! What have I done? Please, please let me go to Susan. She'll be distraught and she's already badly.'

'Look, Sergeant, what if you brought Susan here? I think Hattie is right. They need to be together and the poor woman must be going out of her mind.'

'Well, Sir, if that's what you want, but it is very dangerous. She isn't implicated at this moment, but if police are seen to go to her house and she is seen leaving, well…'

'It won't be like that, Jackson, and you know it. What game are you at playing? Susan isn't meant to know anything so her natural thing to do when her young-un didn't come home would be to call you lot in. So police being round her place wouldn't look suspicious. If you're trying to get at me through all this you're a bigger bastard than I thought you were.'

'Get at you, my dear, why should he…'

'It isn't like that, Sir…Hattie, I…'

'Then, get Susan over here and get Sally out of wherever she is! I don't care about me being safe. Just make it so as they are!'

'I'll get Susan, but Sally stays put. She's all right. She was spotted yesterday evening playing with that Doreen in the yard of the house they took her to.'

'But that was hours ago, they could have told her I was delayed… but a whole night! She'll be scared…'

'Well, according to my man there's been no sound of a young-un in distress…'

'Oh, no! That means they've used something on her. Something to quieten her, they've used it afore on lasses they have brought in. They sleep for hours…Oh Sally…Sally, what have I done?'

'You've done the best thing you could've. And, if they've used something on her, well, that isn't a bad thing. As long as they know what they're up to it'll be like you say and she'll sleep for hours so won't know anything is going on. This'll turn out, you'll see. If we give up now we'll lose. It'll all have been for nothing. We have to get the whole gang. And, get them good and proper and if we get that Lord Marley, an all, well scandal or not, a good job will have been done!'

'But, at what sacrifice? At what sacrifice?' She could no longer stop her tears. Her body folded and she sank down onto the sofa nearest to her. Despair, fear and shame, yes, most of all shame, brought her low. Because, wasn't the outcome of all this going to be her own freedom? Freedom, from Bobby Blackstaff! Freedom, from her life on the streets! Freedom, from the likes of Sergeant Jackson taking her down! Oh God! What had she done?

She felt Arthur sit down beside her. When not trying to stand he had the strength of a man with no handicap. That strength and his gentleness, too, as he took hold of her was a comfort. 'Help me. Oh, Arthur, help me!'

'Come on, my dear.' He rang the bell on the table next to him and Harry came into the room, 'Take Hattie upstairs, Harry. Run her a bath and get her bed ready. She's all in. Go on, dear, leave all this to me. Now, go on, trust me, I will sort it all out. Susan will be here before you know it. We'll look after her. Leave it all to me.'

CHAPTER FOURTEEN

It was dark when Hattie woke. Shocked that she'd even slept! She felt for the matches on the bedside table. Finding them she lit the gas mantle. In its flicker she could see the clock. It was half past nine! It didn't take long to dress.

How was it every stair creaked when it never had done so before?

'Is Susan settled down, Harry?' Arthur's voice drifted up from the drawing-room. *So, Susan is here! She's safe! Thank God.*

'Yes, Sir. She is tucked up and asleep. She took some persuading to take the medicine the doctor left for her and she'd not eat anything. I let her peep in on Hattie and that settled her mind. Hattie's still out for the count.'

Hattie turned and ran back up the stairs. She hadn't thought! Arthur was bound to look in on her. She had to make it look as if she was snuggled up and fast asleep.

Harry crossed the hall when she next peeped over the banister. With her bed arranged in a mound, she hoped would fool Arthur; she was ready to try again to get out unnoticed.

It was a relief to her when Harry didn't stop on his way to bolt the front door. She felt a longing to confide in Harry. But, would he help her? Or, would he stop her and tell Arthur what she intended to do? She couldn't take the chance. Her heart beat like a drum. But, fear or no fear, she had to shift herself. It wouldn't be long before Arthur came out of the drawing-room to retire. He was likely to be drinking his night-cap at this very moment. She had seconds to get out of the door without being seen.

Once outside she took a moment to catch her breath. Which way should she go? If she was caught by any of Jackson's lot she'd be stopped. She had to get to Daisy. Daisy might know where Sally had been taken. But, where was Daisy likely to be?

Making her mind up to go to Ma Parkin's where she might get information of the lasses whereabouts; she sped across the park keeping her route to the darkest ginnals. Coming out of one ginnal to cross over to the next she was startled by a hand grabbing her arm. Pain, more than fear made her cry out.

'Hello, Hattie. You've not been on your patch lately. I've missed you. What were you doing up the posh end? Aye, I saw you running across the park, I thought as I'd head you off here.'

'Kenny! God, you gave me a fright.'

'Aye, and that's not all I want to give you. I can't believe me luck coming across you like this. Come on, there's no one over at my place, the misses has took the young-uns to a show and won't be back till late.'

'I can't, Kenny, I've to be somewhere…'

'Don't give me that. You know what I gave you last time as you was hasty with me. Well, it'll be a darn sight worse if you think as you're not giving me anything at all. And, I'll tell you something else for nothing, I'd drag you to that pimp of yours after and put a complaint in. Here, what's happened to your hands?'

Kenny cut up rough if it didn't go as he wanted it to so she knew he meant what he was saying. He was a man of means. He owned a pawn shop and was a tally man. His business was in lending money to the poor and letting them have goods on tick. Everyone was afraid of him, in particular those who couldn't pay their dues. She must think of something to tell him to satisfy him. She dare not take the time out to see to him. She decided on the truth.

'Me fingers were broke by Bobby Blackstaff's lot. And, they burned me arms, an all. Look, Kenny, I'll tell the truth of it then I'll ask you to be helping me in what I have to do. But, if your need is too much for you, I can send Daisy along to you…'

'Hold on a mo. I don't want to be mixed up in anything as Bobby Blackstaff's mixed up in. I don't mind paying for what he sells, but I want nothing to do with anything else. I'd rather make do with me misses and put up with her opening up under sufferance and making me take it out just when I get to the best bit. But, I tell you something, I'd not let you go if I didn't smell a rat.'

'Thanks, Kenny. I owe you one, we'll do it for free next time you come looking and it'll be good, I promise you.'

'Go on, get going or you'll have me thinking on it so as I'd have you anyroad and right now in the ginnal!'

She was glad to hear a laugh in his voice and waving him a quick ta-rah, ran for all she was worth across the lane and into the next ginnal.

Before she went into Ma Parkin's she peeped through the window, there was no one in the front parlour. Lifting the latch caused her pain, but once the door was open she nipped in as quickly as she could.

'Eeh, Hattie, you gave me a fright. Where'd you come from? I didn't see you pass me windows.'

'Sorry, Ma, is there anyone in your back room?'

'Aye, Daisy's in there, she isn't with a client, though she might be waiting for one, she didn't say.'

Daisy! She couldn't believe her luck!

'I'll have a brew, Ma, and'll take it through and have it with Daisy, ta.'

'You go through I'll bring it in to you. Its quiet the night, don't know where everyone is, mind, there's been a few strangers milling around of late. Some reckon as they're police in plain clothes, so everyone's keeping a bit low.'

This news wasn't welcome. If folk were talking about the strangers being police then Bobby Blackstaff's lot would know of them.

'Hattie! Where've you been? Oh, Hattie, are you all right? Your hands...'

'I'm alright, love. The pain isn't nothing as I can't bear. Arthur got his doctor to look at me and he's put some splints on me fingers and some soothing stuff on me arms. Mind, you're going to have to help me with me tea.'

'Oh, love...'

'Don't be at giving me sympathy it'll get me started. I've a lot more on me plate than what's happened to me hands. Have you seen anything of Doreen?'

'Aye, but not as much as usual and not back at the house. I saw her go into the corner shop a while back. When she came out she had a big brown bag full to the top. I was curious so followed her and she went into an end terrace house up Gollan St. I waited a bit and then seen her come out and go into the one next door, what d'yer reckon as she's up to?'

'Daisy, love, I know what she's up to, and I need your help. Are you on with waiting for a client?'

'Aye, but he hasn't showed. He was a new chap as has been hanging around a bit. There's been a few of them lately. Ma reckons as they're police, but then, you know what Ma's like. Anyroad this...'

'Never mind that now, look, they are police...'

After her telling, Daisy's face showed all she'd felt herself on knowing. 'Aye, I know, love, brings back pain as we suffered, don't it? But, I'm on with having it stopped only I don't trust Jackson. Only thing is as he's scared of Arthur's standing and what could happen to him if he is caught at being in league with Blackstaff, which we all know he is. So, that gives me some clout. If I can get into the house, he'll have to shift himself and do something. He'll know he has no choice. I just hope as I'm in time.'

'But, Hattie…'

'No, buts, I have no choice. Will you help me, Daisy?'

'What would I need to do?'

Hattie could see Daisy was scared out of her wits, but the question hadn't been asked in a way which meant she would make her mind up after she had knowledge of what the plan was. She knew Daisy was with her no matter what.

'That's them, them two on the corner. But, how do we know which house young-un's in?'

They were in the ginnal just across the road from the houses.

'I'm going to make a guess at it being the end one as Sally's kept in. It'd be the best bet, I'd say, as any noise wouldn't matter, there's no neighbours the other side to hear anything and they own the house on this side.'

'I'm scared, Hattie.'

'Aye, I am, an all. Right, as soon as the door opens to me, you run like the blazes. Get to Arthur's as fast as you can. You're sure now as you know how to get there and which house it is?'

'Aye, I does. Oh, Hattie…'

'No more now, love. I'm sorry to put this on you. Let's get it done.'

They hugged each other as best as they could with Hattie's arms, then Hattie crossed the road.

She was amazed to find she got right up to the door without being challenged. There were obviously no police watching the house! God! What was Jackson up to? But then, another thought occurred. Was this the right house? What if these houses were just some that Blackstaff owned, but didn't use for the purpose of sex with young-uns? Well, she was here now.

With a determined attitude she kicked the door hard several times. The noise she made increased her fear; there was no going back…

It was the door of the next house that opened. Doreen stood there.

'Who is it? And what d'yer want?'

The fear died and an anger that made her want to claw Doreen to pieces came into her.

'Where's Sally, you fucking bitch?'

'Hattie! Ha! It's Hattie. Bloody hell, you've got some clout, lass, I'll say that for you… Hey!'

Doreen reeled back. Hattie felt no pain from the blow she'd landed on Doreen's face. It was as if she was out of her body with the anger and fear she held in her.

'Tell me where Sally is, you bastard!'

She stepped into the house. Her mind only took a second to take in the sumptuousness of it, before she was lifting her arm again. Doreen cowered back.

'You idiot, Hattie! For God sake, what're you thinking? Wally and Doug are next door!'

'Where's Sally? Come on, Doreen, if there's a shred of decency left in you, you'd tell me. Where is she?'

'Don't come near me...I'll scream...Let me go. Let me get out of it...Please, Hattie. I promise you, I couldn't help anything as I've done...'

'Then, do the decent thing now, and help me. I can't do much with these hands, but there's nothing wrong with me feet and by God, Doreen! I'd think nothing of kicking the life out of you.'

'She's next door. That Lord Marley's with her...'

'WHAT!'

'No, Hattie, I told you. Wally and Doug are there, they're downstairs keeping guard.'

'No, No! You bastard'

Doreen landed on her back. Hattie couldn't remember pushing her. 'You...you...You vile scum, you...'

Doreen didn't move. She lay in a heap whimpering like a babby and begging not to be hurt.

Hattie took no notice, the feelings in her wouldn't let her, nor would the urgency to get to Sally. Without knowing how, she was standing in front of the door of the house Sally was in. She kicked out with all her might. The door opened like someone had barged against it. Wally stood there a look of astonishment on his face. She knew she'd to act quickly and with the only weapon she had. What's more she'd to hit her mark first off. Wally stepped out of the door and shoved her by the shoulders.

'What's your game, what yer doing here?'

Though she was off balance the railings that separated the pavement from the road stopped her and gave her a leverage making the impact of her foot the more deadly. Wally doubled over whaling with pain.

Getting to the door that led to the stairs only took seconds. And, it seemed she'd flew, not ran up, the steep flight as before she knew it she was faced with three closed doors. A cry came from one. 'Mammy, Mammeee'

A power came into her. The door gave way at her first kick. All the hatred she'd locked inside her for the man who stood there stopped in the act of putting himself away, unleashed. Her body grew as if it

95

wasn't her own. She barged at him. He had no time to steady himself. He landed with his back bent over the bedstead.

Her agony boiled her heart. The source of the beginning of her wasted rotten life exposed in front of her. Her vicious kick found its mark. 'You Bastard!... You Bastard!' Each time the words spat from her she kicked out at him.

He begged her to stop. Tears ran down his face. It was Sally's cry that stopped her.

'Hatttie..ee..ee!'

'Sally, Sally...Oh, Sally, love. I'm here. No one'll ever hurt you again. Sally...'

Sally stared out at her. Her face held unspeakable horror. At that moment it struck Hattie that the poor little mite had had no warning. No knowledge. At least she'd had some. How was she going to help her?

They rocked together back and forth. Not even the torture had hurt as much.

The door opened Doug stood there. It flashed in her mind that he must have been out in the back yard visiting the closet when she'd come in. His appearance gave her no fear. Nothing more could be done to her than the agony of seeing Sally how she was.

'It's over, Doug. Get out while you can. You know about Arthur don't you? Well, he knows where I am. Sergeant Jackson can't save you. So I'd take me chance if I was you and scarper. You might get lucky.'

Doug opened his mouth then, shut it again. His moment of uncertainty was a moment too long. Bobby Blackstaff stood behind him. 'He's going nowhere. And there's nothing as the police can do. I've the lot of them in my hands. I pay them off as you well know having been part of the payment, you fucking whore!'

He shoved Wally out of the way, stepped round, the moaning, Lord Marley and was beside the bed before she could register where he'd come from. He had a knife in his hand. The blade glinted as the gas light flickered over it. She pulled Sally closer making sure she couldn't see. Bobby held the knife with both hands. His knuckles white with the effort of holding the shaft. He raised it above her head. If she moved it would get Sally. The moment froze. Her life and her loves flickered in and out of her mind. She had no scream in her. No begging for mercy. Only a fear for Sally...

The knife came down, her body cringed forward. There was no pain. Had he missed her? She could still feel Sally. See the room. She wasn't dead! Then, a vicious groan assailed her ears and a tearing pain ripped her shoulder. She looked up. The bloodied knife was above her again.

She couldn't move. It descended slowly, very slowly towards her. Then, Bobby fell forward his hands went out as if to save himself and the knife flew through the air. His body lay silent and still across the bottom of the bed. She looked to her left. Lord Marley had hold of Bobby's legs. He'd saved her. Lord Marley had saved her life!

There was a silence. A moment when she looked into Lord Marley's eyes. She didn't feel anything coming from within her but just before he looked away from her she knew she'd seen a flicker of recognition and a deep shame in him. At that same moment the silence was cracked by the clanging of bells. It was over...

The room filled with men. Handcuffs clicked. Sergeant Jackson came into her vision. His face near to hers. 'Are you all right, Hattie? Is the young-un, all right?'

Her mouth dry with fear became wet. She gathered the wetness and spat into his hated face. He didn't react. His hand wiped away her spittle and he turned away.

CHAPTER FIFTEEN

'Megan, you've been quiet since you came back from seeing Hattie.
Are you sure as there's nothing wrong?'

'I can't tell you of it, Ciss. It isn't anything you could understand.
There's stuff as goes on that you've no idea of.'

'Tell me, then. I'm not a young-un anymore, yer know.'

Not a young-un? Oh, if only she knew how young and innocent she
was, and she wished to God she could be like her and not know all that
she did.

'Look, Megan, you've to talk to someone, love, because whatever it
is as is bothering you is making you ill. You're not eating, nor sleeping
proper.'

'Must you girls talk so much? That gown has to be finished for
collection tomorrow and I need you, Miss Tattler, to work on some
designs this afternoon. Here, Miss Grantham, a letter arrived for you,
but I don't want you reading it until your break-time.'

'Yes, Madame Marie.'

Cissy sounded like she was going to do as she was told and picked
up her work again, but the minute Madame's office door closed she got
up, grabbed her letter and went towards the back door laughing towards
Megan. 'She can't stop me going for a pee, and she'll not lower herself
to come out to the closet to see if I'm reading.'

Megan laughed at her, but after she'd gone, her thoughts returned to
Hattie and her worry for her and the little girl she'd told her of. It'd
been all set to happen yesterday. She hoped with everything that was in
her that it'd gone well.

'Megan...'

Cissy's whisper drew her from her thoughts. She looked up. Cissy
was red in the face and all of a fluster.

'It's me mam. Eeh, Megan, you should see what she's wrote. I'll not
be able to go home ever again!'

'What? Is she at pulling your leg again? You're easy pickings for her
fun making, Ciss, as you always take her bait.'

'Not this time. She's got a lodger and she's at trying to line him up
for one of us. Oh, Megan!'

Megan laughed. Come on, it's snap-time. Let's go and get a cuppa and I'll have a read. A lodger! Honest, Ciss, do you really think as she'd do that without asking you? If I know anything, she's been at thinking of ways to make a bit of fun afore we go home. You know what a one she is.'

'Here,' Ciss handed her the letter, 'I'll make a brew and some toast for us whilst you read it. I tell you, Megan, she's gone too far this time.'

Megan smiled as she opened the crumpled sheet of paper.

Dear Cissy,

You and Megan must come home as soon as you can, I've a young bloke lodging with me. He's come to take over your dad's old position as head groom at big house. His name's Jack Fellam.

I told you of poor Mr Harvey copping it, God rest his soul. Well, Henry Fairweather's been saying since it happened as Mrs Harvey is talking of rebuilding the stud, but with Mr Harvey not yet cold nor laid to rest proper, no one thought as it would be just yet. But, it seems them considerations are not for madam posh knickers. She's gone away for a while, sunning herself but before she went she took on this new man. He and his family live in the gate- house and he's running the estate. He's a nice bloke, been badly injured in the war, he lost half of his right leg, but he gets about right well with some crutches and manages to ride his horse around the estate. It was him as found Jack.

Jack's been to war, an all, him and his dad and brother. But his dad and brother both got killed, so they brought Jack home, but then, with all the heartbreak, his mam didn't last long and though he had a position he could've gone back to, he needed a change. He's not down about it all, says he's seen too much for that. That seems a pity, don't it, Ciss, young men who can't feel grief any more?

Don't worry though, about me cottage because I've been told as they'll not be giving Jack tenancy till he marries so until then, as long as I agree to give him bed and board, I'm safe. Mind, I'm pretty sure as he'll be snatched up, and soon, an all. I tell you, our Ciss, if I was just a few years younger I'd snatch him up meself! He's a right handsome bloke, and a cheeky bugger to boot. I've told him all about pair of you, and he can't wait to meet you. I've told him, though, if he takes a fancy to either of you, he's not to muck you about, but to make his choice and stick to it. Write back and let me know when you can come, love, Mam

Megan laughed out loud. Just reading the letter brought Issy into the room; she wrote just as she spoke and her fun-making got at you. 'Eeh, Cissy, its right then, she has got a lodger. I wonder where he sleeps because she doesn't say as he's got our room.'

'Mam'll have put him on the shake-me-down in the parlour I should think, but how're we to face him with what she's said to him?'

'I know, and I bet as she has said it, an all. She'd not think on how she might embarrass us. Let's hope by the time we go home he's forgotten it or he's so used to Issy by then, he takes it as a joke, ay?'

'I hope so. Oh, me Mam! You're right when you say as she's a one. Though, it sounds interesting, don't it? I wonder what he's like and if he will be at taking to one of us.'

***

Megan couldn't stand it any longer. It was Sunday, her half day, and she was going to find Hattie today if she had to walk the streets begging for information.

Cissy came over to her, 'Megan, please tell me what's to do, please! Whatever it is I can take it. I know you say as there are things as goes on. Things as I know nothing of, but how can I know if you don't tell me? Besides, I reads, yer know, I've a lot of knowledge of how things are in London from Mr Dickens's books and I'm for thinking as them sort of things go on in every big city, so Leeds probably isn't much different. This mate of yours, Hattie, the way you keep her secret anyone would think she is a prostitute or something!'

A relief entered Megan with Cissy's words. Not what she'd said, but the matter-of-fact way in which she'd said them. It meant she wouldn't be shocked if she knew. Nor would she be disgusted by the sound of her. Though, she felt a shock of her own. She wasn't a reader herself, not unless it was the magazines on the latest fashions that Madame brought and let them have when she'd finished with them. She couldn't get enough of them. But Cissy always had her nose in a book. She hadn't thought though, that they dealt with such subjects as prostitution! And, they'd been written by a man, too! Still, she'd not comment on it she was just glad to have a chance to talk about everything now she knew she could.

'Aye, she is, but it wasn't what she wanted to be, nor wants to be. It was circumstances, but she's a chance to get out of it.'

Megan sat down and with relief at the unburdening of herself, told Cissy everything. At times during her telling she hesitated as Cissy paled and shock widened her eyes and dropped her jaw, but always she urged her on, insisting she needed to know it all.

At the end of her telling there was a silence, then a stunned whisper, 'Young-uns? And...and, Hattie? Raped! And when she was just thirteen years old? Oh, Megan...'

101

Her arms opened and as Megan went into them she thought of how she was so lucky to have Ciss and Issy and her job. Poor Hattie, why had their lives turned out so differently?

Cissy drew away from her and held her by her shoulders. 'What're you going to do? Are you thinking on finding Hattie?'

'Aye, I have to, I have to know as she is all right. That she's safe.'

'I'll come, an all...'

'No!'

'Please, Megan, I'd be going out of me mind here. We'll be safer together. You on your own, well... anything could happen.'

It hadn't been any use arguing and so not ten minutes later, Cissy, her face pale, but her lips set in a determination Megan knew well, stood beside her in the hall and pulled on her gloves.

'Look, I've been at thinking, Ciss, and I've decided as I'll start me search at Hattie's fella's place. He might know something. After all he knew what she was about to do. He'd backed her in it and his solicitor had sorted things with the police.' She finished buttoning her coat and reached for her own gloves. 'And, I've a mind to take a cab to his place, as I only know his address. I've been there, but I don't know as I could find it again. When Hattie took me we went down ginnals and along back lanes for more than a mile.'

'A cab! By, that'd be something. Do you remember that Sunday as we tried to take a ride in one to the park?' Cissy went into one of her giggles. Megan didn't join in. She knew it wasn't a proper giggle. It was more of a nervous one, so thought better to ignore it and carry on the conversation.

'Aye, I does. The driver looked down his nose at us and gee'ed his horse up and left us standing on the pavement! Well, that won't be happening today. We look like two young ladies in our outfits.'

'That's thanks to you, Megan. And to Madame of course, for letting us have them off-cuts at a cheap price. I love me coat as you cut for me and its right warm, an all.'

'And you look lovely in it. Come on, then, let's go.' Her own nerves were tickling her stomach and she felt if she didn't get them on their way she'd not go through with it.

'Look, Ciss.' They were standing at the side of the road where they were most likely to see a cab pass by. 'Hattie's man, well, he's a gentleman by all accounts. He's rich anyroad. He lives in a big house and has a servant...'

'Eeh, Megan, you didn't say anything about that!'

'I know, but that isn't all. Well, I haven't seen him, but Hattie said as how he's been injured and isn't good to look on.'

'Poor fella. What's going to happen, Megan, when they all come home? Well, them as are coming home. How's it going to be? Who's going to look after them all? This fella at me mam's, he isn't hurt in his body, but from what me mam says, he must be hurt inside. Things as he must have seen...'

'I know, and they say as lasses like us are going to be lucky to get a man, there are so few of them left. It all doesn't bear thinking on. We've been lucky, yer know. War hasn't affected us much and what bit it did were for the better.'

'Well, I'm glad as it's over, well, in the main it is. Will it bother you if you don't get a man, Megan?

'Aye, I've me heart set on getting married and having young-uns of me own, I'm not for thinking as I'd like to be left on the shelf.'

'Well, there's always, Bert Armitage. I'm sure as he's took a shine to you.' Cissy pushed her on the shoulder and laughed.

She shrugged. Cissy often teased her about Bert and she did feel an attraction to him. He wasn't bad looking and he was of strong build. It was his surly nature that put her off. Still, he'd probably change he did seem to like her. He was often standing on the corner when they came out of the station at Breckton, where Cissy's mam lived. She couldn't help but let a big sigh shudder her body. Now wasn't the time for thinking about suitors, and even if it was, she wasn't sure she would really consider Bert Armitage. It was to do with her dream really, she didn't know why, but she felt that Bert wouldn't want his wife following a path she intended to follow. He seemed a proud man, one who would want to be seen to provide for his family. She allowed herself a moment to wonder about him. Where he'd come from, for instance? He'd not been in Breckton long his arrival was just as the war was starting. Not that that was unusual. Miners were badly needed and anyone with flat feet, or some other condition which would make them a hindrance, was sent to work in the pit or in the factories.

'Are you on with dreaming about him, then?' Cissy again giggled and nudged her.

'Go on with you.' She giggled, too, but then, changed the subject

'Anyroad, Ciss, you'll be all right, won't you? With Hattie's fella I mean? You won't cringe or anything? As Hattie says he's sensitive about it.'

'Why're you asking me that? I'll not like seeing him hurt, but I have more about me than to show it and embarrass him!'

Megan had to smile. Cissy was put out of sorts by her asking, but was funny in her indignation. Huffing and pulling a face.

Despite what their journey was about they giggled as they got into the cab and sat holding hands as their bodies jolted from side to side as it trundled along. More than once, Ciss said, 'Eeh, Megan...' She'd no need to ask, what? She knew what was giving Ciss an excitement she couldn't speak of, because she could feel it herself.

Her nerves at why they were here, re-visited her when she stood at the huge front door and pulled the bell cord. Harry opened it as if he'd been standing behind it waiting for her. 'Miss Megan! By, you're a good sight. You're just what Hattie needs. And, who's this, then?'

'She's here, Harry? Oh thank God!'

'Aye, she is. But, she's not well. She's been through a lot. She'll tell you of it. Come in and warm yourself. Let me take your coat.'

After taking her coat he looked towards Cissy. 'Miss...?'

'Cissy. Me names, Cissy, and I'm a friend of Megan's.'

'Well then, as such, you're very welcome. But, not if you stay on the doorstep and let the cold into the house...'

'Eeh, I'm sorry. I'm just in awe of all this. I haven't ever been to such a grand place and now I'm here I didn't expect to have someone to take me coat and such like.' She was giggling again and Megan could see Harry was captivated and Cissy was enjoying his attention. She shook her head at her, but had to smile.

'Right, Megan, you and your friend come along in here and I'll fetch Hattie.'

Megan didn't even notice her surroundings this time, but Cissy did. She gasped as they entered the room, 'I know, it's grand, isn't it?'

'I daren't sit down, Megan. Oh, it's beautiful!'

She'd no time to answer her before Hattie entered the room. A pain clutched at her heart as she took in the gaunt appearance of her beloved friend.

'Hattie, what happened? Your shoulder! You've been injured again. Oh but, thank God you're safe!'

'Aye, safe, but not sound. Oh, Megan...'

'What is it, Hattie? Is the little un all right? Is she safe?'

'She's safe, poor thing, but what she's been through!'

Megan helped Hattie to a chair. They listened as she told them what had happened, though it was plain to Megan that she was not telling all. 'I shouldn't have done it, Megan. And Sue, Sally's mam. She's so ill. She's not going to live. She's upstairs. Her other one...Janey, they found... They found her body...'

The silent tears that fell down Hattie's face spoke of her distress. Megan sat on the arm of the chair and took her in her arms and held her, trying not to hurt her. She didn't know what to say. She had so many questions, but her throat had dried on her and her heart felt heavy. To see Hattie like this. It was not what she ever thought she'd see. It was as if Hattie was broken. Her spirit gone.

'Hattie, you can get through this, you can. Me and Ciss'll help you.'

'Hattie, I'm Cissy. I'm Megan's mate, and I'm for being yours, an all, if you'll have me and like Megan says, we'll help you.'

As she heard this Megan felt a love in her for Cissy that was more than she'd ever felt before. Ciss had risen above the horror the tale had given her and her only thought was for Hattie.

'I'm pleased to meet you, Cissy. I've known of you a good while. And, I've not forgot how kind you was in lending me that half-crown when I most needed it. I've got it for you. It's been kept separate from everything and I've added some to it, an all.'

Cissy giggled, 'You daft thing! I've been at worrying over that, yer know!'

They all giggled at this, and it felt good. Megan took her hanky and wiped Hattie's face. 'See, I told you she was a one. Mind, she's nothing to what her mam's like.'

Hattie's giggle hadn't reached her eyes. She leant her head heavily onto Megan's shoulder.

'It's been a bad time, Megan. I've felt heavy with grief and guilt. After all, some of me motive in doing it all was to get meself out of the way me life was. And, for that I put little Sally in danger and dragged Susan down so far in her spirits she can't rise up again. Oh, Megan, I'm so ashamed.'

'Hattie, you getting free wasn't your main motive, it wasn't! Aye, it was going to be one of the outcomes, but you were at trying to find the other little girl and stopping the terrible things as were happening to young-uns off the poor streets. Oh, I know your life stood to get better if it went well, but don't forget, if it hadn't you were certain to have been killed.'

Hattie looked up into Megan's face. A light was in her eyes that hadn't been there before.

'Hattie, you thought losing your life was worth it if you saved young-uns from the terrible thing as that man and his gang were doing. That's a good thing to have done, not a bad thing. And, Susan, well, poor Susan, you know she wasn't well afore, you knew as she wasn't going to make it, even if you found the other one alive. And, little Sally, she'll forget, she will, Hattie...'

'I hope so. She's young. I mean, she's a lot younger than I was...' Hattie hung her head and the tears that hadn't stopped were silent no more, huge sobs shook her body.

Megan waited. Letting Hattie get to a calm place, a place where she could cope. Her own mind had filled with horror. Poor, poor, Sally, Oh God!

'I was too late....'

Megan patted Hattie and looked over at Cissy. She was held as if in a vice only her bottom lip trembled. Poor, Ciss, she'd taken in stuff she'd no idea of and in such a short time. Megan had an urge to go to her, but she couldn't move. Hattie needed her more. There was a silence. Then, in a stronger voice Hattie said, 'Mind, Megan, its like you say. If there's anything good as has come out of this, it's that other young-uns are now safe. And, I'm for thinking as Bobby Blackstaff'll hang for Janey's murder and that'll be the fate of Wally and Doug, an all, but as for the rest I hope as they rot in jail. Doreen and Lord Marley included. In fact, Doreen more than most, because for a woman to help to get young-uns knowing what was going to happen is vile beyond anything I can think on.'

The door opened and a quiet, refined voice asked. 'Are you all right, Hattie, dear?'

Megan looked up. She swallowed hard. This was the moment she'd been dreading, and she hadn't wanted it to come when she wasn't ready. Her heart went out to the man who stood in the doorway leaning heavily on his crutches. Both of his eye sockets were pulled down, showing the blood red of the insides. His nose twisted to one side and his skin puckered with burn scars. On one side he had no ear, but when her eyes rested on his mouth and chin, these were untouched and perfectly formed as were his teeth. These features told her he'd been a handsome man at one time.

The affect his presence had on Hattie was as if he'd taken away all her troubles. She straightened and dried her eyes. 'Aye, I'm all right, Arthur. In fact, I'm a lot better now as Megan's helped me to look at things in a different way. This is Megan, me mate as I'm always telling you of, and this is Cissy. Cissy is Megan's mate from where she works. Me and her have just become acquainted, but we're liking each other already.'

Arthur smiled. 'I'm so glad, my dear, and I am pleased, too, to meet your friends. In particular you, Megan, I have heard a lot about you. You and Hattie were brought up together, I understand?'

Was he judging her? Was he thinking that she'd done all right for herself? Her mouth dried. She could do no more than smile at him and hoped he wouldn't take her nerves for rudeness, or worse, think she was struck dumb at the sight of him.

'I think it is wonderful how you never gave up on Hattie. Many would have done, given the circumstances. I think you are a true friend, Megan. One doesn't come across friends of your kind very often.'

There was a sad note in his voice as he said this and it was this that helped her find her voice more than what he'd said. 'I'm pleased to be meeting you, too, Ar...Sir.'

'Arthur. Call me, Arthur.'

He'd moved further into the room and came over to her. She stood up and took his outstretched hand. That too, was maimed in that two of the fingers had gone and the skin was wrinkled. But, all she could think of was that it was a funny world, her shaking hands with gentry as if she was his equal!

Arthur extended his hand to Cissy next. As she took it she said, 'I can't believe as I'm meeting someone who's done such a lot to make sure as we are safe from that Kaiser bloke and been through such a lot, an all...I mean'

Megan heard Hattie take in a deep breath and she held her own. She knew what Cissy had meant by what she'd said, but wondered if Hattie and Arthur did.

'Thank you, Cissy. It is nice to know that what I have been through is appreciated.'

Hattie breathed a sigh of relief, but the moment was still tense and Megan was wishing Cissy hadn't brought up Arthur's injuries. She knew he was sensitive about how he looked.

'It is, Arthur, and while I'm on there isn't no-one been at being more of a friend to Hattie than you,' Cissy said, 'Me Mam'd say as you're top drawer, but without the tight knickers pulling your nose high.'

Arthur looked surprised for a moment, then put his head back and laughed out loud. They all joined in and the moment relaxed.

'I'd like to meet this mother of yours, Cissy, she sounds a card! Well, Hattie, I will leave you and your friends to carry on your conversation. No, it's all right, dear. I will see you later. Everything upstairs is fine, Elsie is seeing to that! Anyway, Susan was asleep when I looked in, so she's not having to listen to Elsie preaching, which is a blessing.'

The relaxed and comfortable feeling Megan had in her still didn't stop her being surprised at someone of Arthur's standing giving a small bow to her and Cissy.

'Bye for now, ladies, it was very nice meeting you, in fact it was a pleasure.' He was smiling and it looked genuine and what he'd said sounded genuine. Suddenly she didn't see his injuries, or gentry, just a man. A handsome, young, kind man. And a peace settled in her for Hattie, she'd be all right, Arthur and Harry would see to that.

After seeing Megan and Cissy off, Hattie climbed the stairs and opened the door of the bedroom where Susan lay. Elsie, Susan's sister, rose from the chair next to the bed and put her finger to her mouth in a gesture which told Hattie to be quiet. The gesture, like everything Elsie did, was stern.

She'd been surprised when Susan had said she had a sister living over the other side of Leeds and that this sister and her man had a corner grocery shop, but she'd gladly asked Arthur to contact the sister even though it had set a fear inside her as to Sally's future. With the love she held in her for the child, she'd hoped that future would've been with herself. She'd been further surprised when the sister had turned out to be so different to Susan.

Susan was gentle, fragile and loving whist this one walked like she had a plank stuck up her backside reaching up to her collarbone. Her hair was scraped back into such a tight bun her face was pulled into a permanent expression of disapproval, but then, that was how she was, disapproving. Disapproving of everything she saw. That is, if she looked, which she didn't at Arthur. How she could be a guest in his house and take everything as if it was her right and yet openly and rudely reject him, beggared belief!

She felt every part of herself bristle as Elsie showed her the door. It was as much as she could do to keep her hands by her side and not knock the woman off her feet. In fact, thinking of doing it made her feel better.

Once outside the bedroom Elsie said, 'It is clear to me, Hattie, that me sister isn't long for this world.' She sniffed and used her hanky to wipe her eyes. 'And,' she said, 'I am not surprised after what she's been through!' Her eyes showed none of the emotion she was displaying. She sniffed again only more loudly and held her head high and looking down her nose said, 'I don't know how you are going to live with yourself after this, Hattie. I really don't.'

'Live with meself! I was willing to give me life to find Janey and...'

'Yours AND Sally's! My God, I'm going to have something to say about all this if it's the last thing as I do.'

'Aye, and it might be if you carry on. You know nothing. Nothing! Do you hear me?'

'Don't you dare talk to me of knowing nothing! I know as me sister is lying in there dying! And, me niece is hurting so badly in the insides of her as she's scared even to talk and me other niece lays cold on a slab…God alone knows what she went through afore she died, poor little mite. And as for you! You live here as…as HIS mistress!' Her whole body shook with her disgust, but she'd hardly drawn breath before she continued, 'My God! I know all I want to know or ever thought I would know about life as you lot live, and for decent folk like me who makes an honest living, knowing that much is a mile too far!'

Hattie hung her head. The feeling Megan had given her was leaving her and the guilt she'd born at it all, weighed heavily on her shoulders again.

'Elsie, you may think you know everything. But, all you know is what you want to know, which is just enough to salve the guilt you bear at how little you have cared for your sister and her children's welfare since her husband was killed. And, all you see is what you want to see and how you want to see it.'

Both Hattie and Elsie turned in surprise at this outburst from Arthur. To Hattie it was as though he was a different person, not apologetic for even existing, but forceful and, well, manly.

'I don't know what you mean…'

'I mean, Elsie. That Hattie is not responsible for what happened. She didn't have to listen to your sister when she approached her about Janey. She didn't have to try to find Janey, or put herself in extreme danger to help the police catch the perpetrators of these heinous crimes. And, she isn't responsible for what happened to Sally.'

Hattie stood in awe of Arthur. He was standing squarely in front of Elsie, his body hardly supported by his crutches, forcing Elsie to look at him. His voice, though quiet, was commanding and his stature grew as he went on to say how she'd had nothing to do with how things turned out. That she had been betrayed by the police who were the ones who had sacrificed Sally so they could get the gang they'd been after for a long time.

Elsie wasn't daunted.

'Well, say what you might, but she's one of them… and well, things here are not what they should be!'

'That, may I remind you, is none of your business and whilst it is necessary for you to remain under my roof you will kindly refrain from giving your opinions on anything that is my business and my business alone!'

'Don't worry, I'll not be under your roof a moment longer than I have to be and nor will Sally, because when I leave after my poor sister departs this world, Sally will come with me and live as one of me own. She'll be brought up with decent folk who behave in a Christian manner. And, she'll not be having to look on you every day. Injured through no fault of their own, or not, folk as are like you should be locked away some place where they can't be seen and can't carry on like you do, because not only do you look like the devil, you behave like Him!'

Hattie saw that these last words of Elsie's had cut into Arthur. His skin had paled and his stature shrunk and as he was used to doing he leant heavily on his crutches. But, her own agony was such that she couldn't help him or fight Elsie for him. She just stood next to him and watched as the triumphant Elsie turned and went back into the bedroom. As the door closed a desolate sigh escaped her, bringing Arthur's immediate concern to her.

'Don't worry, my dear, we'll be all right. We don't have to face such people very often. Do you know, Hattie? What she fails to realise is: I am locked away. Wherever I am, I am locked away...'

'Oh, Arthur...'

But then, her mind and heart were agonised by a different thought. Sally. How was she to say goodbye to her? And, to think she was to be brought up by that woman! But, she could do nothing about it. Elsie was kin so had a right and a duty to take Sally. If only she would be taking her as a right and not a duty. All too often duty can become a burden...

CHAPTER SIXTEEN

'He's there!'

'Who?'

'Bert Armitage. I just caught sight of him. He's standing on the corner of the row and it pouring down, an all. He must've asked me mam what train we were coming on.'

'Don't be daft! He's most likely just having a smoke. Old Stan as he lives with has a bad time with his breathing and according to Bert, the poor man's lungs are near gone. Bert has to smoke outside for fear of choking him! Anyroad, how come you sound pleased? I thought you didn't want me to take up with him because of his surly nature!'

'I know, but you said yourself he isn't unattractive and as you thought he'd change his surliness if he was looked after right and had a good wife. So I thought, and with situation how it is, if someone takes a shine then we've to grab them with both hands and take our chances. And, Bert's definitely took a shine to you!'

'Aye, he does seem to have. Oh, I don't know. Anyroad, get your bag down and pass me mine, train's pulling into station.'

Megan looked through the window, but couldn't see much through the cloud of smoke the slowing train belched out. She just made out the sign, 'Breckton' and felt the usual flip of her belly as the excitement at being home gripped her.

As they turned into the street at the beginning of the first of the rows that housed the miners and their families, Bert stepped forward and came alongside her. 'Hello, you got here, then?'

'Why, were you expecting me?'

'No. Well, I've been after asking Issy when it was as you were coming. I've something to ask you.'

The rain was running off his flat cap and his voice and expression was that of a man not happy with his situation. Her asking had he been expecting her seemed to have put him out some, but she wasn't for letting him off the hook.

'I think as you should get on with asking then, because I'm getting soaked and so are you.'

111

'It don't matter none. I'll see thee later.'

And with that he threw his nub end on to the ground and turned and walked away from her. Out of the corner of her eye she saw him cross the road and hurry into the pub that stood just before the turn into the lane where Cissy lived. 'Well! What d'yer make of that, Ciss?'

'It's you as beggar's belief, Megan! You know what he's like, then you taunt him, then you find as he can't take it, which is what you knew in the first place! Anyroad, never mind him, he'll stew or he won't, but isn't this grand, Megan? Just sniff the air. I love the rain. It dampens smell of the pit and freshens everything. Come on.'

She skipped ahead not stopping to adjust her scarf as it fell from her head allowing the rain to plaster her hair to her head in tight curls. Her laughter and joy rang out. Megan shrugged and decided to put Bert out of her mind. She'd not join in with the skipping, though, at least, not until she'd passed the pub. And she couldn't help noticing as she did pass it, that Bert was at the window watching her.

She pulled up her collar and quickened her step. As she turned into the lane, Cissy called out.

'Come, on slow coach. Does you remember song as were sung to us when we was young-uns. Well, it were to me, but I bet as you've heard it.'

And with this Cissy put her arms in the air and twirled round and round singing at the top of her voice:

> *'It's raining, it's pouring,*
> *The old man is snoring,*
> *He bumped his head...*
> *...On the bottom of the bed.*
> *And couldn't get up in the morning!*

Even though the rain and her encounter with Bert had dampened her spirits and excitement some, she couldn't help but feel lifted by Cissy's joy and laughed at her antics.

Cissy didn't see the tall, handsome young man turn on to the lane from the ginnal, but for Megan it was if a bolt of lightning had struck her. She couldn't warn Ciss, she couldn't find enough spittle to wet her mouth to help her to form the words. It was as if her heart had been ripped from the inside of her and given to him.

She stared at him. Every detail of him entered her and gave her feelings she had not known of before. She looked at his hair which lay in flat wet strands over his forehead and noted the rain droplets dripping from his nose. He had the most perfect face she'd ever seen and, even

112

though his body was huddled against the rain she knew that too would be perfect. His smile was broad and his teeth white and even.

His eyes only shifted briefly from Cissy to glance in her direction, but she'd registered they were a deep blue. They hadn't lingered on her, but then, she thought, compared to Cissy the attractive bits she was blessed with wouldn't catch a man's eye at first glance, even if she wasn't looking like a dog coming out of the beck!

A pang of jealousy entered her and she wished with all her heart she'd one ounce of Cissy's beauty.

Cissy became aware she was being watched and stopped dancing. She stared at the young man and then, embarrassment took her. She bent double in a fit of giggles, before taking hold of Megan's hand and running with her over the last few yards to the cottage. The run didn't break the spell for Megan, nor stop the feelings burning her insides.

'That must've been HIM! Oh, Megan, he's so handsome!'

They were shaking their wet things in the back porch. 'D'yer think as he'll like me? Oh, what'll he think of me dancing around like that?'

The sound of the latch told them he'd come in. Cissy looked at her, her eyes wide and more beautiful than she'd ever seen them. Her damp curls framing her lovely face like a halo.

'He'll think I'm a idiot, Megan, I'm right embarrassed. Go in first and get him talking.'

She did as she was bid still not able to speak. As she entered the scullery the warmth that hit her further reddened her already glowing cheeks as she looked into those wonderful blue eyes again. He stood just inside the doorway drying himself on a piece of towelling. Now he wasn't huddled against the rain she could see his size and the strength of his body. She noted the flicker of disappointment that crossed his face.

Cissy's mam had her back to them, stirring something on the stove. 'Right, lad, these are girls as I told you about, this is....' she turned around, 'Where's our Cissy, what's she playing at?'

Cissy came sheepishly through the door. Jack looked at her and smiled. Cissy coloured, and lowered her lids.

'You've a lovely voice, lass...'

'Lovely voice! Where've you heard her sing, Jack? Don't tell me, she's daft as a brush that one. I bet she was singing whilst rain soaked her?' Issy looked over at Cissy, 'You've got nothing up top, lass. I wondered how it was as you were twice as wet as Megan. You'll catch your death!' She nodded in Jack's direction, 'This is Jack as I told you about in me letter.' Her head then bobbed in their direction. 'And this

113

here is, Cissy, me daughter, and her friend, Megan, as I expect you've gathered by now, lad.'

Jack looked over at her and she held his eyes for a moment. 'Hello, Megan, I'm pleased to meet you.'

She could only nod her head at him. It was as if the feelings gripping her body had taken over from her mind. She noticed his eyes stayed longer on Ciss and she heard Ciss say something to him about folk who stare and his head went back in laughter. The sound further danced on her heart, tightening his hold on her.

It was something of a relief when Issy said, 'Well, that's a good start. I think as you'll all get on fine, now get yourselves sat down before me stew is spoiled. By, it's good to have you home, me lasses. Tell us all your news.'

The relief that the activity of sitting down and the serving of the meal and the general banter going on between Cissy and her mam and Jack brought to her, was short-lived. It was replaced by a feeling of something akin to heartbreak as in the time it took to eat their meal it became obvious to her that even though they had only just met, Cissy and Jack were meant for each other.

'You've been quiet all day, Megan. Are you all right?'

They were getting ready for bed when Cissy asked her this after going on and on about how wonderful Jack was and did she think he was taken with her.

'Aye, I'm just tired and worried over Hattie,' she lied. Though, it sounded like a good excuse and Cissy accepted it.

It was in the dark and the silence of the night that the tears flowed. She didn't stop them. She needed the emptying of her pain. She asked herself over and over, how she was going to bear it if Cissy and Jack took up together...or married! She knew without doubt that moving away wouldn't be something she could think of doing. How could she live without ever looking on him? Without being near to him? And, what of Ciss and Issy? She couldn't imagine her life without them in it.

Her last thought before falling asleep, was: There's always Bert...

PART THREE

CHOICES LOST

1920

CHAPTER SEVENTEEN

The wind brushed Megan's hair away from her face. It would look like a mop when they pulled into the station, but she didn't care. After all these years her stomach still knotted in joy as the Breckton sign came into view. She leant a little further out of the window, trying to see over Cissy's head. She caught sight of Bert he was on the station as usual, leaning against the wall at the bottom of the steps. Cissy turned and winked at her as she noticed him and then turned back and strained her neck even further to see if Jack was coming.

As the train came to a halt Bert stepped forward and at that moment Jack came through the gate. Megan looked from Bert to Jack. An: 'if only' came into her head, but she'd have none of it and banished it away. She'd found a place in her where she kept her feelings for Jack and only in the dead of night did she allow herself to visit it.

'Oh, Megan, it's good to be home! Mind, I'll tell you something, by the looks of Bert you've to make up your mind. You can't keep him hanging on forever.'

She didn't answer she just smiled and hoped that the smile had reached her eyes.

'I mean it, Megan, I think as you've kept him waiting long enough. Mam says as Lillian Cole's been at sniffing around of late. And, Pauline Sedgefield. You know. Her from the back row as...'

'You've not been at saying anything of this afore!'

'No, I know, me mam told me not to. She's not for you taking on Bert. She has a feeling in her about him. Only she didn't want to be seen as if she was trying to make trouble between you. She says as you'll do as your heart tells you, and that'll be that. Anyroad, it's bound to happen as lasses who have no man will go after Bert, him being the only unattached male in the town.'

'Aye, I s'pose so and I'll think on. Now, let's get off the train, ay?'

Jack overtook Bert and ran towards them. Taking Cissy's bag from her and putting it on the ground, he lifted her up and twirled her round. 'Eeh me lass, I've missed you.' He hugged her to him. Their happiness nudged at the dull pain in Megan's insides.

'Hello, Megan lass,' Jack had put Cissy down and was holding her close to him. Megan drew on her inner strength and answered him as if she hadn't been affected by his and Cissy's love for each other. 'Hello, Jack, you look well. The sun's been at scorching you as brown as a berry.'

'Aye, it's been grand. You lasses need to get out in it whilst you're home.' He bent down and picked up Cissy's bag and then, looking at her he motioned with his eyes in Bert's direction. 'We'll take your bag, Megan, and we'll see you later, ay? Oh, by-the-way, Issy said to tell you as its cold ham and tatties for supper and it'll be on around six-ish.'

Megan watched them walk pass Bert. They greeted him, but he only nodded. He'd stepped back to his original stance and was leaning back against the wall as if he'd no care as to her being there. Nor did his dark expression change when she walked over to him.

'Hello, Bert. Are you all right?'

'Aye, but not as good as the big fellow by all accounts, but then, it isn't often as the sun gets down in the bowels of the earth.'

'Don't be daft! You look fine...'

'It's daft that I am, is it? Well, I must be, hanging around for the likes of you!'

He turned and walked away from her. For a moment she thought she'd let him go, but a fear gripped her. Did she really want to lose him? Oh, she didn't know what she wanted...

'Are you coming, then?'

'Where to?' She stood her ground. 'And why should I go anywhere with you in that mood? Some welcome...'

He was a few yards in front of her and she could see his anger. He had a funny way. It was as if she was to do his bidding at all times or she'd know to it. But then, he had another side that was sort of...well, vulnerable, like he didn't think anyone could like him. It was this side she was attracted to. Not that it was the only thing about him that drew her to him. No, there was something else. Something she couldn't fathom. She knew it wasn't love. Well, not love like she felt for Jack.

After a moment when it seemed they'd stare each other out he shrugged his shoulders and grinned. 'I thought seeing as it's a nice afternoon we'd take a walk across to the beck and if you're up to it we could take in Mire Hill.'

Her relief came from her in a sigh, which she covered up with a smile. 'Aye, I'd like that. I need to go home and change me skirt and shoes, but I'll not be long. I'll bring some of Issy's ginger beer and meet you at the ginnal in about fifteen minutes, ay?'

118

His grin widened and he motioned to her to catch him up. She did as he bid but left him at the corner and hurried down the lane to Issy's.

It felt good to be held in Issy's arms. To feel the comfort and safety of her love. To smell the familiar, fresh, clean linen and home- baking, smell of her. It was so good the tightness in her nearly broke.

'Eeh, lass, it's good to see you,' Issy held her away from her. A knowing look on her face. 'Bert?'

'Aye, some. I feel I'm not being fair to him hanging him on, but I want...'

'I know. You want what is the right of us all and what so many are missing out on. It's up to you, lass. Think on your choices and when you decide which is the best for you, then that's the path to take. Only don't leave yourself regretting. Put your heart into what you choose and make the best of it.'

She hugged Issy to her again. She knew this wasn't the advice Issy wanted to give her. She knew she'd sooner have told her not to take Bert on.

Bert still had a grin on his face when she met up with him and it settled her some. Though she'd still no knowledge of what she'd say to him if he did ask her to marry him, which is what she suspected he had in mind with this walk he wanted to take her on.

They were standing at the side of the stream, known as the beck, watching the cool water bubbling over the stones when he reached out for her hand. She felt herself stiffen but fought the feeling and let him take her hand in his. This hadn't happened before. He'd never touched her. His hand felt hard and rough. A tremble went through her. She looked up at him. His face was different, there was a longing there. A hunger. The feeling she'd had gripped her again.

'I want to ask...Well... Thou knows...'

She couldn't help him. Her mouth dried and words wouldn't come to her. They stood in a moment that was awkward. Inside she knew such moments shouldn't be like this. Was it because it wasn't right?

'Look, let's climb hill, ay?'

She just nodded.

It was a hot climb and she felt grateful that it didn't give leave for talking. Her thoughts battled on. Should she...?'

'Here it is! This is place I wanted to bring you. Its grand, isn't it? Me step-sister was brought up round here and she was always on about it. Telling me tales on how it was good to come up these hills with her dad and our mam. She said as mam lost a babby at birth and as it hadn't

119

been baptised Priest wouldn't bury it in the consecrated ground so they brought it up here and buried it. She said as they held their own little service for it. I've often looked, but never found anything as could be a grave.'

'You've not said anything of your family afore, Bert. Where does your sister and mam live?'

'We lived down in Sheffield, mam'd come from there, well, not originally, she was Irish by birth. Anyways she moved back after she was widowed and then she married me dad. She'd known him afore she'd left. Me mam and me dad are dead now. Me sister lives somewhere in the Midlands but I don't bloody care about her she's nothing to me. She may as well be dead, an all. She left me with me dad not two weeks after me mam'd died. And after her promising me mam as she'd take care of me and find a way of getting us out of it. I was just on six. She was ten years older than me. Anyroad, I got up one morning and she was gone. Never even said goodbye...'

He was quiet for a long time but she felt he needed to be with his own thoughts so didn't break into them to ask questions.

After a while she poured him a mug of ginger beer and handed it to him. He took a swig and then started his tale again.

'I'd not heard of her for years, thou knows. Then suddenly, I had a letter a bit afore I came here. Said as she'd married some doctor and wanted to get together with me. She said as she'd known as me dad was dead and that's why she felt she could now get in touch. She had things to explain. Ha! That was a laugh! How do you explain leaving a young-un in that hell hole and saving your own skin! She was everything to... Anyroad, I wrote back and told her as she was no sister of mine and I'd sooner she kept out me life and that me dad'd long since made me understand as she'd had what was coming to her when he beat her.'

Megan wondered about the bits of his story referring to 'the getting us out of it' and about his sister being beaten, but thought better of asking. He'd said a lot more than he'd ever said to her before and she didn't want to upset him by probing further. He'd most likely tell her in his own good time.

It was funny him choosing Breckton to come to. And him looking for the babby's grave. It was as if he was trying to be near his mam again. A kinship grew in her. They were not unlike in what they'd been through.

'I'm sorry to hear of all that, Bert. You having no family as such is something as I can relate to. I've no family meself...' She'd not mention her granny and granddad, not yet. 'Me mam died giving birth to me and that was in a convent for them as had no man.'

120

'Well we're in same boat then, so that's a good start. But what I've told you is just for you. I don't want anyone else knowing. No one! D'yer hear? Especially not the likes of Issy Grantham. Because I know as me sister had something to do with her when she was a young-un. I don't want any interference from that quarter. Me business is me own.'

This shocked her. To think that Issy knew of his mam and sister yet knows nothing of them being related to Bert! And she'd not to speak about them either. It wasn't going to sit easy keeping stuff from Issy. She was bound to ask. She's always been curious over Bert.

'You've gone quiet, Megan.'

'I was thinking on me and you not having family as such. Have you pictures of your family? She hesitated. She thought of her locket, but no, she'd not tell of it. She'd been so long keeping her granny and granddad to herself that sharing them would be like spoiling something special.

'No, I did have. I had them in a tin. But when I come here I vowed I'd put it all behind me so I chucked them out. I didn't have a good childhood and it's shaped me. Hardened me. I've no time for anything that has gone. You should do same, Megan. Don't think on what's in the past. Think on what future can be like...' He'd moved closer to her. 'I reckon as you must know what it is I want to say to you, Megan. Are you for it?''

'I want to talk some...'

'Talk? What's there to talk of? We've an idea of each other now. Either you're for being me wife or you're not.'

So, that was it, then? No going down on one knee, no... Oh, well what had she expected of Bert Armitage! He wasn't exactly known for romancing, was he? Hadn't it been on two and a bit years he'd been showing his leaning towards her and today was the first time he'd touched her?

She felt a laugh bubbling up inside her. She swallowed it back. It wasn't right to laugh. Besides, it wasn't a good laugh. It was more of a feeling of ...of anger. Yes, that was it. She was angry. Angry at her mam and Bert's sister and Cissy and Jack, and yes, she was angry with Bert. Bert more than any of them.

'Well?'

She turned and walked away from him. It was all she could think of doing. She'd climb higher. There was still a way to go to the top.

'Where're you off to? Megan! Megan!'

He caught up with her and grabbed her arm and held it in a painful grip. 'What're you up to? You bloody knew how I felt! You bloody had me on, you bitch!'

121

'Let go, you're hurting me. I just want to think…'

'Think?'

They'd reached a small thicket and Bert pulled her in front of him and pushed her back against a tree. His hand was above her leaning on the tree trunk. He was so near she could feel his breath on her and smell his body. It smelt of the coal dust and his brand of smokes, but mostly of fresh washed clothes tinged with fresh sweat. This last was like Jack smelt when he came in from the stables. Her imagination gave her Jack. Something stirred in her belly and a tickly feeling between her legs sent a gripping spasm through her. The feeling surprised her. She dared not look up at Bert in case he knew.

'Megan…'

He lifted her chin. He was gentle, loving…The feeling inside her increased, she couldn't breath! His lips touched hers. She didn't stop him. She wanted the kiss…wanted more…wanted…

'No! Not that! Not afore…' The touch of his hand on her breast had brought her back to reality. The shock it had sent through her wasn't unwelcome, but woke her to what might happen.

'I'm sorry, Megan. I didn't mean…You said afore! Afore what? Are you thinking on marrying me, Megan?'

'I don't know, Bert. Don't get mad at me again. I just want to think on some. I know it isn't being fair on you, but I've things I've to give up and I'm not sure as I'm of the mind to give them up. Not altogether.'

'What things are you talking of?'

'Well, I've talked of them before. You know. Me dream to have a place of me own so as I can design clothes for folk and make them up. Something like where I work, only smaller. I'm good at it, Bert, and I could make a good living for…'

'It isn't a woman's job to make a living! Not a married woman's job. Besides, it'd make me a laughing stock. If you marry me you can forget all that. I'll be the only bread winner. Look, Megan, I want a woman as'll be a proper wife to me…'

'I know and it's that as worries me. Would I be the one as could make you happy? Because I don't know if I could be happy not doing what I love doing. I've had me dream for so long and I've been at saving this good while…'

'Aye, well that'll not go to waste. With what I've got an all we could do the cottage up some. You'll not like it how it is. It needs a good coat of distemper all through. And we'll need some bits of furniture and stuff. Mind, it'll take you a while to get it cleaned up, it's in a bit of a mess.'

'Bert Armitage! You can go and fish! I'll not wed you so as I can be your skivvy! If I do say as I'll wed you, then you can clean up the cottage before I step foot in it!'

'Oh! So it's a possibility, then?'

'I told you; I'm thinking on.'

'You liked it when I kissed you though, so that says something.'

'Aye, I've feeling towards you.'

'Do you love me, Megan?'

The question shocked her. He'd never spoken of loving. She'd only one way of dealing with it. 'Do you love me, Bert?'

He was quiet for a moment. Then looked into her eyes and said, 'Aye, I do, Megan. I have done for a while.'

'I...I'm thinking me feeling for you is love, I think of you a lot and I...Yes, I think I do love you, Bert.' And she knew she did. Not the searing love she had for Jack, but what she felt was a love of sorts. She wasn't cheating him by saying it. And she'd liked the feeling when he'd kissed her. Maybe they'd go along all right together. If only she could keep her feeling for Jack where it was, deep in the inside of her and, if she could live without her dream.

'Well, I'm glad to hear it. But, thou knows, I've no give in me on how I want it to be. If I take you on, you're to be a proper wife and no less.'

'I told you, that's what I've to think on. And I need time. I'll give you me answer when I come home next, I promise.'

'Aye, well I might have taken up with someone else by then...'

'You can if you like! It won't hurt me none!'

His move was quick. He took hold of her arm and pulled her to him. His fingers bruised her flesh. His eyes were dark, deeply dark. And his body shook. A fear trembled through her. Then, he loosened his grip and smiled down at her.

She felt confused. Before she could sort out what had happened his lips came crushing down on hers. He sucked her lips into his mouth and held her so close she could feel every part of him, even... Oh God!

Her body was drowning in feelings she couldn't control. She knew if he tried to go further again, she'd not be able to stop him. Was this, love? Was it enough? Could she give up her dream for it...?

CHAPTER EIGHTEEN

Jack finished the brushing of the hind quarters of the grey mare he'd been grooming. 'There you go, Karinda lass. You're more than ready for your sire.'

'She is looking rather well, Jack. I think Charring lad will be a good match for her. You know he sired Finny boy, the best runner on the flats there has ever been, don't you? I'm hoping he and Karinda can produce something just as special.'

Jack hadn't noticed Mrs Harvey coming into the stable. He felt unnerved and wondered how long she'd been watching him. He nodded and touched his cap. She came closer and took the horses rein from him. Stroking its mane she spoke softly to the horse. 'Good girl. You know I'm relying on you, don't you?'

Karinda shook her mane and whinnied. 'Ha! She knows everything I say to her.' Handing him back the rein she surprised him by abruptly changing the subject.

'How is your wedding plans going, Jack? Has Henry cleared out the barn for you, yet?'

'He was working on it this morning, Ma-am. I think he'll have it ready in time. He tells me it's a job he's done on many occasions and as Cook dresses it up right nice.'

'She does, I've always been amazed at how it looks when she and the others have been working on it. They have different decorations for each occasion. And they are working hard in the kitchen, too, baking lots of pies and cakes. I hope you have a really good time and everything goes well for you.'

'Thank you, Ma-am. I'm sure as it will. And I'm grateful for all as you've done for me and Ciss.'

'Not at all! It's a tradition of the estate. Mr Harvey's grandfather started it. All the wedding receptions of the estate and household workers are held in the barn, as used to be the Spring and Autumn barn dances and a Summer fete. Though we haven't had any of those since... Anyway, your wedding will get us going once more. It's about time there was music and celebrations on the estate again.'

To hide the embarrassment of the nearness of her he fiddled with the horses rein. Laura Harvey had made him feel uncomfortable a few times of late. Standing too close and even touching his arm on occasions.

Her jacket brushed him. There was nowhere he could move to.

'And did you know, Jack, there is also a tradition around these parts that the mistress of the house has the first dance with the bridegroom?'

She was laughing at him. Knew he was uncomfortable. The stable door opening saved the moment.

'Aahh, Gary. Keep Charing lad out there. It is too confined in here. If he has a problem mounting her, he could end up hurting both himself and Karinda. Take Karinda outside, Jack.'

She'd moved away. He could breathe again. He caught Gary's eye, saw the usual teasing grin and the knowing raise of the eyebrow. Gary hadn't missed Laura Harvey's obvious fancy for him and used the fact to have a laugh at his expense. He thought about what had been said and hoped to God that he was right in thinking that she was teasing him about the dance. He knew it was tradition for the gentry of the manor to come to the wedding do, but only for half an hour or so and not to join in!

Concentrating on helping Charing lad mount Karinda, helped him. As a rule the job didn't take long once the stallion was inside the mare, but the eagerness and anticipation of the horse to achieve this could over excite him and waste the sperm. Guiding and helping him was a business that gave no time to chatter or to think of anything until the job was done.

The first experience he'd had in this stables had been a source of embarrassment to him. It was unusual to have a woman boss as it was, but to have her around and helping with this particular task had unnerved him. But, she was matter of fact about it and he'd got used to it.

'Well, let's hope she takes. Gary, get Charing lad back into the box and take him back to Smythe's. We don't want him trying again. Smythe may have another filly lined up for him later today. Well done both of you.'

As she walked away, Gary winked at Jack and in a low voice said, 'She was forgetting who was to mount who I reckon, Jack. I'd say you're in with a chance there.'

'Don't talk like that, Gary! I'll have none of it. Get about your business!'

It wasn't how he usually took Gary's teasing and the lad looked taken aback, but he was angry inside. Not at the lad, he meant to do nothing more than have a bit of banter, but at Laura Harvey! She'd no right putting him in such a position. She was his boss and was taking advantage of the fact. It wasn't unknown, he knew that. Such things went on. And she was a beauty. But he wanted none of it. Besides, she knew he was to be wed soon.

He thought about Cissy. He couldn't wait to make her his wife. He had a need in him and he knew it was this that was letting Mrs Harvey get under his skin. And with the wedding only days away his need was getting more intense. It was the anticipation.

***

'Eeh, Megan, I can't believe it, ten days! Only ten days!'

'Aye, I know, and if you say it once more I'll not finish your gown for you...'

'What's wrong, Megan? Every time I mention me wedding you sound like you don't want to hear of it.'

'I'm sorry, love, I'm at worrying. Everything is going to be different...'

'Aye, that part does spoil me happiness some, but...'

'No, I'm at being selfish. Of course things change. They have to. I'll be right. I'll see you every few weeks and I'll get used to it. I will.'

'You haven't thought on saying, yes, to Bert, then?'

'No, I haven't me mind straight on Bert as yet. I've a feeling in me for him, but anyroad as I said, I'll be right. I'll stay on here a while and keep on with me saving and see how things go.'

'Bert's not for waiting for you, yer know. I told you afore about that Lillian Cole. Well, it seems me mam's seen them together a couple of times and they wasn't at talking neither! Mind, Lilly'd have done all the running. She's had a go at getting Gary Arkwright from Jenny afore now. Me Mam says Jenny moved that quick when she realised. And now she and Gary are to get engaged. She says as Gert's over the moon now it's all settled. And Gert's for living with them, an all. Not like me Mam. I wished me Mam'd think on. I don't want her living so far away.'

'It's only York! It's no different to you being here and her in Breckton!' The sharpness of her tone made her feel ashamed so she changed it to a joke. 'It's a good position she has with them priests, yer know, Ciss. It'll suit her, looking after three men. By, she'll knock them into shape, if I know Issy.'

'Aye, you're right there. But, why doesn't she want to stop with me and Jack?'

127

'She's told you. She thinks as you'll have a better start without her. And I think she's right, an all. If she stays on she's afraid as any advice as she gives could come to be looked on as her interfering. And that could lead to a bad feeling. Anyroad, she's looking forward to the change and she'll have every third weekend off and come and stay with you. And, I reckon as that'll be plenty!'

'Oh, Megan! What a thing to say, even if you are right...'

'Aye, I know, she'd skin me if she heard!'

They giggled at this and Megan felt better. She'd covered up her surliness and hadn't given away the reason for it. She gave her attention back to her work, but her thoughts didn't rest and she didn't feel better in them.

Her mind went to the wedding gown. Madam had allowed her to work on the making of it in the evenings after work and had let her use the work-rooms and the machines. She'd only to finish the bow at the back and then every painful stitch would be done. Though, she'd still to get on with her own frock! She couldn't bear to think about it. Nor on how it will be to be a bridesmaid and watch Jack promise to love and honour Cissy for the rest of his life! Oh, Jack... Would she ever get rid of this feeling she had for him? This longing, this... 'Oh! Damn!'

'Megan Tattler! Was that you on with swearing? Oh, what...? You're crying! Megan, what is it?'

'No, no, I'm not. I... It was the giggling, Ciss, honest... It made me eyes water then, because I couldn't see proper, I stuck meself with me needle...'

'Was it me going on about Bert?'

'Well, aye, it was a bit of that.' She lied, 'I was shocked to hear as he'd taken up with someone. He said as he'd give me some time to think on. Oh! I don't know. I'm in a right tizzy inside. I just don't know what to do. Everything is settled for you, Ciss, and I'm glad, I am, but I just don't know how things will work out for me. If I go for Bert, that's if he still wants me, he's made it clear as I'm to go on his terms. He's a proud man. He talks of me stopping at home and having young-uns and him providing for us...'

'That's at worrying me, an all, Megan. You know...well, having young-uns...I don't know exactly what happens...'

Megan felt a dread in her, she knew what Cissy was referring to, but the last thing she wanted to talk about was her and Jack coming together, not in that way, she didn't.

'Is that what's behind you not wanting your mam to go?'

'Aye, some...'

'Hasn't Jack tried anything?' Oh God! She didn't want to know!

'Aye, he's…yer know…touched me…but…'

'It'll be right, love, don't worry. Jack'll take care of you. I knows of what happens, but it isn't easy to tell of and it sounds bad. Mind, Hattie tells me it isn't. She says if the man loves you and you love him, then it's… Well, she says as it's wonderful. Though it might hurt a bit first time…'

'But what is it? Tell me, Megan…'

'I can't, love, I haven't words as'd sound right, but just to say as Jack… Well, Jack will put something in you…his…'

'Oh! Is that why it… It sort of grows? Only I've felt it against me when we kiss and that.'

The agony in Megan increased. Her heart thumped in her throat. What did it feel like to be held by Jack? To feel him wanting more than kisses…to feel him kissing….No! She must stop this. She must change the subject before the tears came again.

'Aye, that's it, love. Now, talk of something else, ay? You're on with embarrassing me. I don't want to know what you get up to. And don't be at telling me after, either. It's for you and Jack to know and that's that!'

Cissy looked red in the face and put her head down seeming to concentrate on her work. She had a look of rejection about her that caused Megan to once more feel ashamed. Cissy needed her and all she could do was to snap at her. It was as if she'd to punish her because Jack had chosen her. And it wasn't Cissy's fault. She reached out and took her hand.

'I'm sorry, love, I didn't mean it. Of course I'll always be for you. If it…Well, when it happens, if it don't go right or anything you can talk to me. I don't know much, but I can ask Hattie for advice and she'll help. Now, what you're best doing is to think on about Jack. That'll help you to be less worried. Does you think as he's not going to be careful of you? He will be. And men seem to know how to go on, so he'll be at teaching you, an all. Come on now. It's your wedding as you're looking forward to, not your funeral!'

A sudden clapping of hands made them jump. Madame Marie had come into the work-room and stood looking around at them. There was an air of sadness about her and the usual stiff way she held herself was gone. Megan felt uneasy and she saw that Cissy did, too.

'Gels, I have something to say. I'm afraid the garments you are working on are the last. I have to close the business…I…'

'Close! But…'

'Yes, Miss Tat…Megan. I'm sorry. I cannot avoid it. I'll be honest with you all. I just managed to keep going through the war, largely thanks to how hard you all worked. I thank you for that. But the lean times that followed, and the continuing worry over the predicted recession is making it impossible for me to continue. I know you are not altogether knowledgeable about current affairs, but things are not good for businesses at the moment and I am not capable of fighting through a recession. The cutters and pattern-makers have already been given notice earlier today and will be gone by the end of the week. You gels in here will be kept on for a further week. Miss... Megan, when you have done the trimming on that frock you can work on finishing Miss Gr...Cecelia's wedding gown and your own gown. I want you to be able to finish them in time. The cutters will help. That's all I have to say...I'm very sorry...'

She turned and almost ran back into her office.

There was a silence. Megan wasn't sure what part had shocked her the most. The being told they were all out of work or hearing Madame using her and Cissy's first names!

Gradually the chatter started up again. Some in the room seemed happy to be escaping. Megan wasn't. With a realisation that put a sick feeling in her belly she knew her choices were gone. She'd only one path she could go along. Her life was suddenly mapped out for her.

CHAPTER NINETEEN

There was a disappointment in Megan as they left the station. But then, she shouldn't have expected him to have been there. He'd be in the pub with that Lillian Cole if he wasn't on his shift.

'Are you all right with that box, Ciss?

'Aye, Jack should be along. Oh, Megan, I can't wait for him to see me in me gown, and you look lovely in yours, an all. How you got them both finished I'll never know. I'll not ever be able to thank you.'

'Just make sure as Jack don't see it before the day! It's unlucky that, yer know.'

'I'll not let him. Or more to the point, me mam won't!'

'Aye, you're right there. She's got him lodgings at the pub from Thursday, hasn't she? There's not a chance you'll see him after that until you walk up the aisle.'

'Well, it'll not be so bad. We'll be back at work till Friday. Oh, I wished we hadn't to go back. There doesn't seem much point now, does there?

'No, but it'll make the time pass. We've a lot to do to help Madame pack everything up.'

'What're you going to do, Megan? Have you thought on?'

'Aye. I'm going to see if Bert's still for me and if he isn't I'm going to go round the mills and see if I can get set on and get some board and lodgings for meself.'

'So, it's you as is after me now, is it? Well, I've not been for waiting round for thee, thou knows.'

'Oh, Bert! You made me jump. Sneaking up on me like that!'

He'd no time to retort before Ciss jumped in. 'Hello, Bert. Have you seen Jack?'

'Aye, he was just coming down the road. Does you need an hand? I'll help you.'

'No, ta. I'll wait for Jack. Put that box down here with mine, Megan, and leave them to Jack to carry. You go with Bert. I'll be right.'

'I haven't heard meself invite her anywhere as yet...'

'You needn't be like that, Bert Armitage. I know as you haven't been waiting for me, even though I did ask you to give me some time!'

131

'Well, what did you expect? You weren't at encouraging me, were you?'

'Will you walk with me to the beck, then? I've to talk to you.'

'I don't see as I can be at refusing, not when I'm being asked by such a pretty lass.'

He was grinning, but Megan felt hot with embarrassment and Cissy's giggling didn't help matters!

'Well, here we are again. Though it seems as boots on other foot and you've to do the asking this time, Megan.'

'Aye, I know.' She'd waste no time. She'd no choice, she knew that. She deserved the humiliation she felt. 'I...I was at wondering if your offer to take me on was still open to me? I have to be truthful and tell you as something has made me mind up to come to you...'

'What's that, then? Are you saying as you don't come willing, like?'

'No, I'm not saying that, Bert. It's that something has happened as has helped me in me decision.'

He was quiet for a while after she'd finished telling him. She waited, holding her breath.

'But you were leaning towards coming anyroad, you say? And it isn't as I'm your last hope, is it?'

'No, you're not. I've a plan of what I'm to do if you'll not take me on. And I know as you've other choices in the offing. It's up to you...'

'Come here...'

He reached out to her and pulled her close to him. 'Course I'm for taking you on. Lillian isn't anything to me. I was just not for having no one and chancing losing me cottage.'

He held her close. It felt good. She tried to take something from the strength of him to banish away the feeling of dread inside her. She was to make the best of this. Because despite her words about going into the mill; it wasn't really an option. She would find it difficult to pay lodgings out of what she knew of the wages the mill workers were paid.

When his lips came on hers she didn't let it be just him who was doing the kissing. And as feelings woke inside her she allowed them. She didn't stop his caress of her breast. She wanted to know the longing. Wanted to be sure he could rouse in her feelings that would help her to be a good wife. And he did. She was near to begging him to take her down before she gathered all that was in her and pulled away.

'Christ! You're on with being a tease! Well, you bloody well needn't think as I'll take them games when we're wed!'

'I'm not at playing games! I...wanted to. It's just...I want to be wed first.'

'Well, I'm not bloody going to say as I'm sorry for me actions. You were to blame just as much as me...!'

Though his reaction wasn't what she'd wanted. And his quick temper was frightening. She understood. She knew she hadn't been fair to him.

'And, I'll tell thee something else while I'm on. I'm not for waiting no time to be wed.'

'I know, Bert, and I want to be wed as soon as it's possible. I'm sorry. I've no experience of it all. I was letting me feelings carry me, but then, I suddenly realised what I was doing....'

He shuffled the dirt around with his feet. It seemed an age before he spoke.

'Aye, well, I s'pose as it goes good for us, at least I know as you have feelings in you for me and you weren't just for taking me on because you've no other choices. Let's talk on the arrangements, ay?'

They sat down on the grass. There was a relief in Megan. It seemed Bert could come out of his temper as quickly as he could go into it. But, her body didn't let go of how she'd felt. She still had an urge to take Bert to her. There was a need in her, not just to do it, but to know if it was like Hattie had said it could be. But, most of all, to know, if it would be enough to stop the longing and the pain in the inside of her

'We can arrange it all in three weeks, thou knows. I was asking Father O'Malley about it afore I brought you up here last time.'

For a moment she was unsure what Bert meant. His words didn't seem to go with her thoughts or with the feelings going on inside her.

'The wedding, Megan...'

'Oh! Sorry. I was at daydreaming...'

'Aye, well. I know, lass. But we've to sort things out. I need to put in for me cottage proper to make sure on it...'

'Three weeks, is that all it takes? Well then, let's do what we have to. There won't be a problem with you getting the cottage, will there?'

'No. It's mine for the asking, only thing is I have to have a wife or be getting married. I've been on with getting it all cleaned out. Well, best as I can. And I've the two bedrooms white-washed...'

'You took on what I said, then?'

'Aye, I did. Even though, I wasn't sure of you. Mind, I'm not for doing women's work. I've only shifted stuff out as was of no use. As I see it. I'll do the distempering, but any cleaning is down to you.'

His mood had changed again and she felt a feeling of dread in her for it. But, she'd to get on with it. If she was to take him on, she'd to take this side of him, too.

'How about I stay in the cottage until we're wed? I've nowhere to go after next Friday. I mean, if you could move out for a couple of weeks. Stay at a mates or such like…'

'That's a good idea, love. I'll soon find a place to kip or I could take a room at the pub. And as you'll be at home all day you can really get things sorted.'

'We've to post banns, an all. What about we do that on Sunday? We'd have to attend mass. And it's like as not as Father O'Malley'll need us to go for some lessons.'

'Lessons! What's he going to be on with teaching us? I reckon as we could teach him a thing or two even afore we're wed! Ha! That's a turn up. Lessons, from a Catholic priest!'

Megan had to laugh with him. It did sound funny. 'I think it's on the religious side of stuff. Cissy said as he talks about the sanctity of marriage and bringing young-uns up in the church. It's got to be done or he'll not marry us.'

'Aye, all right. Anything as long as it gets settled. Come on. Let's get ourselves away afore I start in on you again.'

He stood and offered her his hand. She took it and he helped her up. For a moment he looked like he was for, starting in on her, as he put it, but she didn't dare visit the feelings again so covered up by making a joke.

'You needn't look like that, Bert Armitage! You've on three weeks to wait so from now on until we're wed, no more meetings without Father O'Malley being present so as to bless us!'

Bert put his head back and laughed out loud. It was a good sound and she couldn't help but join him. She felt a happiness inside her, where before there had been a dread. Things would work out. She was sure of it.

CHAPTER TWENTY

Hattie sat up in bed.

'What is it, my dear? You often look so sad. Is it me?'

'No, Arthur, no. You couldn't be at making me unhappy. Its, well, I'm worried about me lasses. It isn't working out as yet and they're not getting enough to line their pockets. Some of them are getting grumpy about tipping up me due and others are not making enough to tip up anything. I'm at digging into me standby money to keep them in food and pay me bills.'

'Well, it will take time to get known. It's not as if you can advertise. I hadn't thought that you were struggling. You haven't said anything before.'

'I know, but I didn't want you to worry, and besides, you weren't for me taking on this business, even though you helped me to get it.'

'That wouldn't stop me helping you again.' He hauled himself up so he was now sitting. His sigh told her he'd other things on his mind besides talking.

'Yes. I do hate the thought of you having to be involved in a business such as you have. I worry. It isn't legal to do what you are doing. Oh, I know, the girls would do it anyway and you are providing a safe place and care for them and I strongly believe it can be a necessary service. No one knows that better than I do...did. Anyway, I'm surprised that after being up and running for eighteen months you're still not breaking even.'

'It's like you say. I can't advertise. Some of the lasses have kept in contact with old customers and they're visiting. And, I'd hoped as the word would spread that way. Mind, I've been at vetting all the customers first. I'll not have some of the bas... I mean...blokes in the house as used to use them.'

'Look. I'll go round to my club tonight and drop the word in an ear or two. It might help. There are a few members that have been saying they are missing out. Most upper-class wives are the 'lay back and think of England' type and it is less than satisfying after a while. Only the other day I heard a remark on how the street girls were missed since the

Lord Marley busi... Oh! I'm sorry my dear. I shouldn't have mentioned it...'

'It's all right. I know as it's still talked of. Besides, if they're at talking because there's nothing available on the streets, then it shows as there is customers looking. Though, I don't want the Lord Marley type...Anyroad, would you try that for me, ay? I mean. Don't embarrass yourself, but...'

'Oh, don't worry. I'd only have to mention it to one chap I know and the word will get round to the right ears. Let's hope it works. But, I am sorry. Really sorry to have mentioned...'

'I know. And honestly it's all right. It's funny, but it don't bother me so much now. In fact I've hardly thought on it since the executions. The day Blackstaff, Wally and Doug hanged seemed to bring an end to it. And with Doreen serving a long sentence and Lord Marley rotting in his grave, I feel free of it all. I never stop thinking of Sally of course and it all comes back when me hands are paining me, but...'

'I know, my darling, though sometimes it doesn't feel as though justice was done on account of David...I mean, Lord Marley. Him, keeling over like he did seemed to have let him off the hook. And you, my poor darling, left with the legacy of your painful hands...'

Arthur took the hand nearest to him and gently kissed it, letting his lips travel up her arm. It felt good. He was the only person she'd let see her hands and arms and her scarred shoulder. He understood how she felt about the ugliness of the gnarled fingers and the red, raw stretched skin, on her arms.

When his lips reached her shoulder he kissed her scar, then he turned his body and pulled her into his arms. 'Hattie...Hattie...'

His lips; his perfect, firm lips were on hers and she tasted the sweetness of him as his tongue explored her mouth and she sucked gently on it. She had a need in her to talk, to tell him of all her worries. Of her fears for Megan and her longing to know if Sally was being cared for, so it wasn't with an easy will that she lay down beside him. Arthur changed that. It was as if he'd a notion he was fighting for her attention.

His caresses were caring of her and helped her to come to a quiet place. His caring of her always filled her with love for him.

She was ready. Relaxed, and yet, heightened with intense desire. She let her kisses tell him he could come into her. Helping him to do so was something she'd perfected to make it a pleasure for him rather than a struggle and enhancing her own enjoyment of his entering her. Once achieved, he found the strength he needed to thrust her body with such deep pleasurable intensity to bring them both to a release.

Lying in his arms afterwards, she felt safe and would've chosen to lay there forever if she could. But Arthur wasn't for lazing about. After kissing and thanking her he move his arm from around her.

'Well, my dear. I'd better make a move. You know how long it takes me to get ready.'

'I'll be at helping you. I don't want you to be calling Harry in. It spoils it for me. Brings it to an end and puts me back in your world. I want us to be staying in our world.'

'You are funny sometimes, Hattie. All right, you go and run my bath whilst I get myself out of this bed. And, Hattie…You won't go home will you? Not tonight. I'll give Harry an early night and we can have some supper when I get back. What do you think?'

'Aye, I'll stay, love, and be glad to. I've things as I need to talk of. Nothing as you can do anything about. Just me concerns. And I'll cook supper. I've never cooked for you afore, have I? Will Cook be gone, an all?'

'Yes. I'll send them all to their rooms with strict instructions not to come out until further notice!'

'Oh! Poor things. They'll be on with starving afore I've finished with you.' This set them giggling and even more so when Arthur swung out of the bed and made as if to chase her forgetting his crutches and falling straight back on the bed.

Making her way home two days later she felt better and more settled in herself.

They had made love so many times they were both exhausted and when they weren't making love they'd talked through her worries. He'd said the club had been buzzing with the news of her facilities and he'd every confidence she'd see a difference and her business would pick up.

This hadn't stood well with how he'd tried to persuade her to give the business up, or at least, let one of the girls run it. He'd told her he wanted to set her up in a place of her own where he could look after her and visit her freely. He was no longer pressing her to move in with him. He'd accepted that that arrangement didn't suit her.

She'd told him she'd think about it, but if she did accept it wouldn't be for a long time in the future. She'd to be sure of making her money first. She never wanted to be in the position of not having any choices. Not ever again. *'No. If she had anything to do with it she'd be a woman of means as could take care of herself afore she went to Arthur proper, or to any man for that matter..'*

They'd discussed Megan and Sally, too. And he'd said he was sure that Megan was capable of making a sensible decision. He reckoned she had a good head on her shoulders. He was right in that but he had no notion of how being left on the shelf feared lasses like Megan and made them make the wrong choice. And something told her that marrying this Bert Armitage wasn't going to be good for Megan, even though she'd never met him herself.

And as for Sally, he'd said she was best not to interfere, but to let her settle in her new family. He thought that Sally had already forgotten them all and what had happened to her. It wasn't what she'd wanted him to say. She'd been hoping he'd make enquiries as to how Sally was. Her love for the little lass was like a gnawing pain in her breast. But, though she'd thought to go to see her on many occasions, she'd never got further than within a half mile of the shop. Fear had always stopped her. Fear of upsetting Sally. Of perhaps bringing memories back to her. And yes, fear of fully opening up her own wounds. Places within her she didn't want to visit.

The house was quiet when she opened the door.

'Daisy, Phyllis! Where are you?' Lazy bitches! I'm at making things too easy round here. 'Dais…'

'What's all the shouting? Eeh, Hattie lass, you're in a mood. What's up?'

'Up? It's gone twelve and this place looks like it hasn't seen a duster in days! You know as you're all to muck in. I especially rely on you, Daisy, when I take a couple of days away. And yet, I come back to find this mess and you still in your robe. It isn't right. It isn't what we agreed!'

'Sorry, love, we were busy till late. It seems as word has got round that we're here. Last night we had a crowd from that Gentlemen's Club. You know, that one around the corner. I tell you, lass, they were all top drawer. And they all went away pleased. I reckon as some of them'll become regulars.'

'Aye, well, that's good.' She didn't tell her it was down to Arthur's help. 'But yer know how I've been worried of late as to whether I'd done the right thing. It's been a while taking off and one good night don't make a good business! Besides, if we let standards slip we'll not keep good customers. Now, get the windows open, it smells like a brothel!'

There was a silence and then a howl of laughter. Hattie was bemused at first, but then, she saw the funny side of what she'd said and joined in the laughter. As they quietened down and controlled themselves, Hattie slumped into the nearest chair.

'Oh Daisy, love…'

'Is anything wrong, lass?'

'No. Well, nothing as we can have any bearing on.' She stood up again. 'Get Phyllis up and tell her to get the rest of them roused and start cleaning up. Tell her I want every room in the house shining and clean afore I walk round on opening time. You leave them to it and come to me room once you've them organised. I'll make us a brew. I need to talk to you about Megan. I'm right worried over her.'

***

The kettle was whistling on the hot plate when Megan entered Hattie's room with Daisy.

Hattie had her back to them.

'I've someone here with me, Hattie,' Daisy said. 'She was knocking at front door as I came across the passage.'

Hattie turned. Her surprised look turned to a grin and Megan felt the warmth of her welcome.

'Megan! Eeh, it's good to see you. I've been on with worrying over you. And me and Daisy was on with fixing up a mo to chat over me worries and now you're here! It's as if I've conjured you up! What's to do? I thought as you'd be gone back to Breckton by now for Cissy's wedding….Are you all right, love?'

Hattie'd let her out of her hug and stood back looking at her.

'I've lost me job, Hattie. And with it; me choices. Me and Ciss are catching train to Breckton later today. I'm going to marry Bert.'

'Lost your job! Sit down love. Daisy, pour tea out, there's a good un. Tell us what's been happening, Megan.'

Megan didn't take long to tell about Madame Marie having to close the gown shop and how she'd been and asked Bert if he'd still take her on.

'Oh, Megan, are you sure as that's what you want?'

'No. Oh, I don't know. One minute I am and the next I'm not. I've just no other road open to me. Besides, me minds made up and I've to get on with it. Me wedding day's in three weeks…'

'Oh, love. Did you tell Bert as your mind'd been made up for you?'

'Aye, I did. And he was all right about it as I said I had other plans if he'd not have me so he didn't feel as though he was me last hope.'

'Well, if your minds made up, and as you say you haven't got much choice, I hope as it goes well for you, love. But if he ever cuts up rough don't be for taking it. Walk out and come here. We'll sort something out for you.'

'That's a funny thing to say, Hattie. I know I said Bert is surly, but I don't think he'd hit me or anything. He's been through a lot…Anyroad, I'm going to do me best to make him happy.'

'Well, you know best, love. So, wedding'll be in three weeks then, you've not much time to get sorted.'

'It'll not take much organising. Madame gave me a gown she'd had on display, when she heard about it. Mind, that'll take me some time in sorting. It's a gown as a young miss would go to a ball in. But it'll be right when I take all the flounces and bows off it. And it'll be a quiet do, not like Cissy's. Me and Bert have no family, well, Bert has, but...'

She took a moment to tell of Bert's sister and wasn't surprised to hear them speculate as to what had caused her to go off.

'Anyroad, the only close friends as I have round Breckton are Ciss and Jack and Issy, Cissy's mam. Bert has a couple of mates as he works with as he wants to ask. Would you come, Hattie? And you, Daisy?'

As she asked she wondered if Breckton, or Issy or Jack, or even Bert, was ready for the sight of Hattie and Daisy and she nearly giggled at the thought.

'We can't, love. I think you know why. Besides, there's not a chance we can be away for a Saturday. That's a busy night. I'm sorry.'

'But, I never thought as we'd not be at each others wedding day, Hattie!'

'Well, you'll not be at mine and that's for sure, lass, as I'm not destined to have one. Now come on. Be sensible. How would your Bert deal with the likes of me turning up at his wedding, ay?'

Megan rocked with laughter at Hattie's antics as she thrust out her ample bosom and wriggled across the room.

'Aye, and me, an all.' Daisy joined in flashing open her robe to reveal underwear, the like of which, Megan had never seen before. That's if you could call it underwear! Because it didn't cover anything that underwear was meant to cover. There was, well, what she could only think of as, 'peep-holes', everywhere that was meant to be particularly private!

They all collapsed in a heap of giggles and Megan felt more akin to Hattie and Daisy than she'd felt for a long time. Some of the reason for this was that she was now in the same position they had once been in, she too, had lost her choices in life. And with the realisation the guilt she'd shouldered for many a year, especially where Hattie was concerned, lifted from her.

CHAPTER
TWENTY-ONE

The bells clanged in Megan's head. The sound that was meant to be joyous increased her pain with every peal. How was she to get through today?

'Come on, Megan. Turn round so I can fasten you. Oh, Megan, you look beautiful.'

'Go away with you, Ciss. I'm not beautiful!'

'You are, Megan. You look grand. The gold colour of that frock does something for you, lass. And your hair scraped back like that, well, it gives you've an oriental look, even though we can't get all of the frizzy bits tamed.' Issy was holding her shoulders and looking into her eyes as she spoke. 'You know, you have a look of someone as I once knew...And funny thing is he had a name similar to yours, he was called Hadler, Will Hadler, that was it, sounds like Tatler, doesn't it? And another thing, his wife, told me her mam was called Megan. In fact, they put it in their little girl's name. Bridget, her name was. She had four names...'

'Mam! Don't be going on with that. Take no notice of her, Megan. She'll have you on with thinking as she's found your family next!'

'Eeh, I'm sorry. That wasn't right for me to say such a thing. Anyroad, Megan, I think as Bert's going to be surprised when he sees you. You look a picture. He's going to be feeling his need and wishing as it was his wedding day, today.'

'Mam!'

Megan laughed. Though, inside she'd felt a feeling that was like a piece of lead falling into the pit of her stomach. Issy was talking of Bert's sister! She couldn't acknowledge that she knew of her and tell Issy what had become of her. She couldn't break Bert's confidence. She'd promised! But, it didn't sit well in her. She was always open with Issy and Ciss... She pulled herself up quickly before she weakened and covered up her guilty feeling at knowing something these two didn't know of by chastising the pair of them. 'Stop taking her bait, Ciss. And, Issy, you behave!'

'Why? You've got to have a laugh, yer know!'

Issy went over to the window. 'It's a lovely day, lass. June's a nice month to get married in. Me and Tom was married in June. Happy the bride that the sun shines on, ay, love?'

'Aye, Mam, me and Jack are going to be happy, an all. I....'

Megan cut her short. 'Come on, Ciss, let's be at getting you ready, I've a mind to gather your hair up and let the curls tumble down at the back, what d'yer think, ay?'

As they walked down the lane to the church, which stood in the grounds of 'the big house' as Mrs Harvey's house was always called, instead of, Hensal Grange, as it was really called; the local children ran in front strewing petals.

Cissy was a vision in her long cream gown, her face and hair covered with the beautiful lace veil that'd been Issy's.

Every step caused pain to Megan's heart. But she kept a smile on her face and teased Cissy as was traditional.

Issy walked beside her, mopping her tears. Some were for joy, but some Megan knew, were for her Tom too. She must be feeling it today, after all, her life was set for another huge change. She made a mental note to take special care of her once her duties to Cissy were done.

The route they took would pass by Tom's grave. Cissy stopped when she reached it and took a flower from her posy and laid it near to her Da's headstone.

Henry Fairweather stepped forward at that moment and offered her his arm. As Cissy's mam and dad's life long friend, the honour of giving her away had fallen to him. 'Are thee ready, lass? Jack's waiting for you.'

'Aye, I am, Mr Fairweather. Ta.'

When they entered the church and Jack turned round, Megan felt like she'd never catch her breath again. To her, he was beautiful. The sunlight beaming through the stained glass windows lit the whole of his body. It was a picture she wanted to keep in her forever. She let the tears run down her cheeks. It was a release. And she wasn't the only one crying. Even Jack had tears glistening in his eyes as he looked at Ciss. No one would know hers were due to her heart breaking in two.

She fell into step behind Cissy and walked slowly towards Jack. She couldn't take her eyes off him. Without warning he looked at her. The usual smile he was about to give her died on his lip and a look of shock flashed over his face. He looked like he was seeing her for the first time. She hadn't imagined it. The way he turned his attention quickly back to Ciss told her that. Her spirits lifted. It wasn't much, but it was enough. At least he'd noticed she existed and was more than just, good old Megan…

'*What was she thinking!*' Shame washed over her. He was more than likely surprised at the look she'd given him! Oh God! Suddenly she wanted to be anywhere but here. How could she have let her feelings for him show like that? And on his wedding day! On Cissy's wedding day!

The nuptial mass went over her head. Not even when they exchanged their vows did she register what was happening. So deep was the shame in the inside of her. What would he think? What would everyone be thinking? They must have seen how shocked he'd looked.

The bells started again. It was over, then? She'd to face the world without the man she loved by her side. In two weeks she'd stand here again and make her own vow. To love honour and obey a man she didn't love. The thought at this moment was unbearable.

They were on the porch of the church. Everyone talking at once and congratulations and kisses and laughter were all around her.

'By, you look bonny, lass. I reckon as you're the most beautiful bridesmaid as there's ever been. And we're lucky at having her as ours, aren't we, Mrs Fellam?'

He'd said she was beautiful! She couldn't speak.

'Aye, Jack, you're right there. Megan's done us proud. She'd not believe me when I said as she was beautiful. Eeh, Jack…Megan. Mrs Fellam! I can't take it in as that's me name at last! I'm so happy…'

'Aye, lass, you're me own, Mrs Fellam.'

The pain that ripped Megan's heart was short lived as her arm was grasped. She turned to see Bert. His face red with anger. Her shame increased. Had he seen? Had he heard Jack?

He pulled her away from the crowd. 'What's your game? What're you playing at, ay?'

'What? What d'yer mean, Bert? I'm not playing at anything. I'm just doing me bridesmaid's duty and…'

'So, it's your duty to ogle the bridegroom, is it? And to have him tell you as you're beautiful, ay?'

'Well, he's probably the only man as is going to tell me anything like that, because you're not for noticing!'

'I wasn't given a chance, was I? You never even looked round the church to find me. So, now I know how the land lies. Well, thou knows, you can forget being wed to me. You can go on with your other plan and you can get out of me cottage, an all!'

143

Shock held her from going after him. *Oh God! What had she done? How could she have let her feelings show after keeping them locked up inside her for so long!*

'Are you all right, Megan lass? What bee's got into His bonnet? Eeh, he's a funny cuss. Come on. Don't let Ciss and Jack see as you're upset.'

'Oh, Issy. He says as he isn't going to be marrying me and I can get out of the cottage! He thinks…he…'

'Aye, lass. I know what he thinks. And he isn't wrong at that, now is he?'

Megan's head dropped in shame.

'Look, you aren't the first lass as is in love with another's man, yer know. It happens all the time. And, in particular when that man is as handsome as Jack is.'

'You knew?'

'Aye, I knew, lass. But I also know as you're not one to do anything about it and hurt our Cissy. So I had no worries on that score. Me worry was for you and your feelings not being met and making you settle for such as Bert Armitage,'

'He isn't so bad, yer know, Issy. He loves me and I have a feeling for him. There's another side to him that I can love. I don't know what to do. Should I go after him? Will I be missed?'

'If you're on with being sure as you can make a go of it, then go after him. I'll cover for you. They'll be dancing and doing afore we sit down for the meal. Just make sure you're back for that, ay? And, Megan, if it's what you want then do your best. Tell him as you was daydreaming that it was him as was standing at the alter waiting for you and as you got a shock when reality hit. And say the words, say you love him. Because he strikes me as one as hasn't had much love in his life. Go on, lass. And good luck.'

He was where she thought he'd be. In the pub. She couldn't go in after him it wasn't done for a woman to enter the pub on her own so she stood tapping on the window. He turned round as did all the men who had escaped the wedding party to get a quick jug of ale in before the formalities.

Bert went red in the face and she guessed by the laughing men around him that he was taking some leg pulling. She hoped it wouldn't make him angrier.

As he came out of the door he was on the attack. She'd expected that. He'd to save face.

'What d'yer want? I've said me piece.'

'Aye, you have, but I haven't been at saying mine so I came to say it.'

He was put out by her retort, she could see that. He didn't like her chatting back at him, but he'd to get used to it because he wasn't going to have it all his own way.

'Well?'

'Bert Armitage, you've got it all wrong. I walked into that church in a dream. I was on with imagining as it was my day and it was you waiting at the altar for me.'

The words Issy had given her were having an affect. His expression softened.

'I haven't ever been to a wedding afore and I haven't ever dressed up like this neither. Or have folk tell me as I'm beautiful. It all went to me head. I felt like I was somebody. I started thinking of me own day as is to come. My look at Jack was one of shock as I come to me senses and seen as it wasn't you! I felt daft and confused. I...I love you, Bert Armitage and if you were to say as I was beautiful then that would mean everything to me...'

A cheer went up, then calls of 'Go on, Armitage!' and 'By, you've caught a fiery one there, Bert! And 'She loves you...Aahh.'

Bert's expression changed. He looked like he'd explode. His anger bulged his eyes and the sweat stood out on his face. He grabbed her arm so fiercely she cried out. The men quietened down and one by one went back into the pub.

Bert dragged her along the road. Her heels caught on the cobles making her stumble, but he took no heed. When they reached the cottage he opened the door and flung her inside.

'You bitch!'

'But, Bert...I'

His hand shot out. Her face stung. Shock held her breathless.

'I'm sorry...I'm sorry... Megan, Megan me love, forgive me. Oh God! I can't believe as I did that! Megan... I do love you, lass. And you are beautiful. You're the most beautiful thing as has happened in all me rotten life. I'll never be at hurting you again. I don't know what come over me...'

Tears streamed down his face.

The shock of the slap was making her body shake. But, the shame she felt at having brought him to this was crushing her.

'It was my fault, Bert. I've kept you unsure of me. And...and then today...well, saying all that stuff in front of your mates. It's me as is to be sorry, Bert.

145

They held each other close. Bert slowly stopped crying and telling her how sorry he was and a love deeper than she'd felt for him before kindled in her.

His kiss took her to a place her body wanted to be. Yes, Jack was there, and yes, it was him caressing her. But the feeling was so good she responded with all that was in her.

The removing of her frock was all that held them back. Her senses were enough to make sure it wasn't crumpled.

'Megan, Megan lass, you are beautiful. You're, me beautiful lass.'

It was the pain that gave her reality. She stiffened and tried to hold him back.

'No, Megan, no. You're not stopping me now. Stop fighting...lay still.'

'It's hurting. Bert...You're hurting me.'

'I'm not for stopping. ..Oh, Megan...Don't stop me...'

'Slow down...stop...Bert, please stop...'

'Christ! Megan, you're a bitch...A cock tease! Well I'm having none of it. You're having it now and that's the end of it.'

He pushed her back down and forced her legs open. 'Come on...Megan, I'm telling thee...'

'No...No...'

Pain shot through her as he forced his way into her. 'Oh God!'

He stopped pushing and lifted his body. 'It'll be all right now, lass. It's just the first time. You're mine now. I'll not take long. Just be a good lass and let it happen, ay? Next time, you'll be at liking it.' His kiss was soothing. She felt her body relax. It was going to be all right. She had a shame in her that she'd not been wed before she'd allowed it. But it'd be all right.

As Bert moved on her the pain lessened. There was a soreness. But that was how it would be. Hattie'd told her. She was daft not to have remembered and to have fought and made Bert angry. He was all right now, though. He was enjoying it. His moans told her that.

When it was over he lay on the floor next to her. His face red, but his expression the happiest she'd ever seen it.

'That was grand, lass. I reckon as I'm going to like being married to you, Megan.... Ay, look at you. You've to get some work done to cover up what you've been up to, thou knows.'

There was an emptiness inside her. It pushed the shame away and left her feeling as if she was nothing. She hadn't wanted to feel like that. It wasn't how she should feel. 'But,' she thought, 'she only had herself to blame.'

CHAPTER
TWENTY-TWO

Megan could see Cissy from her window. She was hurrying up the lane. She had a lightness to her step as if she would have liked to have broken into a skip.

Megan's cottage was on the road that ran along the top of the lane where the farm cottages were. There were no houses opposite hers as she was on what was termed, the front row. The pub was the only building on the side of the road where the lane emerged. As she was a little way up the road she had full view over the hedge and behind the pub so could see the comings and going in the lane. The lane was a nicer place to live than these endless rows, though she knew she was luckier than those who lived behind her. The outlay gave the feeling that the farm labourers were up above the miners. The farm labourer's cottages were bigger, too. They had a parlour and a scullery as well as a back porch covering the coal house and their own closet. And they were only joined to one other cottage. Whereas the miners cottages were in back to back rows some twenty or so in a row. And to Megan's disgust, had only one closet between two cottages and that backed on to the closet of the row behind.

It was nothing to be sitting out there and have your neighbour from the back row doing his business in the closet that backed on to yours. And worst of all, they always wanted to carry on a conversation whilst they did it! She knew she'd never get used to it and always tried to time her visit to when there would be no one around to join her.

Keeping it clean, she found, was a task only she took on. Mrs Braithwaite, who lived next door, laughed at her for this and only yesterday had said, "Eeh, lass, it'll only get dirty again, thou knows. 'Specially when me man comes home and does his business. You'll never keep it clean. I should give up like the rest of us."

But she knew she wouldn't. As much as it sickened her stomach to scrub and swill it out every day. She'd never give up trying to keep it clean between the times the cart came and it was emptied.

When she opened the door there was a look of joy on Cissy's face. It brightened her out of her thoughts. Though, of late she wasn't at her best in the mornings. Not since she'd taken to emptying her belly into the bucket as soon as her feet touched the floor.

'You look bright, Ciss. Come in love. I needn't ask if everything's all right with you. I can see as it is.'

'Aye it is. I've missed me bleeding! I think as I'm going to have a babby, Megan! Oh, I'm so happy!'

'Ha! You won't be in a week or so, not when you're reaching for the bucket like me every few minutes!'

'You mean? Megan!'

Cissy was round the table and holding her in a hug that felt good. So good she nearly let the tears come. They'd been pressing to for weeks. But she swallowed them back and tried to hook on to some of Cissy's happiness.

'You never said! When...I mean, when did you miss yours?'

'I haven't seen anything since I was wed and...and it was some weeks afore that when I last seen.'

'You'll have tongues wagging if your babby comes early, Megan lass.' Cissy giggled. 'You must have caught first off. By, Jack'll be jealous of Bert. He thinks as he's the best stud in the town getting me took so quick!'

'Ciss! You sound just like your mam. We'll not be at missing her with you around. If you were in the convent as I was brought up in you'd have your mouth washed out with soap!'

They both started giggling then, and somehow Megan didn't feel quite so alone. She and Ciss would go through their pregnancies together.

It wasn't that Bert didn't try. He just had no understanding in him of such things. He'd not ever been around women before. And well, it was his way... His temper! He did try to keep it under. And he was always sorry. Anyroad, it mostly was her fault when he snapped...

'Is something up, Megan?'

'No. I was in me thoughts. We'll be right, won't we, Ciss? We'll get through, ay?'

'What is it, Megan? Is there something you're not telling of? We said as we'd tell each other and we said as we'd see Hattie if we needed help. Does you need... What's that on your arm! Megan, it's a bruise! How did that happen?'

'It's nothing. I...I banged meself. I'm always at banging meself. You know how clumsy I am. I was like a pin cushion at work.'

148

She swallowed hard. The tears were going to come. Damn! She couldn't stop them.

'Eeh, Megan love.'

She sat down on the fireside chair. Cissy sat on the arm and leant over her and held her close. Megan could no longer control her sobs. They racked her body.

'He didn't mean to. It was me. You know how I get his eckles up. I've always done it. I rub him the wrong road. I should learn. You told me of it afore. You remember?'

'Aye, I did. But it doesn't give him leave to hurt you. It isn't right, Megan. He can't have things his own road all the time. You've to have your say, an all.'

'It's not just that. I…I'm not much good at…Well, yer know…'

'It probably isn't your fault, love. He's the man. He should be patient and be on with teaching you. Jack…'

'It's all right. I'll be right. Don't… Don't let's talk on it. It was only the once. Let's put kettle on, ay? We should be at celebrating!'

'Aye. It'll turn out. How about we do go and see Hattie, though? She'll have some tips for us. Because though I'm at being happy, I don't feel as I have it right as yet. I'm still at trying, yer know.'

Megan doubted Cissy was telling the truth, but loved her for what she knew she was trying to do.

'I think a trip to see Hattie is just what we need. And she must be dying to hear all our news.'

'Let's go tomorrow then, ay? Only…Well, Jack doesn't know anything of Hattie. I've not been at telling him of her. That sounds bad, doesn't it?'

'No, I understand. I haven't told Bert of her either. So we're in same boat. Let's just say as we've some shopping to do on account of our conditions. That should satisfy them and stop them being curious. Mind. I can't be going until after eleven. I can't leave me bucket until then.'

They were giggling again and Megan was glad for it. She'd had a fear in her of Cissy and Jack finding out about how Bert was when he lost his temper. The fear was rooted in them thinking to try to help her. That couldn't happen because she knew it would only make things worse. She hoped Ciss would just take it as something that had only happened the once, and besides, Bert had said as he'll never do it again. Oh, she knew he'd said that the first time. But, she believed he meant it this time. He was in such a state after and so loving towards her.

***

149

Doing as Hattie'd said, relaxing and letting it happen and then, gradually taking more of an active part had made Bert much happier when they coupled and over the last few months it had made a difference to his mood and to how he viewed her feelings for him. It'd pleased her, too. It wasn't what she could call, wonderful, but it wasn't without some pleasure for her.

The trouble was it was getting more difficult and uncomfortable to take him. Her pregnancy had swelled her so much, she was like a barrel.

As she dipped doorsteps of bread into the hot fat for his breakfast she could still feel the pain he'd put her through during the night. He'd wanted her to turn her back to him. They'd done it a few times in that position since she'd got bigger and she'd liked it. But with the babby so low it had hurt and she'd suggested she used her hand from now on. Hattie had told her about it and how to do it. Bert had liked it as part of their love-making. He wasn't for it being all he had though and she'd ended in tears after taking a clout as well as the pain of him forcing her to let him enter her.

He didn't speak to her the while she'd been cooking his breakfast. Neither did he speak whilst he ate it. She decided to leave things and got on with putting his snap tin up. She wasn't for saying anything if he didn't.

He was putting on his boots before he said, 'Are thee all right, Megan?'

'Aye. I'm right. We've to talk though, Bert. I'm not for going through what happened last night again. I'm not saying as I'll leave you wanting, but there's other ways.'

'I know. We'll talk on it. But it seems as it isn't right having a wife as you can't use. I can do the other meself if I want to. And you've two months to go as yet.'

'So you use me, then? It's for your pleasure only, is it? Not to show me your love or anything.'

'Don't go twisting me words, Megan. You're good at that. I just can't see me getting by for two months having nothing, and besides, you'll not be ready for a few weeks after babby's born either.'

'Well, you'll just have to go calling on Lillian then, won't you? I'm sure as she'll be willing to let you, USE, her. Because I'm telling you, Bert Armitage! I'm not for it. Not until babby's born.'

'Aye, I might just do that. Like you say, she'll be willing. She's always hanging around me. She showed willing afore you decided you wanted me and it was good, an all. It wasn't given under sufferance either!'

He slammed the door as he went out. Megan sat down. What had she done? If anybody should be accused of using anyone it was her. Hadn't she used Bert because she'd nowhere to go? And he might have been happy with Lillian. It seems they had been at it and he'd liked it. But, what if he went off with Lillian? What then? The cottage was in his name. Could he chuck her out? No, he'd not do that. He'd be an outcast amongst his own. It wasn't done. Oh, having a bit on the side would be accepted. Some would even put him on a pedestal for it. But, would she be able to stand the shame? No. She knew she wouldn't. She'd just have to let him have his way. She would have to bear the pain and pretend it was good. It was the only way.

Waiting for Bert to come home when his shift was done, Megan looked anxiously at the clock. He was late. He was never late. He'd often go out again for a walk or, if it was later, to the pub, but never until after he'd been home and eaten his meal and had a swill.

She'd been thinking about what had happened between them as the morning had gone on and had made her mind up to say she was sorry and to tell him she'd try harder.

But now it was four o'clock and he'd been due back before three! Was he with Lillian? Had he taken what she'd said, as his right to do it? Oh God!

She looked out of the window again. Lillian walked by. She smiled. Was it a satisfied smile? One that said, 'I've got your man?'

Bert came in just after. He looked sheepish.

'Did you do as you said, then?'

'What was that?'

'I saw Lillian go by just now, she looked like she'd been made happy.'

'What yer talking of? I haven't been near her. But, I tell you something, Megan. I will if you keep on.'

'Well, that's up to you, isn't it? So where have you been, then?'

'Oh, I'm not to be trusted now, am I not? Some marriage this is turning out to be. No having what's me right to have. No trusting me. And, I'd like to bet as me dinner isn't on either! By, I took something on when I took up with you, Megan Armitage!'

He came towards her. His anger rising with his every step. 'So, you want to know where I've been, ay?'

'No, Bert. It...it's all right, I was just on with worrying about you.'

'You bloody wasn't! You thought as I was with Lillian Cole, didn't you?'

He pushed her in the chest with each word until she had her back to the table edge.

'Don't, Bert. Don't get all worked up. I'm sorry...I'

'Sorry, is it? Thou knows, if anybody's bloody sorry it's me for taking you on. You bitch!'

His fist dug into her stomach with such force she crumpled to the floor.

'And that's where you bloody belong, an all. You're nothing but a cock-teasing bitch! I'm off. I'm going to see if I can find Lillian and see what she's got for me.'

Megan thought the pain would never stop. It cramped every part of her. She felt a wetness between her legs. Oh God! The babby! No. It's too soon! No...No... She tried to sit up but couldn't move. Waves of pain took all her strength. Panic rose in her. It couldn't happen. Not here on a stone floor and her all on her own. Her babby would die! 'Help...Help me. Oh God! Someone help me..eeee!'

The door opened. 'Oh, Megan lass, what's to do? Is babby coming?'

'I...I think so, Mrs Braithwaite.......Oh! Help me, please help me...'

'Can you get up if I help you? You need to be on your bed, love.'

'No...no don't move me. Oh...Oh... It's coming...IT'S COMING....'

'I'll fetch Gertie. Hang on. I'll not be a mo.'

'Don't leave...'

Despair entered her as the door shut on Mrs Braithwaite. But it didn't last long as an urge she couldn't stop took her and a pain more intense than any she'd suffered made her push down with all her strength. The baby slid from her onto the cold floor.

Gertie Ardbuckle and Mrs Braithwaite came in just at that moment.

'Eeh, Megan, love.' Gertie moved swiftly picking up the baby and grabbing a towel off the fire surround wrapped it around the little form.

'Get water from kettle into that bowl, Bertha. Come on, move yourself. We've to act quickly, yer know.'

Bertha Braithwaite did as she was bid, as she did for all the instructions Gertie called out. Megan daren't ask any questions as they worked. It was as if she was frozen. Suddenly there was a mighty yell from the baby and Gertie said, 'It's a boy, lass. And he's right bonny. You must've been at getting your dates wrong. He's a good size for an early one. I'd say he's on five to six pounds.'

With the relief the cry of her babby gave her, her body started to shake and through chattering teeth she asked, 'Is he all right, Gertie? There's not anything wrong with him, is there?'

'No. He's perfect. He's a might sleepy, but then little ones are.' She cut off there and shouted at Bertha. 'Put him down on the settle, Bertha and run upstairs and get the bedding. We've to get Megan warmed. She's on with the ague. Don't worry, Megan lass. It's a thing as happens. Especially when babby comes quickly like that. We're to get you warm and get something hot into you. You'll be fine.'

Megan didn't think she'd ever be fine again. She couldn't keep a limb still and drinking the hot tea Bertha was offering her was not easy.

Gradually she felt her body steadying.

'Right, that's good lass. Now, we need to get you cleaned up and get you to your bed. You need a good rest.'

Megan found she couldn't speak as they washed her down and helped her into her nightgown, securing a clean rag between her legs. Weariness flooded over her and it took all her effort to get up the stairs. Gertie walked behind her. Her hand steadying her.

Once in her bed Bertha gave her, her son.

As she took him and held him close Gertie said, 'He'll take some raising at first on account that he'll not be able to take much food all at once. He'll be at your breast near on every hour of the day and night. You've your work cut out, lass.'

She just nodded her reply.

It was a strange feeling. A strange, but wonderful feeling! To be holding her child! She couldn't believe it and neither could she take her eyes from him and a love she'd never ever felt for anyone in the whole of her life entered her.

'There! It was worth all the pain I'd say, wouldn't you, lass.'

'Aye, I would Gertie. And thanks. And you, Bertha. I'd not have known what to do without you.'

'Go on with you. Anyroad. I'm to go now. I've to call at the corner shop, which is where I was going when Bertha stopped me. I've nothing for Gary's tea on the go yet. But, before I go, tell us what you're going to call him. Then I can have the full story for anybody as I see on me travels.'

I don't know... I've not thought on. I thought as I'd ages to go. I'll see what Bert thinks.'

'Is he on shift?' Gertie asked.

'No...He...he went for a walk...'

'Don't be on with worrying, love. I told Mr Braithwaite to be going after him as soon as I'd got Gertie to come. He said as he would when he'd finished his dinner! Bloody men!'

Gertie chuckled at this from Bertha, but Megan didn't smile. All she could think of was: Please God, don't let him be found with Lillian. The shame of it would be too much to bear.

'Megan! Megan...' The sound of Cissy calling from downstairs stopped any further thoughts or worries.

The bedroom door burst open, 'Oh, Megan. I've just heard. I was in the village and I saw Mr Braithwaite. Oh, love! Babby's here, then? What is it? Are you all right? Oh, let me see.'

'I'll leave you to it. She's fine, Ciss, and so is the babby. So don't be fussing. Happen she could do with another brew. One as she can enjoy this time. I'll see you later, lass.'

'Aye, and I'll be off, an all. I've to do me pots. I'll look into tomorrow after Mr Braithwaite's off on his shift.'

'Thanks, Gert...thanks. Thanks, Mrs Braithwaite. Thanks for all as you've done. I'll see you both right.'

Bert was in within the hour. She didn't ask him where he'd been. He sat on the end of the bed holding his head in his hands. Ciss had left when he'd come in.

'Don't take on, Bert. I shouldn't have said what I did. Things'll be better for us now babby's born. You'll see.'

'Oh, lass. I never wanted to be one as knocked you about. You've to stop getting at me, thou knows. You make me that mad at times.'

'Aye, I know. I was for saying sorry when you came in last time. But, you coming in late set me off with imagining things and me mouth ran off with me.'

'Well, I knew as you was spirited when I took you on. I haven't been with Lillian, thou knows. I missed cage as come up and got on a later one. First time as that's happened to me. And just now, I went for a walk up Mire Hill. I was on me own. Anyroad. I'd better be at getting me swill and then I can have a look at the babby.'

'Have you a name as you'd like to call him, Bert? '

'Aye. Me sister told me of her Da once. He died young, but was a good bloke. He was foreman at pit. And though folk don't know as I know of him, he's still talked of. And what they say is good. He was called William. Folk called him Will, but I like the short form, Billy. So, how about that, then?'

'Aye, that's grand. Billy it is, with his Christened name as William.'

'I'll bring you a brew up, lass.'

How was it he could be as if nothing had been his fault? He hadn't been sorry or asked how it'd been for her. Their babby could so easily have been born with things wrong with him. He hadn't thought about that and the last thing she'd expected was for him to want the babby called after his sister's father!

He'd a funny side had Bert. Look how he tries to find the grave of his mam's lost child. It was as if he wanted some link with family. Mind, she could understand that. He was like her in that. And, she had discovered, even though he'd not got any photographs of his family he'd kept his sister's letter. It was hidden away just like she kept her locket. She had found it when she was cleaning things out. She hadn't told him, but she'd read it and by the looks of it, Bert had read it more than a few times. It was that crumpled. Like as if each time he'd been of a mind to throw it away and then had changed his mind and straightened it out again.

It had been strange reading about her sister-in-law's life and funny to think she knew nothing about her and her marriage to Bert. She wondered about Bridget, and what she was really like. She didn't sound as bad as Bert had painted her. Her letter read as if she'd been forced to leave him for some reason. Happen it was to do with the beatings Bert had spoken of.

She made up her mind she would write to her. Tell her she and Bert were wed and he was all right. And tell her about Billy and how he got his name. She wouldn't be able to give their address, nor post the letter in Breckton. She'd have to post it in Leeds when she went to see Hattie.

And, another thing, it wasn't going to be long before she went to see Hattie. She was going just as soon as she was allowed up. She needed her help on what she had to do so as not to get her belly up again, because she was never going to bring another babby into this world. She had feared for Billy before he was born and something in her feared for him in the future and she wished she never again had to have that as had made him....At least, not with Bert. But then, that wasn't something she had a choice about.

PART FOUR

THE PARTING

1927-28

CHAPTER
TWENTY - THREE

'By, you're beautiful, me little lass, I couldn't believe me eyes when I turned the corner and you stood there waiting for me.' Jack pulled Cissy to him. His heart swelled inside his chest and his love for her burned its intensity through his body. 'I love you, so much, Ciss.'

'I know you do, Jack, and I love you, an all. I thought as we could walk over the field by the thicket and back through the ginnal. Have some time on our own next to the beck.'

'Will Sarah be all right?'

'Aye, I've left her with Megan. Bert's on late shift so Megan's on with her sewing and Sarah and Billy are playing on the green. Megan's keeping an eye on them from the window.'

'Bert's never found out about her sewing, has he?

'No. And I hope as he don't. Megan's on with making a nice bit of money, yer know. Oh, I hope as she gets enough soon to get out of it.'

'Aye. She's no life with Bert Armitage. There's many a time I'd like to sort him out. But, it's like as is said, interfering will only make things worse for her. Still, at least we're doing something to help with letting her use our parlour and ma's old sewing machine. And she seems to get a good bit of work from Manny. What's she on with now?'

'It's Manny's second grandson's bar mitzvah and she's making the frocks for the womenfolk. It's a big order for her. I've been helping her out though, with hems and stuff. And Manny's good. He lets the women come to the rooms above his shop for fitting and he tells no one. I took the last batch over. Jenny was in the garden and she asked a few questions, but I just said I was taking in some washing and ironing for Manny, as his wife misses me mam doing for her. She took that as a truth. No one else has said anything. There's not a soul as knows, I'm sure.'

'Well, that's good, though I don't like to think that folk think you have to work, but if it helps Megan I'll put up with that, because if anyone does find out and drops the word into Bert's ear, she'd suffer.'

Talking about Megan, he knew, was only delaying things. He was to face what was troubling him. 'Right then, lass. Shall we make a move, ay? It's a lovely evening, but nights are starting to draw in and its on six now.'

'Aye, we best had as I've brought a picnic for us. And I've brought a towel so you can swill yourself under the waterfall.'

'That sounds grand. It's been a hard day, and this heat doesn't help. And besides that, I've things on me mind to talk over with you'

'I know. I mean... I know as something's been at worrying you, love. That's why I thought up this idea.'

He didn't answer her just took the basket from her and held her tiny hand in his.

As they made their way to the beck he hoped with all his heart that there was no one else with the same idea of picnicking. It was a favourite spot for the folk of Breckton. But then, if there were others about he and Ciss could make their way up Mire Hill after he'd freshened himself under the waterfall. There was always somewhere up there to be on your own.

'Jack, whatever it is as is bothering you, you can tell me of it. I might be able to help some.'

He smiled down at her and wished he could tell her all. But she'd be hurt if he did and he couldn't bear that. He'd tell her though, of his main worry and that would relieve his troubled mind some. But on how Mrs Harvey was with him. Well, that would have to be kept from her.

They were settled on a flat grassy area some way up the hill. There'd been one or two out for a walk so they'd had to walk on up a bit to find some privacy. He felt relaxed. They wouldn't be overlooked as they'd had to climb round some rocks and walk through a clump of trees before they had come to this clearing.

Cissy handed him a cheese doorstep, and then surprised him.

'So, come on then, out with it. Are you on with planning to leave me for another....'

'No! I...I mean. Don't be daft. I'd never leave you, Ciss. You're me life...'

'Jack, you scared me. I was at fun making...'

'Aw, me little lass. Come here.' He took her in his arms. The guilt he felt crept over his whole body. Damn, Laura Harvey! Damn her!

'I was on with being shocked at you saying such a thing, that's all.'

She moved in his arms and lifted her head. Her beautiful eyes misted over. His heart wrenched with pain. He'd never hurt her. Never!

Without either of them seeming to move, his lips were on hers. At first the kiss gave him reassurance, but then, deepened and filled him with a longing. Only Cissy could make him feel like this...Only Ciss. But then, how was it Laura...

160

Cissy's soft moan banished all the doubts from his mind. The silky feel of her hair and the hardening of her nipple as he cupped her breast in his hand set up feelings in the heart of him that he couldn't deny. And as he gently eased her down to lay in his arms the feeling in him became an urgent need.

Cissy moved, looked up at him and giggled, 'Here?'

He couldn't answer her but eased himself over and undid his trousers. Tracing his hand up her thigh he felt her legs were bear. She didn't resist as he rolled on to her and pulled her knickers aside. Her cry of joy as he filled her, told him that she wanted him. The writhing of her body to meet him and her calling of his name told him she was reaching her special feeling.

He moved himself forward to help her. Knew the place he needed to thrust would be better reached like that.

His own feeling was akin to agony. He needed to burst into her. . Her legs wrapping him like a vice pulled him ever deeper into her. His agony increased when her body stiffened and he felt the pulsating of her. Her cry filled his ears. 'Jack...Ooh, Jack.'

An intense pleasure as he came into her took over his whole being. He couldn't speak the love that encased him. His body shuddered a moan from the very depth of him.

They lay still a while unable to part, unable to descend the ecstasy. After a moment he gently eased himself out of her.

Cissy curled up into him. Her breath wafted his face. Her sweat mingled with his. He tasted the salt of it on her as he kissed every part of her face. They spoke of their love and how it deepened not lessened as the time went by, but then, Cissy brought them back to reality.

'I haven't me protection in place, Jack.

She didn't seem concerned, but he knew a fear to set up in him.

'But, what if you get caught? Oh God! Why didn't you tell me?'

Memories of the pain they had been through with two lost babbies after Sarah was born cut into him. They had vowed never to put themselves through that again and Cissy had sought Megan's help. He'd no idea how Megan had known about the contraption or where she got it from and he hadn't asked. He'd just been pleased there was a way that they could make love without him having to pull himself from her at the very moment he needed to thrust deeper into her.

'It'll be all right. It's been on three years now since I was caught last. And Megan says as it happened once as Bert took her afore she'd had time to put her protection in, on account of him not knowing as she uses anything. And she didn't get caught. We were on with thinking that after a time it makes you so you can't have babbies.'

'Oh, lass. I hope so. I'd never be at forgiving meself. I can't bear to think of you going through all that again. I thought as I was going to lose you the last time. How soon will it be afore we'll know?'

'Look, Jack. As I see it you've enough on your mind. Just forget that. Besides, you'll be at spoiling the feelings as are still in me. Tell me what's at worrying you instead, ay?'

Ignoring the fear that lay in the pit of his stomach he put his mind to telling her part of his worries.

'It's me job, lass. It's likely as its going to be changing some.'

'Is that all? Why didn't you tell me afore?'

It wasn't all. And he wished to God as it was.

'Well, it wasn't something as I could say much on, I'd heard rumours. But there's been them afore and I didn't want to worry you on rumours. But, Mrs Harvey's had a word with me. She's no choice but to sell the stud horses. She says, it's the recession and the miners being out for so long last year that's brought it about.'

'But what will your job be, then? You will have a job, Jack?'

'Oh, aye.'

He'd have a job all right, but not one that he wanted. In fact, how Laura Harvey had said it would work out; he was worried to the heart of him.

'Mrs Harvey's on with thinking of buying a motorcar and I'm to learn to drive it and take care of it. I'm to be a chauffeur!'

'But that's grand! I can't understand how you're on with worrying. It's like a promotion. Oh, I know as you love the horses, but...A chauffeur!'

'That's not all there is to it though, love. It'll mean me going away a lot. Taking her places as she now takes train to and staying away nights to be on hand when she needs me to be...'

'Oh, no! Oh, Jack! I couldn't bear it. Is there no other job in the offing? There'll still be horses to be seen to. The farm horses and...'

'No, love. It's the only option she has for me. Gary's to take care of the horses as are left, you know, the farm horses and Mrs Harvey's own horse and I think she's keeping another two for when her sister visits.'

Ciss was quiet for a long time and he didn't break the silence. He held her close trying to put out of his mind what might happen if he was days away from her and Laura Harvey got up to her tricks. To his shame, she was getting at him. Oh, God! He held Cissy even tighter.

'No wonder you were on with worrying. Let's think on it some, ay? How long will it be afore it happens?'

'Oh, it'll be a good few months. It'll take a while to sell the stables and then the motorcar has to be made. Them as top drawer have are made to order.'

'Well, we've time to think on. I'll write to mam and arrange a visit to hers. She might know of something going on the estate as she works for. We've not been since the beginning of the summer. It'll be good to see her. It's been hard since she changed her job. We hardly ever see her now and it'll make a nice day out for us.'

'Eeh, me little lass. Nothing gets you down for long. You're always at seeing another road. I feel better already. Come on. We'd best get back as the sooner you write to ma the better.'

He hoped with all that was in him that his ma-in-law would know of something going. There was something in him that was unsettled by Laura Harvey. He didn't know how it could be so. But, Laura Harvey wouldn't let up on him and he wasn't in a position to do anything about it.

CHAPTER
TWENTY-FOUR

April 1928

'Megan! Oh, Megan, love. Come on in. It's good to see you. It's been a good while.'

Hattie's heart lurched. Megan's eyes pitted with pain sank into her hollow face. She thought better of asking how she was, at least, not until they were in her rooms. She had a feeling that broaching the subject would undo Megan. She'd give her time to compose herself. Talk about other things for a while.

'Cissy hasn't come with you this time, then. Is she all right?'

'No. She's having a babby. And I'm worried over her. She's not carrying good again. She's not expected until June, some eight weeks or more, but she's had a couple of shows already.'

'Oh, no! I'm sorry. Please God she'll be all right this time, ay?' The thought crossed her mind as to how it was that the cap had let Ciss down, but her worry for Megan didn't let the thought stay in her.

As soon as she opened the door to her room she took Megan in her arms.

Oh, Megan lass, come here.'

Megan winced in the hugging of her.

'Oh, Hattie, Hattie...'

'It's still going on then, love?'

'Aye. It's got worse as times gone on. There seems no pleasing him. I try, Hattie. I do try...

'I know, love. Don't cry. Come on, sit down by the fire and warm yourself.'

She helped Megan off with her coat. As she did so and the pain showed again in Megan's slow movements, she felt a deep anger against Bert Armitage.

'If I could get me hands on the bastard he'd not hit you again. I could get something done, Hattie, I know folk...'

'No, Hattie, don't...'

'I won't. Though, I don't mind saying as nothing'd give me more pleasure. Oh, Megan, I wish as you'd leave him.'

'I am on with a plan to, Hattie.'

'Really!'

'Aye. It was Cissy's doing. It was back-end of '26. Just after strike finished. Me and Ciss, was on with remembering how it was when we worked at Madame Marie's and I told Ciss as I still did me drawings. When she saw them she said as I should be doing something with them.'

'And you have? Oh, Megan lass, I'm so pleased. I can't believe as it's more than a year since I saw you. I've been on with worrying meself sick. Couldn't you at least write to me, love? Just to let me know how things are with you.'

'I'm sorry, but with Ciss as she is and me sewing and everything, it's not been easy to get away. I thought meself about taking your address down this time so as I could write. It's funny as I've never taken it down afore. I just knew where it was and that was that. Mind, you'll not be able to write back. Unless... I'll tell you what. I'll ask Ciss if I can have letters at hers. Because if Bert found out about you, I'd never get to see you again, Hattie, he'd not like me having a friend, he hates me seeing Cissy and I've never told him of you.'

'I know. But, me mind would be at rest if I heard from you. Now, I'll make us a brew whilst you tell me of what you've been up to, ay?'

At the end of her telling of how Cissy had shown her drawings to Manny and he'd taken them home to his wife. And, as to how she now sewed for Manny's family and friends, Megan said, 'Eeh, Hattie. Its like me dreams come alive again.'

'Good for Ciss. It sounds just the thing. I'm right glad for you, love. So, what're you aiming for?'

'I keep thinking on getting a place. A shop. P'raps with some rooms above as me and Billy could live in.'

'That'd take some money wouldn't it, love?'

'Aye, I know. But, I don't care how long as it takes. I'm not going to give up.'

'What have you got so far?'

'Six pounds. I know it isn't much, but I only have the one lot of customers. I know as I'd have a customer in Mrs Harvey at the big house as she was a regular at Madame Marie's. And though, she didn't know they was mine, or know me, for that matter, she liked me designs. But, with half the daily staff at the house coming from, The Row, it'd be too risky. And, lasses round me can't afford to have clothes made. They get their stuff from jumbles and the tally man.'

'Aahh but, my lasses can afford to have clothes made for them. And, they'd pay good money. They have to get what they want from a catalogue, as they can't get it round here. Stuff comes up from London and it's at a price, an all. You'd have no trouble making what they like.'

'But how? I mean. How could I do it? I couldn't come here. And...'

'Why not? It's perfect! You could have my rooms. I'm not here often now. I've to tell you of it, but as it happens you're lucky to catch me. There's plenty of room for you and Billy. And Bert'd never find you here. You could be at making a good bit of money and have your own place in no time...'

'Oh, Hattie. I'll never be able to thank you for making me the offer. But, I can't. I couldn't be bringing Billy here. He'd not settle and though you say as it's separate, he'd see things.'

'Well, I'll help you find a place nearby then...'

'No Hattie. It's not just Billy. It's Cissy as well, I can't leave her.'

'What about Issy? Won't she come back and look after, Ciss?'

'I'm sure she would and be glad to, but there's not much room at the cottage and Issy has a job. They don't let her have much time off. I've not seen her for on two years. Mostly Ciss goes to visit her. Besides, even if she did I'd still not leave Cissy and... I mean...Well, not until babby's born and she and babby are all right.'

'Were you going to say, Jack? Oh, Megan, love, you got a raw deal in the end. But listen, I know as it'll turn out for you. Though, I wish as you'd think on. You can't go on like this, yer know.'

'I will. You've given me some hope, Hattie. And, aye, I was on with thinking it'd be hard to leave Jack, an all. Though, in the end it'd be for the best and it will come as I have to leave them both. It isn't easy seeing Jack all the while. Anyroad ta, love. But, I've always known I could come to you, it goes without saying.'

'It does, Megan. I wish...'

'Let's leave it there, love, I haven't got much time. I'm to be back afore Billy and Sarah come from there lessons and Bert'll be in on six. So, tell me of your news and where it is as you are, most of your time.'

'Arthur's set me up in a house. Oh, I know I said as'd never go to him on these terms, but its different now. I've me own place here and money enough to take care of meself if anything goes wrong. And, this house as I have is going to be mine, not Arthur's. He'll still own it, but it's to be my home. I'm on with getting it just how I want it. It's not far from Breckton. It's out in the country on the way in to Leeds. In fact you'd see it from the train. It stands in its own grounds. It's grand, Megan. Arthur comes to stay as often as he can. He's happier, as he never liked staying here with me and he knows as I didn't like staying

167

at his. I always felt as though I was his visiting prostitute, well, I know I am in some ways, but in most ways I'm not. And now, I feel I have more of a position in his life.'

'It sounds wonderful, Hattie. I'm so pleased for you.'

'Only thing is as Arthur does some sort of secret work for the foreign office and that takes him away a lot. He says he could be away for months at a time in the future.'

'How does he manage? Its years since I've seen him. Can he get round and that?'

'He's doing grand. He went off to America. He was gone just on six months. They're on with pioneering some work as can remould people's faces. You'd not know him. He looks so much better. They've managed to make his eyes so as red bit don't show and that's at making all the difference to his appearance. And his hair's grown back so that covers where his ear was. Not that it ever bothered me how he looked. But it's given Arthur all his confidence back. I don't know anything of what he does at the foreign office, as I said, its secret work, but it must be important or he'd not leave me so often. It was hard for us both when he was in America.'

'I'm glad for him. I never saw him much but I liked him. So, what happens here when you're away?'

'Daisy takes care of things. Though, she's had enough. And Phyllis has, too. I'm thinking on taking them to me house to take care of it for me so it's not shut down and empty when I'm not there. They...Well, I don't know if you can understand this or not, Megan, but they've become a couple.'

'A couple! How? I mean, well, that don't sound right... A couple, like...'

'I know. But it goes on. There are men as only likes other men and women as...'

'No! It...It sounds...'

'Look. Don't take on. It's a fact and there's nothing as can be done about it. You just have to keep quiet about it. It's up to you whether you accept it or not. It's asking a lot I know, but they're still the same lasses as they've always been. In fact, better. They're right happy now. And I'm not going to be looking at them any differently. They're family to me no matter what.'

Hattie could see as Megan was struggling to understand. She may go through hell in her marriage, but in many ways she has led a very sheltered life. Hearing about Daisy and Phyllis was bound to be a shock to her.

'I have to be going now, Hattie. Will…will you give Daisy me love. Tell her I'll happen see her next time, ay?'

'All right. Now don't let it go bothering you. And think on about me offer. And, love, there'll be plenty of room at me house for you as well. In fact whilst I'm think on it, there's some outbuildings, I could…'

'Oh, Hattie. Thank you. Look, I'll come and see you again after Cissy's babby's born and she's coping. It'll most likely be around July time. I'll see how the land lies then, I'll write to you in the meantime.'

After hugging and kissing each other, Megan hurried out. Hattie stood on the doorstep to watch her go. She looked like she was hurrying as much as she could. She was most likely afraid she would bump into Daisy. She couldn't blame her. It wasn't an easy thing to come to terms with.

The concern she had for Megan, felt better for knowing that she was on with a plan and she hoped there would be a way that she could work for the lasses. The way they spent money on clothes, it would take Megan no time to get her dream.

Megan waved as she reached the corner and then disappeared out of sight. Poor Megan, she'd to take a lot on board from the differences in the way their lives had turned out. She knew of things other lasses of her own standing knew nothing of and each new thing was always a shock to her.

Once back in her room Hattie warmed herself for a few minutes in front of the fire. She had to get back to doing the accounts that she had been doing when Megan had arrived.

It had been Arthur who had advised her to keep books on all the money that came in and went out so that she knew what was needed to keep the place going and what she could take as her own, especially for when she wasn't here as much.

Hattie had hardly given her attention back to the task when she was startled to hear someone knock on her door. She sighed. *The lasses knew what she was on with and had been told not to disturb her!*

Daisy opened the door and put her head round. 'Was that Megan going up the road?'

'Aye, it was. Look, Daisy love, I'm busy. And Megan'd no time to wait for you returning.'

'Oh, I'm sorry as I missed her and I know as you're busy, but I have something as can't wait.'

'It'd better be important, lass. I've to get these books sorted.'

'It is. Mavis has heard as Doreen's died in prison and…'

'Doreen! Well, that isn't anything as'll make me sorry. In fact, I'm glad to hear of it as that means we're not faced with her release coming up. What happened? And how does Mavis know of it?'

'It seems as it was a bit back. Mavis's mam has a mate whose just been released from the same prison and she told of it. She said Doreen just took ill and that was that. But there's something else as well...'

'Are you sure it can't wait, Daisy love?'

'Aye, I think as you're going to want to know this and'll skin me if I keep it from you a moment longer. Mavis reckons as she saw Sally...'

'Sally! Good god! Where?'

'She...she was on the old patch...'

'The patch! But...Well, how did Mavis know her? And what was Sally doing there? And come to think on it. What was Mavis doing there?'

'She has to go that way to visit her mam and she said as she was just crossing over by Ma Parkin's when she saw this lass sort of peeping round the corner. Like as if she didn't want to be seen and....'

'Get Mavis in here. Let her tell me of it all. Oh God! Sally, Sally!'

Her anguish was such that as soon as Mavis entered the room, she blurted out, 'Tell me of this young-un as you saw. How do you know as it was my Sally? I mean...'

Mavis's eyebrows arched in surprise. 'Well, when I first saw her I thought I was at imagining it to be Sally because her mam, Susan, was in me mind. You know, with me mam just on with telling me as Doreen was dead. It'd brought all what happened, back into me.'

'Did you know Susan, then?'

'Yes. She lived on the next estate to ours and when her young-un went missing I saw her trawling the streets and folk pointed her out and she often had Sally with her. She had a go at me mam, an all, on account as she'd heard as I was making a living on the streets.'

'So, knowing what you knew of Susan and Sally, you're for thinking this lass might have been Sally, even though it was some nine years or so ago, now?'

'Aye, she has the look of her mam. She ran off when she saw me looking at her, but I followed and called out her name. She stopped when she heard it and turned and looked at me. Then, she ran off again.'

'What do you think she was doing?'

'Well, at first I thought as she was after learning the game, but I'm not so sure. She seemed as though she didn't want anyone to see her.'

A worry set up in Hattie. If it was Sally, what was she doing? Was she starting on the game? Or was she looking for... *God! She might have been looking for me! Oh, poor Sally...'*

170

'What are you thinking on, Hattie? Are you all right?'

'No, this news has upset me. I...Well, I came to love that little lass, and I've missed her every day since it happened. She mustn't be allowed to be on the game. I won't let it happen. Did she look cared for?'

'No. She looked like a street urchin. I'd say as she was living rough somewhere.'

'Why didn't you bring her in? Oh God! I can't bear it...'

'To tell truth, I didn't know how things were between you and her. That's why I told Daisy first. I mean, we all knew what happened, but with how it turned out, well it isn't spoken much of...'

'It's not your fault, Mavis. I should've been on with finding Sally this good while, but I was always counselled to leave well alone. I'll get me coat. Come on. Take me to where you saw her... I just hope as we find her afore it's too late.'

They'd been searching for over an hour, when Dolly Makin, or Dolly, the bag lady, as she is known, came round the corner.

'Eeh, Dolly, you always come as if from nowhere, how are you, love?'

'I'm at being right at the moment, Hattie. I've got meself a companion. I lost me Posy yer know and I've been at being lonely ever since.'

Hattie had to smile. Posy, was the name of Dolly's cat, but the way she spoke you would think as a man had took her down! Dolly was what was termed as: a penny short of the full shilling, in the way her mind worked. She had been part of street life for as long as Hattie could remember. Her many nooks and crannies she called her homes were in places such as, derelict buildings or railway bridges. Each one was decked out with an oil stove and an armchair.

Dolly would call at Hattie's a couple of times in the winter for a hot meal, but she would never stay the night. She preferred her own cubby holes and her bottle of meth's. She dressed in a confusion of colours and a variety of garments all worn at the same time. And the smell of her was enough to knock you off your pins at times. For all that, she was loved and many folk took care of her in the best way they could without her knowing it.

'So you've got yourself another cat, then?'

'No. It's a young-un. She was on streets so I took her in.'

'A...a young-un?' *Sally...Oh God! Sally with Dolly!* 'Dolly, you can't look after a young-un. Where is she?'

'I didn't say as it was a girl!'

'It's just that I'm looking for a girl, Dolly. Her name's Sally. I've got to find her to take care of her.'

'She's mine! She don't want to be found. I'm taking care of her right enough.'

'How will you feed her, Dolly? And keep her warm? It's only April and it gets cold and wet at night, you're used to it. Please let me see her. Let me see as she's all right, ay?'

'I'm not giving her to you to turn her into the likes of your lasses, so go away!'

This shocked Hattie. For all that she was it seemed Dolly had morals. Not that they stopped her from visiting when she was hungry.

'I'd have thought as you'd have rather have another cat. After all, they can fend for themselves. Get their own food and then, curl up on your lap for stroking. Not a grown lass as'll take some feeding and'll be on the want all the time.'

'Aye well, I haven't got another cat, have I?'

'I'll get you one, Dolly. I'll trade you for the lass, ay?'

'When?'

'Tomorrow. But, only if you let me see the lass tonight and, if she'll come with me, you'll let me take her.'

'Aye, all right. I can trust you, Hattie, for all what you are.'

Hattie wasn't sure how to take this. She never thought to be looked down on by the likes of Dolly.

They followed Dolly for what seemed an age. She would be going along one way and then would suddenly turn and retrace her steps. Hattie tried to keep her patience but in the end felt she would have to say something.

'Dolly! Stop playing your games. We all know where your homes are. You've took most of us in them when times were hard and given us a brew. It's getting late and its cold, an all. Just take us to Sally, there's a good lass.'

Dolly let out a bad tempered groan and then turned down into the next ginnal that led to some tumbled down sheds. As soon as they were within a few yards of them Hattie called out, 'Sally, Sally...Its Hattie, love. Do you remember me? Hattie; as used to take care of you...'

An animal like scream filled the air. Sally, hardly recognisable, Sally, crawled out of one of the sheds. Her scream held pain and tears as she lunged forward, 'I hate you...I hate you...' Her fists flailed Hattie's body.

'Sally, love, no. no...I...'

Daisy moved forward and grabbed Sally. 'Hey, stop that, lass. Come on now. Hattie's come to help you.'

172

Sally collapsed in a heap. Her wretched sobs shaking her tiny body. Hattie knelt down beside her.

'Sally. It wasn't my doing, love. I'll tell you of it. Oh aye, I was one as thought up the plan. But, it didn't go as it should've.'

'How...how could you do that to...to me? I thought...I thought as you loved me...'

'I do, Sally. And I've never stopped loving you. I was let down. How much of it are you on with remembering?'

'Everything...Me Aunt Elsie would never let me forget...She told me how dirty I was every day of me life...And...and how what you did to me made me dirty...And...and how as me actions killed me mam...'

Her sobs tore at Hattie. 'How did you get here, love, did you run away?'

'No. He kicked me out. Me, so called uncle. Me Aunt Elsie died. She had a sickness and I nursed her. She spat at me everyday and told me vile things about you and me mam and when she died me uncle showed me the door. Said he was keeping me no longer and I'd to make me own way. He put in me head to come to you. He...he said as I was as rotten as you are...And you are...I know that from what you did to me...'

Sally's hands clawed out at Hattie's face.

'Please don't, Sally.' Hattie caught hold of her hands. 'Give me a chance to put it all right, love. Let me take care of you...'

'I want me mam. I want me mam. MA..A..AM!'

'Oh, Sally, Sally, I'm so sorry. Please come with me, love. Please, just give me a chance.'

Sally rolled herself into a ball. A small defeated ball.

Hattie put her hands gently each side of Sally's head and lifted her face till they were looking at each other. Her own tears streamed down her face. Her heart felt as if it was breaking. To see Sally in such a state! She prayed like she'd never prayed before, *'Oh God! Forgive me and be at helping me. Please help me.'*

'Oh, Hattie. Make it all right. Make it as it was...'

'I will, Sally, me little love. I'll do everything I can. And I mean it when I say as I love you. I've been where you are, Sally, and I know that someone loving you is the best thing anyone can give you and you have my love. You have my heart for your taking. Come home with me. Please, please come home with me...'

CHAPTER
TWENTY-FIVE

Laura Harvey sat back and stretched out her limbs. She had a smile on her face that spoke of how she felt.

'And, what is making you so pleased with yourself. Did you enjoy your ride?'

'Umm, very much, thank you, Daphy, it's a lovely morning, but it's what transpired before my ride that is pleasing me so much.'

'Oh? What have you been up to? Darling, you haven't...?'

'No, but I'm making progress.'

'I wish you wouldn't, Laura. He's your groom, for heaven sake!'

'I'm not going to marry him, you goose! I just want some fun. And it just happens to be Jack Fellam I want to have that fun with.'

'But, have you thought how unfair your actions are on him and on his wife? Didn't you tell me a while back that she is pregnant?'

'Yes, she is and he is missing out, I'd say, as she hasn't long to go. What's unfair about it? I'll make sure he enjoys it as much as me!'

'Laura! You're incorrigible!'

Daphne's mock indignation set them both laughing.

Laura stood up and walked over to the window. There was an impatience in her to bring all this to a conclusion. She'd played around at first, amused at Jack's embarrassment. Enjoying the little gains she made. But now, she was serious. Really serious.

She held her stomach as a trickle of desire clenched her muscles at the thought of the chances she'd have when he became her chauffeur. The prospect almost made up for the loss of the stud farm.

As if she'd read her thoughts, Daphne said, 'How are things progressing with the sale? Charles tells me there is a serious buyer in the offing.'

'Yes...but I can't say I am happy about it. It happens to be my rival, Smythe. It took a long time to build up to take his place as the best stud farm in this county. Bloody miners! If they had just gone back to work when the rest of the country did I might not have had to sell! They want too bloody much these days. Why can't they be satisfied with their lot?'

'I know, dear. They nearly brought the country to its knees. But, it isn't just commodities and manufacturing that is suffering, you know. Charles is very upset about having to even consider selling shares in his bank. He feels he is letting his Father and Grandfather down. They wouldn't allow anyone to muscle in on the family business, but the general strike has changed things and he may have no choice.'

'I'm sorry. I can be selfish in what I say sometimes. It's just that things were going so well. Anyway, darling, I have to go back to the stables. I...' She floundered, desperately trying to think of a plausible excuse. The feeling inside her hadn't gone away. She wanted to try once more. He was weakening. She might be lucky. They could ride out together. 'I forgot to tell Fellam that Diamond stumbled. He may have hurt himself. I'd just like to make sure that he is all right.'

'But, I thought you said you were going to get changed and we would go shopping...'

'Yes, I haven't changed my mind, darling. I just wouldn't be able to relax and enjoy myself unless I sort out diamond first. I won't be long. That is, unless we have to call the vet in. I'll send a message back to you if I'm going to be delayed.'

***

Jack felt his stomach turn over. He looked at Gertie Ardbuckle unable to take in what she'd come to tell him. Cissy, in labour! My God! The babby coming early! Cissy had at least three weeks to go by their reckoning and she had been all right when he'd left her this morning.

'You say as Megan's with her, Gert? Are you sure Ciss is all right?'

'Yes, she's doing well, by all accounts. Megan just asked me to let you know. She said as Ciss'd said as she hoped you could get home for a while sometime today. I reckon as she's a few hours to go yet, so don't be on with worrying just now.'

'Thanks, Gertie. I'll go up to the house and see how the land lies and see if I can get an hour off. Tell, Cissy, I'll try me best.'

As Gertie left, Jack turned happily back to the task of grooming Diamond.

'Well, what d'yer think to that, lad, ay? Me Ciss is having the babby today. By, that's good news is that. She'd not have been able to go on much longer.' He patted diamonds rump. 'There you go. Her ladyship must've ridden you hard this morning; you've a right sweat on.'

The happiness inside of him at the news clouded out the guilt he'd been feeling. Nothing'd happened. He'd let his guard slip, but he'd given Laura Harvey short shrift in the end. He'd get through. It was nearly over. Cissy would soon be back to normal and she'd be feeling more like helping him get his release before long. He couldn't wait. It'd been a long time since Ciss'd even felt like getting close let alone anything else.

'Aahh, there you are, Fellam...'

Jack stopped his wiping of the saddle and turned in surprise to see that Laura Harvey was back in the stable so soon.

'I forgot to say that Diamond had stumbled whilst we were out. Is he all right? Did you notice a limp or anything?'

'No, Ma-am. He seemed in fine fettle. Though, glad of his rest.'

Laura Harvey had moved closer to him. He felt the familiar twinge in his inside. It came alongside the guilt that burned him up. He turned his attention back to the saddle.

'I'm not surprised. We really had a good time and set a good pace. Diamond was anxious to please me.'

He looked down at her. She was so close. His mouth dried. She smiled up at him.

'Is Prince ready? I thought I would accompany you on the exercising of the horses today. Lady Crompton is planning a shopping trip and I'd like to delay it for a while. I feel very restless...'

The way she said this last further got at him. He needed to do something to change things. But then, something in him didn't want to...

There was a look in her eyes; a longing. She was different. She wasn't playing games. She... Oh God! What was he thinking? Ciss...Ciss, I'm sorry, lass.'

'You seem very distracted, Fellam. Is there something troubling you?'

A relief entered him. She'd given him a way out.

'Aye, me lass is having her pains. It seems as babby is likely to come today, Ma-am, and I was wondering on whether I could...'

'Oh, I see.'

The expression on her face changed. She wasn't going to agree to him going! She turned from him. There was anger in her movement.

'Very well, Fellam, bring Prince out. I will exercise him. And then, get Ardbuckle to see to the exercising of the other horses.'

By the time he brought Prince out her mood had changed.

'I'm glad for you, Fellam. It must be a relief to think it is soon to be over. Especially after what has happened in the past. Of course you can go. And I do hope it all goes well for you.'

177

'Thank you, Ma-am.' The happiness in him at her decision seemed to relay itself to Prince. The horse became frisky and shook and nodded his head, then pulled on the rein in an eager manner. They both laughed at his antics.

'Hold him steady, Jack. I'll never mount him whilst he's like that.'

He was shocked at the use of his first name and how it sounded in the posh tones of her voice.

'I'll tether him to the post a while and give you a lift up, Ma-am. By, the fella's lively. Steady boy.' He took a sugar lump from his pocket and fed it to Prince. 'There you go, me lad. Quieten down now and you'll get your rein.'

With the horse tethered and Laura Harvey ready to mount, he bent down and cupped his hands. His confidence in handling the nearness of her boosted him.

But then, she slipped and he was forced to catch her. She was in his arms, the velvet of her jacket brushed against his cheek. It was like no other cloth he'd ever felt and it affected him in ways he didn't want to be affected. He swallowed hard. Her feet touched the ground. But she wasn't for moving away from him and he wasn't for letting her go. After a moment she turned, released herself, but stayed close. Her eyes, her beautiful violet eyes, were looking deeply into his. He couldn't breathe. Of all the tricks she'd played he'd never been put in the position of holding her before. The feeling it gave him blocked out any guilt. He couldn't move his eyes from hers. He looked at her parted lips. If only he dared to kiss them...

'So, the coat of armour you wear does have holes in it then, Jack?'

She was mocking him. She'd known the effect she'd had on him and it was enough for her. Her bloody games were undoing him. Turning him from his Cissy! God! He hated her.

'There's isn't any holes in anything I wear, Ma-am. I'll fetch the mounting stool.'

It was a relief to get away from the nearness of her. He felt sick in his stomach. Why was he so weak? How could he have let her have even a part of him? Because he had given something of himself to her when he'd held her.

When he returned she was already mounted.

'Call at the kitchen on your way, Fellam, and give a message to Hamilton. Tell him to tell Lady Crompton I am delayed. I will see her in about an hour. I'll expect you to be back in the stables for bedding the horses down later.'

Jack watched her ride away. Heard her soft laughter. Saw the pace she set once through the gates. He allowed the anger in him to have its way as he threw the stool against the stable wall. He'd finish a few chores before he sought Gary out. He needed to calm himself and get himself ready for... For being good enough to stand in the same room as his Cissy.

***

Laura Harvey rode to the southern most part of her estate, a secluded haven surrounded by old trees, a place where no one, other than the family was allowed to go. A place where she could indulge in the only activity that gave her body sexual release.

As she unsaddled Prince she thought over what had happened. The look on Jack's face came back to her. His humiliation and shame had reddened his face and his expression had changed to one of contempt and dislike. Why had she mocked him? 'You're a bloody fool!' she told herself out loud. She should have realised that he hadn't the sophistication to cope with the subtlety of her double meanings.

But then, she remembered the feelings and the sensations she had experienced when he'd held her and a pulse of desire throbbed inside her with the memory.

Prince pulled on his rein and shook his head. Laura laughed at the pleasure the horse was showing at being free and knew a yearning to feel that freedom herself. Her desire intensified with each restricting riding-garment she removed. She looked around. There was no need to, the place was very private. But, she wanted to take everything off and ride Prince with just her loose silk, French-cut knickers on, so needed to be sure.

The sun caressed her naked skin and enhanced her desire dispelling any niggling voices inside telling her this was wrong.

She led Prince over to the tree stump she used to help her to mount and pushing herself off from it, seated herself, straddling her legs across his bareback. Slowly she trotted him round the clearing. The heat penetrated her as the friction gradually stirred her senses. Her thoughts drifted to Jack. In her imagination it was him caressing her deeply.

Pressing her knees hard into the horse she urged him to go faster. Her hair came lose and the cascading locks stroked her shoulders and licked the dark tips of her breasts. Sensation built on sensation. Soft moans escaped her lips. Beads of sweat trickled down her face and neck and found the deep valley of her cleavage.

'Yes... Yes!' Her breathless plea urged her body to accept the almost painful crescendo of feelings that burned her loins and gripped her whole body in a spasm of thrills she could hardly endure.

179

She desperately hurled in the reins and brought Prince to a halt. Holding herself still and taut, she allowed the thrills to pulsate through her. The agonised cry that came from her, held Jack's name.

As the feeling subsided, her body slumped forward and shame washed over her. Damn this loneliness! And damn this longing she couldn't deny! A tear ran down her cheek.

She closed her eyes, then let out a deep sigh and brushed away the tears. What was the point? Thank God Daphy was here. She'd go home now. She'd tell Daphy what had happened at the stable between her and Jack. Make a joke of it. She needed some light-hearted banter, something to lift her. Then, they would go shopping and everything would be all right again.

CHAPTER
TWENTY-SIX

When he reached home Gertie was coming down the steps of his cottage.

'Oh, Jack. I'm right glad to see you. Things are not going well. I'm to fetch the doctor. Megan said as you've enough to pay for him.'

Shock held him from speaking.

'Go on up, lad. You'll be a comfort for her.'

He took the stairs two at a time.

'Megan, what's to do, lass? What's happening?'

'I don't know, She's been at pushing some good while, but there's nothing to show for it and just now a lot of blood came from her. Oh, Jack...'

'Ciss, Ciss lass...Ciss...'

There was no response.

'I'm sorry, lass, I'm sorry. Oh, Ciss, what have I done?'

'Don't take on so, Jack. Doctor'll not be long. He knows she's labouring. He passed this way earlier and Gertie told him. Things were going as they should've been then, but he said he'd be on with being ready to come and assist if we needed him and we weren't to hesitate to call him.'

Cissy stirred. Her body bent in pain. Her face reddened with the effort to push but the weakness took her and she slumped back.

'I'm here, me little lass. Everything'll be right. I'm sorry, lass...'

'It's not... Not your fault...I...love...'

Cissy's eyes closed. Her hand went limp in his.

'Oh God! No...No, Ciss...'

The door opened. 'All right, Jack. Let me get to her. Anything else happened, Megan?'

'She just had another pain. She tried to push but...'

'Aye, I can see. She's haemorrhaged. It'll have weakened her.'

Jack had moved to the other side of the bed. He felt despair enter his heart. Cissy had lost the colour from her face. Her eyes were sinking into her sockets and her lips were blue. He heard the clinking of the doctor's bag and saw the shiny instrument he held, but couldn't register what was happening.

***

Megan's every nerve felt tense to the point of snapping. The babby wrapped in her arms slept as if nothing was going on. It hadn't taken her long to get her cleaned. She'd had everything ready for the task. Throughout she'd kept her attention and her heart with what was going on across the room. Her whole being, willed Cissy to respond.

'I'm trying to release the afterbirth...'

Doctor Cragshaw didn't seem to be speaking to her or to Jack and neither of them answered him. She looked towards Jack, her heart jolted painfully in her chest. The ever-present guilt she felt at her feelings for him increased with the jolt, causing her to bow her head and close her mind to him.

'I'll have to get it away or I'll not be able to stop her bleeding.'

The doctor's anxious words bounced off her closed mind. After a few minutes he stopped massaging Cissy's stomach, and took hold of her wrist. The wait seemed eternal. A deep pit of fear knotted her insides. When he looked up his face told her before he spoke that her fear was going to be a truth.

'I'm sorry...'

There was a pause when it seemed as if nothing in the whole world moved nor made a sound. Doctor Cragshaw broke the silence, said something, but the feeling deep inside her welled up and drowned his words. A hollow moan filled her. Had she made the noise or had it come from Jack?

She forced herself to look over at him. Watched his face stretch and twist in a contortion of agony. His body slumped and he sank to his knees and buried his head into Cissy's still breast.

His pain entered Megan and she knew it to increase her own. The doctor spoke again, 'Megan... Megan, come on now, lass.'

Her mouth opened and closed, but nothing came out. She could only shake her head.

'I know, lass, I know. Have you seen to babby? Good. Put her in the cot for a moment while I clean myself up, and then, I'll take her downstairs so I can have a look at her.' He turned towards the dresser where the bucket of hot water stood. There was still some left in it. He plunged his hands, then, looked back at her as if a thought had struck him. 'Do you feel up to fetching Father O'Malley? If we get him here quickly he can give Cissy a blessing and baptise babby.'

She nodded, she knew his urgency, it was said the body didn't give up its soul for some hours and its anointing would send that soul straight to heaven. She wanted that for Ciss.

The brightness of the outside world shocked her. What time was it? She hadn't counted the hours. The light in Cissy's bedroom was such as she'd had to light the mantels, but then, the small window in that room never gave much light.

She looked over at the gathering of women in the lane. They were all there. The women from the row and those from the tied cottages. Gertie would have put the word round that things weren't going right.

The group moved towards her as she went down the steps. 'Will one of you go for Father O'Malley? Tell him to come as quick as he can.'

'Oh no! Is it Cissy or babby?'

'It's Cissy, Jenny. She's...'

'Don't stand there asking questions, lass.' Gertie stepped forward and took hold of Jenny's arm. 'Get yourself away, you're youngest and'll be quickest. Go on now.' She turned to Megan. 'Is there no hope, lass?'

'She...She's gone...'

Their gasp cut through her.

'Gone? Eeh no! No! Oh, dear God, why? Poor Jack. Is babby all right, Megan?'

'I don't know, Gertie, she seems all right, but...'

'Come on, lass, I'll come in with you. You'll need a hand.'

It was quiet in the cottage, quiet and unreal. Even the babby, lying on the kitchen table being examined, was quiet. Neither Megan nor Gertie spoke, though questions of all kinds were popping in and out of Megan's head. It was a relief when the doctor finally stood up straight and put his stethoscope back in his pocket.

'Is she all right, Doctor?'

He didn't answer but stood with his forefinger and thumb each side of his mouth pulling at his lips. After a moment he shook his head.

'Not totally I'm afraid, Megan. She's not in any danger though, but things are not right with her.'

She knew that already, inside her she'd known. It was in the babby's face. It'd seemed sort of flat. And her eyes, the shape of them had reminded her of the pictures of the Chinese boys and girls in Billy's school book. He'd brought it home once, it was all about other countries and the people who lived there.

'What's to do? Is she badly, Doctor?' Gertie asked.

'No. Not ill as such. Anyway, we'll not worry ourselves over it now. We'll talk about it later. Let's take her up to Jack, shall we?'

They followed him up the stairs and stood just inside the door. The gentle pressure of Gertie's hand on her arm steadied her, but didn't stop the strange feeling that flooded her body. It was as if she'd gone out of herself. None of the things that was happening seemed anything to do with her.

'You've another little girl, Jack,' Doctor Cragshaw said.

Gertie went over to Jack and patted his shoulder. 'Jack lad, I'm sorry. Poor Ciss. What can I say?'

Jack looked up at Gertie, his face wet with tears. He made no sound only nodded his head.

Megan closed her eyes. It was all too much to bear. A knock at the door made her jump. Father O'Malley entered the room. The strange feeling that had taken her deepened.

She couldn't have said what happened in detail after that. The anointing, the baptism, it all seemed to go on without her, though she knew she'd acted as godmother. Her mind seemed to leave her body doing things, and travelled its own road back in time. Pictures of Cissy as a young-un of just thirteen came to her. Her sweet and infectious giggle drifted into the space around her.

Cissy couldn't be gone...She couldn't...Ciss...Oh Ciss... Tears streamed down Megan's face. They wet her neck and her breast, and yet, she wasn't crying. Not crying the kind of tears that would help. Instead her body was emptying itself, leaving her stranded and alone. More alone than she had ever felt in her life.

The terrible sound of Jack's sobs penetrated her thoughts. The rituals were over. She looked over to him. He was standing, but it seemed his large frame had shrunk with the weight of his grief. Gertie and Doctor Cragshaw were supporting him.

The ache of love her soul held for him almost moved her body, but she stayed still. Knew her soul would betray her if she went to him. Knew, too a moment of intense guilt. She looked over at Cissy. Cissy's beauty and goodness was locked in her waxen and still face. She silently begged her beloved friend for her forgiveness.

'Megan' Doctor Cragshaw held her gently by the shoulder and spoke to her in whispered tones. 'Take babby downstairs Father 'O'Malley will help me to bring the cot down. She'll be better in the kitchen.'

After the Priest had left, promising to call in on the undertakers and to make sure Jenny knew to keep Billy and Sarah away until Megan could see to them later, she gave time to the worries she held in her. Her fingers found the corner of her pinny and she twisted it in her hands. 'Doctor, what's to do about babby? She'll need feeding and...and caring for...' She willed him to understand. As Cissy's best friend it would be

184

natural for her to take the babby and care for it, but she couldn't. Bert wouldn't stand for it.

'Don't worry yourself on that score, I know what's in your heart and I know it isn't possible for you to do what you'd like to.' He snapped his case shut. 'If she's fretful in the next hour or so give her some boiled water with a little sugar in it. I'll call in on Franny Bradshaw and arrange for a supply of breast milk for the first few weeks.'

The relief that entered her was taken away with his next words. 'You've seen how things look for the babby, haven't you?'

'You mean her eyes and that?' Suddenly it dawned on her, the slanting eyes the flat features. 'Oh, no! Oh, poor little soul! She's...she's a Mongol!'

'Aye, I'm almost certain she is. The signs are all there.' He heaved a huge sigh. 'Anyway, like I said, Franny'll help, though I don't think she will take the babby in. Wet nurses can be funny over putting these children to their breasts. That wouldn't be Franny's feelings, but she'd have to consider the feelings of the other mothers she is nursing for, especially those of the gentry.'

'But, what'll become of her, Doctor?'

'I don't know, like I said, we'll cross that bridge later, I know of a couple of places that take them, but...'

The door between the kitchen and the stairs opened, and Jack and Gertie came through. Jack held himself together, though the effort of doing so was showing in the strain on his face. Gertie would've had a hand in helping him. She was kindly was Gertie and always seemed to know what was the best thing to do. She was already busying herself filling a bowl with hot water from the pan on the stove.

Jack put his hand out to shake the doctor's. The doctor took hold of it and held it in both of his. 'I'm going to miss her, Jack, she was a lovely lass everyone loved her. I wish I could've done more. I'm sorry, man.'

'You did all you could, I know that, Doctor.'

'I did, Jack, I did. But, it's heart breaking for me when I fail. I've had to learn a hard lesson over the years. I can't change God's will.' He took out a large hanky and blew his nose loudly. 'Well, I've to finish my rounds, not that I feel like it, but it has to be done. I'll call up at the house and let them know what's happened. I'll tell them not to expect you back to work for a few days, they'll understand, and Father O'Malley said he'll...'

Megan left them talking and went upstairs to help Gertie, she didn't want to find herself alone with Jack.

185

Gertie had started to wash Cissy's body. The sight nearly undid her. 'Oh Ciss...Ciss...'

'Come on, love, get yourself busy. Let's make her look right bonny, ay, lass? Get her best outfit out. Go on now.'

When they'd finished Cissy did look bonny, dressed in the pale blue, Sunday best dress Megan had made for her just last year. It wouldn't fasten up at the back, but it was as Gertie said, "They'd not notice that in heaven."

Jack sat at the table in the kitchen. He hadn't stirred from the same position that Megan'd seen him in each time she'd come down the stairs to refill the bowl. The task of laying Cissy out was done and she'd to face talking to him.

'We're all done, Jack. Shall I put the kettle on and make a pot of tea?'

He didn't move or acknowledge that she'd spoken to him.

'He could do with something stronger than tea. I'll not be a minute, Megan. Put kettle on and make a pot and I'll fetch a drop o' whisky to go with it.'

'Right, Gertie.' Her voice sounded normal, but she didn't feel normal. She bustled around the kitchen. Everything she did felt like the first time ever. Jack's desperation filled her every pore. The task of laying the un-responding body out, had given her the truth that Cissy had gone, but there was the now to deal with, and she couldn't. She could find no words to say. No comforting gestures to make.

The bubbling of the boiling kettle broke the silence. The act of making the tea helped her to gain some control and she felt able to speak at last.

'I'll be fetching Sarah after a while, Jack, do you want me to bring her here or take her home with me until after doctor's been back?'

'Oh God, Megan, how will I tell Sarah? How am I going to make her understand? She worshiped her mam.'

'I don't know. I don't know how you'll cope with everything. I... I'm sorry, Jack. I just can't think on not having Ciss. She was everything to us, wasn't she?'

'Aw, lass.' His arms enclosed her. His tears dampened her hair. 'How could such a thing happen? Our Ciss, oh God!'

Her heart drummed a feeling round her body that threatened to engulf her. Her throat constricted. Her tears fell on his shirt as her sobs joined his and their bodies closely entwined shook with anguish.

Suddenly she felt a new strength enter her. She had to be strong for him. She must keep her despair locked away. She had enough practise to call on to help her. She could cope. She would concentrate on his needs.

'Sit yourself down, Jack. I'll help you all I can. I'll fetch Sarah from Jenny's and give her some tea and I'll bring her over when I've Bert off on his nightshift. I'll be with you when you tell her.'

'Oh, Megan, it's good to know as I have you by me.'

Jack sat down and wiped his face with his hanky.

Gertie came in at that moment. 'I'm back, Megan. Have you brewed, lass? Oh good. Pour tea out and I'll get some tumblers down for whisky. We'll all feel better after a nip.'

Jack drank his whisky down in one go, but put his hand up in refusal to a refill. 'I'll just have me brew now, thanks, Gertie.'

After a couple of sips he picked up his baccy tin from the table next to him. His hands shook as he rolled a cigarette and lit it. After a taking a few deep intakes of smoke he threw the nub end into the back of the grate and went over to the cot and peered down at the tiny form.

The babby stirred. One little hand broke free from the shawl and stretched out to him, her tiny eyes looked towards him. Jack took her hand and rubbed his thumb along her fingers, his other hand brushed the tuft of dark hair from her forehead.

Megan looked over at Gertie. Gertie nodded and smiled. She must have been worrying, too. Things were bad, but they would have been twice as bad if he'd have taken against babby.

CHAPTER
TWENTY-SEVEN

The smell of freshly lit tobacco tinged Megan's nostrils. Apprehension knotted her stomach. Bert sat at the table. He rose as she entered. The sound of his chair scraping on the stone floor grated her frayed nerves. 'Where've you bloody been till now? It's nigh on half-past four and no bloody tea ready. I'm on shift while six, woman.'

'Aye, I know, tea'll not take me long. I left stew on side simmering. I've only to pull damper out to have it boiling. You'll not be late.'

As Megan walked passed Bert she held herself ready. The expected blow didn't happen. Her relief, she knew, would be short lived. From one of the shelves of the cupboard next to the grate she took down a clean pinny. The thought of the other one in her bag, red with Cissy's blood, caused her to pause a moment to compose herself.

'You've been seeing to Cissy haven't you? Huh? And don't bother lying about it. I got up earlier to use lav and Mrs Braithwaite said as Ciss was labouring.'

'I had to, Bert. There was no one else as could. I...'

'No one else! No one else! I've bloody told you afore what folks say haven't I? You can't drop any of your own, but you can see to others. You're a laughing stock, and you're at making me one, an all.'

'I'm not. And that's not what's said. That's all in your head! Lasses round here are grateful for me helping them. And, as for me not having me belly up like rest of them every year, they know as I was damaged when I had our Billy. Aye, and they know whose fault that was, an all! Don't, Bert, I... I didn't mean...'

Bert yanked her round by her hair. He'd pounced so quickly she'd no time to stave off the blow. The back of his hand stung the side of her face. Her body reeled backwards. The edge of the table jarred into her. Her breath caught in her lungs.

'You're no proper wife, d'yer hear me? Going all over seeing to others whilst your own man has no dinner or snap ready. How did I ever saddle meself with you?'

He grabbed the bib of her pinny and pulled her roughly towards him. She looked into his eyes. The darkness of them seemed to be pulling her into the darkness of his soul.

'Womenfolk might let you think as what you tell them is right, Megan. But does thee know what they bloody well tell their men? Does thee know what talk at pit is? That you turn your back on me and as I have to beat it out of you and they're not wrong, are they?'

He raised his fist again, but she was ready for him. She placed her hands on his chest and pushed forward with all her might, he staggered back.

'Cissy died!'

The statement hung in the air between them. He stared at her. His mouth slack his head shaking in disbelief.

'What? What did you say?'

'Cissy's dead! She lost too much blood. Babby was wrong ways up, she couldn't shift it, and I couldn't help her. Doctor cut babby free! He cut Cissy with a pair o' scissors! He said as how something or other had ruptured.'

The words tumbled from her. Now they were released, her throat constricted and her body shook. She could no longer control the sobs that racked her. She had a feeling on her that she couldn't have cared if he pummelled her to death with his bare fists, but he didn't attempt to hit her again.

'Eeh, lass, I'm sorry. I didn't know as you'd been through that. I thought as you was on with defying me again.'

'It's all right. Sit down and I'll get your dinner.'

She wiped her face on her pinny and looked over at Bert. She'd a wish in her that it was her that had gone. It was getting harder and harder to take his sudden changes of mood and now with no Cissy...No, she'd not think on. She'd to get on with doing for Bert. She didn't want him to get angry again.

Her actions were automatic. She put the kettle on the grate-plate and pulled the damper out. The fire jumped into life. The stew started to bubble. There was a nice fresh loaf in the pantry. She had made up the dough the night before and had left it to prove in the bottom oven. She'd cooked it off before Bert had come in from his shift this morning. She got it out, took it from the muslin cloth that kept it fresh and cut thick doorsteps and spread them with mucky fat. When his snap tin was full she piled a plate high with the rest and passed him a bowl of stew. He hadn't spoken the while she'd carried out these tasks, but after a couple of mouthfuls of stew he surprised her by saying, 'Come on, sit yourself down, lass, and get some of this stew into you, you looks done in.'

She did as he bid her. She didn't feel like eating, but it was better to pretend than to protest. They ate in silence for a while and the knot of fear in her stomach began to release its hold on her.

'She was all right was Cissy, thou knows, Megan. You're going to miss her.'

'Aye.'

She could say no more. She didn't want to break again. She stood up, 'I've to go over to Jenny's to fetch our Billy and young Sarah. She's taken care of them since after school. You won't say anything to Sarah, will you, Bert? Because she doesn't know as yet.'

'No, I'll not say anything poor little lass, ay? Eeh, its sad news, sad news. Don't be long. I'd like some time with you afore I go on shift.'

As she walked she pondered on how he'd taken it. It was like living with two different people. The one she hated and the other who touched something in her.

'Megan...'

Helen Bray. A woman who lived three doors down was calling her over.

'I'm sorry to the heart of me to hear of Cissy's passing, Megan. I don't know what to say. Shocked everybody it has. Anyroad, love, I'll not keep you talking, just to say as Jenny said to tell you she's taken young-uns round to her mam's. She said as her cottage being next door to Jack's she'd not be able to stop Sarah from going round.'

'Thanks, Helen. I hope you don't mind if I get on. I've to be back quick.'

Helen just nodded at her. It was a knowing nod and ground humiliation into her.

She hadn't far to go. Jenny's mam's cottage was just two rows away from her own and only cobbled paths separated the rows. She glanced down the lane opposite as she walked passed. Her eyes rested on Cissy's cottage. It didn't look any different. Somehow she'd expected it to.

As she rounded the corner Sarah broke free from Jenny and flung herself at her. 'Oh, Aunty Megan, me mam isn't dead, is she?'

Large blue eyes looked up at her and the stains of recently shed tears washed away as fresh ones streamed down the little face. Megan pressed Sarah against her waist and looked over at Jenny.

'Young Graham Pike told her, he said as how he'd heard Gertie tell Manny at corner shop.' Jenny shrugged, closed her eyes, and bit on her top lip. Her head shook from side to side. 'Eeh, Megan.'

Billy's proud claim broke into their pain. 'I hit him, Mam, knocked him off his feet I did. And I told him as his tongue'd split with lies as he tells. It'll not be right, Sarah, me Mam'll tell you.'

Megan didn't answer the appeal in the upturned faces, nor did she go for Billy, as she would normally have done when he boasted of fighting. Instead she bent down and lifted Sarah up. 'Come on, love, I'll take you to your dad.'

Sarah clung to her neck, her sobs so wretched they tore at Megan's heart. She was right to take her home. Right now she needed her dad. Needed to be told from him that her mam had gone. The decision wasn't without its worry.

'Billy, be a good lad and run and tell your dad as I have to take Sarah straight home. Tell him she's upset, he'll know what's happened. Tell him I'll not be more than a few minutes.'

Billy went to protest, but there was something about the way everyone was acting that stopped him. Was it right, then? He wondered. Was Aunty Cissy really dead? His mam hadn't said different. He thought about what being dead meant. His mind gave him a picture of Graham Pike's pet rabbit. He'd made that dead. A smile came on his face at the memory. He walked a few paces in front of Megan, but put no particular hurry into his steps.

He hated Pikey and he'd especially hated him that day because he'd been round to Sarah's and got her to play and they'd left him out of the game. He'd made Pikey pay though. He stole his pet rabbit from its hutch and bashed its head against the wall. By, he could still hear the crunch it'd made. He'd wanted to tell Sarah about it. Usually he shared everything with Sarah, but she'd have gone mad. He didn't understand girls sometimes. Ha! Pikey's face when he'd found out his rabbit was dead! He chuckled to himself at the memory.

CHAPTER
TWENTY-EIGHT

Megan stood on the steps of Cissy's cottage and glanced up the lane. There was a thread of worry mixed in with her sorrow. It was nearly five thirty. She should've gone home. But, how could she have left Jack and Sarah whilst the undertakers had put Cissy in her coffin? She hoped with all that was in her that Bert would understand.

All was uncannily quiet. The womenfolk had gathered at the top end of the lane ready to follow Cissy. They made no sound.

Into the silence came the sound of wood sliding along wood, bringing her attention back to the cart and the long thin wooden box. She held herself together as the undertaker coaxed the horses and the cart drew away taking Cissy to lie in the church.

It had surprised her when Jack had made that decision, but like he'd said, it was better for Sarah, and Cissy loved the church. She wouldn't be alone. She and the womenfolk would take turns to keep watch over her when Jack couldn't be there.

The sound of the horse's hooves on the cobbles, and the steel rim of the wheels rolling over the stones, echoed round her. A cry from one of the women broke the spell that held her. It brought into focus the sounds of the lane: the birds singing, the trees rustling and a gate swinging in the wind. Normal sounds of a normal day. But, it wasn't a normal day. Would she ever have a normal day again?

Without warning Bert's crude threatening voice cut through the air.

'You bloody can't wait to fit into her shoes, can you? After I told you to come home afore I was to leave, an all! Get yourself home I'll deal with you in the morning.'

Megan's breath caught deep in her lungs. She held her burning face cupped in her hands, '*Oh God...Oh God....*'

'Leave it, Armitage.' There was a tone of desolation in Jack's voice.

Bert didn't respond. His glare burned through Megan before he turned and walked away in the direction of the Mine.

Nobody moved until he'd rounded the corner. Once he was out of sight the women's pitying gaze came on her. Her humiliation increased. She wanted to hide away, to disappear and for none of it to have happened. She dropped her head into her hands and ran towards the gate.

Jenny broke away from the group of women following Ciss and caught hold of her. 'Come on, Megan. Don't worry, he'll be forgotten about it by morning. You've had a long day, lass.'

She slumped into Jenny's arms.

'Aye, come on, lass.' A bigger pair of arms took hold of her and she looked up into Gertie's kind face. 'Run on ahead, Jenny, and get tea brewed. I'll bring her along.'

As Jenny did as she was bid Gertie turned and called back to Jack. 'She'll be right. Me and Jenny'll take care of her.'

Megan looked back at Jack. What would he think? Please, God, don't let him have taken in what Bert'd said. She couldn't bear him suspecting her feelings for him. It would be a betrayal of Cissy.

It was around five when Megan woke. She didn't want to open her eyes and let in the day. The memory of Bert's attack came to her and shame filled her body. But then, what did it all matter compared to losing Cissy? 'Oh Ciss, Ciss.'

If only she could go to Hattie, Hattie would help her. The tears welled up and filled her eyes. She wiped them away with the back of her hand. *'Come on, lass, don't start! Get up out of it and keep yourself busy. Don't give in.'*

Flinging the grey woollen blanket back, Megan swung her legs out of the bed. Her feet welcomed the feel of the cool boards. The thought came to her that she must finish the rag rug she was making before winter as the boards weren't so welcoming then. She shook her head. It was as if her mind wasn't right, thinking of rag rugs when she had so much on her plate, and Bert home in just under an hour! She would be better served making sure everything was just right so as not to cause him to lose his temper, because if he did, he'd harp back on what had gone on and that would make him worse.

She would try to say she was sorry, but it would depend on his mood as to whether he accepted her apology. She should've thought on and fetched Gertie to stay with Jack and Sarah. Bert had asked her to come home and be with him before he went off on his shift. Cissy's death had been a shock to him, too. He would most likely think she had put Jack's needs before his... Oh, God! This thought increased her fear. Bert had a thing in him where Jack was concerned, always had, had.

After doing all the chores she'd to do for Bert coming in, dressing herself didn't take long. Even on a warm morning such as this washing in cold water was not something to dawdle over. She wouldn't let Bert wash in cold water though, that would be a starting point for him.

It didn't take long to rekindle the fire, she had banked it up before she had gone to bed. The hob was still hot. On the back of it was the large iron pot she kept topped up with water so that Bert always had enough for his wash. She manoeuvred it further towards the middle. That would ensure it was piping hot. Hot enough so that she could add some cold to it. Bert would have plenty for swilling himself, then.

As soon as it started bubbling she moved it to the back of the hob and swung the grate-plate with the full kettle on it over the heart of the fire, and then, reached down a heavy, iron frying pan, melted some fat in it and fried off some sliced potatoes. She'd just put them on the side to keep hot when the door flung open.

'Huh! I s'pose as you thought to soften me up by feeding me as soon as I come in, ay? Well, you bloody well thought wrong! I've had all night to think on how you took no notice of me telling you to keep away from that bigheaded sod! Aye, I know he's lost Cissy and I feel sorry for him, much as I hate him. But, you chose to do what other's could've done for him rather than come home to me. Me needs are nothing to you, Megan. Nothing! Well, I'm gonna change that once and for all. When I'm done with you, you'll not go against me wishes again. I can tell you.'

Terror gripped her heart. Bert unbuckled his belt and pulled its length from around his waist. 'No, Bert! No! Not that... Please, Bert. I couldn't take it. I couldn't.'

Fear weakened her legs and swayed her body. She groped behind her for the table edge. Finding it, she steadied herself.

'Don't do it. Please, Bert, please don't.' She edged round the table trying to put something between them.

Her pleas didn't stop Bert's snake like advance towards her. His body curved round the corner of the table. His belt a snakes tongue snapping in the palm of his hand. The sound gave her the despair of acceptance and stilled her. Stale smoke, coal dust and the sweat of a nights labour gave her senses his nearness and retched the bile to her throat. She swallowed hard. 'I'll not go against you again, I promise. I...I've thought on and know as me action was wrong. I just wasn't thinking straight when I did it.'

The belt whipped passed her face and cracked on the table.

'Aye, you're right, Megan, You'll not go against me...' His voice lowered till it was no more that a whisper. He wet his lips with his tongue. 'Come here.' He dropped his belt and took hold of her pulling her against his body. She could feel the hardness of him.

The disgust of her knowledge of how his need was heightened by the beating of her never lessened in her. But, this time, he hadn't beaten her. Was the thought of doing so enough to rouse him? The hunger of his groping of her body gave her a relief that it was.

The relief was short lived. A new fear set a panic in her. She hadn't her protection in place!

'Bert, I... I've everything ready for your wash, and I've fried off some tatties. Have them first, love.' She kept her voice soft and let her breath fan his ear. 'Then, after I get Billy off to his lessons I'll come up to you, ay? It'll be good...'

He pulled his head back from her. His eyes smouldered with renewed anger. 'Does you want belt first? Is that what you want, eh? Does you have to push me as far as I'll go, ay?'

'No...No, I thought, well, Billy might come down and...'

Bert pushed himself forward. Her body was held as if in a vice between him and the table edge, 'Well, it'll be more of a lesson for the lad than he'll get down that bloody church hall then, won't it?'

She didn't answer.

Bert gave a small laugh and then sunk his mouth onto her neck. She felt the wetness and then a deep bruising sucking. At the same time he fumbled with his trouser buttons.

'No! No!' She pushed with all her might, then lifted her legs and kicked him away.

'You bitch! You bloody, cock teasing, bitch!'

The back of his hand stung her face and sent her body reeling backwards. She landed on the table, her legs bent over the edge. Bert forced them open pinning her down with his body. He pulled the elasticated leg of her knickers aside. The damp hardness of him brushed the top of her leg. She could do nothing.

The harshness of the shove that pushed him deep into her, rasped her back against the wooden tabletop. Her moan of pain joined his one of pleasure.

'That's right, lass, thou knows you likes it. Well, you've got it now, so just relax. Come on, Megan lass.'

Her thighs stung. The course material of his work trousers chaffed them as he thrust in and out of her. The pain in her back increased with every thrust, as did her anguish.

'Stop, please stop, you're hurting me. No! Bert, don't...'

Black droplets of his sweat spattered her frock. His thick moans mingled with her cries of pain.

'Good girl. I knows as you likes it rough.'

She sank into despair. Her tears salted her tongue and trickled like beads of ice into her ears. A blackness that promised peace loomed in the distance. She wanted to go into its depth. But, her own wretched cry penetrated the blackness and drew her back. 'Oh God! Oh God, help me!'

The cry triggered the end. His body became rigid. His face contorted with agonised pleasure. A sound like an injured animal came from him and a hot wetness entered her. Her mind screamed, *'Please please don't let me be caught!'* His body slumped. The weight of him was unbearable.

There was a silence. Her body released his weight. 'You enjoyed that didn't you, love? You like to put up a fight, don't you? It seems to make it better for you. Well, I'm pleased, an all. Come here.' He pulled her up and took her into his arms and held her close. There was a comfort for her in his warm body, though no peace in her mind.

His hand stroked her hair. 'Megan, we could go along together all right, couldn't we? You only have to think on some. You can have it rough when you like, but there's no need to rile me so as I do something as I regret, is there?'

She couldn't answer him.

He pulled away from her. 'Don't think, though, Megan, as that's changed anything. It was good, I'll give you that. But, I still want you to think on and put me needs first, not everybody else's.'

'I will, Bert. I told you I'd been on with thinking about me actions afore you came in.'

He held her close again. 'Eeh, Megan. You were moaning with pleasure all the while I was doing you. I liked that, love.' He tapped her on the bottom. 'Get yourself cleaned up, lass. I still might have you come up to me when lad's away.' He winked, picked up his baccy tin and went out of the door.

Megan eased herself across the kitchen holding on to a chair to steady her. She was near to the sink when the room spun and her body fell forward onto it. The edge dug into her ribs. Red streaks ran down the white surface and disappeared down the plughole. She tried to control the nausea that waved over her. She grabbed the bucket of cold water that stood on the side of the sink and tilted it so that it splashed over her head. It went some way to clearing her senses. Her only thought now was to get him away to his bed so that she could see to herself. Maybe she'd be in time.

His water was all ready for him by the time he came back in. The smug expression hadn't left his face. She managed a smile that told a lie to the hate she felt.

197

He didn't speak whilst he went about the business of washing, and only grunted something about the tatties being good while he eat them. She poured him a second mug of tea.

'Will you take it up with you?'

'Aye, I will, I was going to have another smoke, but I feel right done in. I'll get forty winks whilst you get Billy off, but come up after, ay?' Again he gave her a wink and his face took on the same smug expression. 'I've some more in me for you, Megan.'

His smile told her he'd forgiven her. She wanted to cry out that she'd done nothing that needed forgiveness, and that he should go on his bended knee to her, but she just smiled back at him.

After he'd gone up she stood a moment and listened for the sounds of him settling. When all was quiet she dragged a chair to the stairs door and wedged it under the handle. Billy would be stirring soon. If he tried the door he'd know she'd be at washing herself. He'd wait till she finished.

She lowered the bucket on to the floor. Peeled her coal black knickers off, and stood astride the bucket and douched herself the while praying she was in time to wash out his seed before it planted itself firmly in her.

This done, she went to the bottom cupboard of the dresser fumbled amongst the clean cotton towels and found her cap. Once it was in place she saw to her other wounds and prepared herself to get Billy up for his lessons.

***

Billy couldn't look at his mam. He didn't want to see how hurt she was. It was a game he played. If he pretended he knew nothing then, there was nothing to know. But, he did know and he felt confused. The sound of his dad having a go at his mam had woken him earlier and he'd crept down the stairs and opened the door just enough to peep through. It'd been a surprise to see his dad going at his mam like the dogs in the lane did at the bitches. It'd scared him some as his mam hadn't liked it and was calling out to his dad begging him to stop. He'd gone back to bed to try to pretend it wasn't happening.

Him and Tommy Braithwaite had watched a couple of dogs once. Tommy had told him babbies were made like that and when he was older he'd be doing it to some lass. The tale had made him feel funny and had made his willy go hard like it did when he played with it or he needed to pee bad. Not that he was worried over his mam having a babby. He'd heard his dad say she couldn't drop any young-uns.

At times he wasn't sure whether he minded his mam getting a good belting from his dad. It did make him feel a kind of hurt inside, but it was mixed up with his anger. Because his dad said it was his mam's fault that he got so mad and his mam always said she was sorry, which meant his dad must be right. And, another thing, if his dad was mad and he was around then he got a belting and that was his mam's fault, too!

'Right, son. Have you got your snap tin, then?'

'Aye. Will I call in and get, Sarah, Mam?'

'Well, it won't do any harm. Though, she might not be up to going. Look after her if she does go with you, Billy. She's very sad at losing her mam.'

Billy pulled on his boots and grabbed his snap tin. He'd to get out before his mam talked some more about his Aunty Cissy dying.

'Ta-rah, Mam. Eeh...gerroff...'

His mam had tried to kiss him, but he still felt cross at her for making his dad mad. He'd to get out as fast as he could.

Once outside he felt sorry and decided to go back and give her a kiss. But, as he turned to go back in his mam was just going through the door that led to the stairs. He'd not bother to call out to her.

CHAPTER
TWENTY-NINE

'Shift up, Megan, you're taking all the step up.'

'Me! I like that! There's not much room for me as it is.' Megan dug a finger into Issy's large frame, but she squashed herself up some more. She didn't mind. Issy's soft body was comforting. Having her close made up some for the loss of Ciss.

'You're cheery the day, Megan. Did Bert pop his clogs in the night?'

Megan laughed out loud.

'No. Though, I don't mind saying as I've wished many a time as he would. And then, at other times, I wouldn't wish him any harm. But, I'm feeling glad because me bleeding started this morning and I've been at worrying.'

'I s'pose how you're fixed you'd have that worry every month.'

'No. If I'm ready for him it's all right, because I have ways of preventing anything happening. Mind, Bert don't know of it. If he did he'd go mad so don't say anything in his company.'

'Huh! Can you see me discussing having babbies with Him! In fact, I'd not talk to him about anything I could think on. Eeh, Megan lass, you took on something there. I always knew as he was a bad un, but he seemed that struck on having you I thought he'd change when he got you.'

'Me, too. But, I should've known. The signs were all there. Anyroad, I've to get on with it. Is Bella all right?'

'Aye, she's sleeping. It was a lovely thought of Jack's, to remember Ciss'd wanted to use me name for the babby. I remember telling her once a long time a go that me mam used to call me Bella and as Issy was just something as started when I got older. There's only Priests and folk such as that as have ever called me Isabella.'

'It's a lovely name.'

'I wonder how things will turn out with little Bella. In the future, I mean. Doctor was on with saying as Mongol children don't live long lives. Oh, Megan. We've a lot to face.'

'Is there no cure?'

'No. Doctor says as not a lot is known of the condition. He says they're called Mongols because their features resemble folk as live in Mongolia, wherever that is. He says she's physically all right as far as he can tell, but he could give no knowledge on her future.'

'Well, I can. She'll be very happy. They are, yer know. And she'll be very much loved and cared for. And, she has an adoring sister and Dad, not to mention Granny and Aunty Megan. It'll be all right. We'll take it a step at a time, ay?'

'Aye. One day at a time. It's the only way to get through. I can't believe it's on three weeks since the funeral. It was a good turn out, wasn't it, Megan?'

She nodded. They sat in silence for a while but then, Megan saw Issy wipe away a tear.

'Are you all right, Issy?'

'No, lass, I'm going to be a long time getting right I'm afraid.'

'I know, love.'

'I was thinking what a hard time I had having babbies. I lost me first at birth, a little lad. And then, there was a couple of misses. I was on with being in my thirty second year when Cissy was born. Funny, how Ciss suffered in that way, an all. Yer know, lass, maybe if Ciss had known how to stop getting caught she'd be here today.'

'Aye.'

They fell silent again. Megan didn't want to tell her that Ciss had known. She'd wondered herself how it was that Ciss had got caught. She'd had a chance to ask her a couple of times, but she'd never done so. It was always painful to her to talk of such things with Ciss.

The sound of a motorcar coming up the lane from the direction of the big house broke into their silence. It was the one that had been sent to bring Issy from her home the day after Ciss had died. It belonged to Mrs Harvey's sister.

'Well, would you credit it? Me chauffeur's come to pick me up again.'

They both laughed at this and it lifted them. But, Megan's laugh was cut short by the look Mrs Harvey gave her as the car passed by. It was a look that made her feel uncomfortable. Like as if she'd no business sitting on the cottage step or even existing for that matter.

'You know, I still can't get over them getting chauffeur to bring Jack to get me. Gentry act in funny ways at times. She must think something of Jack, though, as he said as she'd told the doctor that she couldn't afford to lose him so it was important to get me over to look after young-uns. I wonder what the real reason was. I've never found it in me to trust lady high and mighty. I mean, it isn't as if Jack's invaluable with stables going. And, he don't know first thing about motors.'

'Well, happen as it was a case of her knowing him and she'd not know who she might get if she put out for somebody else. Besides, she owes him a chance. He's worked for her for a good many years now.'

'Aye, happen. Any road, I'm not complaining. I was struggling, yer know, lass. I'd no job and me reputation was gone. Them as I worked for put some stealing down to me. I haven't ever stolen anything me life! Anyroad, I was trying to manage on parish relief, but they give that grudgingly. Last means test as I took they found out as I had a son-in-law in work and told me I'd to put meself in his care.'

'Oh, Issy. If Ciss and Jack'd known that...'

'I know. I was on with being stubborn. I didn't want to be a burden. Mind, if I'd have known what was going to happen I'd have come like a shot.'

'You couldn't have done anything, Issy love.'

'I could've looked after her. Ciss said nothing in her letters about not carrying well. Though I did wonder why she kept putting off trip to see me that she'd been so keen to arrange. I didn't push it because I knew I'd not be able to help with putting a word in for Jack to get a job on the estate as they'd wanted me to. Anyroad. Let's talk of something else. Are you still on with your sewing, Megan? Ciss said in her letters as you use the parlour and you've a nice few customers. Only you've never said anything.'

'I didn't like to, not with how things are, but aye, I've garments waiting to be started on. Manny at shop asked me some two weeks back to see about making frocks for his wife and her friends for a wedding as is coming up.'

'Well, what're you waiting for? Nothing need change along them lines. Whatever Ciss arranged with you still stands and'll always stand.'

'Ta, Issy, I don't know as I could carry on without me dream.'

'What dream's that then, lass?'

'Didn't Ciss say why I was doing it all?'

Megan told about her dream for the future. Somehow, speaking of it made it seem silly and impossibly out of her reach.

'Crickey! That sounds a right good idea, love, and I'd back anything as'd get you away from that Bert Armitage, even though it'd be a scandal to some. But, your own shop! That'd take some money. Can you earn that much?'

'No, it's not possible, it'd take at least a hundred pounds I reckon and I've been at it for near on eighteen months and I've only got nine pounds sixteen shillings and sixpence so far. '

'That's not much, lass, is it? I mean, you've done well, but you're not going to get far at that rate.'

'I know, but Manny's wife and her friends are me only customers, and they only want frocks now and again, for do's and such like.' She paused, wondering whether she should tell of Hattie. Then felt cross at herself for feeling embarrassed to talk of Hattie, so ploughed on.

'Mind, I have had another offer, but I'm not sure how I could do it.'

'Why's that, love?'

'It's for Hattie, a friend of mine as I grew up with. Well, she's more of a sister really.'

Megan took some time telling Issy about Hattie. She wanted to put it all as best she could. Wanted to justify what Hattie did and wanted Issy to see Hattie in a good light.

'Look, lass, I can see how you're thinking and that you've been at worrying about telling me of this lass, as you've never mentioned her afore. Nor did my Ciss come to that. But, don't worry on account of me thinking badly of Hattie. I've known of her kind afore. A long time ago. Its circumstances, like you say, as gets a lot of them into it. With Hattie it was gentry as was to blame and with lass as I knew it was her own da as took her down and then killed himself in front of her, poor lass. Mind, he'd left her some money but that was stolen from her and like Hattie it was a prostitute that helped her and she landed up on the game. There's a lot as goes on as shouldn't. And this Hattie's involvement in stopping that vile bloody racket and getting them beasts to the gallows, well, that's to be commended. At least with Hattie, lasses are being looked after, as long as her business isn't enticing others into prostitution.'

'Oh, no! Lasses were in a state when she took them on. Their health is better, they're well looked after and them as want to get out of the game have every chance because they can save and better themselves. She does get new ones in, but it is only when they are seen on the streets prostituting, and then, it's only those as has no other way. She won't take lasses as are just after making money and aren't in dire straits. She's funny in how she looks on them as being sinful and the others as having no choice and in need of help.'

'Well, there you go. It strikes me as what Hattie does is a good thing and if she makes money from doing it, well, good luck to her. If I was you I'd get started as soon as you can on making clothes for her lasses and get this future of yours sorted.'

'There's more to it though, Issy. How will I sort everything? I mean without Bert finding out? I'd have to make trips to Leeds, and on a regular basis, an all. That wouldn't pass his notice, and if it did, someone would soon make sure as he knew.'

'Look, don't put hurdles where there mightn't be any! Get yourself off to Leeds and talk to this Hattie. There might be a way round problems as you're thinking of. And, if there isn't, well then, at least you tried. What shift's Bert on today?'

'He's on days. Six while six, for the next two weeks.'

'Couldn't be better then, it's only just on ten and there's a train at eleven fifteen, if I remember right.'

A fearful excitement shot through Megan. Suddenly it wasn't something she couldn't do it was a possibility! But, going off to Hattie's at a moment's notice! That was something she'd never done before. She'd always taken time to make sure everything was in place so she wouldn't get caught out by Bert and to be sure that Hattie was going to be in…

'What's wrong? You're not having doubts, are you?'

'Aye some, I'm not used to doing something on the spur of the moment and I'm thinking as to whether I'll catch her. As I told you, Hattie was planning to spend more of her time at the house she has. What if she isn't in Leeds?'

'Well, leave a message with whoever is there to tell her to contact as soon as she can to let you know when she will be in. You said she writes to you here so that won't be a problem for you. Look, lass, if you doesn't go today, right now, you'll never go. You've got money, so use some of it to further yourself. Think of your dream. Go on, lass.'

Issy wriggled her body and clumsily stood up.

'I'll tell you what. I'll come, an all. It'll give me an outing, and I can give this Hattie a once over. Besides, I'll be an excuse for you to use to Bert. You can say as you went with me to Leeds as I had some things to do and didn't feel up to going on me own. You could say as I paid, an all, so he'd have no questions to ask.'

'Oh, Issy, would you? Would you come?'

'Aye, I would. Come on shift yourself. I'll just pop round Gertie's and ask her and Jenny to look after babby and look out for young-uns when they come in from their lessons.'

Megan rose and went towards her cottage. She could do this. She could really do this. And she prayed as she walked, *'Please God help me. Help me to take this step to get meself free.*

CHAPTER THIRTY

Not two hours had passed since she'd sat on the step talking of it, and here she was standing in front of Hattie's house.

'Well! This is something. I didn't expect a place like this. I tell you, Megan, they says as we're sitting on a fortune and by eck they're right, an all. Mind, I've sat on mine too long now it'll not be worth anything, but it gets you thinking don't it?'

Megan giggled and tucked her arm into Issy's. 'Aye, it does, but, I wouldn't swap with them, not even my life, I wouldn't.'

Issy patted her hand. 'No, lass, you're right, neither would I.'

A young girl opened the door. She didn't look much older than fifteen or so. 'What do you want here?'

'Is Hattie in, I'm a friend.'

The girl looked her up and down. 'What's your name, then?'

'Tell Hattie as Megan's here from Breckton, she'll know me.'

The door shut.

'Well! She was no more than a snip of a lass, but she had such a side to her. Surely lasses of that age aren't working game, are they?'

'No, I expect as that's that Sally. You know, the lass as I told you of. Hattie wrote and told me as she'd found her.'

The door opened again. Hattie stood on the step looking down on them. For the first time Megan noticed her appearance and how Hattie looked exactly as you'd expect a... She floundered in her thoughts. What is someone who does what Hattie does, called? The answer came as a shock and had never entered her head before. Hattie was... A Madam... And that's what she looked like. Her dark hair cut short, tightly curled to her face and her figure squeezed into a red satin dress which showed almost all of her ample bust. Lashings of dark red lipstick framed her even white teeth. And as always, she wore the long white gloves. For the second time today Megan felt embarrassed.

'Megan! Oh, Megan love, it's wonderful to see you.' Hattie's arms engulfed her. Her sweet smelling perfume filled her nostrils. It felt good. Her embarrassment left her and she hugged Hattie back with just as much enthusiasm.

'Oh, Megan. I've been worrying over you. And, me worry hasn't been without cause by the look of you. You've took another beating, I see.'

'Oh, that was a bit back. No, things have been all right of late.'

Hattie sighed and shook her head, 'Anyroad, that's not all I was thinking on, how's....

'Hattie, this is Issy.'

'Issy! Well! What I haven't heard of you wouldn't be worth knowing of. I'm right glad to meet you. Come in, both of you. I hope you've come to say as you're leaving that bastard and coming to stay with me, Megan love.'

Megan went to speak, but when she looked over at Issy she stopped. A feeling of uncertainty entered her. She couldn't seem to find her voice to answer Hattie. There was a dread in her as to how to tell of Ciss. She'd not had time to write to Hattie to let her know of what had happened.

'Is there something wrong, Megan? You haven't said yet how....'

'That young-un as answered door, was that Sally, Hattie?'

Hattie gave her a quizzical look, 'Aye, it was.'

'Oh, Hattie, you must be so happy to get her back.'

'I am, Megan, I can't say how much. It's like me life's complete. She's on with wanting to stay now she understands about how I tried to stop what happened. And, how the plan I'd made to save her sister and others went wrong. She's coming to a forgiveness of me and we're on with getting on together. It's going to take a time. She's been through a lot and for years she's been told as it was all my doing by that spiteful Elsie. You know? Susan's sister as come and took over.'

'Well, I didn't meet her, but I knew she was causing you and Arthur a lot of problems and I know as you were heart broken to lose Sally to her.'

'I was and I was right about Elsie's motives, an all. She's used Sally as a skivvy and didn't feed her right and she's filled her mind everyday with how she was on with thinking as things were. She never even set Sally to her lessons! The poor lass can barely read and write. Anyroad, we've a long road to travel, but like I say we're getting along in the right direction now.'

'Can she remember...'

'I think so. We haven't talked about that part, yet. It was so horrific for her. What he did to her and what took place after, with me being stabbed...Oh God! I feel so bad about it, Megan.'

'You mustn't, love, you went through hell. Your poor hands. Oh, Hattie, I wished as you could get to a place where you can see that what

Sally suffered was not your fault. It was that police officer, he took a risk with Sally. You know he did.'

'Maybe I will if Sally does. Like I say, we've some way to go as yet. Now, tell me, how Ciss is! Has babby been born? I take it as so with Issy being over. What did she have?'

There was a shocked silence.

'What's wrong...Is Ciss not well? Oh God! No. Oh, I'm sorry. Oh, Issy, Megan...'

Megan had been dreading this moment and now it had come she didn't know how it should go.

'You knew my lass, I understand, Hattie?'

'Aye, I did, Issy. She was a good friend to me when I most needed one. Tell me what happened, I take it as Ciss... Well, is Ciss no longer with us?'

'Oh, Hattie. I miss her. I haven't thought right since. I should have written...'

'All right, Megan love. Come on. Let it all out. Have a good cry. It's the best thing. Oh, Issy, love...'

Megan told of what had happened. She had her arm around Issy the while she spoke. Issy sobbed throughout her telling. Hattie sat on the other side of Issy stroking her hair.

When she'd finished Hattie said to Issy, 'Ciss was a lovely lass. When I was just thirteen and had just been taken down, I had nothing. Not even the means of feeding meself and Ciss sent over a half crown for me. And that was without even having met me! That says a lot about someone don't it? And you have babby, and Sarah and Jack and Megan. You'll be all right, love. You will.'

'I know.' Issy blew her nose, though it sounded more like she was blowing a fog horn. 'It's just at the moment I can't see a time. One minute I'm fine and the next I'm like this.'

'That's how it will be and it's not a bad thing. You can't bottle it up or you'll be ill. I'll go and sort a brew and some sandwiches out, ay? I bet you could do with something. You've been here all this while and I haven't offered you even a drop of tea. I'll not be a mo.'

When she came back Hattie was bright and breezy and Megan had managed to comfort Issy the while she'd been away.

'Right, get your teeth into this lot, girls.'

Hattie placed a tray on the occasional table in the centre of the room. It was piled high with sandwiches and cakes. Sally walked in behind her carrying a tray with a large pot and cups and saucers on it. Her hands were shaking. Megan jumped up to help her.

'Hello, Sally. You'll not know me. I'm Megan, Hattie's mate. Hattie and me grew up together.'

The girl smiled. 'Was you an orphan, an all?'

'Aye, we're all in same boat. I could tell you some tales of Hattie when she was a young-un. I will one day. They'd make your hair curl even more than it does already!'

'Oh, no! Don't say that, Megan. She's forever on with trying to straighten her hair. She wants one of these bobs as they're all wearing.'

'Huh, and there's me tying mine in rags every night to get this frizz to form proper curls. I'd give anything to have your mop, Sally.'

Sally giggled at this.

'I don't like to push in, but if we don't tell of what we come for we'll have to go for our train and'll miss the opportunity.'

'Oh, yes, Issy, you said as you'd come about Megan getting her life sorted. Does that mean as you're leaving Bert and coming here, Megan?'

'No, but I do want to take up your offer of making garments for the lasses. I just wondered if there was a way it could be done with me staying where I am. Issy needs me around. She needs help with the babby and well, everything...'

'Aye, I see how it is, for you, Megan. Look, I'll show you catalogue so you can see for yourself the sort of clothes and undies lasses like. There's nothing that will be a problem to you. You could make them easily, I know that.'

Whilst Hattie was looking through a pile of magazines, Sally said. 'Are you a seamstress, Megan? I like sewing, and I'm good at it. I had to do all mending when I was with me Aunt and she'd accept nothing unless it was perfect. She'd rip it undone and make me start over. And when I got really good she'd take in mending from her customers and set me at it.'

'She sounds like Madame Marie as trained me.'

'Here it is. Have a look.' Hattie passed the catalogue to Megan.

After a moment Hattie asked, 'Well, what d'yer think, now you've had a flick through?'

'I'd have no problem copying any of this stuff. I could do some designs of me own along the same lines, too. Trouble is I just don't know how I'd go about it all. I mean, there's a lot of problems like getting cloth lasses choose back to Issy's and they'll have to have fittings. There'd be such a lot of comings and goings, I'd not be able to keep it all from Bert. It's hopeless, I shouldn't have come.'

'It's not hopeless, Megan, we can come up with something. For a start, I'd take care of getting cloth to Issy's. I've a car now and a driver.

I had to have, so as to get back and forth to me house. Daisy and Phyllis are there now. I try to get Sally to stay, but no, she'll not leave me side so comes and goes with me. Isn't that right, lass?'

Sally looked embarrassed, but smiled at Hattie. The smile lit her face and held what Megan saw was a love in it. Things were a lot better in that quarter than Hattie seemed to realise. If only Hattie could get the guilt to leave her. It was the guilt which made her see things that weren't there.

'Now, about fittings, Megan, how would it be if the lass having something made came to your cottage, Issy? I mean it wouldn't be often, would it, Megan? Once you've got the size of them all, they'd only need to come when they're having something special made.'

Issy looked up from the catalogue she'd taken from Megan, 'I don't see why not. After all, nobody knows who me friends and acquaintances are. Lasses could be passed off as them as I worked for. And, I don't see how Bert can find out either as you'll be doing nothing different to what you've been doing over these last months and he's not cottoned as yet. I'll tell you something though, Megan. If lasses are willing to pay prices in this here catalogue you're soon going to be rich! Nine and eleven! For a pair of knickers! And they'd not cover anything neither. You'd catch your death in them. They haven't even got elastic in the legs!'

Megan and Hattie burst out laughing.

'You're right about prices, Issy, they are steep for what they are. Though, there's quite a lot of work in some of them pieces. I'd have to be considering that lasses would be buying their own cloth and that Hattie'll have cost of the delivery.'

'You come up with a fair price, but don't stint yourself, Megan. You must know going rate for making up? Well, take that rate and double it and my lot'll be happy. They'll still be making savings and they've money to spend. And plenty of it, an all.'

'Well! There you go, Megan love. You'll have that shop you want in no time. Eeh, that'll be a grand day, lass.'

Megan felt a smile coming up from deep inside her at Issy's words. It was a smile of relief and hope and excitement. It was mixed up with the thought of handling all the different cloths, the wonderful colours and the creation of frocks. Ideas buzzed around her head and, best of all, it gave her a feeling that the future held better things for her and Billy.

Hattie broke into her thoughts. 'Megan love. I'll be ready in a couple of years to invest in something and I reckon as it'll take you that long to get near to what you need, so how about I become a partner, ay? Whatever you've got in two years time, I'll double it'

'You'd really do that! Oh, Hattie…'

'Aye, I would. It'd give me an income and a means of getting out of this game. Are you sure as you'd have me as a partner? And maybe some of lasses could work for us? Give them as want it a chance at doing something decent for a living, ay?'

'I could help. I've been on with telling Megan about me stitching.'

Of course I'd have you. I'll have you both and be glad to. You say you're good with hand sewing, Sally? Well, how about you do the hemming? That's always a problem if the client isn't present, as getting the right length really needs them there. So that'd be ideal for you as you are here! I'll come over with first batch and show you how to pin up and mark the hem so you get the right length and then we'll see how you go on. If you are good, I'll pay you for every hem. We'll work out how much between us, ay?'

'Well! It seems we've got it all sorted. By, you're full of surprises, Sally. And I'm right glad to hear you putting ideas forward. You can't go wrong having a trade like Megan has. It always comes back to you and is there for you if you need it.'

'You know, Hattie, it's like me dream's come true already, it all seems really possible now.'

'It is, Megan. And I'll be your first customer. I'll study catalogue and pick out some things I like, and you send me some drawings of some winter clothing. We'll make a date for you to come over again and we'll shop for all materials and stuff and we can start from there. How would that be?'

'That'd be grand, Hattie. I'll send you drawings in the post as soon as I get back. I've been on with designing for you for a good while. I've a whole collection just for you. It includes a lot of the kind of frocks I see in me mind for you to wear when you're with Arthur, as well as what I call your working clothes.'

'Fancy that, Megan. You sitting doing stuff for me!'

'I like doing it, Hattie, it keeps you close to me, like I'm with you…'

They held each other. Megan knew there were no more words needed. She'd not spoil the moment by speaking of her worries again of what might happen if Bert found out.

PART FIVE

'THE AFFAIR'

1930

CHAPTER THIRTY-ONE

Megan drew in a deep breath in a fruitless effort to quell the excitement in her that had caused her to touch on Issy's, rarely seen, raw edges.

"Look, lass, wait and see! Hattie'll be here any moment." Issy had said when Megan had broached the subject again a few moments ago.

Megan didn't blame her, she hadn't been able to talk of anything else since she'd received the message that Hattie had news, and that she, and not one of the girls, would be coming on the next visit. And that next visit was to be today!

Her concentration was nil and for the umpteenth time she stuck the needle into her finger. She winced and then jumped up. *'A motor engine! At last!'*

After a flurry of cuddles and kisses with Sally and Hattie, Hattie held her at arms length.

'Well, lass, I've brought good news and I hope as you're ready to take on the next stage of our plan.'

'I am, Hattie. Every stitch I've done in this last two years has been for bringing me to this moment.'

'And, you've done a few, love. How you've managed to keep it all from Bert has been a miracle.'

'I know. I've had a few scares. Especially with Billy. He's getting to be a handful. But, he knows as he always catches it if his dad gets mad, so that's been at stopping him saying anything. Mind, he's not been above using blackmail. He worries me at times, Hattie. He seems to have a lot of his dad's traits.'

'He'll be right. He's just at that age I reckon. Not that either of us has had any dealings with lads afore, but I've heard as they're a handful when they're growing up. Sarah and Sally get on well with him so he can't be that bad!'

'He's, all right, Megan. He's no different to any lads as I've known.' Sally chipped in.

'Happen you're right. I hope so. And, I hope as getting him away from his dad will make a difference.'

'Well, love, if you're ready I reckon that can happen now.'

Issy stopped Megan from replying to Hattie. She'd been out the back filling the kettle and now came in with it. 'Hello, Hattie. Am I glad to see you! Megan's been driving me mad over this visit! I expect as you'll be ready for a drop of tea, ay?

'It's good to see you, an all, Issy. You look well. I'll not have tea, though. It's too hot for tea, thanks love.'

'Well, get yourselves into the parlour, it's cool in there, and I've some lemonade as I've made. It's in pantry on slab so'll be nice and cold. I'll bring some of that in to you.'

Megan felt her bottom lip drop without her seeming to let it. Had she heard right?

Hattie had been keeping all the money she'd made in a bank account for her and had helped it to increase quicker than it would've done by using her contacts to get material direct from the warehouses that supplied the trade. And, here she was now, saying she had a total of, one hundred and fifty pounds!

'...So, with me doubling that. We have a grand total of three hundred pounds and I reckon that's enough to start on looking for a place. What do you say to that, 'Madam Megan'!

Megan couldn't speak. Though, a giggle did rest in her. 'Madam Megan!' Hattie hadn't forgotten what she'd said she was going to call her dream place, then? But, had the saying of it been with thinking it could really be true? At this moment she felt inside her that it could. She looked down at her hands. Her own contribution was visibly etched there. At times they had been sore and bleeding with the amount of sewing she'd done and her back had ached till she'd hardly been able to straighten it. Her throat dried, tears welled into her eyes.

'Well, lass. Are you ready?' Issy asked.

Three faces looked at her. Three very dear faces waiting for her to speak, but she could only nod her head to tell them that, yes, she was ready.

Sally clapped her hands. Hattie let out a relieved sigh. Issy stood still her hands clasped under her bosom, her head shaking. 'Eeh, lass, lass...'

Hattie took charge. 'Right! That's settled, then. I'll get me solicitor on to looking out for a place for us. I thought we'd stay in Leeds, in the suburbs. Somewhere as moneyed folk'd find acceptable. Though we'd not want to pay a big rent.'

'Leeds? I hadn't thought to stay that close. What about Bert?'

'He'll not find you. For a start he'll not think for one moment as you've your own business, how could he?'

'No, you're right...But, oh, I don't know! It all seems frightening now it's likely it's going to happen. Me inside's churned all up. I can't think straight.'

You don't have to, love. I'll do all the thinking. You just have to be ready to leave when I come for you. It's as simple as that! And, remember. It's your dream. It's what's kept you going and it's about to come true!'

Hattie's words brought a realisation of the truth of it. 'Oh, Hattie, Issy, it is, isn't it? My dream. I'm about to catch me dream!'

Issy's jaw dropped.

'What's wrong, Issy, are you all right?'

'Aye. It was just what you said, about, catching your dream, I've only ever heard that saying once afore. A long time ago...'

'Oh, I know, it's an unusual saying, but... Well, I've only heard it once meself and it just seemed right for what's happening to me.'

Issy didn't say anymore. And Megan was glad. She didn't like lying to Issy and didn't understand this compulsion in the inside of herself to keep the locket a secret. Nor could she understand how it was that Issy often caught on to something she said or a way that she looked and went on about folk she'd known in the past. It was unsettling.

Hattie smiled, 'Well, Megan. You're happy, I can see that.' She took hold of Megan's shoulders and looked into her eyes. 'But, love, your happiness is no more than mine. Because what you've done, Megan, has given me hope, an all. I've come to see that in the future I really might be able to change me way of life. The business will grow enough to keep us both in time, I know it will!' She hugged Megan to her and as she squeezed her, her voice filled with emotion. 'We're going to win through, you and me, Megan. We're going to win through.'

There was an unease in Megan for a moment, something... But it passed as Hattie said, 'So, Megan, that's it, then. Everything's coming together. Well, we'd better be getting back.'

Sally had already set about the task of emptying the large shopping bag of the paper it'd been stuffed with and filling it with the garments that were ready to take back. The shopping bag ploy had worked well. When there was no material to bring in, the girls always stuffed the bag with paper, that way no suspicion had been aroused as to them coming empty handed, but leaving with a full bag.

'By the way, I forgot to say about another idea as I've had,' Hattie said. 'I was thinking of telling the girls they're not to order anything for a while, Megan. And if you've nothing on for your other customers, I thought maybe you could make up a couple of your designs from the material you have in stock. Something really special, say, a day-wear outfit and an evening frock? Then we'd have something to dress the window of the shop to give folk an idea of what we're about. What do you think?'

'Yes, I've always thought that's what I'd do and I've nothing on at the moment for Manny's lot. You know something, Hattie? I've always wanted to drape the background of the window with swathes of cream satin. Would you get me a few yards ordered? It'd make a really grand background to me designs.' Warming to her theme she went on to say. 'Oh and we'll need...'

'Hold on, love, this is your dream, remember? So, I'll find the place, then if rooms above aren't what you can live in straight away you can stop with me a while whilst we get it all just how you want it, ay?'

Megan laughed, 'Aye, you're right. Ta, Hattie, me dream wouldn't be mine if I didn't see it through to the end.'

When they'd waved off Sally and Hattie, Megan clasped her hands together.

'Oh, Issy? I never thought this day would come, but now it has, I'm ready! I didn't think I was at first. I felt scared like, but I am, I can do it. I know I can. Me heads buzzing with lists of things I'll need and...'

'Megan, I'm right happy for you. But, by eck, I'm going to miss you, lass.'

'I know, love. And I'm going to miss you and Jack... I mean... Well, all of you. You're me family.'

'I know how it is with you where Jack's concerned. I've known as you've never stopped your feelings for him and it's a credit to you as you've never done anything about it. It couldn't have been easy with Ciss gone this two years and the way being clear so to speak. But, I knew as you'd think on where the young-uns were concerned and not cause a scandal as'd outcast them. You've done well, lass. And now as you're going to be away from him it'll be easier. He'll soon be something of your past.'

'Happen...' She could think of nothing else to say. The way Issy had put it was how it should be. But, she knew it wouldn't be. Not ever. Jack was part of the very being of her and would always be.

Issy had set about clearing the tumblers they'd had their lemonade in. Megan gave her a hand. They were by the sink when Issy spoke again. 'You know? Gert'll be at questioning me again now as Hattie's been. She always gets tongues wagging does Hattie.'

'I know. Though she'd not looked so bad today, she had one of her 'Arthur' frocks on.'

'Well, I don't know. There's just something about her. She gets eyebrows raised.'

'Aye. Happen she thinks as she looks right. Maybe if she could get out of the game things'd change. Funny though how she put so much store on the shop being her means of getting her free of it all. I thought she was giving up and selling to Mavis and moving into her house. You know? She never mentioned Arthur. Do you think as there's something up?'

'I wouldn't think so. They've gone along nicely for years. I'd not think as anything would upset that apple cart.'

Megan didn't say anything else, but a feeling told her things weren't right. A guilt entered her with the feeling. She'd always cottoned on to Hattie being in trouble. But she'd been so caught up with the excitement of what was in the offing for her she'd not taken any notice of the alarm bells when Hattie had hugged her.

'We needed some good news, didn't we, lass?' Issy said, 'Its all seems doom and gloom sometimes. Especially with Jack as he is. I wonder sometimes if he's ever going to come out of his sadness. He's just not the same bloke.'

Issy's sigh shuddered through Megan, but she didn't comment. She just nodded. She'd put aside her niggling worry about Hattie and didn't want to give thought to Jack's sadness, not now. Not now she was going. Her heart had been soothed of late as he'd taken to sitting in the parlour with her if she was in there when Bert was on lates. He'd talked and talked to her. Oh aye, it'd been about Ciss and times as they'd had, but his need to be with her and his words as to how it was a comfort to him had gladdened the insides of her. Talking to Issy now, of how sad he was and how wrapped in Cissy's memory he was, would put a sadness in her. And she didn't want to be saddened. She didn't want anything to bring her down from the feelings she had in the inside of her. In fact, she wanted to be alone for a while. Alone with her thoughts, and her hopes, and her dreams. She wanted to hold her locket and talk to her granny and granddad and try to imagine what her mam was like and who had been her dad. And, to get the unsettled feeling Issy's memories had given her, to quiet down.

***

Hattie sat in the back of the car. Sally always liked to travel in the front and today she was glad of that. She was glad too, that Megan nor Issy had mentioned Arthur. The excitement of the moment had not given time to speak of him. She tried to relax, but it was hard. Her mind gave her no peace.

Arthur hadn't been in touch this good while and she'd assumed he was still abroad, where she'd thought he'd been for the last four months. The last letter she'd received from him had been from Italy and that had been some four weeks ago. But then, not more than a week ago, she'd seen his picture in the paper under the heading:

'WAR HERO, LORD ARTHUR GREYSTONE, GRACES SOCIETY ONCE MORE'

A lord! Arthur had never, in all the years she'd known him, told her he was a lord! In fact, he'd lied to her about his name! Captain Naraday! At least he'd had the decency to give her his true first name. Her heart throbbed painfully in the inside of her as she remembered the picture. There was Arthur gazing down lovingly at the beautiful woman in his arms. She knew by heart the piece describing who she was:

'Lady Greystone, who, throughout Lord Greystones' painful and long recovery from his many operations, and the dark days before, when he would hide himself away, because of the horrific injuries he'd sustained in the great war, has stood by him lovingly. Helping him to get through that terribly period of his life, a sacrifice for which she is now richly rewarded, as his devotion to her is there for everyone to see. Society once more is graced with Lord Greystones' charming presence. Lady Greystone wore...'

Bloody there for him! Huh! And who bloody cares what she wore! Why? Why, all the lies? Why, all the hope? Because there had been times when Arthur had given her hope. Hope that she would one day be his wife. *'You bloody fool, Hattie Frampton!'* She wiped away a tear as she silently admonished herself.

There was a letter waiting for her when she arrived at her house. It was Arthur's writing. She went straight up to her room ignoring Daisy fussing over her. She and Phyllis had been doing that ever since the day the picture had shattered her dreams.

My dearest, Hattie,

This is a letter I never wanted to write or never thought I would write.

I can do nothing more than be truthful with you, my dear, but our relationship has to end.

I know this will come as a blow to you. I can assure you I am equally saddened.

My life suddenly changed. Nothing was planned. Matilda, my wife, attended a dinner party, not knowing I was to be a guest also.

Because of my trips abroad and being with you it had been over two years since we had been in each others company and had conducted our marriage by letter only.

Seeing me as I am now, Matilda is able to cope with my injuries and we have found much happiness.

I will never have the love I had with you ever again. But, we could never have a compatible life, my dear. You would not have been happy in the circles in which I move and in which my friends move, and you know I am not happy with the lifestyle you chose to continue in.

Harry will come to see you in the next few days and inform you of the arrangements I have made for you. I trust you will not ever let the press, or my wife, know of our liaison. My friends in the north never knew of our relationship, other than to know that I did use your services. They will not let this be known publicly. They have many things in their own lives they would not want making public. I say all this, not because I looked on our liaison in any other way than a loving and wonderful experience, but I know you will want me to be happy and I could not attain that happiness if my wife found out about you.

I will always love and miss you, my dearest, Hattie.

Yours, Arthur.

The tears dripped on to each beautifully written word. Part of the enjoyment she'd had at receiving his letters had been to gaze at his writing. Oh, Arthur...Arthur.

There was no anger in her, only a deep sense of loss. He was right. She knew that. Oh, but the pain of losing him. How was she to bear it? And, describing what they'd had as a liaison! But then, he was top drawer. She'd always known that, even if she hadn't known just how much top drawer he was! To think that she was saving the fact she was giving up the game as a surprise to tell him when he came home! Mind, it wouldn't have made any difference, she was sure of that now.

Thank God, she'd insisted on keeping her business, because it was likely that this was always going to happen and then where would she have been? At least she was a woman of her own means. Aye, and it was a good thing she hadn't yet gone ahead with her plans to sell to Mavis. But, best of all she had plans for the future. They would help. She'd throw everything into making hers and Megan's business succeed. Though, she'd always give Megan the lead, as it was her dream. She'd not take that from her. But she'd work hard and she'd give herself no time to dwell.

It was funny how life had come round. Her and Megan back together again! They needed one another and always would. That was something. In this new venture, she had all the business knowledge, the contacts, the money to back the business and Megan had all the talent and knowledge of how to go on in the clothes business. They'd do all right. She'd be all right! *Oh, God! Oh, Arthur...Arthur...*

CHAPTER
THIRTY- TWO

Jack was surprised to hear himself whistling. He'd been doing so for a good while and hadn't even noticed himself doing it. The realization gave him the knowledge that he felt better. Something in him had changed. He thought of Ciss, as he had done every minute of the two years he'd been without her, but the memory didn't bring the usual dull ache. Instead, he was thinking of how she used to make him laugh and how she'd always see a way out of things or a different road they could travel. Nothing ever got her down.

'Uncle Jack... Uncle Jack'

He looked round, knew it was young Billy but wasn't able to see him.

'I'm here.' Billy came from behind the big oak tree that stood on the back lawn of the house.

'What're you up to, lad?' How many times have I told you not to come that way? You're trespassing. You're to come over field and down through stables. That's if you come at all, which you shouldn't.'

'It's quicker this way and Mrs Harvey didn't see me. She was at day dreaming. I saw her through the window. Anyroad, I haven't got nothing to do and I wanted to know if I can be on with helping you some?'

'I thought you were playing with Sarah?'

'I was, but she had that thing...She had Bella with her and I threw a stone at cat and it hit Bella and Sarah went mad at me.'

'Aye, she would. She'd not have Bella hurt nor any animals. You know that and should've thought on. And if me little Bella is hurt, I'll be mad at you, an all, and be at giving you a clout.'

'She's not, Uncle Jack, honest. It only skimmed her and she gave me that ug...that smile as she gives.'

Jack felt a worry in him. Young Billy was taking against Bella. He'd nearly used the term Megan had said Bert used when talking of her. He'd have to watch him.

'I'm finished here now, so I haven't anything for you. Look at car you can see your face in it. But I'd have been glad of your help to get it like that, lad. I could've used some of your elbow grease instead of all of mine.'

'What's elbow grease?'

'Ha, never mind now, I'll show you some next time. Now get along with you. I'm to take Mrs Harvey out shortly and I don't want you hanging around here.'

'At least you laughed, Uncle Jack. You haven't been doing that this good while.'

'Aye, I know, lad. I'll tell you what. When I go fishing next week on me days off, I'll take you with me. How will that be, ay? Keep you out of your mam's hair for a day.'

Billy ran off shouting back, 'Ta, Uncle Jack...Ta, ever so much.'

Jack shook his head. 'Young-uns!'

His thoughts turned to Megan. Billy had triggered them.

Megan had been a God send to him and she'd been a comfort to Ma. She'd always been there to listen to him going on. He was going to miss her. He wondered when it was she'd be going. Something in him didn't want her to go. She was a good friend. And he'd noticed of late the beauty of her. He'd been shocked a few times at the picture she made as she'd sat with the light from the window behind her. Funny how he'd never noticed that before. Accept...Well, there was a moment on his wedding day ...Fancy that coming to his mind after all these years. It wasn't a comfortable memory. Happening as it did on that day of all days! He remembered how he'd had a shock when he'd turned and caught her eye. It was as if she'd felt it, too. Eeh, Megan, lass, it's a shame as you're wasted on that Bert Armitage. By, it'll be a good day when you get away from him no matter how much I don't want you to go.

He leant back on the car door. He'd a few minutes before he'd to take the car around the front of the house. His thoughts turned to Laura Harvey and he realized the change in him, that he'd thought was a sudden one, had been coming on a while. Because though she'd been up to her tricks again lately they hadn't been unwelcome to him. He'd even liked being in her company. Though there was a fear in him as he remembered how she used to mock him. He wasn't to forget it was all a game to her. She wouldn't really be interested in the likes of him.

'Jack... Jack'

For the second time he was surprised to hear his name being called, only this time the call held a fear and an urgency.

'Henry! What's to do, man?'

'Gary's been thrown off Diamond. He's in the lane.'

'Aw, no. Is he hurt bad?'

'He was out cold. Young Billy came screaming into to the stables, I sent him running for the doctor.'

'Right, get up to the house and tell Hamilton. I'll get to Gary. I'll lift him into the stables as they're nearest.'

By the time Jack reached him Gary was conscious.

'All right, lad. I'm here. Can you stand? Doctor's on his way. I'm to get you back to stable.'

'Me leg's badly, Jack, and I'm still at seeing stars. I'll kill that lad when I get me hands on him. He's turning out to be a right one. Takes after his dad if you ask me.'

'Who, Billy? Was this his doing?'

'Aye, he came out of bush screaming and yelling, right in me path. He proper spooked Diamond. And just afore I hit the ground I heard him laughing his head off. I tell you, he isn't right in his head. He'll have done this because I caught him in the orchard scrumping the apples and clipped his ear. He said then, as'd he'd get me back or he'd tell his dad and he'd be for getting me. Something needs to be done about him, Jack. He's been at scaring me little lad, an all.'

'I'll see to it. Don't be saying anything to Bert, otherwise Megan'll most likely cop it. And punishment as lad'll get at Bert's hand will be far worse than what his deed deserves.'

'But...'

'I know. You could've been killed. But, you've not. You're still here to be at your moaning.'

'You're a cheeky bugger, Fellam! Ouch! Be careful, I reckon as I've broke something.'

'You will if I drop you, lad. Ha, I've never met such a softy!'

'I'll say something, Jack. It's good to hear you funning again. Are you at feeling better?'

'Aye, I am of a sudden. I feel I'm able to get on with me life some. Funny that. It was a sudden feeling, like me sorrow was lifted from me and I can think on Ciss without wanting to break me heart. By, lad, what've you been eating? You're like a ton o bricks!'

Gary laughed out loud. Jack joined him. It felt good to be having a joke with Gary again. Gary was right though, to be worried over Billy. He'd definitely to do something about the lad. He'd talk to Megan and perhaps find time himself to pay Billy a bit more attention. Take him fishing regular and spend some time talking to him. Give him another way of looking at things to what he sees and hears at home.

***

Laura had been deep in thought. She'd decided recently that it was time Jack came out of his morose and had renewed her attempts to seduce him. The signs were encouraging.

These last couple of years had been a real trial on her, though she'd had some relief from her frustration. Apart from her work she'd amused herself with Daniel, Charles younger brother. He was far too young for her of course, but it had been fun. The thrill of contrived meetings, the teaching him to become a skilful lover without Charles and Daphne having an inkling of what was going on! And, his mastering the art of satisfying her, had all served to help keep her yearnings at bay. But, it was over with Daniel now. He'd written her a sweet letter telling her about a girl he'd met and how wonderful she was. She'd written back saying she would never forget their encounter and hoped he would always keep it in his heart as a beautiful shared secret, and not let it become sordid in his mind and a source of embarrassment whenever they met. That had put it to bed nicely, she thought.

She sighed heavily. It had worked well, Jack being her chauffeur. There were ample opportunities for her to have exactly what she wanted with no chance of anyone on the estate or from the village finding out, or for that matter, Charles. She didn't mind Daphy knowing. It'd be quite fun actually, someone to talk to. She'd missed that during her tryst with Daniel.

The trouble was that since his wife's death Jack had built an even thicker barrier around himself. *Damn it! All I need is an opportunity to present itself, a chance happening! Something! Anything that would pull him out of his morose and get him thinking like a man again!*

She impatiently lit a cigarette and inhaled deeply. She'd another few minutes before she needed to leave for the meeting with her works and estate managers.

To her annoyance the hot smoke started her coughing. She stubbed the cigarette out and struggled to catch her breath. The linctus Dr. Cragshaw had given her was having no affect. She half thought about asking him to prescribe her something else, but knew all he'd tell her was she'd have to give up smoking. He'd talked about her seeing a specialist, which had worried her. She lay back in the chair, her breathing calmed. She let the niggling worry over her health drift out of her thoughts and turned her mind back to her quest for Jack.

A knock at the door made her jump. Hamilton, at her bidding, entered.

Now what? If he'd come complaining about the kitchen staff again, she'd go mad! Oh, God! Her life was so boring. She needed something to happen. Anything! Even if it was the completion of the Byron

Electric Company, deal. Though, at least, the wrangling going on at the moment gave some respite to the boredom. Thank God, she was going away with Daphy to her holiday cottage in Scarborough, soon.

'I'm sorry to disturb you, Ma-am'

'What is it, Hamilton?'

'Henry Fairweather's in the kitchen, Ma-am, he's come up from the stables...'

For a moment she couldn't take in what Hamilton had said. Diamond, rearing up and throwing Ardbuckle off his back! It didn't seem possible, Diamond was a gentle creature.

'Where is Ardbuckle, now?'

'Fellam has carried him into the stable, Ma-am.'

'Thank you, Hamilton.' She was already standing and reaching for her cardigan. Throwing it around her shoulders she ran towards the stables, calling out to Jack.

Gary tried to sit up when he heard her voice. 'Oh, no! That's Mrs Harvey, Jack. Now I'm for it. Ouch!'

'It's all right, Gary. Lie still, she'll not blame you. Now just leave this to me, and mind, don't be mentioning anything about young Billy. Just say as horse stumbled, ay?'

'Aye, I will, but lad...'

'Shush now, she's here.'

'What happened, Jack? Is Diamond all right?'

'I haven't had time to look at him yet, Ma-am. It seems he stumbled on a lose cobble or something, Gary's not sure.'

'Well, where is Diamond now? Has someone seen to him?'

'Henry said as how he galloped off down the lane. He said he was limping slightly, but we were more concerned for lad here.'

Laura Harvey looked uncomfortable and unsure. He could see she hadn't missed the inference he'd put in his tone as to her thinking more of the horse than of the lad.

'I'll stay with Ardbuckle. You go after Diamond. Oh dear! I hope he's all right!'

Diamond hadn't gone far. Jack found him standing near the gate of the bottom field. By the time they were back at the stable the doctor had arrived and was checking Gary over. 'How is he, Doctor? Is it bad?'

'Well, he'll not be riding horses for a while. It's a bad sprain you have there, Gary, you must have twisted it when you landed. You're lucky you haven't broken it! And I'll tell you something else, lad.

227

You're going to have a headache to boast of in the morning! You've a right bump on top of your head. You're to rest up and call me if you feel sick or if your head ache persists. Is the horse all right, Jack?'

'Aye, he seems to have escaped injury.'

Laura held Diamond and was busy checking him over. Dr. Cragshaw went over to her. It was well known as he knew as much about animals as he did humans, his dad being a local farmer. Jack watched him check the horse.

'You're right Jack, there's not much up with him. He's a little shaken, but nothing serious. Now, Gary's a different matter. He's going to have to rest up for a couple of weeks, and in fact, he shouldn't walk on that leg for a few days, so if you can arrange to get him home, Laura?'

'I'll take him in handcart, Doc, he'll be right.' As Jack spoke he lifted Gary, and, ignoring his protests placed him in the cart. He laughed loudly at the lad's plea to be put down. But, once in the cart, Gary stopped moaning and grinned up at him. 'By, like you said, you've certainly changed of a sudden, Jack, but its good to see, man. It's that good its taking me pain away.'

Jack caught Laura Harvey's eye at that moment. She had a pleased look on her face which changed in an instance to a look he'd seen many times before. He didn't shy away from it and though he was embarrassed to hold it with company being around he managed to let her know he understood by giving her a quick nod of his head. He hoped as the others would just think he was being polite. Something in him told him she'd taken it for what it was. A tingle of anticipation shivered through him.

Issy was leaning over the gate chatting to Gertie. Jack called out to her as he passed, 'Any old rags, Ma? 'Cos, I've plenty of bones.'

'What's you up to, Jack?'

'I'm running a regular ambulance service, Ma, and Gary here's me first customer.'

'Has he had a drop too much?'

'No, he just thinks as he can ride a horse as well as what I can, but he found out different, didn't you, lad?'

'Shut up, Jack, and get me home. You're making me a laughing stock.'

'I'm sorry, lad, but you had it coming. By! I've been waiting to get me own back on you for pinching me job from under me nose.'

'Aw, I didn't, man, I didn't.'

'I know as you didn't, I'm only funning. I miss it, though, lad, I'm not much for this driving lark. It was good when we had the studs, wasn't it?

'Aye, it was.'

'I'm coming for you next, Ma.' Jack called back to Issy as he manoeuvred Gary into the gate Gertie held open for him. 'I'm going to take you to Knackers Yard. Mind, I'll fetch a bigger handcart first, as I'll never fit you in this one.'

Issy's laugh resounded down the lane. Her body heaved and she dug her fists into her side to ease the ache her laughing gave her. It was good to listen to. Gertie laughed, but not as loudly, she'd taken charge of her son and was bossing Jenny around as to what was best to do.

Megan turned into the lane at that moment. 'Hello, Megan,' Issy called out. 'What d'yer think of these pair of daft idiots?'

Jack stood still when he saw Megan. It saddened him to have to land her with the fact that Billy had caused Gary to be injured. He looked down at Gary and spoke quietly to him.

'Don't forget, as you're not to say anything.'

'He's not to say anything about what, Jack? Gertie asked.

'Aw, nothing, Ma. We were messing about. We don't want Mrs Harvey knowing anything.' Gary told her.

'Eeh, Jack Fellam, have you been up to your tricks again?'

'Aye, I have Gertie. I'm sorry..'

Gertie took Gary inside, 'Well, its good to see you're feeling better, lad, but you should take more care.' With this she banged the door.

Jack turned back in the direction of Megan. She had a lightness about her. It was probably the hope she'd been given for her future. It shone from her. Something stirred inside him. She was close now. Her eyes were beautiful, deep and dark. She was laughing, and the sound was lovely.

'What's silenced pair of you? Was it sight of me? 'Cos, you was making more racket than a playground of young-uns, afore.'

'I've just been told off by Gertie! But I had it coming. Mind, your beauty had something to do with quietening me, it took me breath away.'

His tone was light, but he knew inside he'd meant the words. He heard his ma laugh, but not Megan, she looked up at him. A warmth flowed between them. It was only a split second, but he felt inside as if he'd been punched.

Megan's nervous laugh broke the spell. She moved away and called back at him. Her words bringing him back to normality. 'Go on with you, taking rise out on me. I'll get you back one of these days, Jack Fellam!'

He didn't answer her, but instead covered his confusion by laughing out loud.'

Megan almost ran over to his ma. He could see her face was red with her blushing. He winked at her and she smiled back at him.

'Well, lass, isn't that a sight to gladden you? Our Jack, laughing and carrying on! Just like he used to. We were only saying about it earlier, weren't we? And I never thought to see day come again, did you, Megan?'

Megan was still looking at him as she answered. 'No I didn't, Issy. Then she called over to him, 'Let's hope as it's a turning point for you, Jack, ay?'

He went to answer but his Ma in law got in first, 'Aye, and for us all, too, lass because I feel as though me laughing parts have been drying up as quick as me fanny this past while.'

Megan's laughter joined his Ma's.

Now who sounds like a playground of young-uns? Talk about calling pot, black! Your noise is worse than any I was making.'

'It's your mam's fault, I can't repeat what she said, but it feels good to have a laugh.'

'I heard her. By, you're crude at times, Ma. You should be ashamed of yourself!'

'Well, it's good to have a laugh and I'd like to bet as our Ciss, is laughing, an all, lad. She liked a joke did Ciss.'

'Aye, she did…'

Megan was looking at him with a concerned look on her face. Issy had shocked them both talking so lightly about Ciss. But he was glad as she had. It'd take away the awkwardness he felt at talking of her when she was around. He smiled at Megan and felt a gladness in him that things seemed normal with her, too. He'd been letting his imagination take hold of him with this new light feeling he had in him. Megan was like a sister to him.

'You know, Ma, I feel better of a sudden, I can't explain it, but it feels good. I s'pose as I haven't been much fun to be around this last two years, ay? And you've not been able to talk to me about Cissy, well, that'll change now, love.'

'No, lad it hasn't been easy for any of us. We suffered a big blow when we lost Cissy, but like I say she'd be laughing with us now, especially if she knew as I'd wet me knickers!'

This set them off again and Jack thought as it was a healing laughter. For them to mention Cissy's name in merriment was something he'd not ever thought to happen again. He knew from now on he was going to find it easier to live with Cissy's memory. It was as if she'd found a place in him that would always be hers but was letting the rest of him go free to live his life as he wished.

His mood was still light when he arrived back at the stables.

Laura Harvey was there tending to Diamond. 'He seems no worse for wear, Jack,' she said as he came up to her. She'd taken to using his first name of late when no one was around. 'All the same, I will ring the vet to check him over, just to make sure. How was Ardbuckle when you left him?'

'He was in some pain, Ma-am, and he was worried as to how they were to get by without his money coming in. There's four in the household with his wife and his ma and lad, an all, and they only have what he tips up to manage on.'

'Oh? Well, call by the kitchen before you go home and pick up some provisions for them, and see if they are all right for coal, if not, let me know and I'll have some sent round to them.'

He nodded, unsure what to say, he'd not thought she'd offer help. He'd spoken boldly and made up Gary's words, because he knew they would find it difficult and in the hope to nudge her into thinking about what it would mean to Gary to be off work a while, but he'd not expected her to take him up on it. She broke into his thoughts.

'Do you think you can cope with the horses while Ardbuckle is off work? I'll need you to drive me into the office first thing each day as I have important meetings going on this next week, but we could arrange a time for you to pick me up so you could return here. What do you think?'

'Aye, I could manage easy, and I'd be glad to.' He patted Diamond's rump, 'I've missed looking after you, lad.'

'So you haven't enjoyed your job as my chauffeur, then?'

'I haven't enjoyed anything these last two years, Ma-am.'

'No, I can understand that.'

She was looking directly into his eyes. He held her gaze. She'd travelled the same road as he had. She'd lost her husband and son. She understood, he knew that, and the knowing gave him a kindred feel for her.

She was closer to him now. He hadn't noticed her move or felt himself lean towards her, but when she put her hand on his arm he could feel its warmth, knew it would be soft to hold.

'I'm glad you're feeling better, Jack...' Her cheeks reddened and he saw the hunger deep in her eyes.

'I'll have this business at the Mine sorted out in a few days then we'll be able to exercise the horses together.'

He held her gaze. She'd said enough. He understood. He felt acutely aware of her. The calculated woman he'd known seemed to melt in front of him, and he saw a beautiful, vulnerable woman. She removed her hand and held out the reins to him.

'Will you see that Diamond and Prince are bedded down for me?'

Her words, though routine, were spoken in a soft appealing voice. He felt an urge to touch her. As he took the reins, he brushed his hand against hers. She flinched. A fear clutched at him. He'd overstepped his mark. He turned and led Diamond away. The relief to escape the nearness of her quietened his insides some.

He'd a need in him and he'd wanted to take her in his arms there and then. But then, he wasn't sure if it was just for her or if his need was general, because he'd had a feeling for Megan earlier. But, that was different. That was... He pulled himself up. By, lad, what're you thinking on? He shook his head and raised his eyes heavenward. He'd not felt feelings like he'd felt today since Ciss had died. 'Me little lass, I miss you.' But even as he said the words the effect they had on him was different. Different to the way he'd felt the other thousand and one times he'd said them. His confusion deepened. It'd been a funny day.

CHAPTER
THIRTY-THREE

Laura's problems at the Mine had been escalating over the last few weeks. Demand was down, and yet the cost of labour was soaring. She had though, received the boost she'd been hoping for. The contract to stockpile and supply the Byron Electric Company had at last come to a conclusion. She'd made many visits to the new company, negotiating the price per ton. Her chief engineer had worked hard to perfect a screening that would produce the exact quality of coal the company would require. At last it had paid off. The deal was to include them putting an electricity supply into the Mine. This would mean she could install one of the new power driven cutting machines, which would enable her to get rid of a good number of the workforce, while at the same time increase production.

Sitting in the back of the Daimler on her way to sign the last of the contracts, she felt relaxed.

'So, how are you feeling, Jack? A little saddle sore?

He looked at her through his driving mirror. He looked unsure of himself. Probably due to what had happened when he'd brushed her hand. She hadn't withdrawn her hand because she hadn't wanted him to touch her. It'd just been so unexpected.

'No, Ma-am. I thought as how I was going to suffer with it being a while since I'd last ridden, but I've been all right.'

'Is Diamond doing well?'

'Aye, he's grand, Ma-am.'

'Good, I'm glad to hear it. I've been worried in case he'd suffered any after affects from that incident with Ardbuckle. I understand from Doctor Cragshaw that Ardbuckle is doing well, but won't be back at work for at least another two weeks.'

'Aye, but he's managing to get around, though, Ma-am. He's made himself some crutches.'

She could see he was beginning to relax. He glanced through his mirror at her. She held his gaze then, deliberately, she put one hand behind her neck and started to turn her head from side to side as if to relieve tension. She sighed and arched her back. Her breasts strained against the restriction of her blouse. He'd noticed. He averted his eyes.

'Actually, I haven't much to see to at the office, so I'd like you to wait for me. I think today, we'll ride out together. I could do with the exercise'

Jack knew what she meant. She had a way of putting so much into a few words. Things that were nothing to do with what she was actually saying. He glanced in his mirror again and once more met her penetrating gaze. He held her eyes for a moment before his attention was taken. They had reached the Mine. He manoeuvred through the gates and eased the car to a halt outside her office. He didn't look back at her again, but got out of the car and opened the door for her.

'I'm looking forward to our jaunt out, Jack.' Her body swayed towards him, 'I won't be long.'

The nerve that had tingled when he'd seen her stretch herself turned into a vice and gripped the muscles in his stomach. He walked round the car and leant heavily on the door with his back to the office. He rolled a cigarette, lit it, and drew deeply on it. He paid no heed to the noises of the Mine or to the screen boys to the left of him, picking over the coal.

There was no doubt in his mind about what was about to happen, nor did he want to deny it happening, but he had a fear in him. His imagination wouldn't give him an idea of what it would be like to couple with a lady like Laura Harvey. His only experience of love-making had been with Ciss. A picture of Cissy came into his mind. It didn't come with guilt nor pain, but a kind of peace. Not that she'd approve of what he had in his mind, but she wasn't intruding on the new freedom she'd given him.

He jumped when Laura Harvey finally came out of her office and called his name. If she noticed she didn't comment. Once settled in the car she leant forward.

'I think we'll ride out to the south of the estate, Jack, to the paddock we have for family use. You know the place. You took picnic baskets there for us on several occasions a few years ago. It's very secluded. I often ride there when I want solitude.'

Jack thought to try to play her at her own game, he wasn't used to talking in subtle riddles, but he'd understood her meaning and hoped she'd know his, too. He turned and looked into her eyes. 'Aye, I know the place, Ma-am, it'll be right suitable.'

Laura's blushes surprised him and, as he had once in the past, he saw how beautiful and vulnerable she could suddenly become.

They had reached Hensal Grange, and were turning into the gates before he again looked through the mirror at her.

'Will I saddle horses then, Ma-am?'

'Yes, Jack, thank you, I'll just need to go to the house to change. I won't be long...I promise. '

This last she'd said with a cheeky grin. Something in him felt at ease. The grin had put them on two footings; one where he was master and the other, where she was. It was going well. Better than he thought it would.

As Hamilton came down the steps to help her alight from the car, Jack turned in his seat and smiled at her. He'd never done that before. They'd had laughs together over work things. But, this smile was from a man to his woman. She smiled back in the same way.

They met in the stables half an hour later. He noticed that Laura still had a nervousness about her and he liked it. It was easier for him than if she was her usual high and mighty self.

'You're all ready then, Jack?'

'Aye, and you'll be glad to know as smell of mothballs housekeeper had tucked around me riding gear whilst it was in storage, has all gone. It was right strong last week when I first put it on. It made me eyes water.'

Laura laughed.

Making sure his riding habit didn't smell of mothballs hadn't been the only thing on his mind whilst he'd been getting himself and the horses ready. A weird sensation had taken him at the way things were changing between him and his boss. Had he really spoken to her like he spoke to his Ma or Megan?

They went into the stable together to lead the horses out. He helped her to mount. This time she hadn't need of any tricks he held her waist and lifted her onto Diamond as if she was a doll. He slid his hand along her thigh as he released her. He saw the pleasure this gave her. But then, she frowned. 'I think it best that you ride behind me in the manner we were always used to, Jack, just until we're out of sight.'

She had to bloody do it! She had to put him in his place! He'd not answer her for a moment. Make her see she'd put him out by not trusting him to know how to go on. He was in the saddle before he said, 'I wouldn't have it no different, Ma-am. I'd not embarrass you, or meself for that matter, in public.'

'I...I didn't mean to upset you. I just wasn't sure. I mean, well, with the new relationship we have, I'm feeling a little unnerved...' She smiled at him in that cheeky way he'd only just found she had.

'Anyway, it's about fifteen minutes hard riding to the paddock, you know. Do you think you're up to it after your easy driving job?'

The moment had passed. Her smile and her joke had made him feel settled again. He'd give as good back. 'Aye, I think I'm up to that. Mind,' He winked at her, 'I'll most likely be in need of a rest when we get there.'

'Yes, I think you will.' She pulled on the reins and set off at a fast pace, her laughter hanging in the air.

He didn't take up the challenge, but followed her as he always would have done, until they were about a mile away from any possible prying eyes, then he urged Prince to go faster and came alongside her. She smiled at him but didn't speak and they rode on in silence until they reached the clearing.

Once there, a deeper silence fell between them, both were a little out of breath and hot from their ride. An embarrassment hung in the air. Laura was the first to speak.

'I usually unsaddle Diamond when I arrive here and give him some freedom to roam.'

'Aye, ok, I'll see to them.' He looked around him. 'You're right, I have been here afore. I'd forgotten how beautiful it is.'

She didn't answer him and this increased his embarrassment. He stood a moment and watched the horses gallop away to the other end of the clearing his stomach clenched with nerves. He glanced at her, she looked hot, and he could tell she was feeling as nervous as he was. Her voice shook a little when she spoke.

'I've brought a flask with me, would you like a drink?'

'That'd be right welcome.' He took off his jacket and laid it out near the tree stump. 'Sit yourself down, lass, I'll get it.'

He found the flask in her saddle bag and undid the cap, the smell of good whisky wafted up at him. He turned to offer it to her. He was stunned for a moment at how different she looked. She'd taken off her jacket and had let her hair lose. It shone in the sun as it cascaded around her shoulders. He sat down beside her and watched as she took a deep swallow of the neat spirit before handing it to him.

The whisky was the smoothest he'd ever tasted and as its warmth settled in his stomach, he felt his nerves calming. He touched her hair, ran his fingers along its length. 'By, you're lovely, Laura.'

Her name rolled off his tongue as if he'd always used it. She turned to face him. Her body swayed towards him. He kissed her hair, her forehead, the tip of her nose and then cupped her face in his palms and brought her lips to his in what he meant only to be a gentle caress. A testing. But, Laura melted into him and the kiss deepened to a passionate hunger.

The hunger released the last of his tension. She was no longer his boss, but his lover. It felt so natural to caress her body. To feel her soft breasts through her linen blouse. Natural, and yet, the urge in him was so strong he was afraid he'd not conduct himself properly. It'd been so long... He fought for control as without releasing her mouth from his, soft moans of pleasure came from deep within her throat. Her tongue prised open his mouth. He tasted the whisky on it as it moved in and out of his mouth sending sensations shivering through his whole body.

They parted to remove their clothes, the while they did so, he couldn't resist touching her and planting small kisses on her breasts. The feelings that built in him deepened his fear. Could he hold out long enough to give her a full satisfying of her need?

He needn't have worried. The moment he entered her she cried out with joy. Her body stiffened beneath him, her thighs clenched him in a vice like hold. He felt a spasm pulsating deep inside her, gripping and releasing him as she reached instant release. The sensation was too much. His cries joined hers as he came deeply into her bringing him an almost agonizing pleasure that he could hardly bear.

As the feeling subsided he looked down at her. Her hair was pressed to her face and her eyes were moist and beautiful. He kissed her gently as he eased himself out of her, then, still holding her to him he lay back.

After a moment Laura stirred and turned towards him.

'That was wonderful. It was beyond all my expectations and I loved the way you took charge from the moment we kissed. And I like being called, lass.' She stretched herself and for a fleeting moment he thought of the yard cat whose actions were the same after she'd had a satisfying meal. He smiled at Laura and kissed the end of her nose. 'Nice of you to say so, Ma-am.' She laughed and snuggled back into him.

He felt happy and relaxed, he'd expected a wave of guilt or sadness, but neither came, just a peace. He supposed this was because it hadn't meant anything to him other than a giving and receiving of pleasure and a release of pent up feelings. He hadn't given his whole self to her and he knew she was content with that. He was under no illusions. This was just an affair. She was his boss and they both had a need on them. They'd hurt no one so he hadn't need to worry. He hitched himself up on his elbow and looked down at her.

'Are you all right, lass? You've gone very quiet.'

'Yes.' She put her hand up and ran her fingers over his brow and down to his chin. 'Thank you, Jack.'

'Thank you? What's that for?'

'For everything. The way you handled things. I couldn't have blamed you if you'd have taken me out of duty. Just another thing your boss wanted you to do, or if you had treated me like a whore. God knows I behave like one sometimes.'

'No.' He took her hand and kissed the palm. 'I wanted you as much as you wanted me, and for longer than you might think. It was just as time wasn't right.'

'You knew I wanted you, then? I'd made it that obvious?'

'Aye, you did, and I'm sorry as you had to wait so long. As I said, it was too soon after I lost me lass. And afore that? Well, I don't know to be honest. I'd like to think I would've held out against you because I wouldn't have wanted to have hurt my Ciss, but you were getting to me even then.'

'I...I'm sorry. I behaved badly. But, well, I was very lonely.'

'No, lass, you've no need to say as you're sorry, it was very flattering if truth be known.'

'But, I know how much you loved your wife, and I could have been the cause of you hurting her, or even....'

'Don't fret yourself. It's all right. Nothing happened now, did it?'

He lifted her head and kissed her eyes and then the end of her nose and then her mouth. Her response surprised him. The kiss became achingly deep and demanding. Before it was over they were coupled again in a frenzy of pleasure.

A fear welled in him, her giving of herself to him in this second coupling was more than he'd expected or wanted. He felt as though his very being was being sucked from him. And then, as her body stiffened with her release, his fear deepened. Her cries were of love for him.

When it was over she clung to him. He laid still for a few moments and then took himself from her and lay back. Nothing had prepared him for what he'd just experienced. He'd been shocked by the depth of feeling she'd shown. He tried to tell himself all women reacted like that when they reached their special feeling. He hoped that's all it was because he couldn't cope with anything more. He'd a strong feeling on him for her, but it wasn't like he had for Cissy... Or Megan. 'Megan'? He sat up as this last unprovoked thought hit him. 'Megan? What had made him think of her? And, in that way, an all!' He shook his head.

'Are you all right?'

'Aye, it's nothing. Just me thoughts haunting me.' He gave his attention back to Laura. Her face looked fearful and he felt sorry he'd caused her distress. 'Aw, lass.' He stroked her damp hair from her face and smoothed her brow. 'You were bonnie afore I made love to you, but you're beautiful now.'

Her naked body felt small, damp and warm in his arms as he held her against him, and he realized how vulnerable she'd become in his eyes in such a short time. He'd always been used to looking up to her, being in awe of how rich and powerful she was. And aye, he'd not always liked her. But then, he'd not understood her.

He'd had a strange day, strange thoughts and ideas as well as what had happened here. He'd have never have thought it would've been like this. His mind brought a picture of Megan to him, *'What would it be like to hold her like this?'* Sadness made his heart heavy, as he remembered she was going. And soon! *'Oh God! He couldn't imagine what his life without her in it would be like'!* Knew he didn't want it to happen. He held Laura even closer, but the action didn't help. The unsettled feeling inside him didn't go away, but he wouldn't let the reason for it become a truth to him. He couldn't.

'Well, lass, are you right?' He released her as he spoke, and eased himself up. He had to busy himself. He gathered up her clothes and passed them to her. As he stood up he noticed the horses standing together looking towards them.

'Well! I didn't know as we had an audience!' He bowed to the horses. 'That's your lot lads. They'll be no more curtain calls today.'

Laura burst out laughing. Her laughter released any tension there was between them and Jack felt glad for it.

When they were dressed he lit a cigarette. It'd been a good decision to bring a packet instead of his baccy tin. He'd have been embarrassed at this moment to have to make a roll up. He offered Laura one.

'I'll have one of my own, thank you, Jack, I only smoke one brand.'

Laura found her cigarette case and they sat down together. Inhaling deeply set off a fit of coughing that racked her body. Jack felt at a loss as to how to help her, he could only rub her back until the spasm passed. He'd heard her coughing before and had noticed a rattle to her breathing sometimes when she'd come back from riding Diamond, and just now when the excitement of their love-making had made her short of breath, but nothing as bad as this.

'You shouldn't smoke, lass, if it does this to you.'

'I know, I've been trying to cut down, but it's not easy.'

She stubbed out the rest of her cigarette and wiped her streaming eyes. He clipped the end of his half smoked capstan and put the nub end into his pocket. 'Well then, we'll make a pact. When we're together; no smoking!'

'All right, but if we're together as often as I'd like, then I might not be able to keep to it.'

239

Jack smiled at her and then awkwardly broached the subject that had been niggling at him. He'd intended to talk to her about it while they relaxed and smoked, but her coughing had stopped him. He didn't usually feel embarrassed talking with her on such subjects, but it'd been a while since the stud had gone and they'd had any reason to discuss things of this nature. Right now he felt a bit sheepish.

'I was just thinking…. Well... We didn't take any care. Against you having a babby…'

Laura smiled. 'Trust a man to think of that after the event! It's all right, Jack, I can't have any children, not after…'

He took hold of her and pulled her close to him.

'I'm sorry. We've been through same mill, you and me.'

They held each other and it felt to him as they were comforting each others hurts.

A slight breeze that hadn't been there before rustled through the trees above them and the birds that had provided the background songs to their love-making were becoming quieter and finding somewhere to settle. A dampness entered the air.

'You know something? If we stay much longer they'll be sending a search party for us we'd best head back.' He felt a regret in him as he said this, he'd not wanted to spoil the peace he'd found with her. He stood up and called the horses to him and began saddling them. Laura held each one steady for him. There was a comfortable silence between them.

They'd been riding for a while when Laura slowed her pace. Jack dropped back until he was alongside of her.

'I've been thinking. I'm going away in two weeks time with my sis…I mean, Lady Crompton. We're going to her holiday cottage in Scarborough. I was wondering… I could arrange with her for me to go a week earlier. She wouldn't think anything of it. She knows I need a rest and she herself isn't free until the following week. And, of course, it would mean I would need you to take me and to stay over to drive me around.'

He smiled, he was getting used to her double meanings. He nodded his head.

As they trotted along she told him more about Lady Crompton's holiday cottage. 'And,' she said as she finished her tale, 'there are no servants to worry about. There is only a housekeeper who comes in on a daily basis. Nobody sleeping in, so we'll have it all to ourselves at night!'

'It sounds right good.' He smiled his knowledge of her meaning. 'It'll be something, an all, to go to seaside. I've not been afore, except when I went to France in the war, but that don't count, it was right dark when we boarded ship, and we never stayed long on beach when we got t'other side.'

'You'll love it. It's right grand...'

He laughed out loud at her mimicking of him. For a moment he felt like a young-un who had been given a treat to look forward to. An urge to ride as fast as the wind assailed him. It was as if he did it would bring the treat to him sooner. 'Come on, slow coach. It'll be dark soon. I'll race you back.'

'I don't give much for your chances. Diamond can out pace Prince any day.'

'That depends on whose riding. Are you ready, or does you want a few paces?'

'Ha! Cheek of you, Fellam! Oh, Jack, I'm so happy I feel happier than I've felt in years.'

'Come on then, gee up.' He tried to sound light hearted, but her words had dampened the excitement in him and a heavy feeling settled in him. She was putting a lot more into this relationship than he needed or wanted. She could end up getting hurt. He didn't want to be the cause of it. But, would he be able to stop himself from being? At this moment he didn't know. There was so much confusion in him.

241

CHAPTER
THIRTY-FOUR

Hattie poured the tea. She was on her own territory. Oh, aye she'd left this patch behind many a year ago, but she still came and had tea at Ma Parkin's now and again. It was as if she'd been lifted from here in body but not spirit and from time to time she needed the comfort the place had often given her in her dark days.

'How've you been, Hattie?'

Harry didn't look comfortable and something in her felt that that was as it should be. He'd not warned her. And yet, he must've known.

'It was a shock, Harry, as I'm sure you knew it was going to be, but I've had some two week to get meself to a place where I can cope. I'm not saying as me heart isn't broke, it is. I miss Arthur everyday. Not like the way I was used to missing him because then I knew as he was coming back to me...'

The tears she'd not shed threatened to stream from her. It was hard. For all her words of getting used to it, she wasn't. Not really. She was still in the shock of it and had read the letter over and over to try to get it to sink in.

'I never dreamt as this would happen.'

'I didn't know, Hattie. I promise you. I didn't know. His Lordship...'

'You knew that! You knew he was a Lord using a false name!'

'Aye, I did. I was his batman. Me loyalty was to him through and through. I didn't like it and many a time I wanted to tell you...I did, Hattie. It worried me because though I could understand it at first, I couldn't understand it being carried on when you got so close. When he didn't tell you it occurred to me then, as he might one day do as he has. I don't think as he ever got over his wife's rejection and I think as he didn't lose his love for her, or his hope as one day...'

'Don't! It...It's too painful...'

There was a silence. Harry had his head bowed.

'Just tell me what it is as he's sent you to tell me, Harry.'

'He says to tell you as you are to keep the house. He's put it into your name. I have the deeds here for you...'

243

'I don't want it! My God! He's never stopped thinking of me as his whore and this is the final payment for me services! Well, he can go to Hell!'

The tears spilled over and a huge sob escaped her.

'Hattie...Hattie, don't...don't, me love. I can't take you crying...'

Harry's reaction to her tears shocked her. He rose and came round to her side of the table. He stood behind her and held her to him. Was that a kiss he'd planted on her hair? Oh Harry. She couldn't move such was the unexpectedness of the action. She had always seen him as a dear friend but he wasn't behaving like a friend. His soft words were of love...

'Please don't take on. It'll be all right, I'll take care of you, my love. Oh, Hattie, I could never speak of it, but I've loved you from setting eyes on you. Hattie...Hattie, forgive my lies...forgive me.'

Her crying ceased with the shock of it all. And, with what was happening to the inside of her. She didn't want to stop Harry. She didn't want to reject him. It wasn't just that he was a salve to her heart. It was...Oh God! How was it she hadn't ever noticed his love for her? How was it she hadn't even felt feelings for him like she was feeling now. Or had she? He had been in her thoughts. She had missed him. That was when she wasn't mad at him for keeping the truth from her. But, part of her could understand that. He was loyal and loyalty was a good quality. And his loyalty had come before what was in his own heart. Arthur didn't deserve him.

'It's all right, Harry, love.' Hattie covered his hands with hers. 'Come and sit down again. We need to talk some.'

As he sat down Harry said, 'I'm sorry, Hattie. I didn't ever mean to declare my love for you. It was something I was going to hold inside me forever. I didn't mean to give you something else to worry over. Don't think on it. I can go back to how things were...'

'I don't want you to do that, Harry. I...I'm a bit unsure of me feelings as yet, with everything as has happened. But, I do have a feeling for you, and it's more than I was used to having. I just don't know if it's...well, it might be because you are a salve to me.'

'I can wait, Hattie. Patience is a thing as I've been trained to. I'll be at helping you, though, love. I've not just come because of the letter. I've left Lord Greystones' service. I couldn't carry on knowing what he'd done to you and the part I'd played in it because of my loyalty to him.'

'But, what are you going to do?'

'I've a mind to start up a business of me own. A cobblers shop and a barbers shop. Ha! I've even a name for it. I'm going to call it, 'Harry's, End to End'.

Hattie laughed with him at this and their joined laughter stirred something in her. She'd always liked Harry.

'Laughing apart, I think as I could make a go of it. I'm skilled in both of them trades and I reckon as if one is slack at one time then the other will compensate and I'll make a nice little living. Enough... Aye, well, that's for later...'

'Well, we're on with the same idea. Starting a shop, that is...' Hattie told Harry of hers and Megan's plan.

'It sounds grand, love. I've always worried over Megan. She deserved better than she got. I know I didn't see much of her but I liked her, and her mate. Poor Cissy. It don't bear thinking on. Such a pretty lass.' Harry shook his head. 'I've never forgot time as I met her. She sort of got to you.'

'Aye, she was special. And, you're right, Megan does deserve better...'

'You do, too, Hattie. What're you going to do about the house and...and well, this other business of yours?'

'I'm not for keeping the house, it has too many memories. It's in me just to tell Arthur what he can do with his gift, but I've to think on. If I sold it I could get out of game as I'm in. I've wanted to this good while and I even have someone willing to take it on, but after I lost Arthur, I pulled out of the deal and was at hoping as me venture with Megan could give me a way out sometime in the future. But, though I feel as Arthur is giving me, me final payment for me services and it don't sit right, I'd be a fool not to take this chance.'

'In this future you're planning, do you ever think a time will come when you could consider me...Well, you know...'

'Are you honestly saying as you'd take me on, knowing of everything? Because I've a past as you'd have to live with, Harry.'

'I know you have, and it's never stopped me loving you. I don't know how it was that you come to be a...well, you know what I mean...but I can bet it wasn't of your choosing. In my reckoning you've paid the price, lass. You've suffered more than most.'

'Aye, and you're right, this life wasn't of me choosing. I will tell you of it one day, but I've a lot on me at the moment. Only to say as Arthur's not the first lord to have ruined me life.'

'Don't think on it as ruined, Hattie, what are you, thirty? No more than that I'm sure. We... You have the most of your life to live yet.'

245

'You should know as it's rude to ask a lass her age, Harry! But, you're right I am on thirty. And, you're right in what you say as to me having a lot of me life left to live. It's just that at this moment in time I can't see forward without Arthur and all we had together. But, I will. I'll take you up on your offer of being patient with me. Because I've a need in me to make sure as what I feel for you isn't clouded by the circumstances as I've been brought to. I don't want you to be just someone as fills a gap in me. That wouldn't be fair.'

Harry just nodded and Hattie thought her life was going to be more bearable for having him with her and there was a hope in her for the future, but for Harry's sake she'd take it steady.

CHAPTER
THIRTY- FIVE

Megan froze. Her hand motionless over the pot of stew she'd been stirring. She held herself stiff and unyielding.

'Oh, aye. It's like that is it? You can't even bear me to touch you now.'

'No, Bert. I... You made me jump. You took me unawares. I'm sorry.' She made an effort and turned round to face him. He'd not approached her in this manner for sometime. His need was usually satisfied by rolling on her and pounding away until his finish and then turning over and sleeping. Or after a beating. He still had that sick trait. The beating of her always roused him. But, to show a simple affectionate gesture like coming up behind her and stroking her was something he'd not done for an age and had shocked her.

'Aye, well, you don't give me any encouragement, thou knows.'

'Maybe I would if you didn't treat me like you do, Bert. You've never been right with me. It isn't just a clout on a Friday night with you, is it?'

'Oh, here we go. You have to bring that up, don't you? You have to get me going. By, Megan, you've a lot to answer for. You've made me what I never wanted to be. And yet, knowing what riles me, don't stop you, does it?'

'Things could've been different, Bert. We started off all right. When things started to go badly, there were times as it could've been put right. I've not wanted to live like we do. I've not wanted to be beaten from pillow to post, despite your thinking to me liking it. What you did just now was a nice thing. Something as should be natural atween husband and wife, but instead, it was something as I wasn't expecting and that's what caused me to stiffen.'

'Well then, perhaps I should do more of it, ay?'

Bert pulled her roughly to him. His hands cupped her bottom. She felt the hardness of him dig into her. She wasn't worried. Coupling with Bert was the last thing she needed, but she'd not deny him. She'd do anything to keep the peace and to get through these last weeks.

'Oh, Megan. We'll make a fresh start, ay? Come on, let's go upstairs. Lad's out playing, he'll not bother us.'

The kiss he gave her was a gentle one and despite everything roused something in her. Something she longed for. A loving. It wouldn't hurt to respond. She could do so, too. The knowledge surprised her. But then, it'd been so long since she'd had anything like this and she was a normal woman, wasn't she? She wasn't the nothing Bert had made her feel she was. Even Jack had shown her something of late. Thinking of Jack made her respond with more passion.

'By, Megan, lass. Come on.'

She giggled at him. 'In broad daylight? Bert Armitage, what's come over you?' She was enjoying herself. 'Go on up, then. I'll just see to stew so it don't burn. I'll not be a mo.'

Bert kissed her again. 'Eeh, lass. Don't be long.'

It only took a minute for Megan to see to the stew and within no time she had her cap in place. How was it she could feel like this? Here she was plotting to leave Bert, and yet, she was all roused up by him and for the first time in years, wanted to take him to her! Well, she'd not dwell on it. Just let it happen. It might be nice to take a happy memory with her.

The shock she'd felt at Bert touching her was nothing to what she experienced when she reached their bedroom. Bert was hopping about on one foot. His anger burned from his face.

'I've just caught me bloody toe on that fucking loose floorboard! I've a good mind to rip it up and have done with it. I think I bloody will, an all.'

She held her breath as he bent down. Oh, God! No...No!

'Leave it now, Bert. We've something better to be getting on with.'

'Aye. And that's a wonder, an all. What's made you so eager of a sudden? You've wanted nothing to do with me for years. You've bloody needed it beating out of you for me to get anything other that a quick release. I haven't forgot that, thou knows.' He sat down on the edge of the bed and rubbed his toe. 'I've a bloody splinter. Fuck it!'

She held back the retort that had come to her. She'd to handle this right. Somehow she'd to get Bert out of this mood and his attention off the floorboard. It didn't bear thinking about what he'd do if she didn't and he found what she had hidden there.

'I'll get a bowl of water and you can soak your toe. It'll make it easier to get the splinter out. And, Bert, you're right about the other and I'm sorry. Like you said, let's make a fresh start. You've brought it about with your being nice to me and touching me, like, so don't let's miss the chance, ay?.'

Bert didn't answer. His expression hadn't softened. She ran from the room and down the stairs. When she came back, Bert was having a go at the floorboard.

'Here, Bert. Leave that. Come on get your foot in here. You don't want it to fester. I'll put rug over the floorboard from my side of the bed. I can make another one...'

'That won't fix it. It'll still stick up...'

In her desperation she came up with a crudeness that wasn't her nature.

'Aye, but YOU won't by the time you've sorted it. Are you going to let me down now you have me going, then, Bert Armitage?'

'Ha! Megan Armitage! I never thought to see the day! Bugger the splinter. Come here.'

She made herself laugh with him and went into his arms. It wasn't unwelcome to her. Her shock had for a moment taken from her the feeling she'd had and Bert's anger had put her back into reality. But, as he kissed her the longing rose in her again and she did want the loving he was offering her.

'Eeh, lass. Let's take it slow, ay? It's always over quick because I've not felt welcome, but with you being willing, well, we can have some fun, ay?'

'Aye, we can.' She could say no more. Bert's hands were giving her pleasure like she'd not ever had and his kisses were gentle and loving. Only once before had she felt feelings rising in her like this. It'd been a long time ago, when she first learned from Hattie to lay back and let it happen, and then, to try to take a more active part. Not that she knew what it was her body wanted. Only that she'd never reached it and that the wanting of it had left her feeling unfulfilled.

Bert was in her now. His movements slow. His kisses deep. The feelings in her built and built and demanded of her to be released. She arched her back, thrusting herself towards him. Wanting him deeper and deeper inside her. Wanting him to go faster and to thrust harder. Knew there was something going to happen. Something wonderful. She wanted it! She must have it! But then, Bert cried out and his body stiffened. *Oh God! Not yet! It hadn't happened! It was so near... No...no...*

'Aw, Megan...Megan, lass. By, that was something.'

He rolled off her and, once more, surprised her by holding her to him. He was used to just turning over when he was done.

'Thanks, lass.' He kissed her hair. 'It could always be like that, thou knows. It was as good as what you've given me after I've beaten you. I've never wanted to beat you, Megan. I'd seen so much of it and been at the brunt of it and I used to vow as I'd never treat me own wife like that. It's just as something snaps in me. It won't again. I promise.'

She was lulled by his words and his loving of her. The throbbing ache she still felt clouded her better judgement. She put her lips to his and as he responded she deepened the kiss. Her body wanted more. Taking his hand she placed it between her thighs.

Bert pulled his lips from hers. 'What's up? What're you doing? Wasn't I enough for you? After all what we've just done and all as I've said, you have to bloody throw it in me face, don't you? You're a bastard, Megan. A fucking bastard!' He turned away from her.

'No, Bert!' Megan grabbed his arm. 'I...It was lovely. I didn't want it to end. You've often took me a second time. It was so good. I wanted to feel it again...'

'It wasn't enough for you, you mean. Get out of it. Go on. I've had me belly full of you.'

Was that a sob she'd heard? Oh, God! What had she done? The feeling that had fuelled her action was gone and she couldn't bring it to mind now. And yet, it'd been so strong.

'I'm sorry, Bert. I'm so sorry.'

The words were heartfelt. She was apologising for bringing him to this. For being the wrong person for him. For all the beatings she'd taken. It wasn't that she deserved them or had provoked them, but she knew now that she'd not helped him in any way to overcome his anger. Most of all she was apologising for not having loved him enough and for losing whatever love she did have for him in the past without even putting up a fight to keep it. She'd known he was the wrong one for her. He hadn't known.

She swung her legs out of the bed. They felt like two sacks of coal they were that heavy. Her whole body was heavy. Heavy with her guilt. It was a good thing she was going. Maybe then, Bert's troubled soul could find some peace.

If in the future she did well from her business, she'd make sure as he was all right. She'd make it her business to save for a divorce so as he was free to find happiness with someone else. Someone who didn't rile him. Suddenly she wanted that for him. Wanted that for herself, too. Freedom. Freedom to find happiness. It wasn't much to ask, was it?

As she put her feet to the floor she caught sight of the floorboard. She was shocked to see it was sticking up at an angle. Bert must've got further with his prising of it than she'd thought! Her heart thudded against her chest. For all her new thinking about Bert she'd not be able to deal with him finding her money and her locket. Most of all her locket!

What should she do? If she tried to put the board back down and he heard her he'd start again. As it was, he only needed an excuse. The floorboard would give him one. Could she get her hand in without making a noise and remove the wrap of money and the envelope containing her locket? She'd have to try.

Every board squeaked her progress. Why hadn't she noticed the noise they made before?

'Where're you going? You said as you're sorry and now you're trying to get away from me.'

This shocked her. Something had changed. Bert sounded distressed.

'I thought as I'd let you sleep. I've to see to getting dinner done. And, I am sorry, Bert. I wouldn't have spoilt what we did intentionally. It was like I said, it was best as we've ever had and I didn't want it to end. I've a lot to learn still. Many a time you've done it again and I didn't realise as you couldn't always.'

'It was with it being so good. It sapped everything from me.'

'Aye, it was good. Well, I've to get on. You get an hour afore you've to get ready for work. I'll go and put your snap up and have stew ready for you.'

'Just stay until I'm asleep. I'm afraid of losing you, Megan.'

She couldn't speak. He was afraid of losing her? Then, why, why? Why had he done all he could to drive her away? She couldn't deal with this new Bert. What'd happened? Had he found out she was leaving? No, it couldn't be that. He'd have knocked two bells out of her if he'd have found that out. Whatever it was, his manner made her want to comply. She got back into bed and pulled the covers over her.

Bert reached out for her and pulled her to snuggle into the back of him. *Oh, God! That this change should come now! What should she do? What should she do?*

She lay cuddled up to his warm body. The feeling was good. This is how it should always have been. Instead she'd spent the whole of her married life lying on the other side of the bed, afraid to move in case she disturbed him. Afraid that if she did he'd become angry and she'd be for it. And, afraid of provoking the frustration of being pounded, for no other reason than to give him his release. She had a release of her own that she needed...No, she'd not think on that. She didn't want to wake up the feeling again.

Though more comfortable and soothed than she'd ever been. Her mind wouldn't rest. The floorboard and the consequences of Bert finding what it hid put a fear into her and kept her alert. She willed Bert to fall into a sleep. He was capable of taking naps and of getting into a deep sleep in a short time and waking refreshed after only having an hour or so. Please God let that happen now.

His snoring told her he'd dozed off. She took her arm from around him. Fear tightened her throat. Should she roll over and lay for a moment? Check if he noticed. It seemed as that was the only choice she had. If he woke she could say she had pins and needles and had had to move.

Nothing happened. She lay with her bottom touching his for what seemed like an age. He'd not noticed her moving. She edged herself towards the edge of the bed. Bert snorted. There was an irritation in the sound. Her body froze.

His breathing became steady again. She inched away from him. Please let her find the boards that didn't squeak!

She'd done it! Her hand was under the board. She could feel the money. Slowly she pulled it out. She could hardly breathe! As it inched towards her she kept her head high so she could see any movement Bert made. Now for the locket.

Just as it came into sight, Bert moved.

'Megan?'

She was lost. She'd nowhere to put the money or the locket.

'I...I'm just dressing. You go back off...I'll give you a call in plenty of time.'

'Aye, all right, lass.'

Bert turned back into the position he'd been in. She looked around hoping an idea would come to her. Her eyes rested on her clothes on the bottom of the bed. She'd have to put the money and the locket on the floor whilst she dressed.

This done, she bent to retrieve her packages.

'Eeh, I can't get back off. Would you bring me a sup of tea, Megan? Where are you?'

'I'm here,' she stood up, the packages once more on the floor. Her lungs felt fit to burst, it seemed an age since she'd taken a proper breath. 'I was just slipping me shoes on.'

'I think as I'll get up after all'

He sat up.

One movement of her foot and the packages flicked under the bed. There was a clunking sound. *Oh God! The pot!*

'What was that?' Bert leant over the side of the bed. Megan collapsed inwardly. It was over. Everything she'd worked for was over. Bert was soon to know it all.

'What's that?'

'What? Her voice squeaked her reply.

'There's something under the bed, a package.' Bert slid off the bed. Megan wanted to run, but her body wouldn't move.

He had her money in his hands when he rose. If she wasn't so afraid she would have laughed out loud at his expression. He counted it licking his fingers to separate the notes.

'Where did this come from?'

She didn't answer, her body shook. She was going to be sick!

'I'm at warning you, Megan. You tell me where this bloody money came from or I'll swing for you.'

'I...I've been at saving it ever since we got married.'

'Saving it! Then, how come we'd to go without day after day and live on handouts all the time as I was on strike, ay? I'll tell you, Megan, it don't make sense! There's twenty pounds here! That's more than I earn in a bloody month! Tell me truth of it, or I'll knock it out of you.'

Megan sank down on the bed. Her mind wouldn't give her a reason to give him. And she wished she hadn't kept so much. A Couple of pounds would have been plenty to take her on her trips to Leeds and wouldn't have needed an explanation. Her only solace was that he hadn't noticed the envelope with the locket in. That was still under the bed somewhere.

'I'm bloody warning you, Megan...'

'Well, why don't you just do it, then? Why don't you just beat me to a pulp? You'll do it anyroad. Your promise not to do it again, was a farce, just like all the other times as you've promised me. You know as you'll be at hitting me whether you find out truth or not!'

'Aye, happen as you're right! Happen as that's best thing. If I beat you to a pulp I'd be rid of you. And, by eck, I'd probably be happier in a prison, even if gallows loomed for me. Because, I'll never be happy with you, Megan Armitage, never in a lifetime would you give me any happiness.'

His voice trembled with his anger, and yet, his words were heartfelt and said in a regretful way. Her guilt clothed her. How was it she was always plagued with guilt? Was it her fault that everything had gone how it had for Bert?

'I'll give you one more chance, Megan. Tell me where the fucking money's come from and what you was at, stashing it away.'

'I...I've earned it...'

'Earned it? Doing what?'

'Sewing...I've been at making frocks for folk this two year or more...'

'What folk? What're you on about...Making clothes? How?'

'I've used Issy's sewing...'

253

'I might of known as that lot'd be involved somewhere along the line! You bastard! And behind me back, an all.'

The blow held all his wrath. It sliced her face and sent her reeling backwards.

She sat back up. She'd to fight him over this. She swallowed the tears down. She'd to stand her corner.

'What's the point in that, ay? You can have it all, Bert. It was going to be for your benefit, anyroad. I was saving it to take us on a holiday to Blackpool. It was going to be a surprise for your thirtieth fifth.'

Bert stood above her. The second blow he was ready to give her held in the air.

'You, what?'

Where the lie had come from she did not know, but even to her ears it sounded plausible.

'I've been on with thinking about how hard you work and how as you've never had a holiday, and yet, what you can tip up hardly covers the basics. So, I thought on giving you a treat. I...I never asked you, Bert, because I know what your answer would've been. So I went ahead. I did something of me own choosing and without your knowledge. I was going to book something for us...'

'Oh, Megan...'

Bert sat down on the bed next to her.

' Why? Why does you do it? Didn't I tell you as I'd not have you working? I know as what I tip up isn't much, but it has to be enough. If it isn't I'll tip up me dog money and give up going to the dog races. Does folk know as you've been doing this? I mean other than that lot over there?'

'No. Don't you think as I'd have been found out if they had?'

Bert shook his head. 'How come you could earn this much?'

'I've been at it some two years.'

'But, who have you been making for?'

What if she told him? Would he do anything to Manny? Part of her was mystified at how he was taking it. His anger seemed to have gone.

She took a chance and told him. He sat in silence a good while.

'So, you mean as every time as I went in for me baccy, Manny was laughing behind me back?'

'No, he wasn't, Bert. He was in on the secret and he was pleased for you.'

Again he was quiet. After a moment he said, 'I can't believe it, Megan. I just can't believe it. That you should have a plan such as this. By, it'd be good to take a break. But, me birthday isn't till back end. We've plenty here. Shall we sort it now, ay? And I tell you what. How

254

about we take young Sarah, an all. She'd be company for Billy. Keep him out of our hair. What d'yer say, ay?'

What did she say? God! She didn't know what to say.

She'd got off with one blow. And, he'd not found her locket! And, he wanted to take Sarah along on the holiday that was never planned! Words failed her. But, she knew what she could do. She could jump for joy! That's what she could do. But, she just smiled at Bert and nodded her head.

CHAPTER
THIRTY-SIX

'What's you got there, Sarah?' Billy laughed. 'He's a tiddler and half, he is. Let me see.'

'He's the biggest catch of the day, and I've beat you, Billy Armitage, and you're a good fisherman, or so you tell me!'

Billy laughed with Sarah. He'd felt cross at what she'd said, but he was that glad to have her on his own that he took it well. She was only teasing, he told himself.

'Throw it back in then, afore it dies. Anyroad, like I said, he's still a tiddler! Not like fish as me and your dad catch when he takes me on river. That's what you call fishing!'

'Well then, next time you go, I'll have to come with you and show you how it's done.'

'Aw, give over. Don't start. We're not for fighting are we? Let's have our butties. I'm right starved.'

As she passed him his packet of sandwiches from her bag Sarah said, 'You know, Billy, it's been good, being out here on our own. I'm glad as your mam sorted it for us. It's good to have a picnic, an all.'

'Aye, it is.'

'Mind, we won't see much of each other when you go.'

'No, in some ways I'm not looking forward to it. Many a time I feel like telling me dad so as it don't happen. I think I might because I don't want not to be able to see you every day, Sarah.'

'Don't do that, Billy. Me granny says as if your dad finds out he'll kill your mam. She says as we have to accept as things change. It happens all through life, she says. Look at me dad he's away more and more lately.'

'Where's he this time?'

'He's took Mrs Harvey on her holidays today and he has to stay for the first week as she'd not have a driver. And something else has changed, too. He snapped at me granny! And I've never heard me dad do that afore. Me granny was having a go over Mrs Harvey. She said as poor thing must be in need of a rest and me dad gave her what for, saying as how no one knows how hard Mrs Harvey works to keep everything going.'

'Well, don't worry. He'll be right. Happen he don't like going away. One thing I do like changing, though, is us being allowed to come out on our own. Especially as we've not much time left afore I go.'

'I know, it's been good, but Bella wasn't for it. She wasn't pleased at me coming out without her. She scared me some afore I came. She got hold of me and squeezed until I thought as me life was leaving me, I couldn't breath! Me granny had to smack her to make her let go.'

'She should be away some place. She takes up too much of your time. She's a nuisance. Me dad says as she should be in loony bin, and I reckon as he's right, an all'

'Don't talk like that, Billy! Bella's not a loony! She's just a little slow that's all. I couldn't have her taken from us. I love her and she loves me.'

'Aw, you're soft, Sarah. You should think on. What if one day she does have a turn, and kills you?' He shivered. The thought of Bella made his spine tingle, and now with this latest. He stood up and looked around. He felt unnerved.

'Don't be daft, Bella'd not hurt me. Not intentional, anyroad.'

He didn't say anything. He just stood looking at her as she gathered the wrappers up.

'Are you stood up because we're going then, Billy?'

'Aye, but I need to pee first. I'll just go into the thicket. I'll not be a mo.'

'Hurry up then, I want to get back to Bella.'

As he climbed the hill an apprehension settled in him. The thicket looked shadowy and menacing. He looked back to where Sarah was. She seemed a long way away. He wondered whether he should wait to pee until he got home, but his nerves had made it more of an urgency. He'd have to go.

When he entered the thicket the eeriness intensified. He picked the nearest tree and went behind it. As he started to pee a squirrel scuttled from behind him. He jumped. Fear tightened his throat. The squirrel stood still. He let out a relieved sigh. Then, seeing a chance for revenge, aimed his pee at the frozen animal. The drenched squirrel scurried a few paces up the tree. He laughed out loud. He felt better. His fear lifted some. He aimed again and hit the animal with some more of his pee.

'Sawah! Sawah!'

Fear snapped back into him. It threatened to strangle the breath from his lungs! He knew that voice. The half-wit! Where was she? He put himself away. Sweat trickled down the back of his neck. He looked around. He couldn't see her! He looked back towards where Sarah was. He couldn't see her either! He must have moved further in than he'd thought. Indecision held him still.

'Sawah! Sawah!'

Bella was getting nearer. He needed to see her. That way he could judge what to do. He moved towards the next tree and peeped out. How had she got here on her own? She must have come down the ginnal and across the field. He didn't feel quite so feared now she was in his sight. He'd have some fun. Scare her a bit like she'd scared him. He crept out of his hiding place and bent down to pick up some cones. He'd chuck them at her from behind the tree.

Bella was in the clearing. She was a bit near to the old Mineshaft. Perhaps she'd fall down. The thought felt good. She turned towards him. She'd seen him!

'Biwwy...?'

He'd have to get away. He'd not ever been on his own with her! The skin on his arms pebbled. He stumbled. He hit the ground hard. Anger and fear welled up in him. He clawed at the earth to regain his footing. His hand wrapped around a solid object.

'Biwwy, fall? Biwwy, hurt?'

The heavy piece of branch burned in his hand. He felt hot all over. His head filled with a redness. It hurt. He stood up. She was near to him. Those beady eyes were looking at him. She stank. He hated her!

The sound of the branch crunching on her head made the redness burst out of him. He could see her clearly again. She was lying at his feet. The branch was wet, and it seemed like the redness from inside his head was all over it. He threw it with all his might and listened to it swishing through the air. It landed in the Mineshaft.

Everywhere was quiet and still. He shivered. Was she dead? The shivering became a tremble.

'Billy! Billy...'

Sarah's voice shook him back to reality. He bent down and grasped Bella's ankles. He felt sick to his stomach at the stench of her. Her clothes were wet with her own pee. She was heavy. The big fat ugly sod, weighed a ton. He was at the Mineshaft. One massive effort and she was over. For a split second nothing. Then, a splattering thud. He wiped the sweat from his brow with his sleeve. It felt sticky. He looked at it. Blood! The fat ugly sod's blood was all over him. He wretched.

Realisation of what he'd done hit him. Tears of panic ran down his cheeks. He'd have to clean himself. He grabbed handfuls of leaves and grass and rubbed his face and arms.

'Billy, where are you?'

'I'm here! Over here!' He ran towards Sarah's voice. 'Sarah. Sarah... Aagh!!'

The earth gave way beneath him. His body slipped and slid, he couldn't stop it! Earth and stones tumbled with him. His body came to halt with a thud. His legs twisted beneath him. He couldn't see. The darkness, cold and smelly, cloyed at him. His screams scorched his throat and blocked his ears.

'Billy! Billy! What? Oh, Billy, I can't see you...'

'Me leg! Ooh me leg. I can't move.'

'I'll get help, I'll....'

'Don't leave me! Sarah don't go... Ooh'

'I've got to, Billy. I'll run, don't worry, I'll get someone...'

Calling her name was no use. She'd gone and left him! He was best to think on and listen out for someone coming. The pain in his leg eased. The cold had numbed him. He thought about Bella. She must be dead! She'd seemed dead when he'd been dragging her. He didn't feel sorry. Mostly he felt scared for himself. He needed to think of something to tell as to what had happened. He could say as she was near to Mineshaft when he saw her and as he ran to save her he fell down this hole. Aye, that was it, that's what had happened.

Drops of rain hit his face. Their pace quickened to a heavy downpour. More earth and rubble slid down round him. Puddles of water formed round his feet. He was going to be buried alive! Or drowned! His screams came back at him through the rain. He couldn't penetrate it. Blind panic gripped him and he screamed louder and louder.

***

Issy was distraught. On seeing Sarah running towards her some hope entered her. But, Sarah was screaming and tears were running down her cheeks. What was it she was screaming? Something about Billy?

'Quieten down, lass. Oh God! Why did it have to start raining? You're soaked through. As if I haven't enough on me plate! Whatever you're shouting about can wait. Bella's gone! Have you seen her? Oh God! Sarah, have you seen her?'

'Bella's gone? Gone where?'

'I fell asleep and when I woke the door was open and she'd gone. Whole streets out looking for her!'

'Oh, Granny! And Billy's...'

'Never mind about Billy, for now. Oh, good, here's Henry...'

'Now then, Issy, what's this I hear about young-un? I've just come in off fields.'

Sarah spoke first. Issy stood aghast at what she was saying.

'Mister Fairweather, Billy's hurt! We were fishing at beck and he went to pee in thicket and he didn't come back. He's hurt, Mister Fairweather. He's hurt bad. He's down a big hole. The ground just swallowed him, he was running towards me then, he was gone!'

'Billy? I thought as it was Bella as...

Issy took Sarah in her arms. 'It is Bella, an all, Henry. She got out on her own and I can't find her! She'd nothing on to speak of. She'll catch her death! And now Billy! God, Henry! What's to do? What's to do?'

'It sounds to me like some of the old Mine seam has collapsed. I'll raise the alarm and rescue team'll soon have Billy out. Stay here now, Issy. Look after little lass. Get in and get her dry and give her something hot and sweet. Aye, and yourself, an all, then if Bella comes back you'll be here for her.' As he turned to go he added, in a softer tone, 'Happen women as are looking will find her afore long. She'll not have gone far. And, if I see Megan round about, I'll tell her of Billy and take her with me.'

CHAPTER
THIRTY- SEVEN

'Well, Jack, what do you think to it? Laura indicated the beach and the sea with her hand, but she'd really no need to ask. It was written in his face and in the joy he showed. He was having the time of his life and was in awe of everything he'd seen since they had arrived in Scarborough just over an hour ago.

'I can't tell you, lass. It's just grand. I feel like a young-un. Come here, I've a mind to dip you in the sea.

'No, Jack. No! Put me down!'

'Not until I've wet your feet!'

'No, no, the water will be so cold!'

She wriggled away from him and ran as fast as she could but he caught up with her and lifted her in the air and swung her round. Her screams were a pretence. The joy she felt was all encompassing.

As he lowered her to the ground he said, 'All right, I'll not dip you if you promise me I can be at making love to you all night!'

'Jack Fellam! You drive a hard bargain! All night?'

'It's your choice, lass.' He turned towards the sea.

'Yes, yes... You can! You can, I promise...Let me go...'

Their laughter filled the air and she couldn't remember when she'd felt so happy. She went willingly into his arms and allowed his kiss, brushing away the feeling of embarrassment she felt at being used so in public. The pleasure of Jack's kiss was worth feeling uncomfortable for.

When he released her he looked out over the sea and on a deep sigh said, 'By, I feel so happy.' He hugged her to him, and then, his voice changed and had a wistful note.

'You know, I'd love to bring me family here. They'd love it. I can just see ma-in-law wobbling along on the sand going for a paddle with her stockings in her hand.'

Laura took this chance to come out of his arms. She could no longer ignore the embarrassment of herself and that of the onlookers. To prevent Jack from noticing she asked quickly, 'How is Mrs Grantham keeping, is she well? I've never forgotten her husband. He was a good horseman.'

'Oh, aye, nothing ails ma, she still misses her old man. But she gets on with things, though I think she's finding it hard to take care of little Bella. She's on two years old now, is Bella. She can be a handful at times. Mind me little Sarah helps. She adores Bella. And she's a sensible head on her has Sarah. Sometimes it's hard to remember she's only just on ten years herself.'

Jack had taken her hand and they were walking back towards the car.

'And then, there's Megan. Ma'll miss Megan. She's a grand lass and for all as she goes through and all the hard work she does, she always finds time to help ma with Bella. And, well, she's a big help to me, an all.'

A small twinge of worry shot through her. Jack talked of this Megan woman with great affection. Even... No! She hadn't let herself think that there could be another woman in his life.

'Megan? I haven't heard of a Megan before, is she a relative?'

Listening to Jack telling of Megan and her life and the beatings she took from her husband deepened the worry she'd felt. His passion when he spoke made it obvious he had a deep feeling for this woman, even if he didn't realise it.

'If I could do anything about how he beats her, I would. In fact, I'd swing for him. And, if I ever did interfere that's what I'd have to do because just giving him a hiding would only make things worse for Megan.'

'You said that your mother-in-law is going to miss, Megan. Does that mean she is planning to leave?'

'Aye, she is.'

Hearing of how Megan had worked hard to earn enough money to better her life put a feeling of desolation into Laura. Jack loved this woman. It was clear in the way he spoke of her. The knowledge of it was breaking her heart. Jack was hers! She'd longed to have him for so many years. Well, one thing she did know. Now she had him, no one was going to take him from her. No one!

'So, she is actually going to leave her husband? Surely she realises that such an action will make her an outcast. I mean. Even amongst the lower classes there is a certain code of honour and a sense of right and wrong. I can't imagine that breaking marriage vows and taking a child away from its father is looked upon in a very good light. She will have to resign herself to being on her own for the rest of her life, unless this...Whatever his name is, gives her a divorce, but really, I can't see it. These things are expensive and very hard to come by.'

'His name's Bert Armitage and he works for you down your Mine and has done for some fifteen years or more. And, you're right. Us lower classes do have a code of honour and a sense of right and wrong...'

'I didn't mean. Oh, Jack, I'm sorry. I was just thinking of, well, you wouldn't want a friend, especially a close friend, to suffer the stigma that Megan is certainly going to suffer. Not to mention her son.'

'No, and she's thought on that. She's going to pass herself off as a widow. Lad'll go along with it. He suffers a lot at his dad's hand so is looking forward to getting out of it. That's why he's kept quiet over what his mam's up to.'

'Well, I hope it goes well for her. Anyway, that's enough talk of Breckton and the goings on there. Shall we have our picnic? I'm suddenly feeling really hungry.'

'Aye, here's a good a place as any. I'll nip over to the car and bring the baskets and the blankets over.'

There was a note of discord between them. Laura was cross with herself for highlighting the fact that they were from different classes. She was troubled, too, because it occurred to her that when the woman had left, Jack may, in the missing of her, realise his true feelings for her. And worst of all, the way would be clear for him! Oh, God! She couldn't bear it! She wasn't going to let it happen!

Laura woke first. She lay looking at Jack. Her mind gave her pictures of the night before and her body tingled with the thrills of remembrance. They had made love three times during the night. He'd completely sated her.

Scrunching up into a satisfied ball of pleasure she pondered on how different things could be if only Jack was of her own class. They could be more open with their relationship, go out socially together. There would be opportunities to stay in hotels without causing a stir. Or even to marry!

But, all that was impossible, just one night away with him, trying to live as equals, had shown her that the gulf between them socially was unbridgeable. Knowing this didn't lessen her need of him or... Or, her love of him. Because she knew beyond any doubt that she did love Jack and would always do so.

The thought brought with it a fear. What of that woman!

She had to do something! Jack had said her husband worked down the Mine and that he beat her, sometimes near to death. A feeling curled her up inside making her think that if this woman's husband didn't 'near kill her', as Jack had put it. Then she would! Well, that wouldn't be possible, but she'd have to think of something! Something that would get rid of this Megan, and scupper her plans at the same time. Because she would need her to have to stay with her husband for Jack to never stand a chance of being with her.

There was only one way. She'd have to sack Armitage and evict them from the cottage! That way the woman would find it almost impossible to get away from him. And, to make sure, she'd see to it that Armitage knew of his wife's plans and the fact that she had money. Yes, that is what she must do. And, the timing was perfect. With her plans already in hand to cut the workforce, Armitage would just be one of many she'd be getting rid of. It would have to be soon as didn't Jack say that there was another woman, a partner of this Megan, who was already looking for a place for her? One had to admire the woman. To put into action such an elaborate plan and to actually pull it off! Well, almost pull it off! A part of her felt sorry for her. This dream she'd been dreaming for so many years so nearly in her grasp! Ha! She didn't think so!

The thought of the battle ahead pleasured her. She turned over to face Jack. Brushing her naked body against his had the desired effect. He opened his eyes.

For a moment Jack was disorientated, but memory flooded in. A little smile curled his lips. Laura raised herself on to her elbow and looked down at him. Her hair tumbled over his face, and as she put her hand up to sweep it back, her nipple brushed his lips. He kissed it gently. 'There's a nice way to be woken up.' He put his arms round her and eased her down by his side and rolled over so he was looking down on her. His throat dried. His body reacted to the feel of her. He'd have thought he'd not have been ready for days to take a woman to him, but he was ready. He pushed the hardness of him against her soft skin. 'I've a feeling on me again, lass. I ....'

'Kiss me, Jack...Kiss me.'

The kiss didn't end before he'd entered her and the pleasure of her filled his being. She was receptive and yet surprisingly demanding. He hadn't expected this after he'd sated her beyond anything he'd known the night before. But, he wasn't for arguing, he allowed her to roll him over and take all she wanted from him. He lay back and soaked up the intense thrills she gave him until her moans turned to hollers and her body stiffened on his and the pulsating deep inside her told him she was done.

Then, he knew the ecstasy of taking from a willing and satisfied woman. A time that was all his own. He'd no need to think of her or how to pleasure her. His mind could wander. She could be who he wanted her to be. Megan...Oh Megan. He felt his pleasure intensify with the thought. He lost himself in the fantasy. He thrust gently, then harder and harder. Oh God! Oh God!

The release brought him feelings that racked his body, and took all control from him. He'd to force enough control not to call out to Megan. When it was over he slumped down on Laura, exhausted.

They lay facing each other. An unease crept into Jack and a guilt plagued him. He wasn't sure if it was that he'd used Laura or that he'd thought of Megan in that way, but it wasn't a comfortable feeling. Suddenly, he felt at odds with himself and with what he was doing and with his surroundings.

This grand bedroom was larger than all the rooms in his cottage put together. Even the sheets, the softness of them had added to his excitement when he'd first got between them last night, but now, they felt strange.

He wondered how it could have all seemed right. He'd excused himself with the thought that he was hurting no one. But, now he wasn't sure. Laura talked as if they had a future together. It frightened him. He wished she would take it all like he did. How could it be any different? They were two people who had a need on them and an attraction for each other. Nothing more! There could be nothing more. Their lives were worlds apart.

'What's wrong, Jack? You look worried. I hate that look you sometimes have on your face. I can't make up my mind if it's regret or if I'm just the wrong woman.'

'There's no look, lass. I'm still trying to get used to the situation, that's all. Me, having an affair with me boss, don't always sit easy. But, we're not hurting anyone, are we? We're free to do as we like, and any one of us can stop it when we want to, can't we?'

Laura looked dismayed and he felt a sorrow in him. He'd to lighten the moment.

'Anyroad.' He sat up and grabbed her pillow from under her and put it over her face. 'I've another need on me just now. And, it's not same as one as I've just had on me. It's for a nice pot of tea!'

He felt Laura push the pillow away in an agitated manner. She looked afraid. He gave her a cheeky look before getting off the bed. He saw her eyes travel over his body. They'd been naked with each other on all of the times they'd been together, but she hadn't actually looked at him, not how she was doing now. He did a turn for her. The smile came back on her face.

'Jack Fellam, you take my womanly pleasures from me and then all you can say is you need a pot of tea! But, I can forgive you as you are so beautiful to look at.'

He laughed at her. 'So, you didn't have any of me manly pleasures, then? By, you're a hard woman to please.'

Laura didn't answer him, but as he left the room he saw that she leant over and took a cigarette from her packet on the side of the bed. The no smoking rule had gone out of the window. He was glad of that. There was nothing more he wanted at this moment than a smoke. Maybe it would ease the unsettled feeling inside him.

As he went along the corridor to the bathroom he heard Laura coughing. He nearly turned back, but as he went to, she stopped. Why she didn't have the investigations, Doctor Cragshaw wanted her to have was beyond him. That cough was more than an infection.

As if he'd been doing it all his life, he ran a hot bath for himself. This, so-called cottage, was like a palace to him. No tin bath to haul in and fill with buckets. '*By, this was the life.*'

After his bath he went downstairs. He knew where the kitchen and everything was. He'd made Laura supper the night before.

Laura had got up and gone into the bathroom after he'd left it, so he took his time making himself a pot of tea and drank a full mug before he went up. His mind was still troubled over what had visited him whilst he was doing Laura. He was to pull himself up. This thinking of Megan in that way wasn't any good. God knows what she'd think if she knew. By, if he knew anything, she'd laugh at him and tell him not to be so daft.

When he returned to the bedroom he found Laura sitting up in bed and looking fresh.

'I just missed the daily help. She was opening back door as I scurried out of the kitchen.'

'I wondered what you were laughing at. Oh! Have you poured my tea?'

'Aye, is anything wrong?'

'No, no. Well, I'm not used to having it poured for me. I'm used to having a tray. Oh, never mind!'

He thought to ignore this. There was a lot of her ways that were different to his and it wouldn't hurt for her to keep being reminded of them. Hopefully, it would bring their situation into perspective for her. Aye, he knew she was used to a tray with a silver pot of tea and a jug of hot water and another of milk, as well as slices of lemon and sugar that was cubed. He'd seen it all prepared in the kitchen back at the big house. But, he was used to a mug of tea and that's what he'd done for her.

'I'd better hop on up to the attic-room where I'm supposed to be sleeping, and make the bed look like as if I did!' He told her. And then, left her to the irritation she showed at his service.

A short time later he was sitting in the kitchen with Janet, as the daily had told him to call her, enjoying the hot breakfast she had cooked for him. She had already served Laura in the dining-room and was having a cuppa before doing the upstairs.

'Do you have far to come?' Jack asked her.

'No. I just live t'other side of park. If yer get some time to yerself, yer want to walk round Peasholme Park, its grand...'

The sound of the front doorbell interrupted her. She got stiffly to her feet. 'There must be some rain in the air, me rheumatics are giving me jip the day.'

She was back in no time. 'It was a telegram for Mrs Harvey. I wonder what's up.'

He felt a tightening in his stomach. A telegram meant urgency. He waited his nerves on edge. Something told him the telegram was about him.

The bell rang and Janet went to rise again. He stayed her, 'I'll go. Whatever it is, she'll more than likely need you to fetch me anyway.'

'Jack, I... I'm sorry.' The hand holding the telegram out to him shook. The edged nerves gripped his stomach. His eyes read the words. His body trembled. Disbelief forced him to read the telegram again. The brutal truth of it sank in. Bella. His little Bella. 'Aw, no. No! No...' He sank down into the nearest chair.

Laura knelt down in front of him and clasped his hands in hers. 'Oh, Jack... Jack.'

He'd not take hold of her hands. He held his together in her clasp. His eyes burned her away from him. He couldn't blink. She flinched under his gaze. She rose and went round the back of him. Her arms came round him and she tried to cradle him to her. He didn't want this. He heard a moan. It'd come from deep within him. His body trembled with pain. He felt her kiss the top of his head and smooth his brow with her hand.

'No!' His body swayed. He stood up. 'How could it happen? A Mineshaft! I thought as they were all covered.'

'It must be one of the old ventilation shafts. A closed seam. Probably from before I took over. But, what would she be doing near one? Did

269

she play that far from home? Oh! I wish to God, Charles had put a telephone in this place so we could find out more!'

'She must've gone with Sarah and Billy to the beck. It says a boy tried to get to her but a seam collapsed and he was hurt. It doesn't give his name, but, if it is Billy, then Megan... Poor Megan.

Jack looked at the telegram again thinking he might have missed something about Sarah, but no. She must be safe. But, how was she to cope with this? His mind gave him one thought. He must get back to her. Guilt flooded into him. He'd left his family unprotected for the needs of his own body.

'Jack?'

Hate welled up in him. He felt the same burning of it from his eyes as he'd felt a few moments ago and once more she recoiled from it and inside he felt it right that she should. Because the hate he held in him came from blame. It was her Mineshaft Bella had fallen down and it was her that was responsible for the safety of the closed seams. It was pleasures of her body that had kept him from his family. Aye, and he hadn't had to ask for them neither! She'd given them to him on a plate.

He moved his eyes from her and went out into the hall. He took the stairs two at a time and made his way to the attic. It only took a minute for him to gather his things together, but in that time he realized the unjustness of his thoughts and sank down on the bed.

Laura entered, 'Jack. Please. I...'

'It's all right, lass. I'm sorry. I shouldn't have looked at you like that. It's not your doing.'

As she came to him he opened his arms and took comfort from her. She was just a lonely lass and he'd taken advantage of the fact that she was attracted to him. Knew now as the blame was solely his own. The warmth of her embrace helped to seep out the cold that had clutched his heart.

'I'll have to go home. And I need to go this minute...'

'Yes of course, darling.'

The endearment gave him renewed guilt. She was getting in too deep. He couldn't cope. It wasn't her, he needed. It was Megan! He let go of Laura and sat down heavily on the side of the bed. He felt as if someone had turned a light on inside him.

In his mind it'd been Megan he'd made love to last night. He could admit it now and feel no guilt. The love that had flowed through his veins had been for Megan and his need at this moment told him the truth of it. He loved Megan. He loved her so much that it hurt. He wished to God it was her by his side.

Laura sat down beside him. He saw a desperation in her, but she didn't question him, instead she went into all the practicalities he couldn't give his mind to.

'You get yourself home right away. I'll be fine, and if things haven't settled down for you by the time you are to fetch me home in a fortnight, just get Hamilton to telephone Lord Crompton and inform him.'

Her voice seemed to drone in his ears. It felt like an intrusion on his feelings. He was confused. He wanted to be away from her. He wanted to be with his little Sarah and his ma-in-law, and he had a desperate need to be with Megan. He wanted to hold them all and say how sorry he was and tell them of his love and how he'd never leave them alone again. Her voice penetrated his confusion.

'Listen, Jack, I know you don't want to think of these things now, but when your head clears and you are faced with them you'll need to know what I want you to do.'

He made an effort deep inside him to listen to her. She was different to him. She was stiff upper lip. He'd listen to her orders, then he could go.

'If you are not feeling up to taking the car into York next week for its service, you remember? I arranged for it to be done whilst I am still here and have the use of Lady Crompton's car. Well, if you are not able to, don't worry. You can get Hamilton to telephone through to the garage and re-arrange a date. But, we do need to concern ourselves with the horses…'

Some of what she was saying was going in. And it helped. It helped him to put up a curtain in his mind. To block out what he really had to deal with.

The curtain lasted until after he'd said good-bye to her, promising he would take care and that he would contact her if he needed any help from her and it didn't lift while he drove himself home. But, the moment he entered his home and saw Issy, it fell away and the pain hit him afresh.

PART SIX

THE CONSEQUENCES

1930 - 1931

CHAPTER
THIRTY - EIGHT

'I can't believe it, Harry! That we should find two shops in the same road! And, both are fit for purpose. But, best of all, I haven't told you yet, but there's a house for sale just two streets away that I'm going to bid for. It'll be perfect. I can have it turned into two flats, one for Daisy and Phyllis and the other for me and Sally.'

'You've not thought on about my proposal, then?'

'Aye, I have. But, I'm still not sure. I need time to get over Arthur. I'm flattered as you want me, Harry. But, still it's only been a short time since it all happened. I want to take it slow. It's for your sake as much as mine.'

'But, I want you so badly, Hattie. I...I need you in all ways. I mean, whilst I was just keeping you hidden in here,' Harry tapped his chest. 'I could cope, but now as I've declared meself and think as I have a chance, it isn't so easy to ignore the nearness of you and...'

'Harry...Harry, stop this. You're not being fair to me or to yourself. You promised me...'

'But, can't I just hold you and maybe a kiss?'

'Oh, Harry...'

'All right, lass. I'll not mention it again.'

Harry turned his attention back to his paper and Hattie poured the tea Ma Parkin'd brought to their table. Her mind was troubled over Harry. She knew she'd feelings for him. He even occupied more of her thoughts than Arthur did of late. *But, what if that wore off? How could she be sure?'*

Her thoughts were cut off by Harry's sudden exclamation.

'Oh, no!

'What is it, Harry?'

'Didn't you say Cissy'd called her babby, Bella? And wasn't she a Mongol?'

'Aye, I did, why?' She almost didn't want to know the answer.

'I'm afraid as she's been killed. Poor, little lass. It appears she was playing near a Mineshaft and fell down it.'

'No! Let me see. Poor Jack and Issy. Oh dear, how will Issy and little Sarah cope? They doted on that young-un.'

As she read the story some gladness came back into her. It appeared Billy had shown his better side. He'd tried to save little Bella and had sustained a broken leg in the process, poor lad. But, at least Megan would be lifted some by him showing he has a good streak in him.

'Oh, Harry. I don't know what to do. That this should happen just as everything is almost ready for Megan! I daren't go to them. They'll be so many folk milling around. How would I answer their questions? I mean, Issy's always passed me and the girls off as lasses as she worked with on an estate out York way. It'd be difficult for me to keep that up as I don't know what she has said about me role and such like.'

'I should write them a letter if I was you, love. They'll understand. And, put in it as you've found a place. Give Megan some hope, at least.'

'No, I don't think that is the right thing to do. Me finding a place is last thing as Megan needs to be thinking of. She'll have her hands full helping Issy and Sarah and Jack. I will write, though and offer me condolences. And then, I think as I'll concentrate on getting all the paperwork for the shop completed and get the upstairs ready for her so as when I do go to tell her she can come straight away.

'Aye, all right. You know best. I've only to sign on the dotted line to finalise the papers on my shop. So I'm going to be busy with buying equipment and setting it all up. I'll not have much time to help you at your business. Will you be all right?'

'I'll be fine. I'm experienced at all this side of things.'

In fact, Hattie was glad that Harry was going to be from under her feet for a while. She needed to sort out how she felt about him and if she was to take him on. Some part of her wanted to. But, it wasn't easy to give herself fully again. Not so soon. She'd no trust in her. That was the worst thing Arthur had done to her. Destroyed the trust she'd had for folk she'd thought of as good folk. And, it'd left her feeling alone. Afraid and very alone.

***

Hamilton's voice droned on. Jack looked around the kitchen at all the familiar faces. He was still closed in the inside of him. They'd all tried to help, but he wasn't for being helped. He needed to work his own way through the grief that held him and he was doing that. Knew he had to. Knew, he couldn't let it take hold of him, as it had done after Ciss had died. His family needed him. He was to be there for them.

'…So, Lady Crompton informs me that Mrs Harvey will not be home for at least another two weeks. Though, she is making excellent progress and is getting back to full health again.' Hamilton said.

Knowing of Laura suffering a bout of pneumonia after he'd left had not touched him deeply. He was sorry to hear it, but that was all. He tried not to think of her or what they'd done. He'd had a letter from her. It was shocking to him in the wording of it. It spoke of her love for him and of how she wanted to be with him to comfort him. He'd burnt it and hadn't replied, even though she'd asked him to.

At this moment he didn't know which way his life was going. The only good thing was Megan had been delayed in going. Hattie had had personal problems and the finding of a shop was not something she could put her mind to at the moment.

He was selfish in feeling glad. He knew that. But, he couldn't have got through without Megan being around. She didn't know how he felt. He'd kept himself closed when he was around her. It wouldn't do for her to find out. He couldn't think on what she'd think of him. She'd more than likely be put out and it would spoil the friendship they had.

'I will speak with you after, Jack. There are some special instructions for you from Mrs Harvey. If you will be good enough to come to my room I will convey them to you.'

Jack nodded at Hamilton.

His thoughts turned to Billy. Poor lad had suffered for his heroics. His leg broke in two places! But, he was getting around some now. Gary had given him the crutches he'd made. He'd cut the length down to size, but you had to smile at the sight Billy made with the top bits being too big for him. He looked like a scarecrow with his arms propped up. He was showing a better side of late, was Billy. He'd have to find some way to thank him. Give him a reward so as he knew that when he was good it was appreciated. If only he could take them all to the seaside. By, that would be something. Give them all something to look forward to.

Hamilton had finished talking and was motioning to him to follow him.

'Come in, Jack. Now, Mrs Harvey is worrying over the service of the car. She says it is getting well overdue. She understands the position you are in, but wonders if you feel up to taking it in, yet?

'Aye, get it sorted and I'll see to it.'

'She has also instructed that you go over to Lady Crompton's cottage in Scarborough and take some clothes for her. Her maid has packed them. Mrs Harvey is leaving hospital tomorrow and will be convalescing at the cottage.'

'Well, if you fix up the service for this week, let's say, Friday. And arrange for me to take clothes and stuff next week. Tuesday'd be a good day. Then car will get a good run after its service. Run any new parts in.'

'Very well, I'll let you know if that is suitable. Thank goodness, Lord Crompton has had a telephone installed in the cottage at Scarborough. It means I can contact Mrs Harvey direct. Well, thank you, Jack. That will be all. I'll confirm all the arrangements with you as and when they are settled.'

Jack's thoughts went back to Megan as soon as he left the office. It was dinnertime and he'd taken to going home to have his snap. He'd found it a comfort to be with his ma-in-law and it put his mind at rest to see she was all right. And with any luck, Megan would be there and he could talk of his idea to go on a day out.

On his way home he stopped off at the graveyard. The mound of fresh earth on Cissy's grave tugged at his sore heart. 'Bella, me little Bella.' He knelt down. 'Ciss love, I'm glad as she's with you, lass. You had no time with her when she was born and doctor said as she'd a lot of suffering to face in the future. Be happy together, lass. And remember, whatever I do in the future or which path my life takes, you and little Bella will always be in me heart.'

He was surprised when he approached his cottage to hear laughter coming from the kitchen.

'Eeh, Jack. You should have been here five minutes ago. Your ma was in full swing. She's had me in stitches.'

'Well, I'm glad of it. Though you needn't be telling me what she's been saying, I can guess as it was on the crude side.'

'Aye, you know Issy. Anyroad, how're you feeling, Jack?'

'I'm all right, Megan. I've been at graveyard. You know, despite everything. It feels good as Bella is with Ciss. I like to think of them together at last.'

'You're right I'm sure of it. And, like you say, it's good to think on. Well, I've to make tracks. I'll...'

'Wait on a mo, Megan. There's something as I wanted to talk to you and Ma about. Ma, what d'yer think on us all having a day out. A trip to seaside?'

'A trip to seaside! Where did that come from?'

'Well, I thought on it when I was in Scarborough with Mrs Harvey. But...'   The memory that he was holding Laura to him at the time shuddered through his body. Never, never again! But then, would he have any choice?

'That'd be grand, Jack. But, how're we going to manage it? I mean, we could go on train, I s'pose, but I've looked into that in the past and with all changes as you have to make it takes hours. It isn't worth it for a day. And what of, Megan? She'd not be able to get out...'

'Oh, Jack didn't mean me...'

'I did, Megan. I was thinking on giving Billy a treat, to sort of thank him, for how he tried to save Bella and for being a good lad this last couple of weeks and I've a lot to thank you for, an all. D'yer think as you could sort something so as you could come? We'd go in car so you'd be back in time for Bert coming in.'

Megan's cheeks reddened.

'Well...I...I s'pose as I could. It'd have to be when Bert is on six while six day shift. He's on that next week. I've managed many a time to get to Leeds on them days and he's known nothing of it. How far is seaside?'

'It's some sixty to seventy mile. I'm to take some stuff to Mrs Harvey on Tuesday of next week and I was thinking on taking you all to the next resort, it's called Bridlington. I don't know what its like, but if its anything like Scarborough it'll be grand. I could then go on and take Mrs Harvey's stuff and be back with you about an hour later.'

'I couldn't get into the car with you, Jack. Somebody'd say something to Bert...'

'No, I know and nor can ma for that matter. I've not got permission to take me family anywhere. Look, I've thought all of this through. You and ma and Sarah and Billy could catch the train to Church Fenton, and I'll pick you up there. The Leeds to York train runs on the hour from six am till last one at ten pm. If Bert's off to his shift by five forty, say. You could be on the seven o'clock train. How does that sound?'

'I reckon as we could do it, Megan. Eeh, lad, you don't know what this is doing for me. Planning something as exciting as a day out! It's bucked me up no end.'

'I'm glad to hear it, Ma. But, Megan's still looking unsure. Come on, Megan love, it's only one day...'

'Aye, it is and if anything goes wrong and Bert gets to know, then so be it. Yes, I'll go. I'll sort everything so as I can.'

'That's settled, then. I can't wait. Seaside! I've never been, have you, Megan?'

'No, I haven't, Issy. We were going once. On a charabanc outing with Miner's welfare, but Bert put a stop to it at the last minute...'

A knock on the door, it opening and Hattie standing there stopped Megan in her tracks.

'Hattie! Oh, Hattie. It's good to see you. I never heard your car.'

'Well, it's outside. And you three look like you was up to something. You jumped out of your skins when I opened the door.'

Issy took hold of Hattie. 'Oh, it's good to see you. Come on in and sit yourself down. And thanks for your letter, lass. It meant a lot to receive it. It was a comfort and we all understood how it was as you couldn't come. Anyroad, you've been through the mill yourself, an all. How're you coping, love?'

'I'm doing all right. It isn't easy, but I have Harry and he's a comfort.'

'Oh, Hattie, I couldn't believe it…'

'I know, Megan. It's still not sunk in with me.'

'But, I'm glad as you have Harry. He's a good bloke is Harry and it was always obvious as to how he felt about you.'

'Was, it?'

'Aye. He was a proper gentleman to us all. Our station being a lot lower than he was used to dealing with didn't matter to him. He treated us all as if we were young ladies, but with you, there was a tenderness in how he was. I hope it works out for you, love. I mean, it's what you always wanted. A proper relationship. A man as wanted you for yourself. A man as you could go to as his wife.'

'I did, didn't I, Megan? And I remember once even saying as I wished that could be Harry.'

'There you go, then…'

'Aye, Issy, there I go.'

'Well, that's poor Hattie sorted out between the pair of you. Now. When's a man to get his snap? I've to go back to work soon, yer know.'

'Trust a man to think of his belly! Your sandwiches are in the pantry under that linen cloth. Now, I'll put kettle on…'

'I'll see to the kettle, Ma, take Hattie through to the parlour.'

'Ta, Jack, you're a good un. Sometimes!'

'Come on. Hattie, before they start up with their banter,'

As soon as they were in the parlour Hattie asked, 'Well, what was you all on with when I came in? You all looked guilty.'

Issy told her about their planned outing.

'That's sounds just the thing. It'll cheer you all. I only wished as I was coming, but some of us have work to do! No, I'm only fooling. I've done it all now and all it needs is your presence, Madame Megan.'

'You mean…'

'Aye, I've found a place and its all ours and, you know what? Harry's place, you remember? I wrote you about Harry starting up? Well, he has a place in the same street!'

Jack came in before they had time to reply. He put the tray of tea down on the occasional table. 'Well, I'll leave you ladies to it. I've to get back to work. I'll see you later, Ma.'

As he went out, his heart was heavy. The joy he'd felt at the prospect of having one day with Megan was gone. Hattie arriving had taken it from him. He'd heard all that had been said. Hattie had news as would take Megan away from him for good. And, he didn't want that. He couldn't even think on it.

CHAPTER
THIRTY- NINE

'You…look ..worse than …I do, Daphne.'

'Well, darling, I have lain awake for most of the night. I'm worried over your health. I've contacted Charles and asked him to make some enquiries in York as to who is the best specialist for you to see.'

'Oh, don't fuss, Daphy…I'm feeling a lot better now. Is… there any tea left in that pot? I'm…'

A fit of coughing prevented Laura from finishing what she was going to say. She held her napkin over her mouth. Daphne came to her side and held her shoulders. The coughing subsided. She lifted her head. The glaring red stain on the napkin filled her with terror.

'Oh God! Daphy, What's… wrong with me? That's… never happened before!'

Tears trickled down her cheeks. Her mind screamed the horror of her own death at her!

'I don't know, darling. We'll have to get to York right away. I'll telephone Charles.' Daphne's arms tightened around her. 'Don't be afraid, darling, it may be that you've an infection in your throat and the coughing has made it bleed.'

Laura looked up into Daphne's face. Read her sister's fear, knew she knew more than she was saying. She let her head droop and rest on Daphne. She didn't ask any questions. Didn't want to know what Daphne knew. Not yet. She needed to gather herself a little.

When her limbs stopped shaking, she lifted her head. 'I'll need to get a little…stronger…Before I travel such a distance and… face what's wrong with me, Daphy… I feel like a caged animal… I need some air. Couldn't we just go…for a drive out… Get my sea-legs as it were?'

'I don't think… No. On second thoughts, I do think that's an excellent idea. Look, it's only eight o'clock. Let's get you back to bed for an hour and we'll see if you still feel up to going out, then.'

As Daphne helped her to rise she heard her intake of breath.

'You've lost so much weight. No wonder you feel weak. We'll get some fish and chips and sit and eat them out of the newspaper! You always like that. I think it must appeal to the bad girl inside you. Anyway, we've to fatten you up.'

'I am a bad girl, aren't I? I haven't told you all about my conquest over Jack yet. We'll have a good gossip as soon as I'm...feeling....better. Is it today that he is coming with... my things?'

'Don't try to talk so much, Laura. Save your breath. Come on, I'll help you back to bed. I'll ask Janet to bring you a tray at about ten-ish.'

'But, if...Jack comes...You will wake me?'

'I most certainly will not! For heavens sake, Laura! Besides, you don't want him to see you in this state. I'll tell Janet we're expecting him and she can deal with him. Now, that's right. Snuggle down. I'll see you later. And, if you are up to going out, Johnson can drive us along the coast. We might even get as far as Bridlington. You remember? We visited it the last time we were here.'

Weakness drained Laura. And, the fear hadn't left her. If only Daphne understood. She so wanted to see Jack. He would settle her mind. But, she hadn't the strength to fight her sister over it. Oh, she couldn't bear this illness much longer. Please God that the specialist would be able to help her. There was so much that needed her attention. She would do some of it when she got up. Things at the Mine must start to move. That Megan woman had to be got out of the way. Oh God! Her head hurt so when she worried over it all.

The thought of the drive out cheered her, and yet, wearied her at the same time. She closed her eyes. Her thoughts drifted to Jack, if only...if only...

'Here we are, Mrs Harvey. I've brought yer a nice pot of tea and a toasted crumpet. I'm to see to it that a hot bath is ready for yer when yer done.'

Laura was surprised to be woken. She hadn't thought she would sleep.

'Thank you, Janet. Put it on the table in the window. Would you get my writing case for me, please? It's in the top drawer of the chest over there.'

While Janet pottered about Laura managed to get herself up. It took a massive effort to reach her chair. She flopped into it feeling utterly exhausted. The nap hadn't benefited her at all, although her breathing seemed better.

The letter to her Manager was hard to compose. She needed to tell him to get rid of twenty men as from the end of the month. He was to notify them at the end of the next week, and tell them she would be looking into vacancies in other areas for them. She would meet with them in about three to four weeks, hopefully to inform them of where they could transfer to. Her Estate Manager was already instructed to make enquiries.

That part was easy enough, but to actually name one of them was more difficult. Eventually she realised the only thing to do was to be blunt.

I want you to make sure that a, Bert Armitage, is amongst the twenty, I have heard stories of him beating his wife and drinking heavily and I do not want to employ such a man, she wrote.

This would surprise her Manager, but he wouldn't question it. She sealed the envelope before she changed her mind. Sure she had covered everything, her mind felt at ease. Though, how she was going to let Bert Armitage know what his wife is up to was another matter. She'd have to think about it more, but not now. 'Oh, how she needed to escape the confines of the cottage, and the fears in her heart.'

CHAPTER FORTY

'Issy, I feel that weird. I can't take it in as we're going to the seaside! And, as for fact as I'm not coming back here! It just don't seem real.'

'Aye, I feel that excited meself. I've mixed feelings on you going, though. Part of me's glad, but I can't get the sad feeling out of me, try as I might.'

'I know. It's a big step. And I'm going to miss you all. And, strangely, I feel bad about Bert in a way. He's been trying to be a better husband lately and he was that looking forward to trip to Blackpool. I've left him all the money, though. And, I don't wish bad on him. I think we were the wrong ones to get together and I blame meself for that. I hope everything works out well for him.'

'You need to stop feeling sorry for him and carrying guilt of it. No one has the right to beat anyone like he beat you. You tried, in fact, you did your best. So put it behind you. And, lass. Think on. You and Billy start your new life today and I reckon as it's all fitted in nicely with us spending our last day together at seaside. I'm right glad you decided to stay long enough so we could.'

'It couldn't be a better send off and I wouldn't miss it for the world. But I've not said anything to Billy yet about us not coming back. I thought to let him enjoy today then, tell him at the last minute. Jack says as he'll help me. We'll tell him in the car as we get back to Church Fenton tonight. He'll not have time to think on it all, then. What did you and Jack decide on telling Bert when you get back?'

'We decided Jack would take me all the way home instead of me doing the last leg on the train. I can say then, that I left you earlier as I wanted to meet up with the lasses as I used to work with and you went to catch the train home and that was last as I saw of you. Did Bert swallow excuse as you gave him?'

'He was over the moon. Mind, telling him as I were going in to York with you to fix up the Blackpool trip for him has made me feel bad.'

'As long as he believed you, that's all that matters, after all, there'd be nothing else he'd let you go for. Let him stew, he's had it coming this good while. I reckon as we can relax and enjoy ourselves. Except, well, I know as I've said it a dozen times, but I am going to miss you, lass. And, I doubt if I'll get to see you for a while as I'm to be careful not to alert Bert as to where you are.'

'It'll be all right, love. We will see each other. Just let things settle down. I'll write to you. I'll tell you everything about the shop and me flat above. Mind, I'm that nervous, I'm shaking. I wish train'd hurry up. I feel as though Bert'll come round the corner at any moment with some reason why I can't go.'

Jack made good time, they were at the seaside and he was back with them having delivered Mrs Harvey's clothes by noon.

Megan saw him arrive. She'd not been able to stop herself looking for him coming every few minutes. As he got out of the car he called over to them.

'Hey, haven't you been on the sand yet, or dipped your toe in the sea? I didn't expect to find you sitting just where I'd left you.'

'No, we wanted to wait for you, Jack. We didn't want to do anything until you came back. We've been for a pot of tea at the café over the way, though. Mind, it's been hard keeping Billy from going off, he and Sarah are that excited.'

'Oh, and you and ma aren't, then? Ha! I bet as your dying to wet your feet! Come on, you young-uns.'

Jack grabbed Sarah's hand and picked Billy up and ran with them on to the beach. Their laughter carried on the breeze.

Megan stayed with Issy. Issy was in awe of it all.

'By, lass, it looks big, don't it? It's most water as I've ever seen in me life. Shall we take our shoes off and go and have a paddle?'

Megan laughed, she couldn't speak. The sight of it all had overwhelmed her, too, and if truth be known she'd felt nervous to go on to the sand until Jack had come back. She did as Issy said and took off her shoes and stockings and clasping Issy's hand, together they picked their way towards the sea.

Jack and Sarah came up to them, they were red with excitement, their smiles lit their faces and their eyes were full of joy.

'Come on, pair of you, come on. Sea's just grand,' Jack said.

'I'll tell you, Jack lad, it's like nothing I've ever imagined.'

'I know, Ma, come and dip your feet.' He took hold of Issy's hand and led her down to the water's edge, then turned and ran back to Megan. 'Come on, me love, come on.'

The endearment came so naturally from him, Megan wondered if he'd realized what he'd said. But, she had, and her heart sang.

'Come on, Aunty Megan,' She felt Sarah grab her hand and she looked down into her lovely little face, so like Cissy's, and knew a warmth and a sadness fill her. It was going to be so hard to part from this little one. She was like her own daughter. The sadness left as quickly as it had come. Jack saw to that. She felt her other hand being squeezed and she looked up at him and smiled. He held her eyes for just a moment and then turned and ran back to the wall to get Billy's crutches.

When he came up to them again he said, 'I'll take these down for lad, then he can have some independence to wander away with Sarah. She's going on about collecting shells or something, aren't you, me little lass?'

With that he took hold of Sarah's other hand, and together they ran towards the sea. They lifted Sarah into the air as they ran. Their joy lifted their voices and made them immune to the cold waves that splashed over their feet as they came to the waters edge.

'Are you all right, Issy?' Megan had let go of Sarah and gone over to Issy, the water lapped around their ankles.

'Aye, lass, I'm just grand, just grand.'

They watched as Jack lifted Sarah and Billy, so he had one child under each arm, and like this, he waded further into the water all the while saying. 'I'm gonna drop you. I am...I am...'

Their squeals were deafening.

'Give over, Jack. You're worse than the nippers.'

'I am? Am I, Ma? Well you wants to thank your lucky stars as you're too heavy, else I'd have dunked you in sea by now'

'Ha! I always knew this padding would come in handy for something, at least I'm safe from your games, you big daft sod.'

'Aahh, but Megan's not.'

He brought the children back to safety, and then surprised them all by bending low and gathering Megan up high over his shoulder and running with her into the water. Megan cried out in mock anger asking to be put down at once! At last he lowered her down. The water lapped around their knees. The silence that fell between them was tangible. Jack looked into her eyes. She couldn't look away even though she knew she was bearing her soul.

'Megan, Megan...'

Her name was a whisper on his lips.

'I...I, Oh, Megan, I love you...'

Her heart swelled within her, constricting her breathing. Tears sprung to her eyes. He loved her! Jack had said, he loved her!

'I love you too, Jack and, I have done since I first met you.'

Their bodies swayed towards each other. Megan's skirt swirled around them. They were oblivious to everything and everyone as their lips met and a deep and unbreakable bond surged through them.

***

I'm so glad you felt up to coming out, darling. It's a lovely day. Oh, look, there's the beach. What do you think? Are you feeling well enough to get out for a while?'

Laura looked wearily out of the window. Her eyes fell on the young couple in the water. They were just parting from a sensuous kiss. She gasped in horror. 'My God! Oh God!'

'What is it, darling, what's the matter?'

'It's Jack. He...' She was stopped from going any further as a spasm of coughing gripped her.

'Where? Oh, dear!'

'H...How could he?' Tears streamed down Laura's face. Through the mist of them she saw Jack release the woman and put his head back. He was obviously laughing with joy. Then, he bent down and lifted the woman up and carried her back to the sand, kissing her face as he did so.

Daphne turned Laura's head away from the scene, 'There, there, darling, come on now, don't get upset it will make things worse.'

'How could he d...do that to me?'

Daphne didn't answer her, but leaned forward and spoke to her driver. 'Mrs Harvey is delirious, Johnson. She is very ill. How long will it take to get to York from here?'

'Well if we get a clear run, M'Lady, it'll take us two hours'

'Right, head for York, Johnson. Just get us there as quickly as you can.'

'No...No...I...I must speak to him...'

'Drive on, Johnson.' Daphne leant forward and pulled the curtain across. 'Oh, God! Laura. How did you get into such a state over him?' Her voice was little more than a whisper.

Laura couldn't answer. The spasm of coughing started up again. Fresh blood tinted her handkerchief. 'I...I...need air...'

Daphne slid the window down. Gradually the coughing subsided and Laura caught her breath. 'Why? Oh, Daphy, why?'

'Oh, darling. I've never seen you so miserable. What can I do to help? How did it get to be like this?'

Daphne slipped off the seat and helped Laura to lie down. She didn't resist. Once she was laid down Daphne wiped her mouth with her hanky and snuggled her up in the car rug. 'Try to sleep, darling.' She whispered. 'We're going home to York. Charles will know what to do.'

Laura made no protest. Her heart was breaking. Her mind was screaming for release from all the pain. Sleep was a blessed sanctuary.

CHAPTER FORTY-ONE

'Look at them, Megan, they're tired out, and Sarah was that insistent on coming on to station to see you off, and now she's dead to the world.'

'Aye, mind, train'll not be more than about ten minutes now. It was a grand day wasn't it, Issy?'

'It was that, Megan.'

'Issy? Well, About what happened. I...'

'You don't have to say anything, love. I've known how you've felt this good while, as you know, and I've seen it in Jack, an all, lately.' She sighed heavily. 'Whether it can lead to anything is another matter, but then, that's up to the pair of you to sort. I will say one thing though, it's only heartache as you'll be getting because you'll not be able to be together, not proper like. It wouldn't be fair on young-uns. Shame, as it would bring down on them, would cast them out. I'm not saying as I'm not for you because I am. I'd not give a damn for what folk'd say, but I'd not be for anything as'd hurt these young-uns.'

'I know, Issy. It means a lot to me that you're not against us and don't be worrying. I'd not bring shame on you all. I don't know what the future holds for us, but just knowing as Jack loves me, helps some. Were young-uns upset? Did they say anything? They've not mentioned it to us.'

'I took their attention away and just told them as Jack'd hurt you by lifting you like that, so was kissing you better. They just took it as it was. Mind, I'm sorry for you both. I am. I tell you what. Put Billy's head on me lap. There's room if I shift Sarah a bit. You go back down to Jack and spend last five minutes with him. You'll hear train coming. Go on.'

'Thanks, I'll not be long, I just...'

She didn't finish her sentence. She didn't have to, she knew that. How was she to live without them all? The next five minutes she spent with Jack might be the last for a long, long time. But, at least she would've had time with him. Time when she would know he loved her. That would have to do for now. She'd to get on with things, as she always did. Her new life was starting. And for that she'd paid a price. She only hoped as she'd no more to pay.

They were on the train. Megan had watched until Jack, Issy and Sarah were lost to her in a cloud of smoke, all the while waving her hand. Her face was wet with tears when she turned and went in search of Billy.

She found him in an empty carriage. He was lying along the bench. Once he'd said his goodbyes Jack had helped him on to the train and he'd disappeared out of sight. He sat up on his elbow when she entered, and she'd hardly sat down opposite him when he spoke.

'Mam, I feel right funny inside. I don't know if I want to go to new life or if I want to go back to dad, I do know one thing, though. I want to go back to Sarah.'

'Aye, I know, I feel the same. But, it's going to be better for us, Billy, I'm sure of that.'

'Does Uncle Jack love you, Mam. You know, like I love Sarah?'

The question and the comparison he'd made threw her for a moment. She sat back and looked at him, uncertain how to answer.

'I'll be truthful with you, Billy. Your Uncle Jack and me, we do love each other, and aye it is like you love Sarah. But, we'd not do anything as would bring shame on you all. We want to be together as a family. But, it's not going to be easy and we don't know how or when, but we will. One day we will, I'm....'

'What about me dad? He'd not have it, yer know.'

'No, he'd not have it. You're right there. And, Billy, he'd not have us living in a shop away from him either. He'll near kill me if he finds us. So we've to be secretive, tell no one where we come from, and be on the look out when we go into Leeds for anyone as knows us and make sure they don't see us.'

Billy's body shuddered and she felt sorry she'd put him through all she had. 'Don't be worrying, I'll take care of you, he'll not find us.'

He just smiled and closed his eyes again and she saw his body relax. Her own body couldn't relax. She felt the tension in every sinew.

The rhythm of the wheels on the track took her back in time. She was ten years old. She and Hattie were part of a group on a trip out for the day, which had been paid for by a charity. Sister Bernadette was there too.

Something about the way she felt today was like the way she'd felt when she'd finally parted from Sister Bernadette and gone to make her way in the world. She put her hand in her bag and found the locket tucked in one of the pockets, pulling it out she put it around her neck. She suddenly felt safer, more able to face the future. Her granny and granddad would look after her.

A little ditty started to go round in her head. She and Hattie had chanted it in time to the noise the train had made that day.

'Where are we going - Hattie and Megan?
Where are we going - Hattie and Megan?'
And, as the train had gone faster, it had changed to.
'You two wait and see. Wait and see...wait and see...'

Where were she and Hattie going? Were they on the up and up? She had to believe they were. She had to conquer the fear and uncertainty that was in her.

***

Issy took the steaming mug of cocoa Jack offered her and he watched as she relaxed back in her chair. They'd been home almost an hour, but had hardly spoken. There was an air that needed clearing between them, he knew that. But, getting Sarah settled and re-kindling the fire, as well as a few chores they'd been doing in readiness for the next day, had helped him to avoid the issues. He could do so no longer.

'Now then, Ma, I s'pose as you've something to say to me?'

'Aye, but it's not what you're thinking, I'm not disapproving, in fact, I'm glad. As I told Megan, I've known a good while how she felt and I've come to see it in you of late, an all. But, I'm worried, Jack. How's it all to work out? You need to think on. Don't do anything as'd bring shame down on them young-uns. Billy's out of it in a sense, as no one knows him where he's gone, but Sarah...'

'I hear what you're saying, Ma, and I agree with you. But, you know, love and need sometimes makes morals take a back seat. And, you've said many a time as God has given Megan a rough deal up to now, so surely she deserves some happiness.'

'You're right there, I've ranted and raved at him above, on Megan's behalf, and I'd have nothing to say about the pair of you finding happiness together. No matter how you found it. Circumstances weren't of yours or Megan's making. But, folk don't take breaking marriage vows lightly. Even if the law does sanction divorce it isn't sanctioned by us Catholics, nor Methodists, and most folk around here are one or the other of those faiths.'

'Aye, I know.'

He sipped his cocoa. The steam from it blurred his vision for a moment. He sat back in his chair. Neither his body nor his mind would relax. His needs conflicted with reality. His affair with Laura ended inside him the moment he'd held Megan in his arms, but, in truth, would Laura let it end? Would she understand if he told her he'd found love? Somehow he knew she wouldn't. And, he knew as having an

295

adulterous affair with him wouldn't sit easy with Megan either. She was made of different stuff than Laura. That wouldn't stop it happening, he knew that. He'd felt Megan's need of him in her kiss, but as time went on the conflict inside her would make her unhappy. His body heaved a deep sigh of frustration.

'Don't worry, Jack, these things have a way of working themselves out. I've told Megan and I'll tell you, I'm for you both, and I'll help all I can. Loves a powerful thing and they say as it conquers all, so just hold on to that. '

'Thanks, Ma. It'd be a lot harder for us if you were against us. I don't know how...' He jumped up. The banging on the door filled the room.

'Fellam, Fellam, you bastard! Open this door, I'm gonna kill you! Open this fucking door!'

'Ma, go upstairs, I'll deal with him. Go on now, you know what he can be like and I'll not have you getting hurt.'

'No, Jack, I'm staying. I'm not afraid of the likes of Bert Armitage!'

Her anger gave fresh life to her body. She shot off her chair, crossed the kitchen and was through the door that led to the out-house before Jack had crossed the room. And, just as Jack opened the front door she was back again armed with her thick wooden copper stick, which, though worn down at one end from poking and lifting laundry, presented as a mean weapon as she swished it back and forward through the air. 'Bugger off out of here, Bert Armitage. We don't want the likes of you in our house, shouting your bloody mouth off.'

Bert stopped in his tracks. 'Get out of the way, you, demented fat bitch! Come near me with that thing and you'll be on your fat arse afore you know it. Where's Megan? And don't say as you don't fucking know!'

He turned. His fist sunk into Jack's stomach. Jack's knees buckled, the air left his lungs. He'd no time to recover before Bert's fist crashed into his left ear and sent him reeling to the floor.

'I'll fucking kill you, you bastard. Where is she?'

The kick he'd been about to give to Jack's head never landed, Issy got to him first. The copper-stick smashed across his back.

'Stop that you bloody bugger. If anyone's a bastard it's you. What are you talking of? We know nothing about Megan's whereabouts. Get out of here.'

Bert turned and raised his fist. Issy was ready. The copper stick cracked down on his raised arm, and then another blow caught his shoulder. 'You just bloody try it, you bastard!' Get out, you filthy scum, you slimy bastard. Only one as is going to get killed round here is you, get out I tell you!'

Jack was on his feet again. He grabbed Bert and locked his arms behind his back. 'All right, Ma, that's enough. Open door and let's get him out.'

Issy did as she was bid, Jack could see as her body was shaking but she stood tall, her head high as she held the door.

Bert didn't struggle. When Jack got him to the door he pushed him so hard he fell like a rag doll down the steps leading to the gate.

'What's to do, Jack? Issy? Are you all right?' Henry was at the gate with Gertie.

Bert got himself up and pushed passed them. 'I'll get you, Fellam, and that fucking bitch of a mother-in-law of yours. You'll not pull one over me. Just watch your backs, because I'll get you!'

'What's going on? Issy, oh, Issy, you're shaking, come on, sit yourself down.' Gertie had almost leapt up the steps. She held the trembling Issy by the arm. Henry had followed behind her. 'What's got him going, Jack?' Henry asked.

Jack closed the door. He'd have to be careful what he said. No one must suspect he and Issy knew where Megan was.

'It seems Megan's left, from what he was saying, but Ma....'

The story they'd concocted rolled easily from him. It sounded that convincing, he almost believed it to be a truth himself and Issy played her part like she was going for an acting award.

'We knew as Megan was planning to go, but that's all she told us, not when, nor how, nor where to, in fact I didn't really believe as she'd do it. God! I hope she finds some way of letting me know as she's all right, she's like a daughter to me.' Issy said.

Jack almost clapped her performance, 'Don't upset yourself, Ma, be happy for her. She deserves some happiness in her life, and she'll not get it with Bert Armitage. She'd have not done this lightly, not leave you, she wouldn't.'

'But, where would she go? She'd no money or anything. She wouldn't go to workhouse, would she? Oh God! Surely not. Even living with Bert would be better than that,' Gertie said.

'Happen she's gone into one of them big houses,' Issy said, 'I was always telling her as they'd snatch her up as soon as look at her. They can't get servants these days and are taking on without references.'

Jack walked over to the sink and turned on the tap. He dipped his head under the running cold water. Their speculation was only the beginning. Talk will be rife tomorrow and for weeks ahead. His actions distracted them. Henry was beside him asking if he needed him to fetch the doctor, and Gertie resorted to her cure for all ills.

'Put kettle back on the hob, Henry.' she instructed. I'll fetch bottle over. It's not the doctor as is needed, but a hot sweet drink and a good stiff tipple!'

When she'd gone Issy asked, 'Is your head all right, Jack? Are you sure you'll not need doctor?

'I'm fine, Ma, anyroad, I bet mine's not as sore as Bert's. Ha, I'm glad as I never made you mad like that, I thought as you'd kill him with that copper stick. And swearing! I've never heard likes of it, nor I bet has Bert, not even down pit!'

Issy laughed with him.

Jack winked at her. It's funny, he thought, but despite the Bert episode they could laugh. They'd had a grand day and Megan was away and safe. He never knew he was such a good liar. Well, before his affair with Laura, that is. Carrying on like he was with her always called for untruths to be told or implied.

Still, all that matters is that Gertie and Henry were taken in. And if he knew anything of Gertie, it'd be round, and be truth of what happened by time cock crew in the morning. He sank back in his chair. *'I'm going to miss you, lass. But, I wouldn't bring you back to that man for all the coal down pit. Things will turn out well for us. I know they will.'*

CHAPTER
FORTY-TWO

It was two weeks to the day before Megan saw Jack, Issy and Sarah again. She couldn't believe they were with her so soon! She'd thought it would be months before she'd see them. After hugs, kisses and wails of excitement, Jack explained, he'd told Hamilton he'd to give the car a good run out to stop it seizing up as with Mrs Harvey still away it was hardly moving.

Issy chipped in with her part of the story. She and Sarah had had to catch the train to Leeds and Jack had picked them up at the station.

'I tell you, Megan, fooling that lot back in Breckton is as easy as taking a babby's titty from its mouth. And Sarah was that excited when I told her on train where we were coming.'

'How's she been, Issy?'

'Not good, she's missing Bella and Billy, and you. Mind, young Annie Bradshaw helps, but...'

'Well, that's good, she needs someone.' She took Issy's hand. 'There's only time as'll heal her. Well, all of us really, Bella's loss is still like a big knot inside me. So God knows how you all feel.'

Issy nodded. Megan knew she was struggling with her emotions. She changed the subject. 'Anyway, let's not waste any of your visit. It's just on eleven so I'll shut early. Its half day closing in this area so I've all afternoon for you. Come on, I'm dying to show you all around. Eeh, Hattie's going to be mad at missing you. Her and Harry have gone off for the afternoon. Things are moving along nicely in that direction. Sally's here, though. She's at stitching some hems, I'll call her. We were both going to be working at our stitching this afternoon, but we'll not now.'

'You mean you're trading already? By, lass, it didn't take you long!'

'Well, not trading exactly, Issy. As soon as the flat was ready and me stock of material and stuff arrived, I dressed the window with the garments as I'd made and within two days I had me first customer call. And, what a customer! It was a ladies-maid. She'd come to see if I'd go to her mistress's house and discuss making her a new wardrobe. Come upstairs and I'll tell you all about it.'

The tour of the shop and flat complete Megan asked Sally to take everyone through to the front room, 'I'll make a brew. Go on, there's a good lass...'

Sally had gone to protest, Megan knew she was about to offer to make the tea, but she needed a little time. She felt suddenly very shy of Jack. She couldn't have said why. But by the time she'd poured the tea out for them all she felt better able to cope.

'So how've you been in yourself, Megan?'

'I've been grand, Issy, better than I thought. Every day's been a new adventure. I've so much to tell you.'

'You're looking lovely, Megan. Your new life suits you.'

'It does, Jack, it does, but you know it's not complete. Not without you. I...I mean...' A hot colour blushed her face. 'I mean all of you.'

'We know what you mean, lass. Look, your news can wait. Jack, take Megan for a walk in that park as we passed up the road. I'll stay here with Sally. And Billy and Sarah can play together. Go on. Get yourselves off. Have an hour on your own.'

'Are you sure, Issy?' Megan's heart leapt at the chance to have Jack to herself, but the feeling of shyness and uncertainty she'd had earlier gripped her afresh. Jack seemed a little distant to her. He'd never been far from her thoughts. And, her body had longed for him at night. But, now he was here she felt unsure.

'Go on pair of you. You're acting like you've just met or something.'

Once out on the street she felt her shyness increase. It was as if she'd imagined what had passed between them before and she was back to the days when she loved him and he didn't know of it. Some of this melted when he took her hand.

'It's good to see you, Megan, and you're looking more beautiful than ever.' He lifted her hand to his lips.

'Oh, Jack, I've missed you.'

Jack did love her. She hadn't imagined it.

'I've missed you, too, me little lass, come on let's get to that park and find a big tree to hide behind so as I can hold you. I'm so near bursting to do so. I'll do it right here in the street if I've to wait much longer.'

The barriers were lifted. The awkwardness had gone. Laughter bubbled up in her and burst out as they ran towards the park. Never before had she been glad of a bad weather day as she was now. The slow drizzle meant the park was deserted.

They found their tree. A sprawling old oak. It stood majestic, surrounded by poplars and elms its wizened roots had pushed through the surface and accepted them like huge arms. Its dense foliage sheltered them from the drizzle.

They didn't speak, just clung together in a kiss so deep, Megan felt her very heart being rung from her and pressed into Jack.

This wasn't a taking of a man from a woman, like she'd only really ever known. It was a giving. A giving of body and soul to each other. Jack whispered his love between every kiss and with every touch. 'This is meant to be, my darling, Megan, tell me you feel it too.'

'I do, I do, oh, Jack...'

Her heart burst her love for him. She wanted him to stay inside her forever. When the sensation rose she did not deny it, she rode the wave of love with him. It was so right that it should be Jack that took her to those heights the first time she experienced them. 'Oh Jack... Jack...Oh...'

She clung to him, as she tried to cope with the spasms of pleasure. She knew she was holding him in a vice like grip, but didn't want him to move. She'd not be able to bear it. As the waves subsided she felt her inner being let go. Her limbs shook, her body heaved, and huge sobs racked her. It was a crying she'd never known in her life, a crying of great joy.

Through it she felt Jack covering her face in kisses and licking her tears, the while calling her, his love, his own sweet Megan, and thrusting himself ever deeper into her until she felt she would die with the pleasure and the love she had inside her.

The feeling started to build again. She heard Jack's name coming in a moan of pleasure from her lips. Heard her own name spoken in love. Felt his movements become stronger and...she was lost. Lost in a world of pleasure so deep she could hardly bear it. Jack was making her his own. Their very souls were fusing together.

There was a quiet moment, a moment broken by the sound of gentle sobs. Her Jack was crying. She moved herself, just a little, not wanting him to take himself from her, but needing to hold him.

'Jack?'

His arms encircled her. His weight pressed her down. 'Megan, Megan, Oh Megan.' He kissed her nose. His tears rolled on to her cheek. She put a hand up and wiped them away. She didn't have to ask. She knew they were tears of joy just as hers had been, but knew too, that there was an anguish mixed with the joy. He smiled down at her then rolled to her side, taking himself from her.

'Megan, I love you beyond anything. You know that, don't you?'

'Aye, I does.'

The small worry she'd had over the anguish she'd detected dissolved and she lifted herself on to her elbow and looked down on him. 'And, I accept your love with all me heart and body. I love you, Jack, and have done since I first set eyes on you.'

'Oh, Megan.' He pulled her down and rested her head on his chest and stroked her hair.

Stillness surrounded them and she knew she'd remember forever the feeling she had inside her and knew the love that encased her body would be with her till the end of her days.

The drizzle had stopped, she couldn't have said when. The sun dappled down through the leaves, and as she looked up the pattern it made looked like a lace canopy. *'Please God let this canopy cover us forever, shrouding our love with protection'*.

Without warning her peace was shattered. An ugly image of Bert shot into her mind and fear rippled through her. Jack stirred.

'Are you cold, love?' He took her hand and sat up. 'I s'pose as we'd be best to get back.' He helped her to her feet, and held her near naked body to his. It felt so right. The fear left her. Bert could never hurt her again, not now, not now that she belonged to Jack.

Her frock was one that buttoned at the front from the hem to the scooped out neckline. Jack helped her to button it up, their giggles at his attempts lightened the moment until he stopped and pulled her to him. 'Are you all right, lass?' His hand came up to her chin and he lifted her head until she was looking at him. 'I mean, no regrets?'

'I've no regrets, love, and I've never been more all right in me whole life.' Some of her shyness crept back in her, but she found the courage she needed and told him. 'I've never had feelings, like you gave me, Jack.'

His kiss felt sweet and yet, she knew a sadness. She wanted to be with Jack forever, but she knew as that couldn't be.

When they returned, Issy busied round them without looking directly at them. Or was it her imagination? Whatever it was she felt a blush redden her cheeks. Jack laughed and winked at her.

'Here you are, we thought as you'd never come back. Me and Sally have made some sandwiches and kettle's boiling for some tea, and I'm starving to skin and bone.'

'Right then, Ma, we're ready and waiting, do the business and serve up.'

Issy huffed and puffed, but didn't pursue it. Jack didn't help matters, he looked like a cat that had just caught a mouse.

'Sally's been telling me more about your first client, Megan. It sounds as though you're off to a good start.'

'Oh, you mean, Lady Gladwyn?'

Jack drew in a loud deep breath as she said this. She turned to look at him. He looked shocked, but then smiled. She didn't have time to quiz him before Issy spoke.

'Sally says you're on with making her a whole new winter outfit.'

I am, Issy. I feel right lucky getting Lady Gladwyn as me first customer. It seems she drove passed me shop and was taken with garments as I had on display. And, best of all is, if she's pleased with what I make for her she's said as she'll recommend me to her friends. In fact, I was surprised as she didn't recognise me. She was a regular at Madam Marie's. I told her as I was trained there and I nearly told her as all clothes she brought from there were my designs, but I didn't. Somehow it would've been like a betrayal to Madam and she didn't deserve that.'

'Well, that's good. Once you get a foot in door with that lot you'll not look back. I'm right glad for you, lass.'

'Thanks, Issy. Like you say, it's a start. I need to build up a few more clients though and fairly quick if I'm to keep going. There's not much left of me start up capital, so it's a bit of a worry at the moment. But, it's worth it. Me life's that different in just two weeks it's like a miracle!' She squeezed Jack's hand. She couldn't help herself, and she looked at him and whispered, 'A real miracle'

He smiled at her. But, once again she felt there was something wrong. A worry entered her. Was, he regretting what had happened?

To cover her fear she chatted on. Telling them about Lady Gladwyn's house and how she and Sally were going to have to work from early morning till late at night to get the work done. It was as much to prove they could deliver on time as the fact that gentry was slow in paying that would be driving her, she told them.

'It'll work, I know it will. I'll make it work,' She said, as she finished her tale. 'Anyroad, that's enough about me goings on here. What's been happening back at Breckton? I s'pose as Bert's created some. Has he had a go at you both?'

They skipped over the incident that had happened just after she left as if it was nothing, but she knew what it must have been like and loved them both all the more for trying to ease her mind.

Their next news shattered that ease and sent a shiver of fear through her. Bert had been sacked! Oh God! He'd be looking for her as it was, but his time would've been limited, but now? He'd not rest until he'd found her, she was sure of that.

'That news has upset you hasn't it, love? We knew as it would, but we decided we had no choice, but to tell you. You're going to need to take care. I'm only sorry as you've already had contact with customers before me and ma could get over to you. We thought p'raps you could change your name or...'

'Change me name? Oh, on shop you mean? Well, I have, Jack. I mean, I haven't put a sign up or anything, as yet. But, I have registered business in Hattie's name. Bert knew nothing of Hattie. We've called shop, 'Frampton's Exclusive Frocks and Gowns.' I know as I'd always said as it'd be 'Madame Megan's' but, thinking on. That'd be daft.'

'And, you've not thought on changing your own name? What does Lady Gladwyn know you as?' Jack asked.

'I don't know as she knows me as anything. Her maid introduced me to her as Megan from Frampton's, but she'd not think on it. She never used it. Well, you know how top drawer are. They can talk to you without really talking to you. Why? Do you think it's important as no one knows me real name?'

'Yes, I think as it'd be best. I think as you should change your name completely, for business purposes...'

'But, why?'

He didn't answer her for a moment. She looked from him to Issy. Both seemed tense. Afraid even. They'd glanced at each other and then looked away quickly. 'What's wrong? What should I know? Issy? Jack?'

'It's Mrs Harvey. She's not back yet from her sisters, but I've heard tell she's coming back soon. She knows folk. Folk as you're dealing with, like this Lady Gladwyn, in fact, she's one of her closest friends. She's bound to tell her about you.'

'But, why are you worrying over her, Jack? I can't see her running to Bert to tell him. She probably don't even know as he exists. I think you're worrying over nothing, love.'

The look passed between them again. This time Issy's held a warning. The fear that clutched at her heart held a more sinister coldness than did the fear of Bert. This was the fear of the unknown. Whatever it was they were holding back held terror for her. *No. She was being silly. There was no chance in heaven or hell that these two would do that to her.*

'Look, lass, our worry is, if Mrs Harvey becomes a customer, right? Well then, her households going to know, at least them as deals with her clothes. And, you know as none of them can keep anything to themselves. They thrive on fact that its news about goings on up at the big house as keeps us all entertained. And, as most of them live in Miner's Row…'

'Oh God! You're right, I never thought about it like that, it was always a possibility I s'pose. Mind, it's not too late. Like I say. Lady Gladwyn'll not remember what I'm called.'

There was a silence for a moment and during it a thought occurred to her.

'Happen as I could stop all home visits. Make it a rule as clients come to me shop. Like they had to at Madam Marie's. Then, if Mrs Harvey does become a customer she won't expect me to go out to hers.'

'Well that might work, but is still has its worries.' Issy said.

'It needn't. I mean they never bring their maids shopping so that's not a worry. And thinking on it, it might turn out in our favour as you might have to pick up stuff when it's ready for her, Jack. Or at least you could warn me if someone was to come with you.'

'It sounds good, I know, but…'

I shouldn't worry, Jack, Mrs Harvey wouldn't recognize me if she saw me. I can only recall one occasion in me whole life that she looked at me. It was a funny look and it made me feel a bit of a shiver run through me body. It was as if she had a loathing of me. It was a long time ago. Just after we lost Ciss and me and you were sitting on step together, Issy. I couldn't understand it at the time and still can't. Though, I'd not thought on it till now.'

Jack once again draw in a deep breath. His discomfort seemed to have increased. *Why?*

'Anyroad, Bert losing his job might turn out for us, too. He'll probably just disappear down to Sheffield or somewhere he could get set on at a pit again.'

'Happen as you're right, lass. We're probably meeting trouble half way when it's not even travelling our road. But, we wanted you to be aware of the dangers.'

'Ta, Issy. I know. And, I'm glad as you've made me think on, but now stop worrying pair on you. Come on, times passing and you've to go in a bit. I don't want to spoil the last half hour thinking about Bert. He's in me past, and that's where he's staying.' She wished she felt inside how convincing she sounded outside.

Jack's hand curled round hers and a warmth entered her. All the talk of Bert had overshadowed what had happened between them. She squeezed his hand. It was going to be hard to say good-bye. Would she ever get used to it? And worse, how would she cope not knowing when she would see them again? And, her body asked, how would she keep her yearnings for Jack's love-making stilled?

***

The time for them to go came all too soon. Jack stood on the steps with Megan. Issy and Sarah were already in the car and Sally and Billy leant through the car windows talking to them.

'I need a few minutes with you, Megan. I need to say me good-byes in private.'

They drew back into the shop. He pulled her to him and held her. His face buried in her neck. 'Megan. Megan....' an anguished love croaked his voice. 'I'd never mean to hurt you ever, Megan. Not ever.'

He felt her stiffen.

'What is it, Jack? I feel as something isn't right. I know without you telling me that you'd not ever hurt me. Oh, me love, when can you come to me again? How soon? I can't bear to be apart from you.'

He skipped over her first question as if she hadn't asked it. How could he do any other?

'I don't know, love, it's not going to be easy. I've to be careful as I'd not be able to live with meself if I led Bert to you.' His heart heavy with guilt squeezed his chest tight. He knew her greatest danger was through his affair with Laura, but how could he tell her?

Johnson had been over to Hensal Grange to collect some things for Laura. It had surprised Jack that he'd not been instructed to take them to her, but after listening to Johnson, he'd known why. He'd told him all that had happened, how ill Laura had been at the cottage and how she'd taken on when she'd seen him kissing a woman in the sea at Bridlington.

All kinds of fears had attacked him since that day. Fear for Megan, fear of losing his job and home, fear for Sarah and his ma-in-law. And fear of Megan ever finding out. Oh God! He held her even tighter, his shame burned him. It'd been bad enough telling his ma-in-law, but he'd had to. He'd had to discuss what Johnson had said with somebody. She'd been shocked, but as ever she'd understood. Like him, her main worry had been for Megan and the danger this all posed her.

Megan stirred in his arms. 'Hey, you're crushing me bones, and well, you're getting me feelings going inside me.' She drew away from him.

'Oh, Megan. Megan.' He drew her near again. 'I'll work something out, lass. I promise. I'll be back soon. Somehow, I'll be back.'

Again she drew back from him. 'Come on, me love, they'll be shouting us. You need to calm yourself.' She took his hand then leant forward and kissed his cheek. 'Just hold on to my love. Hold it safe inside you. Touch it whenever you touch your heart, and we'll always be together.'

They walked back through the shop. They stood a moment together, not talking or holding and yet they were joined, as he knew they always would be.

The parting was happy, full of hugs and kisses and promises to see each other soon, but it didn't lessen his weight of guilt. *'What would Laura do? What would she do? Was the sacking of Bert part of her plan to get revenge? Or was he just being silly? Somehow, he didn't think so....'*

CHAPTER
FORTY-THREE

'Darling Laura, you look much better, how are you feeling?' Daphne held her at arms length and then hugged her to her.

'I'm loads better, darling. Two weeks in this clinic has done wonders for me. My breathing is fine now and I'm eating well. I'm nearly finished packing, so we needn't hang around for too long.'

'Charles is just having a word with the doctor. He wants to know how long before all your results are in. The shadow they found on your lung is very worrying, but hopefully now your infection has cleared, your last X-rays will show that it has gone.'

'Oh, I'm sure it has. I've hardly coughed for a few days now. I'm eager to get home and deal with some important matters. One thing I've done while I've been in isolation this last two weeks is think, and it's been good for me. I have a plan formulated in my head and I now need to get home and put it into action.'

'You don't mean you're going home straight away, dear? You can't, you're not strong enough. Come home with us, stay a week or so. Charles is talking about taking some time off and arranging a cruise for us, somewhere really hot. Now that would be lovely, wouldn't it?'

'It would, and I certainly won't rule that out, but as for staying with you, not possible. There is so much that needs my attention, both on a business and a personal level.'

'Hello, old thing'

'Charles! Come in. Don't stand there with your head poked round the door like that. You look silly! Oh, it's good to see you. I'm going to need someone sensible to help me with this sister of mine.'

'Come here first and give me a hug. You look... well? Better. A lot better, my dear, but you've a long way to go, and I expect Daphne has been trying to persuade you to take it easy? Thought so. I told you, my darling, that you would do no good. Now, now, I'm not going to start a fight with you. I know you mean well and you're right in everything you say, but if I know Laura, and don't forget, I've been in the ring with her when it comes to arguments about what she should or shouldn't do, she's having none of it. Am I right?'

'Yes, you're right. But, I'm not all for saying no to everything. That cruise sounds good and you could do with a rest yourself, Charles. So don't let me stop your plans on that one. But, I have so much to see to. You understand don't you? You know I have such a lot going on. The Byron contract's going to be the saving of me, and I've a lot to put into place for it to happen on time. There's recruiting of experienced men for a start, then accommodation for them. I need some good men in place to oversee the installation of the cutting machines, so that has to take priority and...'

'Hey! Hold on, old thing, you're making me feel exhausted just listening to you. Look, I can take some time, how about Daphy and I come with you, that way I can help you with it all.'

'It's not that simple, Charles, I ... I have some personal things to see to. I need to straighten out my life. I've been silly. Well, Daphy knows what I mean. So it's better that I go home alone and sort it all whilst I'm feeling so well. You are only at the end of a telephone line if I need some advice. Besides, if the worse comes to the worse and I need prolonged treatment, I can have it knowing everything is ticking over well, both in my business and my private life.'

'You know, she has a point, Daphne. What do you say, darling?'

'Oh, all right. But, you will contact us if you need the slightest help, won't you?'

'Yes, of course, darling.'

Charles left them then to go in search of Johnson.

'Darling, how are you really? I mean, well, you know, about... well, that chauffeur of yours, and that awful business of seeing him with another woman?'

'I'm all right about it. At least I think I can handle it. How did I let such a thing happen, Daphy? I feel such an idiot. But, I fell in love with him. I know, I can't believe it myself, but it's true. There's no future in it I know that, and it looks like he's fallen for someone else anyway.'

'He's a cad! No, that's not right. A man of his class cannot be called a cad, but, Oh, I don't know. What do the lower classes call men like him?'

'That's not fair really. Jack didn't ever commit to me. Oh, he said nice things and we were good together, but he always cautioned me about taking it all too seriously, and he was right. It's a pity we can't make our feelings behave to order.'

'I'm so relieved, darling. You seem to be well in control. You'll be fine. Look, just do one thing for me. Stay a couple of nights. I've got something organized for tomorrow night. Nothing big. Only, Charlotte Gladwyn rang. She and Derek are going to be in York and I've asked them to dinner. She can't wait to see you. Now you're set on going home, we could arrange for them to drop you off. At least then you won't have to see Fellam too soon and you will have company on the drive. What do you say?'

'All right, if it will make you happy. It will be nice to see Charlotte. I haven't seen her for ages. And no, I'm not yet ready to see Jack.'

She'd pulled that off well, she thought. Daphy seemed quite happy now, and the coast was going to be clear when she got home. It shouldn't take much to pull Jack back in line. This was only a hitch she was sure of it. That woman would be out of the way in less than two weeks and if she put a threat on Jack of him losing his job and home, he'd be sure to want to carry on with how things were. After all, he'd enjoyed it as much as she had.

Finding something to wear the next evening proved a problem, but she eventually settled on one of the frocks that belonged to her niece.

Daphne's daughter had had her coming out ball the year before and was now enjoying a year in Europe with her twin brother. She was the same height as herself, but tinier in build so the frock fitted perfectly,

Examining herself in the mirror had been a painful experience. She needed to put the weight back on that she'd lost. And, she needed to feel stronger! Her mind was strong, but she tired so quickly.

'Are you ready, darling, can I come in? Oh, you look lovely. No, don't look like that, you do. I think Charlotte and Derek are going to be pleasantly surprised, They've been very worried about you.'

'Is that the truth of why they've come all this way? Oh don't bother denying it Daphy. You've been scheming I can see that. You and Charlotte are as bad as each other. I don't know why I love you both so much. Well, her anyway, I suppose I've got to love you.'

'Come on, we're not up to anything, I promise.'

'No? I'll believe that when I see it. If this isn't a dummy run for something bigger, then I don't know you two as well as I think I do.'

The evening had gone well and they'd retired and left the men to their port when the 'not up to anything', surfaced.

'You know, darling, you look really lovely. I think it suits you. Being thinner, I mean. It shows your lovely bone structure to its best advantage.'

'Come off it, Charlotte, you know I look awful.'

'You don't, darling, really! You should socialize more, we all miss you, and there are one or two interesting men on the scene at the moment...'

'Uh, Uh, here it comes!'

311

'No, really, darling, it's nothing we've planned. But, it won't hurt to enjoy yourself and have a look at what's around. It must be lonely on your own.'

'Yes, it is, but I've no time and I'm not up to doing the rounds at the moment. Anyway, I shouldn't think there's anything interesting going on until the winter season, and I couldn't stand the intimacy of a dinner party. Not with strangers there. All that polite conversation! No. Count me out,'

'Aahh, but that's where you're wrong. You remember Lord Fennington died, oh, about two years ago now? Well his eldest, John, didn't outlive him by many months and so the younger one, David, has come back from France. He married a French aristocrat. Anyway, it appears he is a widower with one son, and is now the new Lord. He's about your age, handsome and well set up, and they say he has started to accept invitations. Jocelyn Withers has taken it on herself to introduce him to everyone. She's giving a late summer ball in about three weeks time and...'

'No. No. And, it's no use you two ganging up on me either, I'm not fit enough yet to think of attending a ball, and you're not going to match make me with this Lord David Fennington, or anyone else for that matter! I knew you had something up your sleeve. You're incorrigible. Both of you.'

'Oh, I see, so you're fit enough for business, but not pleasure?'

'Daphy, that's below the belt and you know it. Besides, I've nothing to wear, nothing fits me, and I'm not going in one of Teresa's coming out gowns. Everyone will recognize it. And, you can pretend all you want to. I know that nothing will look good on me. I'm too thin.'

'Aahh, but I have an answer to that. You'll never believe it but I've found myself a new dressmaker! No, not an expensive London one. It's a new place just opened in Leeds. And, wait for this! The woman who is designing for me used to work for Madam Marie! Anyway, her designs are exquisite, and her materials are out of this world. And the best bit is; they are not expensive! In fact, I've ordered a whole new winter outfit... What's the matter darling? Are you all right? Laura?'

'I... I'm all right. I'm just tired. I'll go up now, Daphy, if you don't mind. It's early days for me yet. But, I will go to Jocelyn's ball, Charlotte, and I will treat myself to a new outfit from... What did you say this woman's name was?'

'Oh, I can't remember...Oh, wait a minute. I wrote it down. Megan. Megan of Frampton's. That's it. I don't know if she's the only designer they have, but as she is so good I made a note of her name. Yes. Here it is. I'll tell you what. I'll telephone you in a couple of days and arrange to pick you up and bring you over to mine. I'll arrange for her to come over as well and bring some swatches and designs and things. We'll have a lovely day picking and choosing something for you. How's that, darling?'

'That would be wonderful, thanks, Charlotte. 'Megan, you say? May I see? Hum, Coppery Street, Bramley? Well I never! 'Frampton's of Bramley.' Quite a posh name for...I mean, well...'

'I know, and this Megan is part owner of it. Though, it beggars belief where she got her money from she's very low class. It would be interesting to find out. In fact, Madame Marie must have had her work cut out getting the woman to such a high standard. Why she took her on is a mystery. I thought she only took on middle class girls whom at least had had an education.'

'No, I recommended a girl from my estate. She took her on and she did very well by all accounts. Now, you'll have to excuse me, darling. Say night, night to Derek and Charles for me.'

'I'll see you up, darling. Oh dear, you're trembling. Here take my arm.'

'Thanks, Daphy, I do feel shaky.'

It took a while to convince Daphy she would be all right, but eventually she found herself on her own. To her amazement tears began to stream down her face as soon as the door was closed. So she'd done it! It must be her! It was too much of a coincidence. The name, Megan! And, having worked at Madame Marie's! Oh, God! That woman was all set up and away from Bert Armitage. Just what Jack had wanted to happen! She'd surely lose him now? How could she keep him? If she sacked him, he'd have somewhere to go, and he'd soon find work in Leeds. All her planning had been to no avail. Although? Wait a minute. What about, Armitage? Surely he wouldn't take all this lying down? Not from what she'd heard of him he wouldn't. What if she was to make sure he found out where his wife was?

The tears dried, and she rubbed a weary hand over her face. Her head ached and her chest felt tight. No! She mustn't be ill again. There was so much to do. So much...

**

Once home Laura found that most of what had seemed like a huge burden during her illness turned out to be simple to achieve. Her manager had already done most of it. He'd found there was a huge number of very skilled men on the market, so the hiring had been easily achieved. Dealing with the union, though, had proved to be a hard task, and costly, as she'd had to agree to meet the cost of relocating the men she'd sacked. And then, there was Jack.

She'd decided she would ignore his presence while she sorted herself out. She needed a scheme. She needed him to need her. To rely on her totally as he was used to doing, that way he'd do as she bid. But, whilst he had that slut waiting to give him a home, what chance did she stand?

It had been planned that her manager was to pay off the men who were to go. But, she decided she'd have to be there, it was the perfect opportunity, and the only one she was going to get. She'd give out the payments herself and speak to each one. She'd have to have the proceedings take place in her own office at Hensal Grange as, not only did she not feel well enough to venture out to the office, but that would have meant Jack driving her and she definitely wasn't ready for that yet.

When the actual time arrived, Laura didn't feel so confident. Her stomach twisted with nerves. Could she pull it off without anyone knowing she was doing it deliberately? But then, it wasn't just Armitage, it was the whole thing. These men had been working loyally for many years for the company. Many started in her father-in-law's day. Suddenly it seemed like a betrayal, and she wished she was anywhere but in this room waiting to face them.

Thank goodness she had been able to put Charlotte off for a couple of weeks. Seeing Megan Armitage would have made her task a little too personal. By the time the appointed day came around again everything would hopefully be sorted one way or the other, if not...No, there was no, 'if'. Her plan would succeed...

Five men had been in front of her when she heard his name. It was turning out to be more of an ordeal than she'd anticipated and one she could have saved herself from if it wasn't for this bloody business of getting rid of that woman!

He was in front of her, and he looked nothing like she expected, he was a strong looking individual. And he had a power about him, an evil power. She shuddered and took a deep breath.

'Well now, I'm here for two purposes, Armitage. One is to express my regret at how progress at Hensal Grange Colliery has unfortunately meant some of you lost your jobs. And, the other is to give you a resettlement payment which I think you will find very generous, and should tide you over for a while. Have you found another position?' She knew he hadn't.

'No, Ma-am'

'You have somewhere to go, I take it?'

His look darkened. Her nerves enhanced to fear.

'Only on the road, and I'll not stand here talking to you, so you can pretend as you bloody care! I'll take me pittance and be off.'

Out of the corner of her eye she saw her manager move. She put her hand up to stay him.

'But, surely you will be going to your wife? I hear she has a nice little place in Coppery Street, in Leeds. I was quite surprised and pleased to hear that one of my tenants had done so well, and that, it had come at such a time when you most needed it. I imagined that it was all planned that way, I...'

The sound of a sharp intake of breath from behind her, interrupted her, she turned and looked at her manager. She feigned a worried expression. 'Have I said something wrong?'

Armitage's raised voice brought her attention back to him.

'What does you mean, a place? What bloody place? And, how come as you knows of it?'

She let her voice falter, 'I...I'm, well, I didn't realize. Perhaps I shouldn't have spoken of it, I...'

He leant forward, his hands on the desk in front of her. He stared straight at her. His blackened evil soul exposed in the depth of his eyes. Her body trembled with the knowledge of her own self. The self, deep in her own soul that had prompted her to do what she'd just done. Oh God! What if he killed Megan? She hadn't thought it to be a reality. Knock her back into line maybe, but now? She wasn't sure. Her legs would hold her no longer. She sank back into her seat.

'I asked you a question, Miss High and Bloody Mighty. What place?'

'That's enough, Armitage. Get out of here. You've got your money.' The Manager stepped forward and faced him squarely.

'I'm not going until she tells me what she knows of me wife and her doings.'

Once more she found herself looking into those black evil eyes. But, she'd composed herself. She may as well tell him, if only to get rid of him. She stood up. 'It's a ladies fashion shop on Coppery Street. Its called, Frampton's, or something like that, Now leave this office at once or we'll call the police.'

He glared at her for a few seconds. His body trembled. His mouth opened and then closed again and then he turned and slammed out of the office.

Her manager looked at her with concern. She sat down, happy in the knowledge that her distress looked as real as it had been a few minutes ago.

'Well! What was all that about? How come he didn't know his wife had set up a shop in Leeds?'

'She'd left him, Ma-am. No one knew where she was. Mind, I'm surprised to hear as she's set herself up like you say. How's she managed that I wonder? Well! Well! Any road, I'm glad for her, but God knows as to what'll happen now Armitage knows of her whereabouts. As thou knows, Ma-am, he gave her a pitiful life afore, but now as she's dared to leave him...'

She looked at him, feigning ignorance.

'You asked specifically for him to be one of the men to go, as you'd heard of his cruelty to his wife.'

'Aahh, yes, I remember, so that was him? And, now I've told him where his wife is. Oh dear! I never dreamt he didn't know. After all, she told a friend of mine that she'd achieved her success by making clothes here and saving the money. How could she have managed that without her husband knowing?' *Jack would rue the day he'd given her this knowledge.* Well, at least he'd learn a valuable lesson. And he'd never, ever cross her again.

'She must have managed it without anyone knowing, because it's first as I've heard of it and there's not much as goes on that I don't to get to hear of. Well, I never!'

'Oh well, what's done is done. She'll probably take him back, they always do. Shall we continue? Who's next?'

***

The banging on the door startled Issy out of her nap. 'What? Who is it?' Before she could rise from her chair the door was opened.

'It's me, Issy, Oh, love, I've bad news for you!' Gertie could hardly catch her breath.

'What is it? What's happened? Sarah? Jack?'

'No, love, it isn't none of them, it's Megan. He knows. Bert Armitage. He knows where Megan's at. Mrs Harvey told him when she gave resettlement money out. Oh, I'll have to sit down.' She pulled one of the chairs out from under the table. 'It all beggars belief! She's in Leeds! And, it's said as she has a shop! How did she manage that?'

'Never mind that now. Oh Megan! Poor Megan. Has Bert gone? Does Jack know?'

'Yes, talk is as Bert went straight to station. When I was told I went over to see Henry to see what he knew. He told me as he was stood

316

talking to Jack in the garage when the Manager of the Mine came out of the house and told them what'd happened. Henry said Jack took off in Mrs Harvey's car like as if the world was on fire!'

'Oh, Dear God! What am I to do, Gert?'

'Happen as you're best leaving it to Jack. He'll get there about same time as Bert, and hopefully sooner. He'll not let him hurt her I'm sure of that.'

'No, I've got to do something, look, Gert, I'm going to Dr. Cragshaw, and I'm going to ask him to take me over there. I'll beg him if I have to. Emotions are too high for Jack. He's in love with Megan...'

'What? Jack...? And Megan...? No!'

'I know, I know. It isn't right, but it is how it is. Neither of them planned it. And, they'd not do anything as'd bring me and young-uns into shame. But, now Bert will know and it was bad enough thinking on what he'd do to her just on her leaving him. But, when he realises as how there's someone else for her, and who that someone else is! It don't bear thinking on.'

'Well! I never dreamt! And, you know where Megan's at?'

'Never mind that now, will you help me, Gert? Will you see to Sarah when she comes in?' Gert was nodding. 'Mind, don't tell her anything, nor no one else for that matter.'

'I wouldn't... I.'

'Now then, Gert. No offence, but like me, you likes a snippet. 'An exclusive' as papers call it. But, I also knows as you don't use anything you know in malice. So think on. You know what this'll do to Sarah. I want no shame bringing down on her. Right?'

'I'll not say nothing, I promise, Issy. Now go on, and go as fast as you can! Oh God! I hope as Doctor'll take you and you get there in time. I dread to think what'll happen if Bert realizes what you've just told me!'

CHAPTER
FORTY-FOUR

'Mam... Mam... Ma..a..a.am!'

'What? What is it, Billy? Have you hurt yourself? Have you been stung? Calm down, love. Tell me what's wrong...?'

'I've... I've just seen me dad! He's coming, Mam... He's coming up street!'

Terror gripped Megan. It tightened her throat and threatened to strangle the life from her. Her legs gave way. She sank back on the chair she'd just risen from.

'Mam? Mam... Mam... I... I'm scared...!'

Billy's fear wrenched her from her own.

'Sally, close the door! Quick, lass! Lock it and put all bolts in place. Billy... Billy.' She stood up and took him by the shoulders. 'Run upstairs, get some money out of me purse and get yourself out of the back door. Take the key and lock it from outside and get yourself over to Hattie's. Go on, lad. Hurry! Hu...'

'Get out of me fucking way! I'm here to see me so-called wife!'

Megan turned. Saw Sally being shoved to the floor by Bert. But, before she could react a piercing scream of terror filled every space of the room. It crushed all movement and froze her body. She was in a cold cocoon, wherein, the only knowledge she had, was the fear of her own imminent death.

'Stop that fucking racket, you bloody little wimp!'

The vicious push Bert had given Billy sent him reeling backwards. His arm raised above the cowering boy. His belt coiled round his fist. The glinting of the buckle caused Megan to come out of the cold fear that had held her.

'No!' She sprang forward, placing herself between Bert and Billy. A tearing pain ripped through her. Her cry of agony joined by Bert's cry of pain. Sally had sunk her teeth into his leg.

'You, fucking bitch!' His movement was swift. His body twisted. The buckle whipped through the air. Sally moved but she wasn't quick enough. The buckle caught her and a gaping raw gash appeared on her head. Her body crumpled.

Releasing the breath the stinging pain had held in her, Megan lunged forward. Bert's boot lifted and was aimed at Sally's head. He didn't find his mark. Instead his body fell heavily, unbalanced by the force of the hold Megan managed to get on his raised leg.

In a flash she was sitting on him. Beating his vile, hated face with her fists. 'You, bastard! You, bloody bastard!'

The spittle ran down her chin. The pain of years oozed from her. She grabbed his hair and banged his head on the floor. 'No more! Do your hear me? No more!'

In one swift movement he twisted his body and unseated her. Before she could right herself he was up and standing over her. The arm she put up to protect herself ripped open as it caught the full thrust of the lashing. 'No…No..o..o.o.o!'

'I'll give you fucking, NO! You, scum! You, fucking whore!'

She tried to crawl away. The buckle stung her buttocks. The stinging unbearable pain took the breath from her. The smarting of her back as another blow caught her drew that breath back, only to be released with an agonized cry, as more crushing blows bore down on her, 'Oh God! Oh God! Help me. HELP.. M..E..E..EEE!'

'You're rotten, Megan Armitage! Fucking rotten through and through! You'll do no more to me, you cow!'

She kicked out, caught his shin, causing him to step back. Using everything she could muster, she scrambled away and managed to stand and face him. Her own broken spirit mocked her. Reduced her to a whimpering begging animal, 'Please no more…I…I'm sorry I left you. I…I'll come back... I'll do anything, anything as you want of me, but…'

'Back? Back to what? I've got nothing. Nothing! Does you hear me? I'm on streets…me family gone. You fucking left! And I thought when I come home me trip to Blackpool would be all sorted! You cruel bitch!'

He sprang forward. She had no escape. His arm was around her neck. She couldn't breathe!

'I'm going to kill you!'

Her body hit the floor. She was nothing…nothing... The flailing of her was his right.

Her blood squirted into her eyes and her mouth. It mixed with her tears and her snot. Her agony drummed in her ears and filled her mind, blocking out all that was human. No begging, no praying… Nothing. She was the vilest of creatures…

***

Jack slammed on his brake. The barrel boomed down the cobbled road towards him. It'd happened, just a few yards in front of him. The car that had hit the dray had seemed to come from nowhere. The horses hadn't stood a chance. The dray had overturned spilling its load of barrelled beer.

Just as it seemed the barrel would hit him head on it veered and the passenger side of the car caved in. The noise deafened Jack. His shock held him suspended.

'Are you all right, Man? Can you get out?'

Jack looked at the policeman unable to take in what he was saying.

'Are you hurt, Man?

Jack shook his head. That such a thing should happen, but he'd not let it delay him, he couldn't. He got out of the car.

'Hey, where do you think as you're off to...'

'I'm all right. I'm not hurt. Look, Constable, I can't stay...I've got to get to Coppery Street...'

'You're going no-where, Mister. You're the only witness. I need a statement from...'

'No! I must go...I must... Me lass is in great danger. Her life depends on me... Please... I'll come to station to give evidence...Please!'

'What're you talking of, Man? Happen shock's playing tricks with you. You can't leave the scene of an accident. Now. What's your name?'

'Jack, Jack Fellam...I'll be in touch....'

'Hey! Come back here...Well I...!'

Jack's body took on the challenge. His legs gained a speed he'd not dreamt of. He was so near. So near...

As he turned the corner he could see the shop door. It was closed. He sent up a prayer, *'Please God let me be in time...'*

'What the..? Jack Fellam! You bastard! You knew all along where she was! Well, I'll do the two of you in one go. Come on then, big fella. Let's see how big you are with no ma to defend you.'

'Jack... Jack? Megan could only mouth the words. Some comfort came into her.

Jack and Bert both leapt at once. Their bodies landed near to her. Her bench crashed to the floor. An echoing loud boom filled her head. The paraffin stove was on its side! Flames flared. Snaked round her workbench. In seconds her rolls of material were alight. Horror engulfed her. Her throat stretched, but no sound came.

Through the swirl of smoke she could see Bert on top of Jack. His fist reining blows down onto his face. He couldn't defend himself. His arms were trapped, one under his own body, the other pinned down by Bert's knee.

'Please God, help him!'

The heat was unbearable. She turned her head to where Billy had fallen. He wasn't in the path the flames were taking. She looked over to Sally. 'Oh God!' The flames were all around her! She crawled on her stomach. The swirling smoke choked her. Stinging tears streamed from her. But, somehow she managed to reach Sally and with every ounce of her being, drag her to the door. Once her head was outside, she had to give up. Had to go back and get Billy.

Billy was on his feet. He was holding something. Through her tears it looked like a huge menacing hammer. 'No, lad... No!' There was no voice for her to use. The smoke smarted her throat and stung her nostrils. A blessed blackness took her into its peace.

***

'You leaning forward isn't going to get us there any quicker, Issy. Rest back, woman.'

'Aye. I know, but I'm scared with every bone in me body.'

'And, with good reason to be.' Doctor Cragshaw shook his head. 'I've not taken in all you've told me yet. It was bad enough Megan upping sticks and leaving. Talk was rife then, though it was tempered by the fact as folk were glad for her. But, Her and Jack! That's not going to be accepted. Folk are going to be on Bert's side. Even those as despise him. If he murders the pair of them it'll be said as he was justified!'

'I know, Philip lad, I know...But, what can I do? I know what you're saying. It isn't right, but...well, they both deserve some happiness.'

'I'm, Doctor Cragshaw now, Issy, not Philip. I know, that sounds pompous but it took me a long time to get the older generation to accept me as their doctor, me being a local lad. But, like you say they both do deserve some happiness and in other circumstances, yes, I can see them together and would be the first to wish them luck. But, I can't as things are, much as I'd like to. I'd be hounded out of my job. Medical Council would...'

'Take it as understood, Doctor. And, I'm sorry me use of your first name offended you, but try as I might, I can't get the cheeky lad as you used to be out of me head, that don't mean as I don't respect you. I respect you more than anyone I know, you getting your scholarship and doing so well. And, anyroad, what you've done today in bringing me will be seen as you going to help your patients. After all, that's what they all are, and I've fetched you to them because they're all in danger. Right?'

'Well, put like that. Yes. I'm only doing my duty. Now then, which way do I go from here? We're in Bramley now.'

'Turn here. Yes, I'm sure it's....'

As they turned into Coppery Street, Doctor Cragshaw slammed on his brakes. 'Oh, No! Is that Megan's place?' He didn't wait for her to answer. 'Stay here, Issy!'

Issy stared in horror at the flames and smoke belching out of every window of the building. Her fear surged her forward. She was out of the car and by the doctor's side in a flash. 'I'm coming with you. Oh, God!' She looked around her, 'There's no car, Jack can't have got here, he...'

The clanging bells drowned her words. A fire engine screeched to a halt in front of them. Two ambulances followed behind.

'Stand back now. Come on everyone, out of the way.'

'I'm a doctor...Dr Cragshaw. I'm from Breckton and I know the owner of the shop. Is everyone out of the building, do you know?'

'I've had no time to check that, Doc, having only just arrived.' The policeman answered, 'I was seeing to another accident and fella as witnessed it ran off. Said his lass was in danger in Coppery Street. I come as quick as I could and...'

'Oh, God, Doctor, there's Jack coming out...He's on fire...Oh, my God! Jack...Jack'

One of the fire officer's leapt from the engine and sprinted across the road taking off his jacket as he did so and in seconds had Jack on the floor and had smothered him.

'I couldn't reach...'

'It's ok, Man. It's all in hand. Don't worry yourself...Doctor quick. Over here!'

The Doctor was just behind him as was Issy. Jack's body was trembling from head to toe. It was impossible to see how badly he was injured as black soot covered all that was visible of him.

'Oh, Jack, Jack love...'

'All right, Issy, leave him to me.'

Issy stood as if in a trance. She looked from the blackened body of Jack to where an ambulance man was working on Megan and it seemed as her world was coming crashing down around her.

'There's another bloke still inside!'

The shout from the fire officer brought her back to reality. Her decision was made in seconds. She could trust Philip with Jack, but she was to see as the ambulance men knew as what they were doing with Megan then take care of the young-uns. She looked over at them. They were sat huddled together. Sally, her face covered in blood sat with her head resting on Billy's her arm around his shoulder. Billy was in a daze. His eyes stared out into nowhere and his body trembled all over.

***

It was two days later that Jack woke. At first he thought he'd had a nightmare, but then his pain gave him the truth of it. 'Megan, Megan…Where…'

'It's all right, Jack. Stay calm. You're in hospital.'

'Doctor, Megan's hurt…'

'I know. Now, I'm here to examine you, Jack. I've just…'

'Is Megan…?

Doctor Cragshaw shook his head, 'I'm sorry, Jack, so sorry, but things look badly for Megan. I can't honestly say she'll survive. It's suspected that there may be internal injuries and there's a very real risk that she'll develop pneumonia. She's very weak from loss of blood. Her injuries are … Well, I've never seen the like. To think as a man could do such a thing to a woman, well anybody come to that.'

Jack sank into himself. His eyes closed. He swallowed hard to try to stop the stinging tears, but they seeped through and ran freely down his face.

Dr. Cragshaw took hold of his hand. 'You've been through a lot, Jack…' He hesitated, and then, took a deep breath. 'I'm afraid there's more, though. I'm here at the request of the police.' He turned and for the first time Jack saw two men standing behind him. 'These men here are detectives. I'm to check you over to see if you are well enough to answer some questions.'

'Questions? Can't they wait? I know I'll have to sort things out, I left an accident just afore I got to Megan, but I had to. I was only just in time as it was. Is Billy and Sally all right? And ma? I saw ma with you.'

'Billy and Sally are going to be fine. Sally has a nasty gash on her head and they're both in shock, especially Billy, he seems unable to speak at the moment. But, that's a natural reaction to the horror he witnessed. And Issy? Well, you know Issy. She has some friends supporting her. Hattie and Harry, I think she said their names were.'

'Oh, thank God. Hattie'll take care of them all.'

'Yes, she's an odd looking character, but she has a kindness and a level head on her. Now, roll over, Jack, I need to check your dressings. You were very lucky. Your burns are only superficial and you seem to have suffered very little from the smoke. Although, how you managed

324

that, I don't know, seeing as you made several trips back into the building and managed to catch your clothes on fire!'

'I only went back in once. Sally was already by the door. And, Billy could hop along whilst holding on to me and I carried Megan at the same time. When I went back for Bert, flames'd blocked me return. I held me breath and tried to get through but...'

'That's why you're to be questioned. You see Bert... Well, he didn't come through it, and it wasn't fire or smoke as killed him...'

'We'll take over now, thank you, Doctor. Now then, Mr Fellam. It was a bad night's work what with fire and cruel beating as lass took. But, more seriously than that. A man is dead and he didn't die from natural causes, neither. So, what light can you throw on that matter, Sir?'

'I...I don't know, I mean... What killed him? I tried to get him out... I couldn't reach him...the smoke...the fire... How did he die?'

'Couldn't reach him? Or didn't want to because you knew he was already dead, ay? Knew blows as you landed him had done him. Isn't that how it was? Nice and convenient if his body was burned up and no evidence to trace. Isn't that what really happened, ay?'

'No! No...'

The larger of the two men who hadn't spoken till now moved forward and sat on the end of the bed.

'It must have been a terrible scene, lass being beaten, young-uns crying and scared, and the man causing it all, half crazed, capable of anything? No one would blame you. What did you use? And, what happened to the weapon?'

Jack didn't answer. Billy's face and the evil intention he'd seen flashed into his mind. Oh God! Billy had killed his dad! Aye, and meant to, an all...Oh God!

'You and lass having an affair, was you? Nice and convenient to have her husband out of the way, ay? And, if body can burn, an all... Well, the perfect crime...'

'No!'

What then? Young lass wasn't one as you went to save was she? Oh, we know you went there intentionally to save someone, you told policeman at the accident scene. In a state you was. Desperate...'

'I...No... Not Sally...Megan. She'd left Bert... He found out where she was. He was going to kill her... I had to stop him...'

'It wasn't enough just to restrain him though, was it? Most would say as he was in his rights. His missus got what was coming to her... That is except you, Fellam. You had other motives. Saw an opportunity, didn't you? Kill him. Get him out of the road and set fire to cover up

325

your crime. And, all under the guise of wanting to save this Megan. Your mistress! Folk'd see you as a hero and the path would be clear...'

'We... we fought. Paraffin heater got toppled. It was an accident...'

'Oh, no! Bloke wasn't killed by accident or as a result of fighting, nor fire. It was blows you landed. Remember? Vicious blows to back of his head. Blows that were meant to kill him...'

'I didn't mean to kill him...just stop him...he was raging... I couldn't get better of him...I didn't mean....'

'Jack Fellam. I am arresting you for the murder of Albert Armitage. You don't have to say anything...'

Jack didn't register what the detective said to him after the first statement. Fear and shock held him rigid and gave him thoughts that intensified his terror. My God, I could be hanged! Megan...Megan, oh God! He looked over to where the doctor was. Saw the look of horror on his face... 'I didn't mean to, Doctor, I...'

Doctor Cragshaw shook his head, 'Oh, Jack, no! No!'

PART SEVEN

THE COPING

CHAPTER
FORTY-FIVE

The clanging of the prison gates grated on Jacks nerves. Each set he went through underlined his dread. He was being taken to the visitor's room. Doctor Cragshaw was waiting to see him. *Please God, don't let him be coming with bad news.*

But then, why else would he be allowed to visit? They'd not allowed any visitors since he'd been formally charged with Bert's murder. They'd said it was on account that all the folk who could visit him were witnesses, or in the case of Hattie, she was refused because she had the witnesses staying with her.

'Jack. How are you, Man.?'

'I don't know to tell the truth, Doctor. I'm in a kind of trance most of the time. I can't feel anything or think on things.'

'That'll be the shock. It's a funny thing is shock. It can in some ways protect us from what we have to face.'

'What do I have to face, Doctor? Have you come with news? Is Megan...'

'Megan's doing well. She's out of hospital and is at her friend, Hattie's house, and as you can imagine she is being looked after well by Issy and Hattie and there are two women living in a flat at the back who seem to know Megan and Issy well and are helping. And, of course, Megan is helping her own recovery. She's a very strong and determined young woman and wants to get better so that she can support you. In fact, she's shocked us all in how quickly she is getting better. Not to say she hasn't still a long way to go, but she will win through.'

'Oh thank, God! Thank, God.' He sank into the chair and put his head into his hands. He'd not cried since he'd been in this awful place. But now, it was as if he was a babby. Sobs racked his body.

'Let it all out, Jack. It'll do you good. Help you to break free of the shock and help you to make decisions about your future.'

'How can I do that? Me future isn't in me own hands.'

'Yes it is. Look, I haven't got long. I am meant to assess you medically. But, I came chiefly to give you news, and in my opinion, you knowing what is going on will help your health, especially your mental health.'

'Thank you, Doctor. Tell me how everyone is.'

'I'll not go into detail...' The Doctor told him how everyone was coping as best they could and that the young-uns had been told he was away at work, so as not to worry them.

'...Billy is worrying us all. He hasn't spoken a word since it happened. It's the shock, as I said it can affect us in different ways. But, Sarah is paying him a lot of attention and looking after him like he was a babby. I'm just leaving him alone at the moment. His physical health is fine. These things often resolve themselves with time.'

This news gave him mixed feelings. Part of him was glad the lad wasn't having to face the truth of what he'd done, *but what that meant for himself didn't bear thinking on....*

'I have other news,' The Doctor continued. 'And, I need you to give me your agreement to it. Mrs Harvey...'

'I want nothing to do with HER! She caused all this. She is the real murderer! Only it was Megan as she'd wanted to see dead.'

'Listen, Jack. She is what she is. Aye, I know the whole story. And, you're right, this was her doing. Though, I'm going to speak straight. You know that's my nature. You, Jack, must shoulder some of the responsibility. Lady Crompton tells me that Laura fell in love with you and you knew and didn't take her feelings into account. In the eyes of her family, you dropped her without as much as a, by-your-leave and went on to your next conquest.'

'What!'

'I'm not here to judge one way or the other. But, from what I have heard you were very insensitive to Laura's feelings. If you knew as she'd fallen for you. You should've been more of a gentleman in how you let her down. And, you weren't being fair on Megan either. Well, I needn't say anymore. The price has been paid as I see it. And now, we've to deal with the mess that has been caused.'

Jack couldn't speak. His guilt hit him like a punch in his stomach. The doctor was right! He did know Laura was getting in deep. He should've talked to her. Written to her. Warned her where his true feelings were. God! He was guilty! He was as guilty of Bert's murder as he would've been if he'd rained the blows on his head himself!

'Well, as I see it, Jack. You're getting a bit of luck. Lord and Lady Crompton are anxious that Laura isn't caused anymore harm. She is quite ill. The shock of what her actions caused, especially what has happened to you, has caused her to collapse. It is confirmed as she has TB of the lung. She is going to Switzerland where she will have the best chance of getting better. Though, in my opinion her chances are very slim. Lord Crompton has asked me to speak with you. He wants to keep Laura's name out of all this. He has asked if you will allow them to pay for a very good lawyer to act on your behalf.'

Jack stiffened inside. Laura had done what she'd done because she was a woman crossed. Aye, he'd played his part. But, the part he'd played hadn't deserved all this. Not for Megan it hadn't.

'Jack, if you're thinking of refusing. Think on. You need help.'

'But, how can anybody defend me? All the evidence is against me.'

'Are you saying as you did it?'

'No! No, I'm not. But, who's going to believe me? I've had it, Doctor. I'm going to hang...'

'You mustn't think like that. Listen, Jack. A good lawyer will help. He might even be able to get the murder charge dropped and one of manslaughter put in its place. You'd only be facing around five years in prison, then. Be sensible, Man. Take the Crompton's offer. All they're asking is that Laura's name and her affair with you is kept out of it all.'

'And, you think that's right!'

'No, I don't as it happens, but if that can keep you from being hanged, then I'd go for it. I'd see it as right in them circumstances. Look, dragging it all out can only make things worse for you. Think about it. Think how it makes you look. Having an affair with your boss, then with another man's wife! It don't look good. Especially as the husband of the woman you had an affair with has been murdered and you are implicated! If I didn't know you and know you are not capable of such a despicable thing, I'd be the first to put the noose around your neck! So think on. Them as are dealing with you. Don't know you. If they get to hear the full story you WILL hang and make no bones about it!'

'All right. You're right. I have no choice. But, it don't sit easy with me.'

'Good. Never mind how it sits. It's your only hope. Now then, the lawyer is already engaged. He's the best. My solicitor knows of him...'

As the doctor told him of the lawyer Jack felt himself going into his own head. His emotions were churned between anger and despair. If only he could lie in Megan's arms and have it all not to have happened. Oh, Megan, me lass, will I ever see you again?

'...Anyway, he will be in to see you tomorrow. Tell him the whole truth, Jack. Don't leave anything out. Then, he will know what he is dealing with and how to deal with it. Thank God, you had the foresight to plead not guilty at your initial hearing. Your trial date isn't set as yet, though, as the police asked for more time. So, you'll meet this lawyer, then?'

'Aye, I'll meet him.'

'Good. Now, that's done, I can concentrate on contacting Bert's sister...'

'Bert's sister?'

'Yes. It's a funny tale. I don't mean funny in an amusing way. But, it turns out as Issy and I know Bert's sister, her name's Bridget Hadler. She was brought up in Breckton. There was a lot of to-do around the time her dad died. All sorts went on. You should get Issy to tell of it. I was only a young-un when it happened. Anyway, it seems as Bridget's mam married again and had Bert. I tried to contact Bridget as soon as it happened, but she and her husband were abroad on holiday. They will be back now. And, nothing is lost as Bert's body hasn't been released as yet. Megan had their address.'

'Megan knew?'

'Yes, but, she'd been sworn to secrecy, at least, where Issy was concerned. Bert didn't want any interference. Megan'd told Hattie, though, and we found the address amongst Megan's things.'

Jack had no time to ask any further questions. The prison officer opened the door of the room and announced that time was up.

'Well, Jack. Think on now, Man. And do as I say, tell the truth.'

Jack didn't answer this. He quickly gave the doctor messages for everyone, especially Megan.

As he was led back to his cell he thought; the truth! How could he ever tell the truth? The truth would kill Megan. Or at least kill all the life that is in her.

***

Jack Looked across the table at James Pellin. The man wasn't much older than himself! It beggared belief that he was a top lawyer of whom it was said could get the devil off a charge of arson if he'd a mind to. Or so Doctor Cragshaw had told him.

Pellin sat in silence. His piercing eyes lowered now. Jack felt a relief in him at that. It was like he could see your soul when he looked at you.

'You're lying, Jack.'

'I'm not. It's the truth. I'm telling you. I couldn't get the better of him. The fire was taking hold. I had to do something. I hit him. I picked up Billy's crutch and I hit him as hard as I could. I did it so as I could save the rest of them. We'd have all burned to death if I hadn't done it.'

'The only thing I believe about your story is the weapon. A crutch could've been used to kill Armitage. And, if you're not for telling me who it was that wielded it, then I have two options. One: I can go for self defence, but given the circumstances I can't see that holding up. Two: I can dig and dig until I find out the truth...' As he paused Jack felt again the feeling that his eyes were piercing his very soul.

'....And, that truth is not going to be that you killed Bert Armitage.'

Jack's body shook, he closed his eyes. His mind flashed the blunt heavy end of the crutch smashing down over and over.... His ears heard the sound, the terrible crunching sound and the moan as air was forced to leave Bert's lungs never to be drawn in again. But, he wouldn't let in the evil. Not the evil he'd seen in Billy. He shook his head and looked up at Pellin.

'Why? Why don't you believe as it was me?'

'Why? Because, I have this thing called intuition. And, that intuition is not letting me believe you. Now, which one was it?'

'It was me. I keep telling you...'

'You can tell me till you're blue in the face. My intuition tells me you probably will. Because, you are protecting someone you love and you are the kind of man that would go to the gallows rather than betray them. But, I won't give up on you, Jack. I'll find out the truth. Unfortunately, the only other two who know, can't remember the incident. But, they will. I'll have to get the Crompton's to cough up some more of their hush, hush, money to pay for psychiatric help for them.'

'Will you be able to keep Lau...Mrs Harvey's name out of all this?'

'I doubt it. I'll let them think so for a time. But, it doesn't matter one jot to me that they are paying. My loyalty is to you, Jack. As I believe you are innocent, I will use every bit of information I deem necessary to use, in your defence. Regardless of who may be hurt in the process! Besides, I may not have any choice. If it becomes apparent that the involvement of Mrs Harvey is crucial evidence I will have to share it with the prosecution. I'm duty bound to do so.' Pellin let out a heavy sigh. 'Jack, you are admitting to having killed a man! You had a motive for that killing. A motive that will be judged as premeditated. There can be only one sentence. YOU WILL HANG!'

Jack watched as Pellin wiped the sweat from his brow and around his neck. The handkerchief he used looked like it had never been used before. Funny that.

'Don't go away from me, Jack. Listen! Let it sink into you that you are going to be hung by the neck until you die! It isn't quick, Jack. You kick and kick! Your body swings. Your head swells. Please, Jack! Look. If it was Megan, I'd be able to get her off with self defence. She'd serve a minimum time. Or more than likely, no time at all, when what she has suffered is taken into account. If it was Billy, well, he's a minor. His mental state will be looked at. It will be considered if he knew his action would kill or not. Umpteen things will be taken into consideration and the worst that could happen is that he would be committed to an institution and helped to get better, then possibly in years to come will be rehabilitated. But, neither of them would die! Do you see what I am saying, Jack. Death is final.'

Jack made no reply, he couldn't. It all seemed so simple to Pellin. And yet, he knew that any of those outcomes would be too much for Megan to take.

'Look, I've done my best. But, this isn't the end. I am going with my gut feeling. I am going to do my best to prove I am right. In the meantime, there is a plea hearing tomorrow. We are going to stick with a, not guilty, plea. I'll see you tomorrow.'

'I don't want you to represent me...'

'Oh, don't try that one, because I'm telling you, it won't stop me digging and digging until I find the truth.'

As Pellin left and Jack was taken back to his cell, he felt out of control of everything. He couldn't contact anyone. He could do nothing. All he could do was hope. Hope that the Crompton's refused to pay for medical treatment for Billy and Megan so that they remained in the world where they had no recollection of the horror of what'd happened. And, he wished to God he didn't either.

***

The phone call was the best news they'd had. Doctor Cragshaw was with Hattie and Issy when the telephone had rung. James Pellin had asked for him. And now here he was telling them that Megan and Billy were to receive help.

'Look, on the face of it, it does sound good. But, this kind of therapy can take a long time to work. It isn't always the best idea to bring back the memory. It may cause worse problems, particularly in Billy's case. So we must all be prepared for that.'

'Shall we see what Megan says? She should be the one to decide.'

'Yes, Hattie, you're right.'

Whether the doctor thought she was right or not, she wasn't for anything happening that Megan didn't know of.

Megan was propped up by umpteen pillows. She looked pale and gaunt and yet managed a smile. The bruising around her eyes was receding and the blue- black colour was fading though her eyes were still very blood shot.

'How are you feeling today, Megan?'

'A little better, thanks, Doctor, but I'm right troubled. I need to know what is happening. Is there any news as yet from that lawyer? Does you think as he's seen Jack?'

'Yes, he has.' Doctor Cragshaw told Megan what Pellin was proposing.

'But, why? I mean, why is Mrs Harvey's sister doing so much? I mean, it's kind of her, but...'

Hattie held her breath for a moment. She looked at Issy and then at the Doctor. Each indicated with a look that Megan shouldn't be told.

'What? What is it? Hattie, don't keep it from me. You know, we never keep anything from each other.'

Hattie took a deep breath. *What should she do? Was it her place to tell?* Megan was right in the fact that they'd never kept anything from each other. Especially something as big as this! Rightly or wrongly she decided she'd to stand fast to what had been the very basis of hers and Megan's life together. The truth.

'Look, love, what I tell you...'

'No...'

'Issy, let Hattie tell me. I have to know. I already know as its something as will affect me by how you're all acting. Go on, Hattie.'

At the end of her telling, Hattie wasn't any longer sure she'd done right. Megan looked devastated. Hattie sat on the bed.

'It doesn't affect how Jack thinks of you, Megan love, Megan...'

The laughter started in her bowels and erupt out of her mouth from that deep point, causing her immense pain, and yet, release. Release from the agony of knowing the truth. The truth that left her feeling cheated. Cheated out of a time she could've been with Jack. Cheated in the fact that he'd lain with another woman. Cheated in the trust she'd had in him. Because that trust hadn't seen him doing something like this. Not just taking to sate his need. Not Jack!

'Eeh, lass, lass, don't take on...' Issy's stroking of her hair gave her no restrictions, only comfort.

Hattie held her hand. She gripped on to it trying to make it the saviour of her.

'Megan, Megan, do you want me to give you something to help...?' The caring voice of the doctor offering her blessed oblivion.

'No...No. No, I've to face it. I...I can. I...I have to. Oh, Jack, Jack...This'll do him, won't it? I mean, if it comes out, how will he look? Oh Jack...Why?' No one spoke. She looked around at them.

None of them could help in a situation such as this one. 'And, to think as he must've talked about me when he was with her!'

'Megan love. Let me tell you, lass, as that woman was after Jack for years. Even when Ciss was alive! And, he stood out against her until Ciss was two years in her grave, but then, well, his need... Well, you know how it is with men...'

Aye, she knew how it was. Only, she'd thought Jack was different. She could understand Issy trying to justify it all, but to her it was hard to accept.

'...Anyroad, he was afraid of something like this happening. That's why he wanted you to change your name.'

'Why didn't he tell me, Issy, why?'

'He was afraid to tell you. He didn't want you feeling badly of him. And I agreed with him as he shouldn't. Not yet. You'd been through so much and you were just starting a new life. He was going to tell you sometime in the future. He'd not live a lie with you.'

'But, he did! He should've told me...'

'Let me give you something to rest you, Megan.'

'No, I...I want to see Bridget. She...She will need me. I need to make her understand. She'll be here this afternoon, you say?'

'Yes, she will. But, she does understand. I have told her most of it. She says she knows first hand what it's like to go through such violence. She doesn't hold you or Jack responsible. Look, a mild sedative wouldn't put you out for long. Just help you to rest a while.'

'All right, thanks, Doctor. Is Billy all right? And, Sarah, and Sally? I haven't seen them today.'

'Aye, they're fine. Billy's happy as long as Sarah's paying attention to him. He shows no sign of remembering. Maybe, it would be the best thing for him to have some help, what do you think?'

'But, isn't he better not knowing, Doctor? What I can remember haunts me whether I'm asleep or awake. Shouldn't we let Billy live without the memory?'

'We can't. We need you both to remember. We need the truth to come out for Jack's sake. Pellin thinks as Jack is innocent. But, he is confessing to it all.'

'Is he? Why? No... No! Doctor, he mustn't, why is he?'

Shock sat her body up. 'He didn't do it!' Picture's shot into her mind. Flashes. 'Oh, God! NO! NO!'

'What is it? Megan love...'

'It...It was Billy...Oh, Hattie...It was Billy!'

The horror of it all played through her mind as if she was there again. Her body retched and retched. Someone put a bowl under her and she retched until she felt her very heart would come out of her.

'Megan, Megan…Oh, love.'

Issy's sobs filled the room. How did we get to this? Megan asked herself. Oh aye, me and Jack sinned. But, did we deserve so much punishment for doing so?

A pin prick of a needle going into her arm calmed the retching. 'Doctor, I didn't want to be put to sleep, I told you…'

'I know. But, as your doctor; I overroad your decision, it will rest you for a couple of hours. You need that, Megan. I don't want you going into shock again. If you get pneumonia we will be lost.'

'Hattie, what should I do?'

'Sleep for a while, love, then if you feel up to it, tell us all about it, and we'll take it from there, ay?'

'I'm sorry, Issy. That I should bring this down on you. I've never told you, but I love you, you are like a mam to me.'

Issy patted her hand. 'Oh, Megan, love. I love you, an all. We'll get through, we will.'

'Doctor, get that help for Billy. The truth has to come out.'

As her body relaxed she felt someone wipe her lips and put water to her mouth. She sipped the cool liquid. She'd let her body rest. But, what of her mind? Would she ever have peace of mind again?

CHAPTER
FORTY-SIX

As she came out of the sleep Megan knew she hadn't rested. Not properly. She'd dreamed. She'd seen horrific images of Jack and Billy hanging by their necks! She'd tried desperately to take their weight, but every time she'd reached them they'd moved. Her body was racked with pain, but her mind was racked with agony. She opened her eyes. Hattie sat by the side of her bed.

'I don't suppose as you're much rested, love. You've been very agitated. I've done wrong. I shouldn't have told you. Issy's out of sorts with me and so is Harry...'

'No, Hattie. They don't understand the trust as we have. Most people have broken our trust, even those as we love the most and should've loved us, but we've not broke each others. That's at meaning a lot to me. Folk have a false sense as they're protecting you by keeping the truth from you. And, aye, they do it for the best of reasons. I just wish as Jack'd told me or if he hadn't the courage, at least Issy should've said...'

'Aye, Issy should've advised him better, but you can't blame Jack. you can't put a woman's head on a man, love. They're not the same. They can justify anything to themselves. Though, I reckon as no one regrets his actions more than Jack. You've put him on too high a pedestal, love. He was bound to fall off. My Arthur did. He crashed right through the floor. I thought as he was different. You'd have thought as I'd have learned about men enough to see the fall coming, but I didn't.'

Megan felt she'd nothing in her to give Hattie so she just patted her gloved hand. It was an action they both used at such times.

'Is it going to be all right for you and Harry? I...mean. Can you learn to trust again?'

'Oh, aye, I think as you can. I'll not bring me pain from Arthur and crucify Harry with it. He don't deserve that. But, I'll be more careful, as I know as you will. I'll not look on Harry as some kind of God just because he loves me. I'll keep in mind that he's a person and can make mistakes. But, I know as what he's offering me is a truth. He don't want to just take me. He wants to marry me. That's first time that has happened to me. And, you know something? I'm not for going to his bed until he does make me his wife! But, I'm not letting him know, so, poor thing keeps trying…'

'Oh, Hattie…Oh, don't make me laugh. It hurts. And, stop messing with him. He doesn't deserve that. You know you love him. So put him out of his misery. You're games might come back to haunt you.'

The door opening interrupted them. Issy put her head around it. 'Megan lass, Bridget and her husband, Edward, are downstairs.' I thought I'd come up first and see as you're ready.'

Megan gave her a smile. She wanted to rest Issy's mind at her knowing all and not telling.

Issy came into the room talking as she came.

'There's something right funny, lass. Bridget looks just like you! They say as men often pick women as look like their mam or their sister. Well, you wouldn't credit it! And, you know, she takes after her da. He comes right back to me mind when I look at her. Though, I've often said, haven't I, as you remind me of someone? And, I still can't get over the coincidence. Fancy, her being Bert's sister! And, fancy him landing up here where she was brought up!'

'That wasn't chance, Issy.' Megan's hand went to her neck. She wanted to hold her locket. Issy's words had given her the need of its comfort. It wasn't there! She looked around her as she told them how Bert had come to these parts because he'd wanted to be near where his mam and his sister had lived.

'What is it, love? Have you lost something?' Issy asked

'Me locket…'

'It's here. They had to take it off you in the hospital.' Issy opened a drawer of the chest opposite the bed. As she brought it over it twirled in her hand, glinting as the light caught it.

'Oh look. There's an inscription on it.'

Issy squinted at the locket.

'To catch a…A dream… Good God! No! It can't be the same one!'

'What do you mean the same one? Hattie asked, 'The same one as what?'

'I…I've seen this afore. A long time ago; where did you get it, lass?'

Megan felt her stomach muscles tighten. She told Issy and Hattie the story of the locket and of her mam dying at her birth.

'Well, well! I'll have to sit down a mo…' Issy shook her head from side to side. '…Megan, love. I feel as though all me coincidences are coming together. But, I'm afraid of the outcome. If this locket holds the pictures of Will and Bridie, then… My God! If they are your grandparents...then...then, Bridget... No! No, it couldn't be. You said as your mam died! And yet, how like Will, and Bridget you are. The same dark eyes, the lovely olive coloured skin and the high cheekbones.'

'What...what're you saying, Issy?'

'I don't know, lass. I need to look inside...Will that be all right, love?'

Megan's, 'Yes' was little more than a whisper.

Issy's hands shook and her mouth dropped open.

'Tell me, Issy. Please tell me...'

Issy stood up and came over to her side. 'Megan, love. I have no alternative but to tell you, but I wish I had. I'm afraid me news isn't all good.' She held the open locket up, 'This here is Will and Bridie Haddler, and they were Bridget's mam and dad. They had no other surviving children, so if they were your granny and granddad....'

The silence that followed was fraught with tension as each absorbed the information.

Megan slumped back on to her pillows. She could hardly breathe. Bert's sister was her mam! She was about to meet her mam! Her mam was alive! Her world had gone mad! Bert's sister...

Nobody spoke. Megan knew they'd already come to realise what had just dawned on her. 'Billy...and me...share the same grandmother! Billy's an inbred! Oh, Hattie, Issy...'

Issy and Hattie both looked distraught. Both seemed dumbstruck.

'What do I do? How do I face her? Will she know me?' The emotions churning her insides gave her umpteen questions, all of which, held some fear for her in the answering, and yet, didn't some of them hold what she'd always longed to know? Who her family are? Who she was?

'One thing you can do nothing about, love, and that's Billy's inbreeding. It wasn't your fault...'

'It was in a way, Issy. I could've shown me locket to Bert afore we was wed. I nearly did. But, I always wanted to keep it to meself. It was the first thing as ever belonged to me, proper like. I kept it from everybody. If only I'd have shown it...'

'If only, begets, if only. But, it don't alter nothing. We've to deal with things as they are. Now, how Bridget and you deal with finding each other and what the tale is behind her giving you up, will soon be on you and that's me worry at the moment. Are you feeling up to it, Megan love? Or does you want us to put Bridget off for a while? After all, you've so much to come to terms with.'

'No! I mean… No, Issy love, I want to see her. I need to…' A cold tear trickled down her cheek and as she'd turned to talk to Issy another ran over the bridge of her nose. 'It should be a joyful time, me finding me mam, but it's not. I have so much inside me. So much to tell…I…' A sob caught in her throat. How much more would descend on her? How much…

'Oh, Megan love…'

'Shift over, Issy.' Hattie stopped Issy's sympathetic flow by pushing her way nearer to Megan then kneeling in front of her. 'Megan, lass, I know it's come at a bad time, but isn't it what we always dreamed of, finding our mams? Well, no matter what else has happened or is happening, surely that's the one bright spark amongst all of it? Think on it, love. You've found your mam!'

Megan looked at Hattie. She was right. How often had they lain awake together into the early hours, two lost little souls, longing to know who they were and where their mam's were? And, in the years since, how often she'd felt the pain she'd felt when she'd been told hers was dead? But, she wasn't dead. She was here. Here in this very house. And, she had no idea what she was walking into.

'Hattie, you're right. I just can't take it all in. I…I mean how will it be when I see her? On top of that, I have something in me as I've not spoken of and I'm scared…'

'Don't be scared, love. Like we said, we're all here for you. We'll help you. Is it about what happened?'

'Yes. Billy did kill Bert. He hit him with his crutch. And…and he meant to. Oh, Megan. He hit him over and over…Me little lad. Me little lad. He… He had an evil in him. And…and it was all my fault.

'It wasn't your fault, lass, it was Bert's. And aye, Jack has some guilt, an all, as does that Mrs Harvey. But not you, Megan love, you were just the victim of it all. Look, love, we had an idea anyroad as that's how it all happened from what you said earlier. Jack has a good lawyer, we'll tell him all about it…'

'But, what will happen to Billy?'

Hattie told her what the lawyer had said would most likely happen.

Megan's heart, though already splintered, seemed to shatter in her breast on hearing this. Aye, Billy had killed his dad. But, the sin wasn't his. It was hers. Hadn't she put a terror in him about what might happen if his dad caught up with them? And, it did happen! In front of his very eyes! He must've felt as he had no choices…Poor Billy… How would he bear being locked up in an institute! No! No… She'd not be able to bear it, either… There would be no help for him. Them places were… No! She couldn't think on it…

She lay back and closed her eyes. She wanted to be alone. She wanted to try to sort everything out in her head. She didn't feel that she could face Bridget or face having her confirm she was her mam.

After a few moments she heard the door close. She opened her eyes. Hattie was standing by the window looking out. She closed her eyes again. Her head throbbed. The turmoil inside was too much to cope with. She longed to be lying in Jack's arms looking up at that protective canopy. She wanted to feel the happiness and peace she'd felt then. Oh, Jack, Jack...

Her thoughts turned to Bert. He was gone, gone forever. The thought should give her a good feeling, but it didn't. Not that she'd wish him back, but in his death he'd won. He'd destroyed Billy and Jack, aye, and her, an all, because she'd never be the same again. None of them would.

The tears she'd stemmed earlier came back to sting her eyes. The pain in her heart twisted and turned to agony as she tried to imagine what it was like for Jack.

She became aware of a hand holding hers and opened her eyes. She looked into Hattie's. Her eyes, too, were misted with tears. 'Don't give up, Megan love. Don't give up. Jack's going to need you, and Billy. And aye, Issy and me, an all. All of us need you.'

The mist dissolved into a wetness and a tear overflowed down Hattie's cheek. Megan leant forward and wiped it. 'I'll try not to, Hattie.'

Suddenly, it was as if they were children again with all the pain of then piled high with the pain of now and Hattie rested her head in her lap and they allowed the tears to silently flow down their cheeks.

'I'm scared, you know, Hattie. After all we dreamed it'd be like. And, it's not. I feel that scared I feel like changing me mind and not seeing me mam. I don't know how it should all happen. Or even if we should tell her what we know. And s'pose as Sister Bernadette was lying to me and the folk in me locket are not me grandparents.'

'No, she wasn't, I know that. Anyroad, Issy said as you looked like Bridget's dad, and you do, them features of his are yours. And, Megan, Bridget herself is like an older version of you. Not that much older. I reckon as she had you very young. Look, love, how about I get Issy to tell her afore she comes up? Wouldn't that be better than dropping it on her in front of you?'

'Aye, it would. It'd be better for her, an all. Give her chance to get used to the idea afore she meets me. It's going to be a shock to her. Her own bother's wife...Oh, Hattie...'

'All right, love. Shall I take the locket with me? I think it would help in Issy's telling.'

Megan handed the locket over and Hattie bent down and kissed her cheek, then left quickly, giving her no time to change her mind. Hattie was shaking she was as anxious as she was. She knew why. Hattie was to face seeing her unite with her mam, whilst still not knowing of her own or ever knowing of a time she would. But then, that's how it'd always been with them. Her getting the best end of the stick. Though, it changed some when she got Bert, but even then, she'd a feeling in her that Hattie would've liked her status as a married woman. Dear God! Status! Oh, aye, she'd had the status. But, for the most part, it'd been a living hell.

To think, Bert was her uncle! Was it bloodline that had drawn her to him? Because she'd always had a feeling for him and she'd known it wasn't love and, despite all he did, she never lost that feeling for him. In a way she felt some pity for him now. She could see the tragedy of their ever meeting up with one another. Maybe, if he'd have met up with someone else who really loved him as a woman should love her man, he'd have been different. And, what of Billy? Was he unstable? Aye, she'd to face it. Deep down inside her she'd known a lot of his actions were not, just a lad's way, as they were put down to. Billy was unstable. Billy needed help. And, it wasn't to be wondered at. He were born to his own cousin and uncle!

The painful laughter threatened to start again, but she wouldn't let it. No. If she did she'd not be able to stop and she'd fall into a deep pit of madness. She was needed. Despite the horror of everything, she had to stay strong. Strong for Billy and Jack. And, strong enough to meet the woman who might be her mam. In some ways it would be better if she wasn't. It would be better if a mistake had been made by Sister Bernadette. At least then, one part of the nightmare she was in wouldn't exist.

CHAPTER
FORTY- SEVEN

'Megan...Megan, love...'

Megan hadn't realised she'd had her eyes closed so tightly. The voice brought them open. And, as the concerned and loving face of the voice came into focus, she knew it was all a truth... 'Mam?'

There was a silence. Megan waited, holding her breath, then sighed with a relief she hadn't expected to feel as Bridget said, 'Yes, dear...'

'Oh, Mam...'

A gentle hand stroked hers. Glistening tears of joy fell down the smiling, beautiful face. 'I can't believe it...It's like a miracle. My own baby...'

They stayed like that for a moment, neither knowing what to say. Megan felt a surge of love for Bridget. It was a love that forgave all. Nothing mattered, not why, not all the loneliness, nothing. All that mattered was her mam was here. Her very own mam...'

It was Bridget that asked the first question.

'Has all of your life been awful, Megan dear? I mean, have you had some happy times?'

She thought a moment. Recent hurts stopped her mind giving her any happy memories to speak of, but then a laughing Ciss came to her and with the image came many happy moments of their time together. And then, she thought of Hattie and all they had been to each other. And, the moment little Billy was born. And, how lucky she was to have Issy and Sarah and Jack, above all, Jack... Yes, she'd known happiness, she'd known the greatest happiness of all, the love given to her by Jack and she nodded, 'Aye, Mam, I've had a lot of happiness mixed in with the bad.'

'I'm glad, dear. Oh, Megan, I'm so sorry, I...'

'No, don't be sorry. It's all right. You're here now and that's all as matters.' But it wasn't, suddenly she did want to know, why she was left, who her dad was, and what had happened to him. What had her mam's life been like? What...Oh God! She wanted to know the answer to so many things that had troubled her all her life. But then, she remembered, her mam had lost her brother without ever being reunited with him.

'I'm sorry about...Bert...I mean...he was your brother and he...Well, I didn't know he was...'

'I know, dear. The fact that we're all blood relatives is marring our coming together. How could anybody ever prepare for such a thing happening? I did tell Sister Bernadette to tell you everything. I told her to tell you about Bert and where he lived and...and about me. And, I contacted her, just as soon as I was in a position to take care of you. She told me you had been adopted and that I should keep you in my prayers, but that I would never be allowed to have the details of your adoption. Why? Why did she do such a thing? I trusted her.'

'She told me you were dead. That I had no family alive. That you'd never told who me dad was, only thing she said was, it wasn't your fault, you had been attacked by someone you trusted.'

Bridget bowed her head.

'Yes, that is true.' She paused and took a deep breath. 'The man who raped me was someone I trusted. I worked for him and his wife at the corner shop on the street where we lived. I'd loved him and his wife, they were very good to me and Bert and they seemed so happy together. It was a shock beyond anything I'd known, not just the rape but, Bert's dad, my step-dad's involvement in it and his future plans for me...' Tears ran down her face and her face filled with distress.'

'It doesn't matter, Mam, I understand, don't distress yourself further. It's in the past. All that matters is you are here now. Have you any other children?'

'Yes, two boys, Richard and Mark. They don't know where we are or anything about their Uncle Bert dying. We will tell them when they are older. They think we are on holiday. They are with their grand parents. They'll be having a good time getting spoilt. Richard is eleven and Mark is ten.'

'That's grand, not only a mam but two brothers as well! Only, you don't have to tell them about me either, Mam. They are too young to hear our tale. Best we give them time to grow up without any complications. We can say I am a long lost cousin or something.'

'No, darling, they have always known about you, though they think I was married before. And every night when we say our prayers, they pray for mummy's lost little girl and brother and, funny this, but after your letter, for their uncle's wife and his son, whom they thought was their cousin. They are going to be surprised how grown up you are as we always spoke of you as a little girl. And now I find I am a Granny, too! That is going to be a shock!'

'That's lovely, thank you, Mam. To think all these years you and my brothers have been praying for me. Mind, it makes you wonder if Him up there ever listens...You know, Mam, there's no need to say who I was married to. You can keep that until they are older and... And about Billy being an inbred. It's too much for them. It's bad enough for us as have to know. And, Mam, Bert...'

She went on to tell Bridget how Bert had kept her letter and how he'd wanted to be in the place where she was brought up and had searched for her sister's grave. 'And like I told you in me letter, he named Billy after your dad.'

'That's a comfort, Megan. Thank you for telling me. If only he'd answered my letter...'

'He was a stubborn man. Billy can be like him. I...I'm worried over Billy, Mam. I've heard tell as inbred children can suffer ...well, mentally.'

'Yes, it is possible. I know what you are worrying over. Issy told me everything. Billy may need help. Edward, I will bring Edward up to meet you soon, anyway, he has friends in the profession. He can see that Billy gets the help he will need. Everything will turn out. You'll see. Now, my dear, you're tired. We've covered a lot of ground. And, we've both been hit by something akin to lightening striking, finding each other like this. It's the happiest and yet the saddest day of my life.'

'I know what you mean, we've lost so much and so much has happened to us and all because of Sister Bernadette's thinking as she was doing right by us. We've a lot to tackle. But, we won't lose each other again, will we? No matter what happens and no matter how all this concludes. We won't lose each other.'

'No. You'll never be able to get rid of me! Even if you find you don't like me. I'll not go away.'

'Mam, I'll never come not to like you. I know as I love you even now. And, I know as I will for the rest of me days. I'm so happy to find you. It's what me and Hattie...Oh, poor, Hattie. We used to dream of this moment. But, I can't ever see a day when she could find her mam.'

'Megan, I think I know who Hattie's mother is. In fact, given that Hattie looks so like her and that you were brought up together in the same convent and are the same age, I'm certain I do. She and I were in St Michaels together. We became very close, like you and Hattie. She was a lovely girl. Her story was heartbreaking in that it was a calculated rape by a member of her own family specifically to get a child. Her name is also similar, it must be something the convent do, change the child's name. My friend was called Lucy Grampton. She died giving birth to Hattie. She came from a well to do family, but there aren't any close relatives alive now. The shock of what happened to their only child and the deceit they suffered through the actions of her mother's sister was too much, both of Lucy's parents died within two years of her death. They were an elderly couple. They'd had Lucy very late in life. So, Hattie really is an orphan with no-one who would care to be found. And though she is probably entitled to a legacy she would never prove it, it was all hushed up and all traces of her banished, she was even named by Sister Bernadette, who worked at the convent at the time. You know, one thing, despite the deceit in not telling you and I the truth, for whatever reason she had, Sister Bernadette, did her best for you both. She used her knowledge of what happened to Lucy to blackmail the Reverend Mother of St Michaels to arrange things so that she was always going to be with you both.'

Megan had lain still throughout the telling, her heart heavy for Hattie. 'It's strange about Sister Bernadette... It will take me a long time to forgive her. We could have been together. She stopped that, and yet, she protected Hattie, well both of us, because she did take care of us and intervened on our behalf if things got really bad. You know, throughout, things have gone better for me than for Hattie and I've always carried a guilt about it.'

'That's not your fault, my dear. And anyway, if Hattie is like a sister to you she can be like a daughter to me. I know it's not the real thing for her, but I'll try to make it the next best thing. And it will be my way of paying back her mother. She was very good to me.'

'But, Mam, I need you to understand about Hattie...' As she had done with Issy so long ago she carefully told of Hattie. It was in her not to have anybody feel bad about Hattie.

'Don't worry, Megan. I'd guessed some of it when I met her. It won't affect me. As I've said before, there's stuff in my past and from what I understand, Hattie is trying to put it into her past...'

'She is. She has a good stash now. She was left a house...Well, sort of. Anyroad, it's been sold. So she's been able to get rid of her old business. Her and Harry... He's fella as loves her. Well, I think...Well, I'm at hoping, as they might marry soon. You know, Mam? Afore all this happened everything was going well for me and Hattie.'

'It will again. I know it's hard to think that it will, but, we are together now and I think that everything will turn out for Billy and Jack and you could start up your business again. You hadn't been going long so you couldn't have lost it all. I mean, orders will be delayed. But, like you told me, your customer was very taken with your designs and is likely to recommend you. Give me her address and I will contact her. I imagine that, as she is a friend of that despicable Laura Harvey, she knows already what has happened and probably feels some guilt and doesn't know what to do about the situation. Did you take a deposit and leave carbon copies of the designs she wanted, with her?'

'Yes, Lady Gladwyn did give me a deposit, but no, I didn't leave copies of what she wanted making. I had them all in a book. Me idea was to have a book for each customer, and then, they could point out things as they'd really liked on one outfit and might want on another. Now I think on it, though, I should make copies.'

'Yes, I should in future, but, it won't matter, I'll try to persuade Lady Gladwyn to see you again and together you should come up with what it was she wanted. What do you think?'

'I don't know, you can't be sure of how top drawer folk'll act over anything, but I'd not be against you trying. It would be grand if she would give me another chance. I've probably got enough of me start up capital to buy the materials and Hattie will help me out. I could use Issy's sewing machine. It's slower than them as I bought for shop, but I managed for over two years on it. And, even if Lady Gladwyn won't have me back, I've still got hope. I can start up again. I can.'

'Well, I'm glad you think so, dear. We all need something we can hang on to. I'm thinking, if you think to re-start in another area rather than stay around here where there are so many memories, it would be lovely if you could move nearer to us. We can build a proper family. Edward and I can help you, I'd certainly become a customer and I know I could get you some business amongst my friends, some of them are on the fringe of being 'top drawer' as you call it and they have some good connections.'

Megan felt her mouth drop open at this information.

'I know. Look, it's all too much for you to take in at the moment. I'll tell you all about it when you are better and I'm more able to tell more of my life. Anyway, I'd better go and bring Edward up to meet you. He'll be worrying about us. We've left them all for such a long time they'll all be wondering how we are doing.'

As she got to the door, Bridget turned back and said. 'I'm very proud of you, Megan love. You know, I think you get your talent for drawing from my dad, your granddad, he loved to make sketches. Oh, and I chose the name of my Granny O'Hara for you...She was my mother's mother... Oh, I've such a lot to tell you...'

Megan smiled. She lay back and allowed the wonderful feeling of really belonging and of being part of a family to wash over her. She knew there was still a lot to face, but she had her mam to face it with her. That was something to be thankful for, she told herself. But then, a thought came to her. 'Mam, will you ask Hattie to come up first, and will you come, too. I can't hold on to the information about Hattie's Mam. She has to be told.'

'Alright, dear, if you are sure?'

'I am, Mam, I am.'

CHAPTER
FORTY-EIGHT

The sweat ran freely down Jack's cold body. His legs shook as he stood looking at the judge whose voice droned in his ears.

'Jack Frederick Fellam. You are charged, that on the 15th day of October, 1930 you did murder, by beating, a Mr Albert Armitage. How do you plead?'

His, 'Not guilty' didn't sound convincing. But then, it wasn't what he'd wanted to say. He'd not wanted to drag it all out. Why had he let Pellin convince him to?

The wrangling didn't take long. Pellin had warned him he'd not have much of an argument for getting him bail.

'Mr Fellam, bail is refused. You will be remanded in custody until the 18th March 1931. At which time you will appear here, at the Leeds Crown Court, to stand trial. Do you understand?'

'Yes, Your Honour.'

He understood, all right! Five bloody months cooped up in that cell! Oh Megan! Megan! A despair entered him. He held on to the message she'd sent him. It added to his shame that she knew of his affair, but to know that she had come to an understanding of it and had forgiven his part in it was a help. If only he could talk to her...

He was glad as Megan had found her ma. Though, her being who she was beggared belief! Still, no matter what the circumstances, it was something that would be a help to her. He wished as it was him helping her. Holding her...Would he ever do so again? And, what of Billy? He was glad it was a friend of Megan's step-dad who was going to help him and it wasn't to be paid for with any more of Laura Harvey's bloody blood money. But, how would the lad cope with having to face what he'd done? What if it tipped him over as Doctor Cragshaw'd warned? *What then? Oh, God! It all seemed so hopeless.*

***

351

'Oh dear, Doctor, will Billy be all right?' Issy asked the consultant psychiatrist, 'Should I go after him?'

'No, we'll leave him for now. But, you must all be prepared for a long drawn out healing process. It is going to take a long time to get through to him. I will have to gain his trust, which I have already damaged. You saw his reaction when I mentioned his dad. He took flight. That's a typical reaction of this kind of trauma. Billy is a very frightened young boy. I'm going to have to go very slowly, very slowly.'

'But, we don't have time...'

'Don't get upset, Issy. Surely, John, there are other, quicker ways. What about the new regression techniques? I was reading something only the other day whereby service men, suffering from similar mental traumas due to their experiences in the war, had been helped by taking them back to their pre-war life and then bringing them forward.'

'Yes, it is an option, Edward.'

'Is it safe, John?' Doctor Cragshaw asked. 'Only I am afraid your field is something I know very little about.

'Yes, the trials have been good, but all of those who were on the trial programme were much older than Billy and they could be told what would happen and talked through all the implications...'

Issy felt all this talk was above her, as were the three doctors talking it. But she knew as Phi...No, she wasn't to think of Doctor Cragshaw as that. It wasn't her place to call him Philip, even in her mind. But, whatever, she knew he'd watch out for Megan and Billy. He knew how far all this should go...

A sudden scream cut into her thoughts. The scream held a terror. It was Megan...What was she screaming? Issy stood as if she'd never move again. But Edward grabbed her as he went by and pulled her along.

Hattie and Bridget came from the kitchen just as they entered the hall. Sarah was just behind them, but thankfully, Issy saw Daisy was there, too, and saw that she took Sarah by the hand and took her back into the kitchen and closed the door.

Edward held Issy back as they reached Megan's room. When he opened the door the sight Issy saw, froze her in fear. Billy held aloft a wooden rolling pin as if he would bring it down on Megan's head. His eyes stared out of there sockets and froth foamed from his gaping mouth. Issy knew she was looking at living evil. Her blood ran cold in her veins.

The door opening had quietened Megan. She turned towards them. She looked desolate, Issy wanted so much to go to her, but knew she'd to allow Edward to get things under control.

'Put that down! Do you hear me, Billy? Put it down! Billy, Billy, can you hear me? Don't be afraid, put...'

Edward had a command to his voice. But Billy took no notice.

'She's got to die...It was her fault...'

'No, Billy, it wasn't your mother's fault, don't...'

'I...I have to...I have to kill her. It's telling me, I'm to do it...'

'What's telling you, Billy?'

'The redness, the red...' Billy's body broke out in sweat and his skin paled. 'The redness says she's to blame! She left me dad! She made him mad...He hit Jack. He...he was going to kill him!' Billy put his arms even further back. Issy felt her body sway. No! Oh God! No...

'I've to get the red out, I...'

'No!' Edward leapt forward.

Billy swung round to face Edward. He felt his arms drop, they were heavy. Everything was heavy. That fella as said as he was his step-granddad was near him. He'd to stop him...

'Get away else I'll do you, an all...' The redness inside his head burned. It swelled... His head would burst! It had to come out. He thought of the first time it had come to him and given him such pain. The thought brought the image of Bella at his feet and he laughed.

'The stinking half-wit. Ha!' His body shook and the laughter took him. The pain in his head increased. The redness was eating him! He needed to stop laughing. It was making him weak... He'd to beat it...Look at them all, he'd have to do them all in...

The redness would help...It was helping him...It was coming back... giving him strength...

He swished the rolling pin backwards and forwards. He could still see Bella, she was looking back at him...The ugly sod. He lashed out at her. Heard once more the crunching sound of her head.

'She's dead! I've done her...Ha! She's heavy...she stinks...The ugly sod, stinks. I've got to get her to the Mineshaft...'

'Billy, what are you saying, lad?' Issy's voice penetrated the redness. He liked Issy...

'It was the redness. It told me to...it come out...it was on the branch...then on me...It come out of me head. I didn't know what to do... I hid her... dragged her to the Mineshaft...

He was losing his power again... He'd only to do his mam in and it'd be over... His eyes hurt. They felt like they were leaving his head! The agony of the redness crushed him. He swished the rolling pin again.

'You killed...'

Shud up! I have to listen...'

'Who are you listening to?'

That was that new bloke they'd brought in. Why didn't he listen to what he told him?

'The REDNESS! I told you! He's in me head!'

A pain seared him. He had to get it out. Had to do his mam in...it was all her fault. He raised his arms. A strength came into him. He felt huge. Bigger than everyone in the room. He looked round at them. They were all staring. He laughed out loud.

Someone was shouting...It was his Aunty Hattie.

'Tell the redness to go away, Billy. Go on. Tell it. It isn't your boss. It'll do as you say, lad. Tell it as you don't want to kill your mam...'

'No! It won't...it made me...it made me kill Bella and me dad...it made me...'

'Well, you bloody well tell it, it isn't going to make you kill your mam or it'll have me to answer to and that'll frighten it. I'm helping you, lad. We can be at beating it together, ay?'

'Billy, I'm your mam, I love you. I'll join with, Hattie. I'll help you fight the redness...'

'We all will, lad. We'll not leave you on your own with it...'

Everybody was nodding. The fella who had been talking to him earlier started to move. He didn't want him talking at him again. He wanted his mam. The redness was going...He'd beaten it. His Aunty Hattie had made them all help him to beat it. He didn't ever want it to come back...'Mam...Mam...'

He was in her arms. He was safe. 'Ouch!' Something had been jabbed into his bottom. It'd hurt...His mam held him tighter. His eyes felt heavy...He couldn't keep them open...

Megan felt a movement beside her. Hattie had come to lie beside her. Her arm came round her and Billy. There were no words Hattie could say. She knew that.

Issy stepped forward. Her body bent over. Her face a mirror of pain. She wanted to take Issy's pain away, but knew she couldn't.

For a moment Issy just looked at her. Her head shook from side to side. Her body sank down in the chair next to the bed. Was it all over? Could Issy forgive? Issy's shaking hand reached out for hers. She gladly took it.

Bridget came further into the room. She motioned with her head to Edward and he steered the rest of the doctors out and closed the door. Bridget came over and knelt in front of Issy.

'Issy, Issy dear.' She brushed a stray strand of hair back from Issy's desolate face.

'Everything will be all right, Issy.' Issy looked up into Bridget's face. Bridget paused a moment, then said, 'Issy, I've never stopped thinking of you as a second mother. I just wished I'd conquered my shame and contacted you. When...When I realised I was carrying a baby I wrote a letter, but I couldn't post it. I so wished I had. I'll look out for you now, Issy love. Just like you looked out for me when I was a girl, remember? You were all I had whilst mother was in that workhouse.'

Issy patted Bridget's hand then turned to Megan. 'Oh, lass...'

Megan understood. It was enough to have Issy's warm chubby hand in hers. It told her she still had Issy's love. Despite everything she had brought down on her, Issy was still with her.

Questions came into her. Her granny in a workhouse? And Issy caring for her mam? But, she didn't voice them. The tears running down her mam's face stopped her.

Megan looked at each of the women. Women she loved and who loved her. She could see the pain pitted into her own heart, was etched into each of them. It was a pain cut deep by others brutal acts.

She held Billy to her. She had no more tears left in her. No more. Surely Jack will come home now? And Billy will get the help he needs.

Megan relaxed back and let her head fall so she was looking at Hattie. Hattie smiled. It was a smile that held courage. Enough courage for Megan to hold on to. Megan smiled back.

355

THE EPILOGUE

A FINDING OF PEACE

CHAPTER
FORTY-NINE

'Megan, love...'

Megan did not turn around to look at him. The distance between her and himself was a void too gaping and cold for Jack to cross.

'What are you thinking, lass?'

'I'm for feeling all the pain again. Not that it ever goes from me, but the letter has opened the wounds and made them sore.'

'I know, lass.

'Why can't she leave it alone? I...I know she's dying...And well, I understand she wants forgiveness, but why does you have to go to her? That woman broke me, Jack. She brought me so low I've never properly recovered. She gnaws away at me thoughts. It's like a war in me. A battle I fight daily with me hate for her.'

'We'll never be right until it's settled, lass. Going to her and giving her the chance of getting our forgiveness might settle it all.'

'She wants you, Jack, not me. You! It says it in the letter.'

'Well, that's not going to be how it is. In the past I had to do Mrs Harvey's bidding, but not now. If I go, you come, too.'

'Wouldn't a letter, do? Did you ask Lord Crompton if we could write a letter saying as we forgive her?'

'Aye, I did. He begged me to consider going.'

'How can she do this? We're just getting sorted. The year you spent in that prison...Oh God, Jack. And...Billy... He's settling and doing well on the treatment. The shop's beginning to show a profit. You have your job...'

'It is as you say, lass, but there's something between us. Something's not letting us be happy...'

'You're not happy with me?'

'I didn't say that, Megan. What I'm trying to say is there are loose ends. Stuff we need to face. Just living with it, isn't working. Once it's done we can...'

'And going to Laura Harvey on her death-bed and giving her our blessing, will end it? I don't know as I can do it, Jack...I don't know as I want to. The hate in me wants her to rot in Hell!'

'That's it, Megan. That's just it. The hate in you. The bitterness. It is eating you away. You are for letting her win...'

'Win! Don't you see, Jack? She has won. She has the power to open all the vileness and lay it raw between us.'

Megan turned to face him. What he saw in her face cut into the heart of him.

Two years had passed. One of those they had been apart. He could still hear the Judge. 'Jack Frederick Fellam, you have been found guilty of perverting the cause of justice in that you withheld information that would have assisted the police in their enquiries. Taking into account all the circumstances and the time you have already spent in prison, you are sentenced to be detained for twelve months...' And so it had droned on.

In some ways they had been stronger during that year. Determined not to let their lives be ruined. It had been Hell, but it was a Hell they got through. Megan kept busy re-building her business. Billy was sectioned for an indefinite period, but with the help of Bridget and Edward, he is in one of the best mental hospitals there is and started to make progress from the very beginning. His new found affection for his mam is a salve to Megan.

On his release from prison, they had married. They'd made it a double with Hattie and Harry. It'd been a good day. A happy day and to top it all not long after and right out of the blue, Smythe had offered him a job. He could never understand why, but it was welcome and he was plodding along there. The other blokes knew all about him and what had gone on. They didn't seem to bother about it all. They respected his knowledge and his skills with the horses and all in all he was all right working there.

On the face of it, everything should be grand. Oh, he'd known as there would be a lot of healing to do. He had thought his love could do that. The letter from Lord and Lady Crompton had shown it hadn't.

'We feel we have no right to contact you, please forgive us for doing so,' the letter had said. Then it had gone on: 'Mrs Harvey is very ill. Her life is coming to an end. She has a dying wish to see you and to ask you to forgive her. She is deeply troubled and holding on to life for this one thing. As her sister and brother-in-law, we appeal to you to on her behalf to consider making the trip to Switzerland and extending your forgivness to her.. We fully understand if you are unable to oblige. Please contact Lord Crompton...etc

Lord Crompton had been very humble when he had contacted him, "I beg of you, Jack, to allow my sister-in-law to die in peace and my wife to be able to know she did do so."

'I need to think, Jack.' Megan's words cut into Jack's thoughts. He lifted his head. The void was still there. Megan walked towards him. She didn't stop by him or speak again. Her feelings were echoed in the slam of the door. After a few moments the front door latch clicked, and then, that too, banged shut. Jack raised his eyes. Was he asking too much? Well, if he knew anything, Megan will have gone to Hattie and that was a good thing. Hattie will help her.

'Is everything all right, Jack?' Issy came into the room. Jack looked at her, saw the worry etched into her face. It was a worry that he couldn't lift for her. If anyone did the lifting it was her. Oh, and Sarah of course. Sarah was growing up with a sensible head on her shoulders. Together, her and Issy kept them all going. Kept some balance in the fraught atmosphere.

'Make us a cuppa, Ma, and I'll tell you all about it. I could do with your advice.'

'If it's advice you need, Jack, then you most likely know what you need to do, you just want me to help you to decide. Eeh, lad. Will it ever end?'

***

'Megan, I'm going to talk straight. It's not likely as you're going to like what I say, but it has to be said.'

Hattie had that look on her face that Megan knew well. Frustration frayed her temper. 'I know you're going to side with, Jack...'

'Look, lass, if you've a mind not to listen, why did you come? I'm not letting you off hook with this one, Megan. Jack is right. The bitterness in you is destroying the person we love. Everyone of us can see it and feel it. Your mam's worried over you... Oh, yes, we've spoken. And, we both agree, you have to have a conclusion to all of this. Some of it you have to live with, but Mrs Harvey's involvement, you don't!'

'But, Hattie...'

'I won't listen to your side, because I know it. Where d'yer think as me and Harry would be if he harboured feelings in him about me past, ay? None of us can alter our our past. Jack had an affair. It meant nothing to him. I've told you afore, men are different to us, but Jack is different to most. He had his chances when Ciss was alive; God Rest Her, but his love for her stopped him. That marks him as a good un in my books. He has told you, that when he spoke of you to Mrs Harvey it was with pride, aye and love. He had no idea it would lead to what it did...'

'I don't blame Jack, Hattie...'

361

'You say you don't, but he feels blamed and that on top of everything is wearing him down. He cannot say sorry all his life, Megan.'

'I...I...'

'Oh, love...'

Megan went into the fold of Hattie's arms. Her tears, locked away so long ago, tore from her body in a torrent she felt she'd never be able to stop.

'Forgive, Megan. Forgive...'

A feeling as if a door had opened in Megan's heart, drained her tears to nothing. Her sobs became sniffles. Hattie was right. Jack was right. Her mam, Issy, all of them were right!

'Why d'yer think you and Billy are at peace, love? It's because Billy has been helped to forgive you. Oh. I know, what the little chap thought was your fault wasn't, but to him it was. Once those working with him managed to get him to forgive, to understand, he was able to return your love. They are working on getting him to forgive his dad, now, and then...'

'How d'yer know all this, Hattie?'

'Yer mam, my pretend mam, bless her. She telephones me and we have long chats...'

'About me?'

'Yes, mostly. As I said, we are all worried sick for you, love.'

'It'll be all right. I can see now. Ta, Hattie. Oh, ta ever so much. I understand. I'll do it. I'll forgive, Mrs Harvey. I will. And, yer know, I need to work through all the folk involved just like Billy is. Mam said not long back she could get that psychiatrist bloke to help me. I snapped her head off. Said I didn't need help, but I do, don't I, Hattie?'

'You do, love. We have all tried, but we are too close, we only make you cross. Oh, Megan, I'm so glad...I'm so glad.'

***

Jack and Megan's journey by rail and sea to Switzerland gave them time to talk. Free from everyday cares they had time to listen, too. Jack told her he'd long since come to an understanding in himself and had found forgiveness for Laura's actions and he hoped she had forgiven him.

Megan wasn't without a pang of hurt as he spoke. Part of her wanted to say he had no right to forgive the woman until she had.

As if he had read her thoughts he held her close.

'Megan, I'm not saying I forgive her for what she did to you, I can't do that until you do. It is what she did to me that I can forgive as I

362

shoulder half of the blame. I should have held out against her. But, in a funny way, I came to understand her. Her loneliness, her grief, all of it mirrored my own, it drew us together.'

'I can only say I want to forgive her. I want to understand. And I will try, though I am hoping something happens that makes it all come naturally.' Megan told him.

They met up with Lord and Lady Compton on their arrival and were taken to a small guesthouse. Arrangements were made to take them to the clinic later that day.

When they arrived at the clinic Jack felt he was entering a gulf of silence. The squeak of their every step on the polished floor of the long corridors deepened the dread in Jack. He held on to Megan. Lord Crompton was ahead of them showing them the way. Lady Crompton had stayed in the car. The fact Jack had brought Megan to the clinic with him wasn't commented on. They were allowing him to handle the situation in his own way.

Lord Crompton stopped outside a small room. The doors were open and Jack could see that opposite them on the other side of the room there was a balcony with a spectacular view across a shimmering lake, with a backdrop of snow covered mountains. And yet, it wasn't cold. The late September sun was shining directly into the room. He had been told that Laura had been wheeled out onto the balcony to receive them.

The moment they stepped into the room a weak but unmistakable voice called out.

'Jack?'

Megan clutched his sleeve. He looked down at her.

'Go in, love. Go in on your own first. I'll wait in the corridor. Fetch me when you are ready...'

'But...'

'It's all right, Jack. Go on. Do what you have to do. Say what you have to say. I am never going to ask you about it. This has to be an end. I will come in...I will, but not yet.'

Jack didn't answer her. He knew she meant it. If it was possible, the understanding she had come to, deepened his love for her. He held her close then waited for her to leave. Lord Crompton went with her. It was Megan who closed the door behind them. At that moment Jack knew her trust in him had been re-forged. He took a deep breath, whatever was to come, he was ready.

Had he said, ready? Nothing prepared him for the sight of Laura. Her features were sunken and drawn. The small amount of flesh left on her bones made her appear skeletal. Her beauty was gone, and yet something of the old Laura remained in her deeply sunken eyes. He hoped she hadn't seen the shock the sight of her had given him or the overwhelming pity that had swamped him.

Pity mingled with other emotions churning inside him. This dying woman had lain in his arms, had made love to him, had loved him and wanted him. He crossed over to her side and sat on the chair provided, he could think of nothing to say other than, 'Hello, Laura, how're you feeling, lass?'

It was a stupid question. He wanted to tell her he would make everything right for her. He'd change things. She wouldn't die. But, that too, was stupid.

Her thin, trembling hand stretched out to him and he took it. 'Oh, Laura lass, I...'

'Shush... You're here now. It's all I wanted...just to see you again...before... And to tell you something...' A bout of coughing attacked her.

He leant forward and held her. Waited while she calmed. When she did she said, 'I've had a lot of time to think...I'm sorry... So sorry...Tell Megan...'

'Megan's here, she's outside, she wants to see you when you are ready. For my part, everything is all right. Don't think on it. It's done with. And listen, I'm not without guilt, I didn't treat you right. I should never have...'

'No... No, don't take on any of the guilt, Jack. It was all my doing...all of it... I want to make amends...'

'There is no amends that have to be made...'

'Tell me, Jack....did you... ever love me?'

This is what he had been dreading. But he'd made his mind up that if he got the chance and was on his own with her, he would lie. If that is what he could do for her to help her die happy, he would do it.

'Aye, I did, Laura. I did love you. It died in me when everything took place, but now I know you are sorry, I can feel it again.'

'You...have made me very happy...very happy, Jack. I have always loved you... Though my love was selfish and made me do things ...to hurt...you. It isn't now. It...' She could not continue, her body was so racked with coughing and her breath so laboured that Jack got up and called out for help.

The room filled with nurses and doctors. Megan rushed in along with Lord Crompton. Once the bed had been dragged back into the room Megan stood next to him on the balcony looking out at the beautiful view. Jack knew his eye's to mist over. The action going on in the room behind him filled him with a sense of helplessness.

The Doctor eventually came to them, and in a heavily, accented English, told them that Laura did not have long. 'Lord Crompton has gone to fetch her sister. It is hoped they will be in time.' His head shook from side to side as he said this. 'We will wheel Laura out here again. She has many times expressed a wish that she be allowed to die, looking at the beautiful mountains.'

Megan held him even tighter than she had done before. The sense of helplessness deepened. He could only stand transfixed as the nurses manoeuvred the bed back out on to the balcony. Once this task was completed Jack looked down at Laura. He would have said she had shrunk even more had it been possible for her to do so. He knelt beside her and held her hand. 'Megan is here, Laura...'

Her eyes flickered open. Her hand clawed weakly at the sheet.

'For..forgive me, Meg...'

Megan knelt down, 'I do. I do. Jack has made me understand how lonely you were and how you had no real idea of what might happen. You weren't used to folk like Bert. You didn't know what your actions would cause. You lived in a different world. I don't think you would have done it if you'd have been like us and knew the way of us. You were fighting to keep your man. I can understand that.'

Laura's half closed, dead eyes showed a flicker of light. Her lips moved, but no words came out, then they closed in a small, but lovely smile.

Jack kissed her hand and assured her again all was forgiven.

This brought a peace to her. She relaxed and closed her eyes. Her hand tightened in his and then went slack as a heavy sigh released her last breath.

They stayed still for a moment and gazed at her. To Jack some of her beauty returned in her death. Her passing had been peaceful, he was glad they had been able to help it to be so. A deep sigh escaped him as he gently placed Laura's hand back on her breast and joined her other one to it, and leaning forward, kissed her still cheek and whispered goodbye. Megan kissed her too as she said her goodbyes. They got up to leave holding each other as close as they could. As they reached the door Lady Compton entered the room.

'Am I too late, Jack?'

He nodded. He didn't trust himself to speak.

'Oh, Charles!' She collapsed into her husband's arms.

'Come on, my dear, she's at peace now.' Charles steered Daphne towards the balcony. 'Jack, will you wait outside for us? I'll need to talk to you.' He said over his shoulder. 'We'll only be a few minutes.'

'Take all time as you need, M'Lord. Me and Megan'll be walking by lake.'

The beauty of the lake and the mountains engulfed Jack. 'This must be the most beautiful place on earth, Megan. Yer know if I could choose where I wanted to die I would choose somewhere like this with you by my side. I love you, Megan, more than I can say. In fact, I'm going to say it as loud as I can. I'm going listen to it being echoed all around the mountains.'

He put his head back, but it wasn't a shout that came. It was a strangled sound and then a sob and he sank down on his knees and wept. Megan sat down beside him. Her anguish wrapped him in concern. His sobs brought out all that was in him.

'Oh, Megan, I'm crying for Cissy, our sweet, Cissy. And, me little Bella...Me mam and me dad and me brothers, all gone. But, they are still all so very dear to me. And Laura, poor, sad and lonely, Laura. But, mostly, Megan, me heart breaks for all you have been through because of me affair with Laura. The deep scars on your back... They're a daily reminder of your pain and of the fact that I so nearly lost you, too. Every night I have nightmares. That prison...Oh, God...and the hell of only seeing you once a month and then not being able to touch or hold you. How could I have opened those wounds again? How could I have thought Laura's forgiveness of me, or us forgiving her, was worth that?'

'Don't, oh, my love, don't. Don't torture yourself anymore. It is over. It is truly over, Jack.'

After a while a calm feeling came over him and he felt cleansed. Knew he and Megan had both been cleansed. There was no bitterness left in Megan to gnaw away at her. He knew that. He could feel it. He took his hanky and blew his nose and then went to wipe Megan's tears.

'Eeh, Jack Fellam, I'm not having that round me face.' Her giggle was the best sound he'd ever heard in his life.

Megan wiped her own tears on her own hankie then snuggled into him.

The peace of the mountains settled in them and they sat in silence allowing the cool air to bathe them. The lowering sun dappled on the lake.

**

'Aaah, Jack, Megan. Here you are. Well, it's a sad day. Poor Laura. She was only thirty-eight you know. Well, well, poor Laura. She had a sad life really. What with everything.' Lord Crompton stood a moment looking at the ground. Megan and Jack rose.

I want to thank you both for coming. All arrangements will be made for your return.' He paused. Neither Jack or Megan said anything.

'Bad business. Sad. Very sad.' He paused again. They could see he was fighting for control.

'We're very sorry, M'Lord,' Megan said. She felt Jack squeeze her hand.

'Yes, thank you, very decent. Well, must be off. I'll send everything you need to your boarding house and I'll contact you when I get back. Did Laura say how she left things?'

'What things, M'Lord?' Jack asked.

'Her Will, Jack. She's... Well, I'm not speaking out of place. I'm her executor. I am charged with arranging everything. The Will is to be officially read of course after... But... Well, she meant to tell you today. She has left the bulk of her estate to be shared equally between you and Megan. By way of an apology. Quiet right, too...'

Megan looked at Jack. He had an incredulous look on his face.

'I can see it's been a shock to you, on top of everything. Laura wanted to tell you herself...'

'But...No, she shouldn't have. We can't accept. It wouldn't be right. We all played our part in it. Me, Bert, Jack... We were all as much to blame. I told her. What she did, she did because she didn't understand. We forgave each other, its over. That money is yours and your family's...'

'I have never heard such generosity of spirit, Megan. But, no. It is what Laura wanted. She has thought of us all, you are not to worry about that.'

'Look, I must get back to Lady Compton. You have everything you need at the Guest House?'

'Aye, we're being well looked after. They told us dinner is laid on for us tonight and a breakfast in the morning.' Jack told him.

'Good, now don't worry, my man will bring over your return tickets and sort everything out for your journey home. And, about the Will. I'll help you. Laura made a couple of requests as to how she would like you to use some of the money, but she stipulated they are only requests. You're not to be beholden by them. I'll be in touch as soon as I have everything sorted. But, Jack and Megan, your life is going to change quite significantly, the sum you will inherit is around £10,000. Take care, and like I say, I'll be in touch, probably be in about two to three weeks. Goodbye and thank you once again for coming, I know your doing so will have helped my sister-in-law to die peacefully. She looked...beautiful. Yes, beautiful.'

As he turned to go, he shook both their hands. They could only nod. Shock encased Megan, and Jack looked as though he'd been all but turned to stone.

'Meg...'

'I know, Jack. I can't take it in.' A nervous giggle escaped her. 'Oh...My...God!'

'Eeh, Meg. Meg...'

Her feet left the ground. She was being held aloft by Jack. The mountain's swirled around her. When he lowered her Megan looked down at the lake. In its depth she saw the reflection of the swishing pines. She was reminded of the pattern made by the sun dappling through the leaves of the tree when she had first lain with Jack. She had likened it then to a protective canopy. That canopy had slipped from over her but it was back. She could feel its protection once more. Everything in her world was coming right. She thought of Hattie. *Oh, Hattie. We came through, lass. Me and you, we came through.*

The end

Lightning Source UK Ltd.
Milton Keynes UK
UKOW052142270613

212921UK00001B/100/P